A Counter-History of Crime Fiction

Supernatural, Gothic, Sensational

Maurizio Ascari
Senior Lecturer in English Literature, University of Bologna, Italy

palgrave
macmillan

First published in hardback 2007
First published in paperback 2009 by
PALGRAVE MACMILLAN

Palgrave Macmillan in the UK is an imprint of Macmillan Publishers Limited, registered in England, company number 785998, of Houndmills, Basingstoke, Hampshire RG21 6XS.

Palgrave Macmillan in the US is a division of St Martin's Press LLC, 175 Fifth Avenue, New York, NY 10010.

Palgrave Macmillan is the global academic imprint of the above companies and has companies and representatives throughout the world.

Palgrave® and Macmillan® are registered trademarks in the United States, the United Kingdom, Europe and other countries.

ISBN-13: 978–0–230–52500–9   hardback
ISBN-10: 0–230–52500–8   hardback
ISBN-13: 978–0–230–59462–3   paperback
ISBN-10: 0–230–59462–X   paperback

This book is printed on paper suitable for recycling and made from fully managed and sustained forest sources. Logging, pulping and manufacturing processes are expected to conform to the environmental regulations of the country of origin.

A catalogue record for this book is available from the British Library.

Library of Congress Cataloging-in-Publication Data

Ascari, Maurizio.
   A counter-history of crime fiction : supernatural, gothic,
   sensational / Maurizio Ascari.
      p. cm. — (Crime files)
   Includes bibliographical references and index.
   ISBN 978–0–230–52500–9 (cloth)   978–0–230–59462–3 (pbk)
      1. Detective and mystery stories, English—History and criticism.
2. Supernatural in literature. 3. Sensationalism in literature. I. Title.
PR830.D4A8 2007
823′.087209—dc22   2007018603

Printed and bound in Great Britain by
CPI Antony Rowe, Chippenham and Eastbourne

Contents

Acknowledgements

Writing is always an enticing adventure. Writing in a language other than your own native idiom – Italian, in my case – is an even greater one, for instead of mastering the language one feels partly possessed by it. Thus while I was writing this book I did not feel like an armchair sleuth whose grip over reality is unfailing, but rather like a hard-boiled detective, who is vulnerable and liable to err, although instead of drinking whisky I occasionally bit my nails. I started from a handful of clues – connections that excited my curiosity, things I had either perceived or simply sensed – and I had this intimidating resource, a language that was both the object and the instrument of my research. Needless to say, this book has been long in the making. It has peopled my winter evenings with suspenseful plots and shady characters. It has kept me pensive while walking in the streets of my home town, Bologna, or driving my car along the motorway. It has been 'rehearsed' in the course of various conferences, where I gave papers focusing on the problems I intended to tackle, although at the beginning my view of the 'case' was rather hazy.

Complexity is often the result of a communal rather than individual itinerary. Therefore I wish to thank all the friends who kindly helped me along the way. First of all Stephen Knight, the 'master of mystery' who generously took on the task of deconstructing my prejudices on 'detective fiction', opening my mind to the wider implications of 'crime fiction'. Without his radiant readiness to share his immense knowledge of this literary field I would never have been able to achieve this goal. I am very grateful to Clive Bloom, whose highly original critical works greatly helped to reshape my approach to the galaxy of crime and gothic fiction, and who kindly accepted this study for publication in the series he edits. Heather Worthington also deserves my heartfelt thanks, for the keen attention she devoted to my typescript and for her moral and intellectual support in the final stages of the revision process. I have truly met with invaluable readers, whose wide perspective has enabled me to expand my horizons and whose advice has prevented me from falling into factual or theoretical traps. This venture also offers me the opportunity to thank Michael Webb, a long-time friend whose 'linguistic counselling' service has helped me to improve my English and to ease my anxiety.

Since writing a book is a painstaking process that often takes up the time one should spend doing other things, my warmest thanks go to

Franca, whose sympathy and patience are the prerequisites of all my enterprises. When a dream comes true I know that I owe it to her.

Shorter versions of various chapters of this book were presented as papers – either in English or in Italian – at international conferences or in foreign universities and/or appeared in proceedings, miscellaneous volumes or literary journals.

Chapter 1 – 'The Detective and the Mirror: a Literary Genre Discovers Itself', in *The Benstock Library as a Mirror of Joyce*, Joyce Studies in Italy, 7, eds Rosa Maria Bollettieri Bosinelli and Franca Ruggieri (Rome: Bulzoni, 2002), pp. 103–20; Chapter 2 – ' "Murder Will Out": Dreams, Detection and the Quest for Revenge in Medieval and Modern English Literature', in *Crime, detecção e castigo. Estudos sobre literatura policial*, eds Gonçalo Vilas-Boas and Maria de Lurdes Sampaio (Porto: Granito Editores e Livreiros, 2002), pp. 17–33; Chapter 3 – 'The Eye of God: Persecution, Omniscience and Detection', *New Comparison*, 32 (Autumn 2001): 17–35; Chapter 6 – 'Che lingua parla Auguste Dupin? Breve indagine sul poliziesco delle origini', 'I Convegno nazionale sulla letteratura popolare: il caso Sherlock Holmes', Roseto degli Abruzzi (TE), 5–7 July 2002; Chapter 8 – 'Londra come "cuore di tenebra": il primitivo nel centro dell' impero', 'Il primitivo e le sue metamorfosi: archeologia di un discorso culturale', Bologna, 17–19 November 2005; Chapter 9 – 'Artisti, anarchici e atavismo: il "degenerato" come mostro', in *Incontrare i mostri. Variazioni sul tema nella letteratura e cultura inglese e americana*, ed. Maria Teresa Chialant (Naples: Edizioni Scientifiche Italiane, 2002), pp. 141–56.

Introduction

In the last few decades the profile of the literary canon has changed significantly, for reasons as diverse as the 'rediscovery' of women's writings that had been previously marginalised, an increasing theoretical awareness, the effort to overcome national boundaries in order to study literature on a European or world scale and the tendency to relate literature to the discourses of science, politics and religion within the framework of a semiotics of culture. This transdisciplinary and comparative cultural climate, which encourages intellectual freedom and subversive readings of the past, is also accompanied by an increasing interest in exploring domains of knowledge and experience that were previously branded as 'unscientific' or 'irrational'.

Important studies have been devoted to the relationship between science and pseudo-science, to the conceptualisation of the supernatural in Victorian culture, and to the development of pseudo-sciences such as mesmerism, hypnotism, spiritualism, physiognomy, phrenology and criminal anthropology. As the organisers of a conference on science, pseudo-science and society remarked as early as 1980, while in the past philosophers of science had aimed 'to formulate a criterion of demarcation that would decisively separate science from every other area of intellectual activity', recent scholarship 'has turned to the examination of pseudo-science and its role in intellectual and social life.'[1] According to Michel Foucault, the Western search for truth consigned a whole teratology of thought beyond the margins of legitimate discourses,[2] but truth cannot be grasped once and for all, and we should unceasingly redefine these borders.

Whatever one's personal beliefs and sympathies, it has to be acknowledged that the vast container of imagination we call literature has always been marked by a wide range of approaches to the human condition and its predicaments. Realism is only one of the sets of conventions that have contributed to the development of literature, while the realm of fantasy has enabled writers to catalyse and express psychic energies that could hardly find an outlet within the boundaries of verisimilitude. In her seminal volume on fantasy, Rosemary Jackson underlines the complementary nature of realism and fantasy, which exists only 'in a parasitical or symbiotic relation to the real'.[3] Jackson also associates fantasy with the increasing secularisation of society, and subscribes to Tzvetan

Todorov's claim that the literature of the fantastic is 'the uneasy conscience of the positivist nineteenth century'.[4] Needless to say, the nineteenth century was also the time when crime fiction gave origin to what came to be regarded as detective fiction. Starting from such a premise, I will explore the centuries-long process leading up to this transition, and so highlight the interaction between realism and fantasy in the development of this genre.

Although the critical emphasis that has been laid for over a century on the association between detection and science might lead us to believe that nineteenth-century detective fiction was unambiguously realistic, in fact it had an ambivalent status. This is acknowledged by Clive Bloom when he claims that 'Other genres owe much to gothic concerns and neither detective fiction nor science fiction can be separated in their origins from such an association.'[5] Elsewhere, Bloom describes detective fiction as a bridge between late romanticism, which was marked by individualism and the search for an organic theology, and modernism, which felt itself freed both 'from a theological moral purpose' and 'from the cult of personality'.[6] According to Bloom, the detective story contributed to this transition by idealising personality as 'pure thought',[7] thereby reconciling 'the contradictions of a society under the dual pressure of eccentric individualism and dubiously safe conformism'.[8]

Having acknowledged the complex nature of crime fiction in general and of nineteenth-century detective fiction in particular, let us now focus on our position as early twenty-first century readers. No act of reading can grasp the multi-layered structure of a text in its entirety. Reading always translates into a selection of elements from the texts we approach, responding to factors as diverse as education, motivation and concentration. We grasp only those aspects of texts that our cultural position and subjectivity enable us to recognise and to relate to other data. Needless to say, I am no stranger to this phenomenon. On re-reading certain stories of crime and detection in the light of further (literary and critical) works, I began to realise how many elements of now-canonical texts did not fit into the literary patterns which I had previously used to interpret them. Likewise, further reading made me realise that works I had formerly discarded as uninteresting actually embodied important aesthetic and ideological tensions. This prompted me to venture into a new critical enquiry, although the many excellent studies that have been recently devoted to crime fiction repeatedly made me hesitate and retrace my steps.

The result is a critical survey that does not aim to study the nineteenth-century development of mainstream detective fiction, but rather to map those hybrid zones where its conventions mingle with those of sensation fiction and the ghost story, or else are conflated with the discourses of pseudo-sciences. This volume is thus governed by the need to uncover areas of cross-fertilisation and to make connections, albeit without sacrificing that sense of categories and distinctions that is a fundamental intellectual tool. Parodies, adaptations, translations from and into foreign languages, as well as the critical works that the ramifications of crime fiction fostered, and that in turn fostered the public recognition of popular literature, will all be taken into account as contributing to the formation and the canonical status of this genre.

This text aims to trace a counter-history of crime fiction, both by disinterring texts that have had little or no critical attention devoted to them and by reinterpreting, in a different light, works that we believe we know all too well. Implicit in the act of naming a genre is the idea of a border which delimits and circumscribes. Since every classification and genealogy involves historically determined criteria that are not a symptom of timeless transparency but which partly construct a phenomenon, tracing the borders of a genre is inevitably a somewhat arbitrary process. Not only is the ever-changing profile of a genre defined by conventional lines which are produced by an encounter between differences and which are continuously renegotiated, but the 'land' that stretches on both sides of the border is also a fertile site of exchange. It is in these border-territories that processes of creative innovation often take place, thanks to acts of transgression and occasions of hybridisation. Moreover, while in the past border-territories were subjected to the scrutiny of normative criticism, in the postmodern age – as Linda Hutcheon writes – 'the borders between literary genres have become fluid'.[9]

This flexibility is linked to another aspect of our approach to culture, that is the tendency to regard 'canonicity' not as an essential property of literary texts, authors or genres, but rather as the result of a cultural process, and therefore as an object of study in itself. Like every other literary canon, that of 'detective fiction' has been increasingly subjected to critical scrutiny in order to make its assumptions explicit and to explore the circumstances of its formation. In the so-called 'golden age' of detective fiction, bodily fluids were 'washed away' from the pages of 'clue-puzzle' novels and crime was increasingly represented – by writers and critics alike – as an aseptic riddle to be solved by the detached mind of an investigating agent. Yet, in the following decades the popularity of sub-genres as diverse as the 'hard-boiled', the 'crime novels' *à la* Highsmith, 'police procedurals', 'thrillers' and 'psychothrillers' – whose main ingredients are the materiality of the victim's body, the physical, emotional and legal vulnerability of the detective and the psychology of the criminal – helped trigger a sweeping change of critical and historical perspective. As a consequence, the early twentieth-century prescriptive view of detective fiction as rooted in pre-modern enigma stories, implying that rationality was the guiding light of the genre, was radically revised by late twentieth-century critics, who conversely emphasised its debt to the early-modern traditions of picaresque novels, criminal biographies and broadsides.

Drawing on the many excellent critical and theoretical works that in the last few decades have shed light on crime/detective fiction, *A Counter-History of Crime Fiction* aims to provide new insight into the development of the genre. A meta-critical approach is at the heart of Chapter 1 ('Revising the Canon of Crime and Detection'), which discusses both the early twentieth-century *construction* of a detective canon and its late twentieth-century *deconstruction* so as to set the theoretical premises for an alternative view of the genre.

The relation between crime fiction, the supernatural and the gothic is explored in chapters 2–5. Chapter 2 ('Detection before Detection') analyses the paradigm of 'divine detection', which underlies several medieval and early-modern stories. Revelatory dreams and the apparitions of ghosts contribute to the workings of providence within fictional and theatrical texts that firmly locate the principles of order and justice in the divinity. Chapter 3 ('Persecution and Omniscience') explores a transitional stage, when omniscience ceased to be regarded solely as the attribute of a divinity that was represented as both benevolent and just. In the eighteenth-century climate of Enlightenment, equality and freedom, omniscience took on different shades of meaning, becoming both a sublime attribute of power and the arch-rational organising principle of Jeremy Bentham's machine for surveillance – the panopticon. Chapter 4 ('Victorian Ghosts and Revengers') describes the resurgence of the supernatural and the motive of revenge in Victorian literature in connection with the representation of crime. The link between this renewed interest in the supernatural and pseudo-sciences such as mesmerism, hypnotism and spiritualism is explored in Chapter 5 ('Pseudo-Sciences and the Occult') so as to reassess the importance of anti-positivist forms of detection, including the late nineteenth-century vogue for 'psychic detectives', dealing with occult mysteries.

Chapters 6–9 examine the multifarious sensational components of nineteenth-century crime fiction, taking into account the commercial aspects of popular literature as well as the developments of criminal anthropology and social science. Chapter 6 ('The Language of Auguste Dupin') focuses on the function of translation in the international growth of crime fiction from the 1840s to the 1880s, delving into the mechanisms of popular culture. Chapter 7 ('On the Sensational in Literature') analyses the development of sensation fiction in the second half of the nineteenth century, discussing the role of women as writers and consumers, the critical debate between detractors and advocates of sensation, the increasing centrality of the professional detective and finally the cultural resonance this genre achieved by means of parodies and adaptations for the theatre. Chapter 8 ('London as a "Heart of Darkness"') explores the pervasive presence of the metaphor of darkness in a series of nineteenth-century – mainly non-fictional – texts denouncing the deplorable conditions of life in the East End, with the aim of analysing the ideological and aesthetic implications of this rhetorical strategy. Chapter 9 ('The Rhetoric of Atavism and Degeneration') deals with the impact of late nineteenth-century pseudo-scientific anthropological categories on the literary treatment of crimes and criminals.

The conclusion ('The Age of Formula Fiction') looks back to the first chapter, focusing on the early twentieth-century formation of the canon of detective fiction as a multifaceted process, involving creative writing, criticism and the media. Doyle's works are thus presented as the hub of a complex cultural phenomenon, the Sherlock Holmes 'myth', while Chesterton's works are related to the development of neighbouring sub-genres such as terrorist/anarchist and spy fiction. Finally, the anthologies that scholars/writers such as Wrong, Wright, Sayers and Thomson edited and introduced are investigated – against the backdrop of modernism, with its search for form – to shed light on the theoretical elaboration that led detective fiction to be identified as a sub-category of 'mystery' – linked with stories of the supernatural – rather than of 'crime'.

This concise profile of my text is in itself a comment on its title. *A Counter-History of Crime Fiction* aims to reassess some of the assumptions concerning the origin and nature of detective fiction, showing that the identity of this sub-genre should be regarded as the result of a cultural construction rather than as a faithful mirror of the 'essential' qualities of a certain number of literary works. For this reason I have preferred to use the comprehensive term 'crime fiction', to permit the exploration of a wider network of texts, including Renaissance tragedies, criminal biographies, *Newgate Calendars*, gothic novels, Newgate novels, sensation fiction, the ghost story and melodrama. The wide scope of this volume is also reflected in its subtitle, *Supernatural, Gothic, Sensational*, where the term 'supernatural' embraces – in Bloom's words – 'all those areas above or beyond the material realm',[10] while 'gothic ' and 'sensational' designate both aesthetic categories and specific literary genres.

A further comment must be added regarding the comparative approach that underlies this study. As an Italian who teaches English literature I could not deny the desire to explore the links between the various national cultures that contributed to the genesis of detective fiction. The result is a book that freely crosses the borders between Great Britain, the United States, France and – occasionally – Italy itself, so restoring detective fiction to the cosmopolitan dimension that presided over its origin, in an effort to attain a better understanding of a genre whose complexity has been underplayed for both ideological and aesthetic reasons.

1
Revising the Canon of Crime and Detection

As Hayden White claimed in *Metahistory*, every historical account combines a certain number of 'data' with 'a narrative structure for their presentation'.[1] So let us now adopt this 'metahistorical' perspective and briefly examine the traditional accounts of the development of detective fiction to uncover the underlying narratives.

At the end of the nineteenth century, detective novelists and critics shaped the identity of what was increasingly perceived as a new genre by denying its sensational heritage – with its vibrant appeal to the emotions – in order to emphasise its rational character. As early as 1892 *The Adventures of Sherlock Holmes* was reviewed by Joseph Bell (a professor of Doyle's at the University of Edinburgh), who drew various parallels between detection and medical semiotics.[2] Only a couple of years later, Watson – another colleague of Doyle's... – opened one of his biographical sketches of Holmes with this declaration: 'In choosing a few typical cases which illustrate the remarkable mental qualities of Sherlock Holmes, I have endeavoured, as far as possible, to select those which presented the minimum of sensationalism, while offering a fair field for his talents.'[3] These words are taken from 'The Adventure of the Cardboard Box', which was first published in the *Strand*. The story, however, was not included in the 1894 edition of *The Memoirs of Sherlock Holmes* because its subject – adultery – was regarded as scandalous.

From its inception, the discourse on detective fiction discarded the sensational lineage of the new genre, grounding its literary status on its association with scientific method and highbrow literature. The melodramatic impact of sensation fiction was superseded by riddles and enigmas which respectably set the mind to work with crystal-clear lucidity. Death and crime – the corollaries of evil – were exorcised by the focus on the enquiry, an incontrovertible proof of the enlightened human potential for good.

1

When Doyle received the honour of seeing his works published in a twelve-volume edition (an important act of canonisation), he wrote a new preface (dated 1901) to *The Adventures of Sherlock Holmes*, which was republished in 1903. Characteristically, Doyle described Poe as 'the father of the detective tale' and associated the brevity of detective fiction to the centrality of mystery and analysis:

> the secret of the thinness and also of the intensity of the detective story is, that the writer is left with only one quality, that of intellectual acuteness, with which to endow his hero. [...] The problem and its solution must form the theme, and the character-drawing be limited and subordinate.[4]

Identifying Holmes with his method, Doyle appeared to forget how important the formulaic details of the detective's house, personal appearance and lifestyle were to his readers, as is proved by the enduring popularity of the illustrations that accompanied Doyle's texts in the *Strand* and elsewhere.

One of the first book-length studies on the genre was published in 1913 by the American writer Carolyn Wells, whose *The Technique of the Mystery Story* is focused on mystery rather than crime, and on form rather than subject. The progressive detachment of the detective interest from its sensational components is apparent in Wells's analysis, whose major concern is to assert the literary status of what was commonly considered as an idle pastime. Not only did Wells regard the literature of mystery as rooted in ancient riddles rather than in the representation of crime, but she quoted several sources to prove that detection is an intellectual problem and as such should be kept separate from sentiment, emotion or desire. Of course, this emphasis on the rational response elicited by detective fiction also amounts to a denial of its sensational components:

> the Detective Story sets a stirring mental exercise, with just enough of the complex background of life to distinguish it from a problem in mathematics. Whatever thrills of horror are excited come by way of the intellect, never starting directly in the emotions.[5]

The critic was well aware of the fact that detective fiction stimulates a competitive spirit in its readers and her words seem to anticipate those metaphors of detective fiction as crosswords or a game of chess that, in the next decade, were to become critical commonplaces, conforming to an increasingly mechanical view of the act of reading as well as to an increasing emphasis on 'fair play', that is on offering readers all the elements to solve the mystery autonomously.

During the 1920s and 1930s detective fiction finally achieved the full status of a literary genre thanks to a rich critical output, including R.A. Freeman's 'The Art of Detective Stories' (1924), Dorothy Sayers's introduction to *Great Short Stories of Detection, Mystery and Horror* (1928) and H. Douglas Thomson's *Masters of Mystery: a Study of the Detective Story* (1931). These critical essays can be considered as symptomatic of the increasing tendency to disparage the nineteenth-century crime tradition in order to promote the more recent 'scientific' developments of the genre. Over the decade, both the theoretical and the historical approach to detective fiction tended to consign it to a space of rigid rules. In their attempt to assert the dignity of the genre, writers and critics emphasised its rational elements at the expense of other components and consequently pushed the more sensational aspects into the background.

In 1946 a large number of these essays were collected by Howard Haycraft in his seminal anthology *The Art of the Mystery Story*, the purpose being 'to bring together under one cover a representative selection of the best critical and informative writing about the modern mystery-crime-detective story, from Poe to the present time'.[6] The canonical import of this anthology is apparent right from the foreword. Haycraft, who had also authored an influential narrative of the genre, *Murder for Pleasure: the Life and Times of the Detective Story* (1941), selected and canonised both literary and critical works in order to sustain a normative view of a genre whose borders were being traced with increasing sharpness.

In *Murder for Pleasure*, Haycraft made two decisive moves. First, he identified very precisely the genesis of the genre, claiming that 'As the symphony began with Haydn, so did the detective fiction begin with Poe. Like everything else in the world, both had precursors.'[7] This was probably designed to emphasise the Americanness of detective fiction, since early critical works dealing with this genre often reveal chauvinistic competition for the identification of the ur-detective story. Second, Haycraft dated 'the earliest critical discussion of the genre'[8] to 1883, thus entirely disregarding all the critical works that had flourished in the 1860s and 1870s as a result of the sensation vogue. He also claimed that on the whole 'the development of any competent body of detective story criticism did not occur until the mid 1920s',[9] virtually erasing from consideration a whole range of critical works whose main thesis ran against his restrictive concept of 'detective story'. Of course this second move had a strong canonical import, for instead of acknowledging the continuity between crime and detective fiction, Haycraft aimed at distancing one from the other.

The Literature of Roguery (1907) – a seminal study in which the comparatist F.W. Chandler had investigated a large literary field, corresponding to what today we label as 'crime fiction' – was excluded from Haycraft's anthology as a work 'of little present-day interest'.[10] A similar fate was met both by those critical works of smaller scope that did not focus on Poe and Doyle (suffice it to mention Walter C. Phillips's *Dickens, Reade, and Collins Sensation Novelists*, 1919) and by various examples of continental criticism, such as Régis Messac's *Le 'Detective Novel' et l'influence de la pensée scientifique* (*The Detective Novel and the Influence of Scientific Thought*, 1929), a book Haycraft disparagingly described as a hybrid, lamenting the 'forbidding academism and esoteric content of these continental considerations'.[11] Needless to say, neither Chandler nor Messac conformed to the restrictive view of the genre that Haycraft supported. Without placing in question the merits of Haycraft, one should acknowledge that his works marked a fundamental step in the canonisation of the genre according to a centripetal view that was not exempt from chauvinism and authoritarianism.

On the other hand, the critical works Haycraft barred from his influential collection offered a radically alternative historical profile of the genre. Considering the literature of roguery as determined 'by subject matter rather than by form',[12] Chandler examined the Spanish, French and German sources of a genre that can be traced back to the early modern period. Chandler's book aimed to study the representation of low life, which accounts for the almost total absence of Collins, who 'preferred melodramatic villainy to roguery',[13] and the greater attention given to authors like Defoe, Fielding, Smollett, Scott, Ainsworth, Bulwer-Lytton, Dickens and Reade, as well as to the Raffles saga. While acknowledging the growing importance of 'the literature of crime-detection',[14] Chandler's wide perspective enabled him to see what the other critics of this period (including Doyle) seemed unwilling to acknowledge, namely that:

> there has been a constant tendency to rise from the sensational to the analytical; and from a combination of the two a third type has resulted. Its purpose is to gratify the reader's taste for the ghastly, the tragic, or the criminal, and at the same time to propose a mystery whose solution shall exercise all his intellectual ingenuity. The supreme example of this mingling of the sensational and the analytical is to be seen in the stories concerning Sherlock Holmes.[15]

Chandler was far from indifferent to the social dimension of the new genre and commented on the difference between the higher-class readers

Doyle addressed and 'the great unwashed', who were 'regaled in shilling shockers and in dime novels'. Curiously enough, however, the insightful Chandler (who had probably grown partial to the central figure of his study – the rogue as an anti-hero, either endowed with romantic panache or represented in a realistic vein) ended his work with a misleading prophecy: 'That this subsidiary genre will attain to the rank or to the influence of its picaresque parent seems unlikely.'[16]

Messac's *Le 'Detective Novel'* also included crime and gothic literature among the ancestors of detective fiction in an effort to understand the multiple components that had contributed to the formation of this new genre. Being a critic rather than a writer, Messac was able to achieve a more detached view, less influenced by the rigorous 'poetics' of the 'golden age'. Messac investigated the relationship between the development of scientific thought and that of detection, contrasting a religious vision based on mystery with a philosophical-scientific attitude which was grounded in the observation of reality. Although the critic defined the origin of detection as the triumph of analysis over revelation, he was well aware that the history of this genre had not been unconditionally dominated by rationality and that the development of detective fiction had by no means followed 'a straight line'.[17] In Messac's study chapters such as 'Miracles and literature', 'Ghosts and brigands', 'The visionary' and 'Natural magic' bear witness to this fact and almost trace a counter-history of crime – rather than detective – fiction.

From detective to crime fiction

Criticism, like literature, is involved in a continuous process of change. As we have seen, in the first half of the twentieth century mainstream critics analysed works of crime interest – or 'criminography' – with the aim of singling out the centrality of detection in order to trace the genealogy of a genre whose borders were firmly and restrictively laid out. Haycraft's defensively normative conception of detective fiction was instrumental in mapping the progress of a genre that was still regarded as unworthy of much critical attention and that was also essentially formulaic in its recent developments. In the second half of the century, however, due both to the increasing public/academic recognition of detective fiction and to a renewed interest in criminals on the part of contemporary writers, this critical approach evolved in the direction of complexity. The literary status of detective fiction became less and less in need of defence, but the very category of detective fiction was simultaneously called into question, as critics – desiring to enlarge the scope of their enquiry – revised the extent of the detective canon, rediscovering books that had never been republished or searching the pages of periodicals for relevant materials. Thus the history of detective fiction was reassessed within the larger literary territory of crime fiction.

Michel Foucault had a major impact on this process, since *Surveiller et punir* (*Discipline and Punish*, 1975) and other writings focus on issues such as the power/knowledge nexus, the body of the criminal and the eye of power, that is, the centrality of gaze in various activities of social/individual diagnosis, classification, surveillance and reform.[18] From the 1970s to the present day, the categories that Foucault elaborated while studying the transition from sovereign to disciplinary power in modern Western civilisation have increasingly influenced the critical debate on detective fiction, which is no longer regarded as an isolated enclave, but as a country whose borders allow frequent exchanges.

A symptom of this new attitude is the increasing scope and importance that the term 'crime fiction' has acquired. While in 1958 A.E. Murch chose *The Development of the Detective Novel* as a title for her history of the genre, in *Bloody Murder: from the Detective Story to the Crime Novel: a History* (1972) Julian Symons acknowledged the complex status of this literary form, claiming that the most sensible way of naming it 'is the general one of crime novel or suspense novel'.[19] The deconstruction of the centripetal view had started and, as a consequence, in the last thirty years crime fiction has become an umbrella term that includes the sub-category of detective fiction, rather than being defined by it as the weak pole of a binary opposition.

Of course critics did not unanimously pursue this new line of inquiry, but a few years later Stephen Knight published *Form and Ideology in Crime Fiction* (1980), where – following in the footsteps of Symons – he invited readers and critics alike to reassess the traditional account of the genre in order to establish 'the nature and ideology of crime fiction without detectives'.[20]

The development of 'theory' – with its new interest in ideology and suspicion of formalist close reading – largely contributed to this change of perspective. In *From Bow Street to Baker Street: Mystery, Detection and Narrative* (1992) Martin Kayman sought to revise the orthodox account of detective fiction as a genre pivoting on Doyle's works. While many scholars had chosen to trace the characteristics of this fully formed model back to its more or less 'imperfect' antecedents, Kayman described such 'anachronistic analysis' as dangerous 'because it collapses and rewrites the period prior to Holmes as a mere anticipation whose significance is valued only through the retrospective teleology'.[21] Refuting this critical stance, Kayman freely mingled gothic, sensational and detective fiction in a study that refuses to abide by any normative view of genre.

Martin Priestman's critical output – spanning more than two decades – likewise reflects the shift in perspective that brought the category of crime increasingly under the spotlight at the expense of detection. While in his early *Detective Fiction and Literature: the Figure on the Carpet* (1990) Priestman intended to deal 'with the relationship between detective fiction and established literature',[22] in an effort to break the academic boundaries between 'high' and 'low' literature, his later *Crime Fiction from Poe to the Present* (1998) testifies to the new canonical status of popular literature and to the increasing consensus the term 'crime fiction' enjoys. The same attitude marks *The Cambridge Companion to Crime Fiction*, which was edited by Priestman in 2003. A major step in the canonisation of the genre, the book expands on the many facets of crime fiction, so as to provide – in Priestman's words – 'a sense of the genre's history as multi-layered rather than unidirectional, and of its criticism as in process rather than univocal'.[23]

To understand this new perception of the genre as plural we should also take into account the wealth of studies that have been devoted to specific sub-genres of crime fiction in the course of the last two decades, ranging from Ian A. Bell's *Literature and Crime in Augustan England* (1991) to the overcrowded shelf of sensation criticism, including works by Jenny Bourne Taylor, Winifred Hughes, Beth Kalikoff, Sue Lonoff, D.A. Miller, Lyn Pykett and Ann Cvetkovich. This critical output made it imperative to reassess the traditional view of the development of detective fiction so as to take into account its relationship and exchanges with the neighbouring sub-genres. A veteran of crime criticism decided to meet the challenge and managed to encompass, with a bird's eye view, the development of crime fiction in its various dimensions. In *Crime Fiction 1800–2000: Detection, Death, Diversity* (2004) Stephen Knight provided readers with a handy yet richly documented guide to the genre, reasserting his choice of 'crime fiction' as the most comprehensive definition:

> there are plenty of novels (including some by Christie) without a detective and nearly as many without even a mystery (like most of Patricia Highsmith's work). There is, though, always a crime (or very occasionally just the appearance of one) and that is why I have used the generally descriptive term 'crime fiction'.[24]

Although in recent years the label of crime fiction has gained wide currency, ousting detection from its central position as the key element in defining the genre, the issue of terminology is still central to the contemporary critical debate and far from settled. Sub-generic labels such as 'hard-boiled' or 'clue-puzzle', for instance, are increasingly put to the test and regarded as interrelated – rather than mutually exclusive – literary forms. Contemporary critics feel the need both to historicise the definitions that were handed down to them and to redefine their meaning according to a more complex and flexible view of the genre as an aggregate of literary forms.

Blurring the boundaries

The issue of reception plays a major role in this volume. Thus, while subscribing to the prevailing view of the genre as composite and recognising the necessity to acknowledge the umbrella term 'crime fiction' to designate a constellation of sub-genres, I have nonetheless chosen to utilise traditional sub-categories such as 'sensation' and 'detective fiction' in order to historicise them, to deconstruct them from the inside, to analyse them as instruments of 'identity', and to retrace the steps that led to the formation of what came to be regarded as sensation or detective fiction.

The concept of literary genre is still instrumental in analysing the historical evolution of crime fiction, but a fundamental premise of this work is the refusal of any monogenetic account of the origin of literary genres such as the one Haycraft offered in *Murder for Pleasure*, where he regarded detective fiction as the product of the genius of Poe. From our more detached observatory, we can only subscribe to Alastair Fowler's polygenetic view of genre formation – 'when remote antiquity does not obscure the period of a kind's beginnings, they can always be shown to have preceded the inventor'.[25] Fowler uses the term 'kind' as the equivalent of 'historical genre', that is to say as a flexible diachronic concept that has 'to do with identifying and communicating rather than with defining and classifying'.[26] Refuting the traditional vision of literary genres as fixed sets of rules, Fowler insists on their organic growth, and also denies a mutual exclusiveness between genres, since 'genres have no clear dividing boundaries'[27] and 'membership of one by no means rules out membership of others'.[28]

As we have seen, Knight and Kayman both consider the traditional account of the origin of detective fiction – that of a genre rooted in a series of 'canonical' texts pivoting on the Dupin trilogy and the Holmes saga – as being far from objective. Knight also draws our attention to the fact that most nineteenth-century detective and crime stories originally appeared in the pages of magazines and newspapers, and these periodicals do not 'when examined produce so simple or so gratifying a genealogy of the detective as the classic account suggests'.[29] This should teach us to nurture a healthy suspicion concerning the outcome of our critical inquiries, which are inevitably 'situated', since when looking backwards we always interpret the development of a phenomenon in an instrumental way in order to highlight those aspects that correspond to our current needs and wishes – ideology and desire both being involved in this process.

Drawing on these principles, then, this book will analyse some of the processes of cross fertilisation that took place within crime fiction between the Middle Ages and the early twentieth century; in other words before the genre was theoretically defined as 'detective fiction' and evolved towards the 'clue-puzzle' as the result of an increasing emphasis on the rational and scientific detection of essentially aseptic riddles. My aim is thus to take into account the heterogeneous components that went into the making of a genre whose formulaic character has not prevented imaginative – or heretical – variations on the theme of crime and detection. Indeed, the main object of this critical enquiry has been to problematise crime fiction in order to probe its multifarious nature.

This attempt presupposes an awareness of the 'political' dimension that crime fiction has had at every stage of its development. Although mainstream detective fiction had a traditionally conservative bias, the genre as a whole cannot be reduced to its bourgeois, capitalist, chauvinist and sexist dimensions, for it may well boast long-standing radical components, as Knight reminds us.[30] And yet we cannot but agree with him and other critics that crime fiction in general played a major role in the process of global policing that took place in the eighteenth and nineteenth centuries, that is, in the secular dissemination of the principles of law and order into various fields of thought, communication and social activity – a process Kayman (the emphasis is his) describes as aimed at '*internalizing* the presence of the Law in the consciousness of that culture'.[31]

Elaborating on these assumptions, I will explore some aspects of crime fiction in order to underline its pliable and permeable character, as well as its sensitivity to external influences. My aim is to study crime fiction as a system of competing and interconnecting sub-genres, which are correlated to other forms of representation and either support or oppose the current social order in a variety of ways. Consequent on this premise, in addition to the intertextual approach that is virtually inherent in any historicist project, two basic strategies of analysis will be adopted. First, texts will be contextualised to investigate the ideological premises and social energies that influenced their conception and early reception. Second, a metacritical approach will highlight the role of the critical and theoretical debate concerning sensation and detective fiction in progressively shaping the genre. This critical heritage not only influenced the development of detective fiction – by helping to create a set of expectations in readers and to define the conventions that writers respected or transgressed – but also refashioned the origin of the genre in order to accommodate it to the identity which the genre had acquired. Borrowing a term which is current in other fields of study, one could say that a 'foundation myth' identifying Poe as the father of detection was created to support a normative view of the genre.

The decision to focus my analysis not only on primary sources but also on critical and theoretical essays derives from the idea that a body of literary works is recognised as a genre not only because its components share a certain number of conventions and intertextual links, but also on account of the discourses it generates. These two dimensions are interdependent inasmuch as literary works trigger critical analysis, which in turn influences their reception and the production of new texts. Thus, a genre may be regarded as a set of models and a theoretical construction that jointly shape the expectations of readers together with the strategies of writers and publishers.

As regards its temporal span, the volume is rooted in the medieval period. Pre-modern and early-modern crime literature will be explored to analyse the revelatory/premonitory value of dreams and the code of revenge – two conventions that intertwined with the belief that the ghost of the victim would haunt the guilty party. It is my contention that far from disappearing completely in the eighteenth-century climate of Enlightenment to make way for an increasingly rational approach to crime these elements retained a powerful hold on readers.

Critical works have all too often emphasised the rational dimension of what they have styled as 'detective fiction' at the expense of other components that also contributed – and still contribute in a significant way – to its success. Reversing this line of enquiry, I will set aside those conventions that became dominant in the evolution of the genre in order to study the persistence of a supernatural element within the tradition of crime fiction. During the nineteenth century the paradigm of rational enquiry did not completely eradicate the search for a higher design ruling the fiction of law and order, and it may well be argued that the enjoyment of readers depended precisely on the interplay between natural and supernatural elements, which engendered a fruitful tension between the domain of the intellect and that of the emotions.

The volume ends at the beginning of the twentieth century, when those crime narratives that were perceived as 'unorthodox' were increasingly being marginalised as part of the trend to normalise detective fiction which reached its climax in the late 1920s. As we know, it was in 1928 that the American writer S.S. Van Dine – the creator of Philo Vance – pronounced his 'Twenty Rules for Writing Detective Stories', while one year later another novelist – Monsignor Ronald A. Knox – included his famous 'Detective Story Decalogue' in his introduction to *The Best Detective Stories of 1928* (1929).

A glance at the present

In order to understand how important the phenomena analysed in this book still are, let us briefly ponder on the ensuing question: how much of our enjoyment as readers – and film viewers – at the dawn of the third millenium AD still depends on forms of syncretism? Sensational elements – connected with the materiality of the body and its fluids, the brutality of violence, the cogency of physical pain – are part and parcel of postmodern culture. Moreover, contemporary crime fiction and films make abundant use of gothic and supernatural elements – sometimes to adorn with an additional frisson the formulas of mass culture, deepening our sense of awe and mystery, as is proved by several best-selling films. *Angel Heart* (1986) dramatises the timeless encounter between a criminal and the father of all thief-takers – the devil himself. In *Seven* (1995) – where a serial killer stages murder according to the gamut of the deadly sins – the religious element accords the gruesome fantasies of murder a sublime grandeur. *Sleepy Hollow* (1999) anachronistically shows a late eighteenth-century police detective who is sent to investigate a series of strange deaths in an out-of-the-way village in the recently formed United States. The son of a woman who has unjustly been killed as a witch, this young *ante-litteram* policeman denounces torture as a senseless abuse and applies rational methods to the detection of crime. Nor does the supernatural nature of the mystery he faces prevent him from solving it.

The supernatural, however, can acquire a more openly subversive character, as in the Mrs Hudson series, authored by Sydney Hosier in the 1990s. In turning the marginal character of Mrs Hudson into a female equivalent of Holmes, the writer offers an alternative view of Victorian detection, refusing to ground this discipline on positivist rationality. It is thanks to the out-of-body experiences of Mrs Violet Warner, Mrs Hudson's friend and assistant (a character who self-ironically moulds herself on Watson) that the female sleuth is able to uncover the mystery at the heart of her first adventure – *Elementary, Mrs. Hudson* (1996). Even one of the most successful and 'respectful' among recent Sherlock Holmes apocrypha – Caleb Carr's *The Italian Secretary* (2005) – relies heavily on the presence of ghosts, a phenomenon which is hardly rationalised at the end of the story, when Holmes concludes 'Are ghosts – indeed, are *gods*, real? We cannot know; but they are powerful facts of human intercourse. And so...'[32]

Other contemporary authors use detection to meditate on our existential condition and on the metaphysical dimension. Umberto Eco's *The Name of the Rose* (1980) owes its charm to a skilful blend of thriller features, gothic elements and a medieval background. One of Eco's enlightening footnotes to the book, however, is devoted to a theme he defines as 'The metaphysics of detective fiction'. After claiming that the public like detective fiction not because of a morbid curiosity for death or because order is restored at the end, but because they enjoy the act of conjecturing, Eco draws a parallel between detective fiction and philosophy, since they are both aimed at answering the same question: Who is the culprit? Hoping to solve the ultimate riddle, human beings enter what Eco describes as the labyrinth of conjectures – a rhizome-like space where everything interconnects.[33] As Michael Holquist wrote in 1971, 'If in the detective story death must be solved, in the new metaphysical detective story it is life which must be solved.'[34] Instead of providing the reading public with ready-made answers confirming their world-views and the existing social order, metaphysical crime fiction focuses on detection as a search for meaning, turning it into a parable of life.

Numerous other examples include Thomas Pynchon's *The Crying of Lot 49* (1966) and Eco's *Foucault's Pendulum* (1988) as well as Dan Brown's unashamedly commercial *The Da Vinci Code* (2003). What these books variously exploit is the sensational appeal of worldwide conspiracies that span the centuries and are imbued with religious, masonic or otherwise esoteric symbolism. In a world that is obsessed with information, where complexity borders on 'disorder', and where knowledge often seems self-referential, the quest for 'truth' and for a 'transcendental meaning' is still a prime motive. In this cultural climate, novelists have repeatedly drawn on the paradigm of crime and detection to stage the adventures of postmodern knights of both sexes, whose tasks prove dangerous and bewildering, and whose ultimate achievements can disappoint those thriller-minded readers who simply look for a good mystery and a satisfying solution.

Although Pynchon and Eco may be regarded as exponents of what Stefano Tani defined as the postmodern 'anti-detective novel', utilising the detective formula to achieve effects which go far beyond the revelation of a mystery and the restoration of order, a latent interest in the super-natural also marks the work of traditional 'clue-puzzle' author P.D. James, whose novels repeatedly capitalise on the relics of the sacred that still haunt our society. Suffice it here to mention *Death in Holy Orders* (2001), with its theological college housed in a mansion on the edge of a crumb-ling cliff, or *The Murder Room* (2003), where murder is described as 'a paradigm of its age'.[35] The contemporary murders that James presents in the latter novel are indeed 'copycat murders' – the emblem of an epoch that incessantly rewrites, mimics, fakes; thus masking (and paradox-ically revealing) its void and meaningless inner core, responding to the absence of God from its cultural horizon.

Characteristically, in P.D. James's earlier *An Unsuitable Job for a Woman* (1977) the person who is responsible for the death of Mark Callender is not brought to justice by Cordelia Gray but is actually killed by a woman who turns out to be the dead boy's mother. Implicitly regarding this act as a just revenge, Cordelia lies to police commander Adam Dalgliesh in order to protect the perpetrator, but a higher court decides the fate of this female revenger, who dies a little later in a car accident. With a last ironic twist to the plot, at the end of the novel Dalgliesh self-mockingly acknow-ledges that the whole development of the case had been decided from the netherworld by Cordelia's former associate – the late Bernie Pryde, a police agent Dalgliesh had fired years before: ' "I find it ironic and oddly satisfying that Pryde took his revenge. Whatever mischief that child was up to in Cambridge, she was working under his direction." '[36]

Sensational, critical or philosophical, melodramatic, nostalgic or ironi-cal, the supernatural plays a central role in postmodern crime fiction, where it fulfils a variety of roles, including, of course, parody and decon-struction. This persistence of gothic and supernatural elements invites us to reassess the binary opposition between scientific detection and revelation as well as that between human and divine justice, for it is in the interstices of these dimensions that the appeal of much contemporary crime fiction still resides.

Part I
Supernatural and Gothic

2
Detection before Detection

Those critics who take an encyclopaedic approach to crime fiction customarily cite among the sources of the genre two episodes from Genesis in the first book of the Bible, which can be read as the religious foundation myth of Western society. It is because of a crime – although in religious terms it is the 'original sin' – that Adam and Eve abandon the condition of perfection they enjoyed in the Garden of Eden in order to enter the time of history. Stealing the fruit from the tree of knowledge triggers an inevitable detection, and the same occurs when, in another episode, Cain is marked and exiled to the East of Eden for having killed his brother. The more crimes the first humans commit, the more punishment they receive and the further they spread across the face of the earth. Incidentally, this cyclic plot has an uncanny analogy with the mechanism of retribution which led to the creation of distant European colonies through the transportation of criminals. What I find particularly meaningful in these ancient stories, however, is the fact that evildoers are doomed right from the beginning since the primal detective and judge is God himself. In other words the construction of Western morals pivots on the idea of omniscience and the certainty of punishment.

What is probably less well known is that the paradigm of divine detection also characterised the Roman world and the stage of syncretism when pagan and Christian cults started to blend. Some of the artefacts found in the Roman temple of Sulis Minerva in Bath are curses, which were written on sheets of pewter and consigned to the waters of the spring that marked the site as sacred. People asked the goddess to redress a variety of wrongs and a common complaint was theft, resulting in messages such as the following, dating from the fourth century AD: 'Whether pagan or Christian, whosoever, whether man or woman, whether boy or girl, whether slave or free, has stolen from me, Annianus, in the morning six silver pieces from my purse, you, lady Goddess, are to extract [them] from him.'[1] The phrasing of these curses was particularly careful, for in order to obtain the desired effect one had to follow a number of prescriptions, and trained scribes took care of this against the payment of a fee. A list of the suspects is often appended to the curses, in order to help the goddess in her inquiry. As we can see, in Western societies, the concept of retribution has long been utilised as a powerful psychological tool, both to prevent socially unacceptable behaviour and to give vent to the anger of the wronged party.

From a Christian perspective, each individual is ultimately destined to appear before a celestial tribunal to account for his/her deeds and this belief in itself represents a pervasive form of inner policing. In a pre-modern world where illiteracy was the norm and access to the Bible was restricted to clerics, the figurative arts and the theatre often fulfilled the 'missionary' task of instructing the people, divulging the spiritual discipline on which the edifice of society rested. In the morality play of *Everyman* (1495), when the hero is summoned by Death he is required to bring with him his 'book of count':

> For before God thou shalt answer, and show,
> Thy many bad deeds, and good but a few;[2]

Spiritual 'accountancy' was far from a jest for medieval men and women, since a powerful rhetorical apparatus was set into motion to make them feel the full force of the judgement that would inevitably follow death. The dialectics between God's justice and mercy provided an appropriate space of uncertainty, enabling the church to evoke the most harrowing eternal torments, but also allowing the individual to nourish hope. Moreover, the emphasis on the resurrection of the body helped make these never-ending tortures particularly 'real', for in afterlife the atrocity of pain would be felt with the full sensitivity of a live organism.

Given the fact that medieval culture was deeply imbued with this religious view, what role did detection play in it? We tend to associate detection with the rational search for clues and a culprit, that is, to regard it as a quintessential product of the Enlightenment and positivism. Yet, if we explore the medieval and early-modern cultures we realise that they expressed a common belief in the power of 'supernatural entities' not only to punish criminals in their afterlife, but also to ensure their detection on earth, notably when they were guilty of murder – the capital sin.

The idea that murder carries the seeds of its own discovery and punishment was reassuring in a world where social control was inefficient and criminals had a good chance of getting away with their misdeeds.

As Foucault reminds us, it was only in the seventeenth and eighteenth centuries that monarchies developed an efficient '"economy" of power', that is, procedures which allowed power to circulate pervasively throughout the entire 'social body'. Before that, monarchies fought forms of subversion – such as criminality – by means of 'spectacular and discontinuous interventions':[3] in other words, punishment was 'exemplary' because it was exceptional.

Literature is inevitably enmeshed in social and ideological structures and it comes as no surprise that in the medieval and early-modern ages crime literature played an active role – together with the church – in the network of social control that was to be subsequently reinforced by the police, journalism and scientific 'disciplines'. Moreover, the idea of divine detection was coherent with the ideological framework of Christianity which conceived truth as the fruit of revelation rather than as the result of a process. Following in the footsteps of Foucault, I am interested 'in seeing historically how effects of truth are produced within discourses which in themselves are neither true nor false'.[4] In other words, I wish to analyse how literature supported a system of beliefs that tended to infuse people with a terror of God's wrath, inducing them to internalise the law.

Dreams and detection

As the English proverb 'Murder will out' illustrates, in the Middle Ages – according to popular belief – the primary agent of detection was divine providence. People believed that God, being inherently just, could not tolerate crime going unpunished. Detection was often linked to the belief in the premonitory value of dreams as divine messages which could, if correctly interpreted, guide us in the right direction. This oracular tradition was rooted on one hand in Graeco-Roman antiquity[5] and on the other in the Bible itself – for example, in the dreams God sends to Joseph and Daniel, who become official interpreters of his will.[6]

The resultant syncretism is epitomised by an episode in Chaucer's *Canterbury Tales*. 'The Nun's Priest's Tale'[7] tells the story of two friends who, while on a pilgrimage, arrive in a city where all the inns are full and are obliged to separate for the night. After falling asleep, the main character dreams of his friend, who invokes his help, beseeching him to run to the stable where he is sleeping and where he is going to be killed; but the protagonist does not heed this warning. The dream recurs until the friend reveals that he has already been killed and implores the protagonist to wake up at dawn and run to the Western gate of the city, where he will find his body concealed in a wagon carrying dung. The following morning the hero looks for his friend at the stable, but the innkeeper claims he has already left. This induces the main character to follow the instructions he received while asleep and when he sees the wagon he starts to shout, asking the passers-by and the guards to help him to empty it. The corpse of his friend comes to light, the driver and the innkeeper are both arrested and this moral is drawn from the story:

> Blessed art Thou,
> O Lord our God, as Thou art just and true,
> Who never sufferest murder to be hid!
> 'Murder will out' – we see it every day.
> Murder is so hateful and abominable
> To God, Who is so just and reasonable,
> That He will not allow it to be hidden,
> Though it may wait a year or two, or three,
> Murder will out – and that's my firm opinion![8]

In the absence of witnesses and clues, the victim himself was regarded as the first agent of detection. This technique recurs in Chaucer's 'The Prioress's Tale', where a child is murdered by a group of Jews who are annoyed by his song of devotion to the Virgin. From the pit where he has been thrown, the child denounces his murder post-mortem, by starting to sing his favourite hymn. In this anti-Semitic tale of martyrdom, divine detection is linked to a miracle, not to a premonitory dream, but the story reiterates the belief that the blood shed will condemn murder with a voice of its own, notably when the sin is particularly offensive to God, as is the case in these two stories, featuring a pilgrim and a pious child in the role of victim.

The revelatory power of dreams also had a comic potential, which was exploited in the miracle play *Secunda Pastorum*. Having decided to steal a sheep while his companions sleep near their flock, Mak runs home with the sheep and conceals it in a cot, asking his wife to declare that she has given birth to a child. He then goes back to his friends and pretends he is asleep. When the third shepherd wakes up, he tells the others that he has dreamt of Mak, who – covered in a wolf's skin – had silently captured a sheep. At that moment Mak pretends to wake up and declares that he has dreamt that his wife Gill gave birth to a child around midnight. Mak hopes that this misleading clue will put the others off the scent, but when the three shepherds arrive in his house to examine the new-born baby, they discover the stolen sheep. Thanks to the glorious announcement of the birth of Christ, Mak escapes the punishment he deserves.[9]

The dream that Mak counterfeits brings us to another aspect of revelation, that is to say its potential unreliability. The Bible repeatedly warns against false prophets who take advantage of the common belief in the sacred origin of dreams in order to turn the chosen people away from God.[10] Dreams can thus be an instrument of deception, both in the hands of charlatans and of the devil, while two successive revelations which convey the same message with different images usually prove true.[11] This ambiguity was to resurface in Renaissance revenge tragedies.

Ghosts, politics and revenge

The popular belief in divine justice is publicly denounced as a fraud by the arch-villain of Renaissance theatre – Machiavel – in his prologue to *The Jew of Malta* (*c.* 1590). Christopher Marlowe was famously accused of atheism by his fellow playwright Thomas Kyd, seemingly under torture, and one cannot help but wonder whether these lines from Machiavel's soliloquy actually betray Marlowe's thoughts on divine retribution,

> I count religion but a childish toy,
> And hold there is no sin but ignorance.
> Birds of the air will tell of murders past;
> I am asham'd to hear such fooleries.[12]

This overtly cynical monologue – deconstructing the detective apparatus of providence – was destined to remain an exception, while most contemporary dramatists preferred to rely on a more orthodox system of values. Nonetheless, Renaissance revenge tragedies often reveal the effort to come to terms with an ever changing view of the world.

As we know, the custom of revenge played an important role in ancient pagan societies, where primitive forms of revenge, exceeding the offence, were subsequently limited by applying a principle of reciprocity (the *lex talionis*) and were eventually superseded by the payment of an indemnity, which the Germans called *wergild*. After the conversion of the Germanic peoples to Christianity, revenge was increasingly stigmatised, partly because of the strengthening of centralised power which regarded the administration of justice as its own prerogative. The earthly and the heavenly systems of values supported one another, insofar as the injunction to leave retribution to God – whose justice was regarded in turn as a form of revenge – agreed with the objectives of sovereigns whose aim was to take the administration of justice into their own hands.

Despite this close alliance between religious and civil ethics, a popular ethic founded on revenge still survived and in Renaissance England the issue was far from being settled. In his essay 'Of Reuenge' Francis Bacon decries this custom as primitive, 'a kinde of Wilde Iustice; which the more Mans Nature runs to, the more ought law to weed it out', but he also mentions various exceptions to this principle, admitting that 'The most Tolerable Sort of *Reuenge*, is for those wrongs which there is no Law to remedy'.[13] In Renaissance tragedies the choice of the revenger is often presented as inevitable because the homicide is close to the top of the pyramid of power and consequently it is not possible to rely on the authorities to ensure that justice is carried out.

Works such as Thomas Kyd's *The Spanish Tragedy* (*c*. 1587), Shakespeare's *Hamlet* (*c*. 1600) and Cyril Tourneur's *The Atheist's Tragedy* (*c*. 1611) – to mention but a few – are all based on the contention between the conflicting moral codes of religion and revenge, as well as on the struggle between the individual claim to justice and a tyrannical apparatus of power. Within this sub-genre detection is of vital importance, since the revenger cannot perform his retributive task without identifying the culprit beyond any doubt. The revenger is often helped in his investigation by the victim, who appears in the shape of a ghost or in a dream. Of course, each tragedy combines these ingredients according to a peculiar recipe.

Drawing on Seneca, in *The Spanish Tragedy* Kyd has the prologue told by the ghost of Andrea and the spirit of revenge. Having been unfairly slain on a battlefield by Balthazar (the son of the viceroy of Portugal), Andrea cannot find repose in the underworld, which is described by him in classical terms. When Proserpine decrees that in order to witness his revenge Andrea should be brought back to the earth 'through the gates of horn, / Where dreams have passage in the silent night',[14] her words echo a passage from the *Aeneid* where Virgil distinguishes the supernatural sources of reliable and unreliable dreams.

Two gates the silent house of Sleep adorn;
Of polish'd ivory this, that of transparent horn:
True visions thro' transparent horn arise;
Thro' polish'd ivory pass deluding lies.[15]

Kyd's prologue exemplifies the syncretism of Renaissance dramatists, who skilfully blended Christian values and classical figures or *loci*, often to avoid censorship, notably when tackling religious matters. Moreover, while the prologue firmly establishes the rightful nature of the ghost's complaint, false dreams occur in the Portuguese subplot of the play, which dramatises the danger of taking revenge on the wrong person. In the scenes set at the Portuguese court, the Viceroy's dreams – apparently revealing the death of his son, but actually embodying his anxiety – temporarily support Villuppo's untruthful version of the facts, perfidiously pointing to Alexandro as a traitor who has killed Balthazar from behind.

Although the prologue reassures the public about the legitimate nature of Andrea's thirst for revenge, in the play there is no communication between the ghost and the revenger Hieronimo. What is more, at the end of the play the tragic hero will not revenge the original murder of Andrea, but that of his son Horatio. By having two characters killed by the villainous and powerful Balthazar, Kyd managed to create a strong link between the natural and supernatural planes, but he also chose to sever any direct contact between them. Thus the revenger, who is a magistrate and embodies the respect for the law, is destined to question painfully and repeatedly his right to punish, until – precisely when he begins to despair of God's justice – a letter denouncing Lorenzo and Balthazar as the murderers of Horatio falls from the sky. Although the agent of this revelation is Belimperia, who has been imprisoned in a tower and has written this letter with her blood, the coincidence is striking. Yet Hieronimo still takes his time, until at a much later stage in the action he appears to be pondering over a book:

Vindicta mihi!
Ay, heaven will be revenged of every ill,
Nor will they suffer murder unrepaid:
Then stay, Hieronimo, attend their will,[16]

Hieronimo is quoting by heart a well known passage from the Bible – 'vengeance is mine; I will repay, saith the Lord' (Romans xii: 19)[17] – which justifies his inaction, but the volume he is reading turns out to be Seneca's *Agamemnon*. Classical wisdom soon prevails over his Christian feelings and he finally decides on revenge.

By artfully combining quotations from the Bible and Seneca with Virgil's architecture of the underworld, Kyd achieved a precarious but effective balance between incompatible sets of values, firmly setting revenge within the frame of supernatural justice. Thus, although Hieronimo first turns murderer to accomplish his revenge and then commits suicide, in the last scene of the play Andrea's ghost is ready to welcome him into Proserpine's kingdom, while for his enemies death is only a prelude to eternal punishment.

Moving on to Shakespeare, I need hardly mention that Hamlet plays the uncomfortable role of a detective discovering the secrets of the court, in particular by staging the play within the play which simultaneously re-enacts the fictional murder of Gonzago and the presumed murder of his father. As we know, Hamlet calls his play *The Mousetrap* because it should enable him to catch the 'mouse' he is chasing, that is, Claudius, whose reactions to the play will hopefully reveal his guilt. Yet the psychodrama Hamlet puts on to induce Claudius to betray himself risks obliterating the supernatural origin of an enquiry which is founded on the revelations of a ghost. Since the scrupulous revenger does not trust the ghost, whose nature may be devilish, it is precisely to assess the spirit's truthfulness that Hamlet has the play performed. By combining supernatural and psychological elements, Hamlet's enquiry is typical of a transitional cultural phase:

I have heard that guilty creatures sitting at a play
Have by the very cunning of the scene
Been struck so to the soul that presently
They have proclaimed their malefactions;
For murder, though it have no tongue, will speak
With most miraculous organ. I'll have these players
Play something like the murder of my father
Before mine uncle. I'll observe his looks,
I'll tent him to the quick. If a but blench,
I know my course ...[18]

Here the belief that murder will talk with a 'miraculous organ' does not evoke – as in Chaucer – a supernatural event, but rather a psychological phenomenon, the impossibility of concealing one's guilt. Hamlet relies on the drama to verify the statement of the ghost, and after spying on the reaction of Claudius at the climax of the play, he exclaims 'I'll take the Ghost's word for a thousand pound.'[19] Needless to say, after achieving his mission, Hamlet dies together with his enemies, since revenge is a self-destructive mission.

The revenge tragedy cycle may be said to reach its anticlimax with Tourneur's *The Atheist's Tragedy; or, The Honest Man's Revenge*, where the incompatible moral codes marking the schizophrenic attitude of the revenger are eventually reconciled. In the course of a dream, the Baron of Montferrers appears to his son, who is far from home, fighting a war. The Baron invites him to return to France 'for thy old father's dead / And thou by murder disinherited', but instead of inciting him to shed further blood, he orders him to abide by the decrees of heaven and 'leave revenge unto the King of kings'.[20]

Like Hamlet, Charlemont questions the nature of this uncanny dream and the explanation he offers sounds quite modern:

... Tush, these idle dreams
Are fabulous. Our boiling fantasies
Like troubled waters falsify the shapes
Of things retained in them, and make 'em seem
Confounded when they are distinguished. So
My actions daily conversant with war,
The argument of blood and death, had left,
Perhaps, th'imaginary presence of
Some bloody accident upon my mind,
Which, mixed confusedly with other thoughts,
Whereof th'remembrance of my father might
Be one, presented all together seem
Incorporate, as if his body were
The owner of that blood, the subject of
That death, when he's at Paris and that blood
Shed here. It may be thus. I would not leave
The war, for reputation's sake, upon
An idle apprehension, a vain dream.[21]

Charlemont rationalises his dream as the combination of the violent impression caused by the blood he has seen on the battlefield and the beloved memory of his father. It is the ghost himself that disperses these doubts, by appearing again – no longer in the inner space of the mind, but as a visible entity, causing a soldier to flee in terror. Here the word of the ghost is proved by repetition and by an experience that transcends subjectivity – two criteria that do not satisfy Hamlet. Charlemont returns to Paris, but when he is about to kill the perfidious D'Amville, the ghost of his father stays his hand, reasserting that revenge belongs to God. And in fact, in the final scene of the play, the murderer is punished by God himself, for when D'Amville raises an axe to cut off Charlemont's head, he accidentally strikes his own instead. Although this unforeseen development proves 'that *patience is the honest man's revenge*',[22] it also deprives the Christian revenger of his tragic character, turning him into the hero of a comedy who is rewarded with a happy ending, while the real protagonist of this tragedy is the atheist D'Amville. Thus it is with a paradox that *The Atheist's Tragedy* marks the ending of the Renaissance revenge cycle. The text achieves the combined effect of defusing a dangerous social practice and ridiculing atheism, while reasserting the supreme power of providence.

'Providential fictions'

In spite of 'atheistic' attacks, the idea of God as the primal revenger was still fertile in the Renaissance period, as is shown by the popular literature of those years, in which murder plays a prominent role. *The Murder of John Brewen, Goldsmith of London, who through the entisement of John Parker, was poysoned by his owne wife in eating a measse of Sugersops* (1592) is a case in point. This tract relates the story of a man who is killed by his wife with the help of her lover, but two years after their crime the widow and her accessory are overheard while they are quarrelling and thus unwittingly reveal their deed. The death sentence inevitably follows and the story ends with this reassuring sentence:

> The Lord give all men grace by their example to shunne the hatefull sinne of murder, for be it kept never so close, and done never so secret, yet at length the Lord will bring it out; for bloud is an incessant crier in the eares of the Lord, and he will not leave so wilde a thing unpunished.[23]

Here detection is the result neither of miraculous events nor of human ingenuity, but rather of an accident, yet the story is firmly framed within a Christian plot of guilt and punishment. We should not forget that according to a providential logic accidents are to be interpreted as signs of God's will, although his ways may appear at times tortuous and his action may prove slow to produce the desired effects.

A providential plot also appears in Thomas Nashe's *The Unfortunate Traveller; or, The Life of Jack Wilton* (1594), a picaresque novel whose ending includes what we could define as a cameo revenge tragedy in prose. The protagonist of this subplot is Cutwolf, who kills Esdras of Granado – 'the emperor of homicides'[24] – in revenge for Esdras's murder of his brother Bartol, one of Esdras's accomplices. Cutwolf himself, however, is now condemned to die for the murder he has committed and the whole episode is presented as a dying speech – that is to say as the public 'confession' a criminal used to give before being hanged. In order to understand the rhetorical strategies that underlie this revenge plot, let us focus on the words Jack Wilton, who is the first-person narrator of the novel, addresses to his readers so as to signal a shift in register from comedy to tragedy: 'Prepare your ears and your tears, for never, till this, thrust I any tragical matter upon you. Strange and wonderful are God's judgements; here shine they in their glory.' In the eyes of the picaresque hero/narrator, by killing Esdras, Cutwolf also revenges the death of Heraclide, a woman who was raped by the bandit and consequently committed suicide. Cutwolf's act thus takes on a wider meaning and this 'wearish, dwarfish, writhen-faced cobbler' becomes somehow the scourge of God, for 'Murder is wide-mouthed, and will not let God rest till he grant revenge.'[25]

Various elements contribute to the highly sensational character of the final encounter between Esdras and Cutwolf, as is recounted by the latter in the course of his speech. Not only does Cutwolf claim to have travelled 'above three thousand miles'[26] to pursue Esdras, but – as in *Hamlet* – the final aim of the revenger is to damn his opponent's soul rather than simply to deprive him of his life. Thus, a sort of psychological conflict takes place between the two men, since first Cutwolf promises Esdras to spare his life if he abjures God, and then he kills him so as to make sure he speedily goes to hell. By setting this subplot in Italy, which was notorious at the time as the land of duels and revenge, Nashe felt free to orchestrate a grotesque climax of horror for, after shooting Esdras, Cutwolf raises this blasphemous paean:

> Revenge is the glory of arms and the highest performance of valour. Revenge is whatsoever we call law or justice. The farther we wade in revenge the nearer come we to the throne of the Almighty [...] All true Italians imitate me in revenging constantly and dying valiantly. Hangman to thy task, for I am ready for the utmost of thy rigour.[27]

The orthodox moral that Jack Wilton draws from the 'truculent tragedy' that Cutwolf invoked in his dying speech is that 'One murder begetteth another',[28] but even more convincing is the message of despair Esdras conveys to his assailant before dying: ' "This murder is a house divided within itself; it suborns a man's own soul to inform against him. His soul, being his accuser, brings forth his two eyes as witnesses against him, and the least eyewitness is unrefutable." '[29] Presenting a murderer as his/her own first accuser was a powerful strategy to instil in readers a principle of self-surveillance.

While in Nashe's novel Cutwolf is at one and the same time the instrument of God's justice and of his own perdition, reiterating the moral ambivalence that is at the heart of revenge tragedies, it is God himself who takes on the role of revenger in the collection of crime stories an Exeter merchant named John Reynolds published in six books between 1621 and 1635, *The Triumphs of Gods Revenege against the crying, and exe-crable Sinne of Murther: or His Miraculous discoveries and severe punishments thereof.*[30] In its long subtitle, the book is presented as '*very necessary to restraine, and deterre us from this bloody Sinne, which, in these our dayes, makes so ample, and so lamentable a progression'.*[31] This advertising strategy both magnifies the phenomenon of crime and offers as a solution a form of preventive psychological policing, firmly establishing an editorial practice that would pervade the following centuries.

As Albert Borowitz claims, although Reynolds presented his collection as the adaptation of criminal cases he had come to know while travelling on business in Europe, 'the entire book appears to be a fabrication'.[32] Thanks to the intricacy of Reynolds's plots and to his compelling rhetoric of revenge, this work soon achieved great popularity. Not only did it provide Thomas Middleton and William Rowley with the plot of *The Changeling* (1622), but by 1670 Reynolds's collection had gone into its fifth edition (the first to be lavishly illustrated with woodcuts) and it continued to be printed well into the eighteenth century. Even William Godwin acknowledged the text as a source of his seminal crime novel *Caleb Williams* (1794), as we shall see in the next chapter.

The thirty stories Reynolds collected combine the tradition of revenge tragedies with other forms of crime fiction, such as the broadside, whose status – between fact and fiction – is ambivalent. As in Renaissance tragedies, here the choice of a distant setting – in terms of space and/or time – makes the literary representation of crime less offensive, for Reynolds's 'Tragicall Histories' are 'acted in divers Countries beyond the Seas', such as Italy, France, Switzerland, Portugal and Spain. Moreover, crime is firmly encapsulated within a Christian ethos where God is endowed with the twin functions of detection and punishment. Interestingly, the words *detect* and *detection* frequently recur in Reynolds's work, usually in passages that reaffirm its exemplary value, 'Which inhumane murther, we shall see, God in his due time will miraculously detect, and securely revenge and punish.'[33] The central message of the book – that is, the idea that 'murther, though never so secretly acted, and concealed, will at last be detected and punished'[34] – is repeated over and over again, with an almost mesmerising effect.

What varieties of foul deeds make up this gallery of horrors? Reynolds often portrays family crimes whose motives involve lust, money, unwanted pregnancy and incest. Female poisoners abound in these stories, where the cunning of criminals makes the final triumph of God even more spectacular.

As regards detection, here the emphasis is neither on revelatory dreams nor on ghostly apparitions. Revenge tragedies set out to explore the inner drama of a bewildered human being whose mission as revenger implies two stages of psychological anguish, concerning respectively the sphere of knowledge and that of ethics – first the drama of uncertainty as to the identity of the culprit, second the doubts concerning the moral right-eousness of revenge. Casting God in the role of revenger changed the rules of the game. Since God is omniscient, the drama that unfolds before the readers' eyes in Reynolds's work does not lie in revelation of the culprit, but in the sensational ways God will choose to punish the impious. 'Historie VII' is a case in point. After unsuccessfully attempting to have her sister poisoned by her maid and after killing this dangerous accessory, the per-fidious Catalina obtains her sister's forgiveness, but God's judgement is relentless. Thus, while on board a coach that is driving her to church, Catalina is struck by lightning:

> but see the providence & justice of God, how it surprizeth & overtakes this wretched Gentlewoman *Catalina!* for as shee was in her way, the Sunne is instantly eclipsed, and the skies over-cast, and so a terrible and fearefull thunder-bolt pierceth her thorow the brest, and layes her neere dead in her Coach: her accident, so they thinke it fit to returne.[35]

As a result, Catalina's body is blackened from her waist up. Her guilt is thus revealed to everybody, but this supernatural punishment leaves her sufficient respite to confess her sins and redeem herself before dying.

This story embodies the typical paradigm of Reynolds's tales, where a crime – often pertaining to the domestic sphere, and therefore doubly odious – is committed and the culprit is subsequently reached by God's justice, often in the form of an unexpected accident injuring or maiming his/her body. Reynolds's criminals go through a variety of ordeals – they may drown or fall from their horse or be killed by a mad bull or other-wise betray one another – and we are always led to understand that the hand of God is behind these events. In 'Historie XV', a man commits the most unnatural crime of throwing his mother into a well to obtain her money and go on with his dissipated life. Having quickly spent all his ill-earned money on drunken orgies, he is imprisoned for debt. While in jail, he falls and breaks his arm (the one he used to commit his murder), which rots and has to be cut off. A descent into madness, a confession of his crimes and a sentence of hanging round off this short biography.

As we can see, in Reynolds's narratives the body of the criminal is depicted as an object of contempt both before and after death. In 'Historie IV', after discovering the crimes the two main characters have committed (and before they also die) the judges have the criminals' corpses disinterred and burnt 'at the common place of execution'. The ashes of the two are finally 'throwne into the ayre, as unworthy to have any resting place on earth'.[36] The body of the victim is occasionally called on by Reynolds to testify to the villains' crimes, both metaphorically ('for the innocent and dead bodies of *Mermanda* and her husband *Grand-Pre*, out of their graves cry to him for revenge')[37] and literally, for example in 'Historie XXVII' a wolf disinters a corpse, thus revealing that a murder was committed.

This brings us back to the role that clues play in these tales, where they occasionally contribute to the solution of the mystery. In 'Historie XXVI', for instance, a pair of gloves is left by one of the murderers at the crime scene and betrays him. In 'Historie XII', letters play a major role both in the action leading up to crime and in the ensuing investigation. It is thanks to the love letters that Baretano wrote to Clara that Albemare becomes aware of their affair and decides to have Baretano murdered by two soldiers, Pedro and Leonardo, in order to marry the girl himself. His plan is successful, but too many people share this dangerous secret. Thus, when Pedro is imprisoned for theft and asks for Albemare's help, the latter sends his man Valerio to the prison and has Pedro killed. Leonardo himself, however, is later imprisoned for debt and sends Albemare a letter, threatening to reveal Albemare's dark deeds unless he pays Leonardo's creditors. When the letter reaches Albemare's house he is not at home and the subsequent chain of events is openly shown to be the result of a providential plot, since it is thanks to a half-witted character that the letter falls into Clara's hands:

> when, behold our sweet and vertuous *Clara* comming from Saint *Ambrose* Church, where she had been to here *Vespres*, and seeing a faire letter fast sealed in the fooles hand, shee enquires of him from whence hee had it? who singing and hopping, and still playing with the Letter, shee could get no other answere from him, but *That it was his Letter, and that God had sent it him, that God had sent it him:* which speeches of his, he often redoubled.[38]

Thanks to the God-directed action of the fool, Clara is informed of her husband's crimes and brings the letter to Baretano's powerful uncle, who has Albemare, Leonardo and Valerio executed.

We can regard Reynolds's collection as an attempt to capitalise on the sensational appeal of revenge tragedies and therefore as an advance on previous 'providential fictions'. As Godwin certainly understood, given the structure of *Caleb Williams*, Reynolds's book derives its strength from the omnipresence of God, who acts covertly behind the scenes, precisely like the hero of a revenge tragedy. Yet, while Reynolds appropriated the popular figure of the revenger, identifying it with God, he also got rid of the supernatural apparatus of dreams and ghosts that characterised revenge tragedies.

Crime literature between tragedy and comedy

In his classic study on the literature of roguery, F.W. Chandler analysed the many provinces that make up this varied literary territory – from picaresque novels to jest-books, beggar-books, cony-catching pamphlets, prison tracts and repentances, canting lexicons, criminal biographies and collected chronicles of crime. Chandler also distinguished the 'villain', whose typical crime is murder, from the 'rogue', whose typical crime is theft.[39] Most of the medieval and early-modern crime literature I have mentioned pivots on murder, which was regarded as the capital sin and was therefore believed to trigger supernatural forms of detection. Reynolds's collection is particularly revealing in this respect, for in order to enhance the tragic appeal of his stories, the author repeatedly relied on the most hateful homicides – those treacherously happening within the domestic sphere, including parricide and infanticide.

While murder was associated with the sublime dimension of tragedy, theft, cozenage and other minor crimes were regarded as closer to lower genres – such as comedy and the picaresque – and recur in various kinds of popular literature that anatomise the underworld, exploiting the sensational appeal of misdemeanours. This shift from tragedy to comedy implies a different attitude both in the conception of the plot and in the world view the texts convey. As Hal Gladfelder puts it:

> Whereas fictions of providential intervention are complexly plotted and highly patterned in their effects – corresponding both to the elaborate machinations of the murderers they portray and to a view of the world as ordered, purposeful, watchfully governed – picaresque stories are episodic and arbitrary in their moral and emotional effects, just as the world they imagine is unstable, disintegrating, catalyzed by chance meetings and clashes. One is tragic, the other comical and satiric.[40]

Starting from these premises, I will highlight three different approaches to the comic treatment of crime. The first is exemplified by Thomas Middleton's *The Last Will and Testament of Laurence Lucifer, The Old Bachelor of Limbo* (1604). Here the criminal is overtly presented as a devil and is therefore implicitly condemned right from the beginning. The testament opens 'In the name of Beelzebub'[41] and testifies to Lucifer's complete surrender of his soul to hell. The humorous treatment of Lucifer – who can be considered as a descendant of the 'vices' we find in morality plays – is aimed to provoke a rejection of evil, and the text itself is defined as 'a harmless moral'.[42]

While this take implies no identification at all between readers and the character portrayed, various early-modern works invite the public to feel pity for the criminal. These comic 'providential fictions' suggest that prevention – rather than detection and revenge – is the primary aim of God. In spite of their past mistakes, many criminals can still be saved, but an exceptional event is often needed to make them abandon the path of vice. A variety of 'special effects' can be deployed by divine providence to convert these black sheep. Many works could be mentioned in this respect, such as Richard Head's *The English Rogue Described in the Life of Meriton Latroon, a Witty Extravagant* (1665), a major example of English picaresque.[43] When the main character is condemned to death and closely contemplates an eternity of despair the story seems to evolve towards a tragic climax, but in the end his death sentence is converted into 'a seven years banishment'[44] and his picaresque adventures can resume against exotic backdrops.

The dichotomy between a tragic treatment of murder and a comic treatment of minor crimes also marks, for instance, Defoe's early eighteenth-century criminal biographies. While Moll Flanders is finally allowed to spend a comfortable old age in England (only 'formally' repenting her former crimes), Lady Roxana – who is guilty of conniving with her maid Amy to murder her own daughter – concludes her narrative with these desperate words: 'the Blast of Heaven seem'd to follow the Injury done the poor Girl, by us both; and I was brought so low again, that my Repentance seem'd to be only the Consequence of my Misery, as my Misery was of my Crime.'[45] Interestingly, only one crime – the unpardonable crime – is mentioned in this passage.

The problem of repentance is central also to Defoe's *The Life, Adventures, and Pyracies of Captain Singleton* (1720), where Singleton – part rogue, part hero – is allowed to make amends for his former life of crime. The climax of the novel coincides with the turning point in the life of the main character, whose conversion follows a natural event of supernatural import, so to speak. The boat on which Singleton is travelling (together with a devout Quaker, who will be instrumental in his salvation) is suddenly struck by lightning, whose heat and flash, and whose concomitant thunder, throw all the men into the utmost terror, while the Quaker preserves his calm and manages to save the boat. This is how Singleton describes his state of mind:

> I was all Amazement and Confusion, and this was the first Time that I can say I began to feel the Effects of that Horrour which I know since much more of, upon the just Reflection on my former Life. I thought myself doom'd by Heaven to sink that Moment into eternal

Destruction; and with this peculiar Mark of Terror, *viz.* That the Vengeance was not executed in the ordinary way of human Justice, but that God had taken me into his immediate Disposing, and had resolved to be the Executer of his own Vengeance.[46]

Once again, God is presented as the primal revenger, but this sublime display of power turns out to be a means of redemption rather than of punishment.

A third form of comic treatment of crime can be identified in early-modern literature. Those criminals who were guilty of theft rather than murder often had an ambivalent status, since they could also be regarded as brave and gallant individuals who rebelled against an unjust society, redistributing its riches, following the archetype of Robin Hood.[47] Works such as Alexander Smith's *A Complete History of the Lives and Robberies of the Most Notorious Highwaymen, Footpads, Shoplifts and Cheats of Both Sexes* (1714)[48] easily turned villains into heroes, surrounding the exploits of highway criminals with a romantic aura and presenting them as part of an aristocracy of crime.[49]

Comedy and tragedy interestingly mingle in Smith's collection of criminal biographies. Although the various histories usually end with the death of the criminal, readers are only occasionally reminded of the wrath of God, while a comic vein is pervasive, and even religion can be the object of a jocular treatment. After being robbed by a highwayman called Whitney, Mr Waven – who is a 'lecturer of the church at Greenwich' – is obliged to improvise a sermon. Drawing inspiration from the word THEFT, Mr Waven divides it into letters, 'Now T, my beloved, is Theological; H, is historical; E, is Exegetical; F, is figurative; and T, is Tropological.' The ensuing speech is a piece of rhetorical bravura. The effects theft produces in this world are described by Mr Waves as follows, 'T, Tribulation; H, Hatred; E, Envy; F, Fear; and T, Torment',[50] but these five letters also 'point towards a tragical conclusion, for T, Take care; H, Hanging; E, Ends not; F, Felony; T, at Tyburn'.[51] The churchman, however, receives but a scant prize for his oratorical virtuosity, since he has been relieved of ten pounds and is handed back only ten shillings for his pains... This is not the only case where Smith dealt ironically with religion. When another highwayman – Captain James Hind – assaults Hugh Peters to rob him, the latter tries to save his purse by appealing to Holy Writ, but a rhetoric duel takes place on the field of faith and the highwayman proves more proficient than his adversary.[52]

As we can see, when the comic treatment of crime (be it the prelude to life and salvation or to death and damnation) prevails over the tragic plot of murder and punishment, divine detection loses its centrality.

The *Newgate Calendars*

Sixteenth- and seventeenth-century crime literature had an ambivalent relation with reality, often claiming to be grounded on facts even when it was actually the fruit of invention. Yet, the space and time coordinates of early crime literature are often distant or indeterminate, as is shown by the works of Nashe and of Reynolds. Between the seventeenth and eighteenth centuries, on the other hand, due to the diffusion of print and journalism, present reality – the reality 'news' deals with – acquired increasing relevance. Smith's *Complete History* exemplifies this trend, since it includes several criminals who had died on the gallows just a few years before its publication, but other early-modern literary texts capitalised even more openly on topicality. As Gladfelder writes, the 'dying speeches' and the Ordinary of Newgate's *Accounts* (reporting the confessions of criminals who were going to be executed) 'had to be printed and sold quickly', for both their commercial and their moral value was tied to their 'recentness'.[53] Claiming that reports of recent crimes fuelled a climate of uncertainty, Gladfelder also calls our attention to the fact that news reports are inherently full of fragmented information, while 'if things are to signify, meanings must be *attached* to them'.[54] Post-execution accounts of criminal deeds managed to circumvent this problem, since they implied a closure and a reassessment of past events in the light of their ultimate outcome – that is, death following a reconciliation with God or a hellish refusal to acknowledge one's crimes, thus preventing the possibility of redemption.

The eighteenth-century *Newgate Calendars* are rooted in this tradition of criminal biographies and can still be regarded as 'providential fictions', for they present a sequence of earthly events as the result of a God-directed script. In these collections of exemplary lives the accidents conspiring to frame a criminal are still conceived as part of a providential design, taking place against the backdrop of what Stephen Knight defined as 'a pre-urban, pre-capitalist, pre-detective world'.[55] The pattern of crime and punishment, however, is less pervaded by God's gaze and presence, and therefore less formulaic than in the previous century, while these narratives are fraught with new forms of anxiety concerning the accuracy and equity of judgement.

Compared with Reynolds's work, *The Malefactor's Register; or, the Newgate and Tyburn Calendar* (1779) features a much wider array of crimes, including 'Bigamy, Burglary, Felony, Forgery, Highway-robbery, High-treason, Murder, Petit-treason, Piracy, Rapes, Riots, Street-robbery, Unnatural crimes, And various other Offences.'[56] We know how heavy the penalties imposed by the so-called 'bloody code' were and a good many of the criminals that the *Calendar* portrays inevitably end their life on the gallows. Yet some escape death, even at the very last minute, as in the case of John Smith, whose reprieve reaches Tyburn immediately after he has been hanged, still in time to save his life and to gain him the nickname of 'Half-Hanged Smith'.[57] All in all, however, the tone of the *Calendar* is tragic rather than comic, as is also shown by its illustrations, which emphasise various forms of execution (hanging, beheading, burning) and torments, as well as the practice of branding thieves.

The purported aim of the editors of the 1779 *Newgate Calendar* was still didactic, although sensational elements obviously play a major role in the compilation. Right from the title page we are offered this view of the book:

> The whole tending, by a general Display of the Progress and Conse-
> quence of Vice, to impress on the Mind proper Ideas of the Happiness
> resulting from a Life of strict Honor and Integrity: and to convince
> Individuals of the superior Excellence of those Laws framed for the
> Protection of their Lives and Properties.[58]

Significantly, Laws, rather than God, are mentioned here, emphasising the secular – rather than the religious – basis of morality, as is apparent also in the accompanying verses:

> Such is the folly, such the Fate
>   Attendant on dishonest Schemes,
> That Villains ever find, too late,
>   An End to their delusive Dreams.
> We see – and oftimes they confess
>   With their departing Breath,
> 'The *Paths* of *Honour* lead to Peace,
>   The *Ways* of *Vice* – to Death.'[59]

Virtue leads to peace, not to heaven, while crime leads to death, not to hell. These words can be regarded as synonyms, but the shift from the supernatural to the mundane is undeniable. The same can be said of the frontispiece, where a mother hands the *Calendar* to her child who is point-ing to a gibbet that can be seen in the distance through a window. The admonitory/exemplary value of the volume is thus underlined, but the scene does not reveal any sign pointing to the presence of God, while behind mother and son four statues are shown, bearing the attributes and names of Justice, Wisdom, Temperance and Fortitude. The statues hint at the four 'cardinal' or 'natural virtues' (prudence, temperance, fortitude and justice), which are not specifically Christian, although together with the three theological virtues (faith, hope and love) they make up the set of seven virtues that counterbalance the seven deadly sins. God, however, is mentioned in the caption accompanying the image:

> The anxious Mother with a Parents Care,
> Presents our Labours to her future Heir.
> 'The Wise, the Brave, the Temperate, and the Just,
> Who love their Neighbour, and in God who trust,
> Safe through the Dang'rous paths of Life may Steer,
> Nor dread those Evils we exhibit Here.'[60]

Although a good citizen is expected to trust in God, the teachings he/she may derive from perusing the *Calendar* are intended as a guide to steering clear of danger along the paths of life rather than to avoiding the wrath of the maker.

What is more, if we compare Reynolds's stories with the 1779 *Calendar* we discover that its compilers were already distancing themselves from the popular idea that truth is inevitably revealed, advancing instead the less reassuring view that 'truth' is the result of a process and thus depends on the faculties of those who are called upon to judge. This is apparent in the case of Robert Fuller, who is indicted for the attempted murder of Francis Bailey. The victim testifies that he recognised his aggressor, but as the judges subsequently discover, a similar accusation had already been levelled by Bailey against another person, who had been acquitted of the crime:

> On this occasion it may not be improper to make a remark on the immense power that is lodged in the breasts of our judges who go the circuits. A great deal of this power is discretionary: it remains with them to reprieve the convict or to leave him for execution: an awful trust! which makes the possessor of it accountable to God and his own conscience.[61]

In the eighteenth century the new ideological climate of European society brought into question the traditional belief in 'divine detection' and fundamentally changed the nature of 'providential fictions' such as the *Newgate Calendar*, where crime is still part of a Christian narrative whose inevitable conclusion is punishment (both on earth and in the afterlife), but whose editors refrained from setting in motion any supernatural machinery.

Towards the 'professional case'

In the second half of the century – as a result of the enlightened and reformist attitude of the public – a more empirical and rational model of investigation was advocated, as is evidenced by seminal criminological works such as Cesare Beccaria's *Dei delitti e delle pene* (*Of Crimes and Punishments*, 1764) and Pietro Verri's *Osservazioni sulla tortura* (*Observations on Torture*, which was written in the 1770s and published in 1804). Beccaria's book in particular obtained such immediate international acclaim that a French translation appeared in 1776, while the first American edition was published in 1777. These authors not only campaigned against the death penalty and torture but also brought under discussion clues and their reliability. They also drew a neat divide between divine and natural justice (which are immutable) on the one hand and human or political justice (which is variable) on the other.[62] According to Beccaria 'As soon as these two essentially distinct principles are confused, there is no hope of reasoning well in public things.'[63] Crime was no longer regarded primarily as sin, but as the infringement of a social pact.

A few years later William Godwin further increased the distance between sin and crime by conceiving of the latter as the product of environmental factors rather than an evil bent. In his *Enquiry Concerning Political Justice* (1793) the Jacobin philosopher claimed that 'the actions and dispositions of mankind are the offspring of circumstances and events, and not of any original determination that they bring into the world'.[64] This principle governs *Caleb Williams* (1794), where Caleb's morbid curiosity and Falkland's obsession with honour are justified by the characters' backgrounds. Godwin, who is regarded as the father of anarchism, considered crime as a social evil, not as an offence against God.

As Gladfelder claims, already in the course of the eighteenth century 'the law prevailed over religion in the struggle for ideological dominance', but crime narratives nevertheless continued to exploit the vocabulary 'of religious terror and longing'.[65] The rhetoric of sin survived despite the progressive assertion of a secular framework considering crime primarily as an offence against the law. For instance, only the transition from the eighteenth-century *Newgate Calendars* to the 1809–26 versions, which were edited by lawyers Andrew Knapp and William Baldwin, would produce what Struan Sinclair called a 'shift from a theological to a mainly legal frame of reference'.[66]

These nineteenth-century *Calendars* once again feature a variety of crimes, ranging from murder to child-stealing, burglary, coining, high treason, forgery, letter-stealing, rape and bigamy. Naturally, crimes against property were becoming a major offence in an increasingly mercantile and bourgeois society. Moreover, Knapp and Baldwin showed a growing concern with the administration of justice and condemned torture as barbarous. The case of Thomas Picton – a magistrate in Trinidad who was indicted for torturing Louisa Calderon, an eleven-year-old girl, to extort a confession from her – is a case in point.[67] Needless to say, the youth of the suspect contributed to the melodramatic appeal of the event.

Torture was also discussed in an appendix in which the compilers of the *Calendar* extolled the wisdom of British laws, which abolished this 'inhuman practice' in 1772, although it still prevailed 'in some of the English settlements abroad' – a comment which clarifies the import of the above-mentioned story. After arguing that 'No man can be judged a criminal until he be found guilty', Knapp and Baldwin went on to trace the practice of torture to its origins:

> This custom seems to be the offspring of religion, by which mankind, in all nations, and in all ages, are so generally influenced. We are taught by our infallible Church that those stains of sin contracted through human frailty, and which have not deserved the eternal anger of the Almighty, are to be purged away in another life by an incomprehensible fire. Now infamy is a stain; and, if the punishments and fire of purgatory can take away all spiritual stains, why should not the pain of torture take away those of a civil nature? I imagine that the confession of a criminal, which in some tribunals is required as being essential to his condemnation, has a similar origin, and has been taken from the mysterious tribunal of penitence, where the confession of sins is a necessary part of the sacrament.[68]

This subversive account of the origin of torture and confession testifies to the free-thinking attitude Knapp and Baldwin applied to the study of legal procedures, in order to get rid of the dangerous prejudices and customs that society had inherited from the past.

In another appendix, the two lawyers set out to disprove the popular belief in ghosts and haunted houses – notably the superstition that the ghost of the victim would denounce his/her murderer – by referring to various cases of 'pretended ghosts'.[69] The most interesting story Knapp and Baldwin relate is that of the 'Cock Lane Ghost', in which a Mr Parsons exploited the credulity of the populace to take revenge on his former lodger, Mr Kent, by having the 'ghost' of his deceased sister-in-law accuse Kent of murder. Needless to say, no ghost haunted the lodgings of

Mr Parsons, who contrived to fake the otherworldly apparitions and messages with the help of various members of his household, including his daughter. Deconstructing this supernatural rhetoric of crime and punishment was an important aspect of the campaign which people like Knapp and Baldwin were conducting to reform the apparatus of justice. In the same period the problem of ensuring equitable trials also attracted the attention of scientists like Laplace, whose *Essai Philosophique sur les Probabilités* (*Philosophical Essay on Probabilities*, 1814) includes a chapter 'On the probability of testimony' and another 'On the probability of judicial decisions' (not to be found in the first edition). After describing the possibility of error in judgement as the main argument in favour of the abolition of the death penalty, Laplace claimed that a penalty ought to depend on 'the measure of the danger to which the acquittal of the accused may expose society'.[70] Probability calculus also enabled the mathematician to ponder the composition of juries and on the majority of votes that is necessary to make a judgement reliable.

Thus, science was starting to assert its role as the guiding light of detection and punishment. Unsuprisingly, these decades were also marked by the rise of a new narrative formula, the 'professional case'. In a recent book, Heather Worthington analysed the serial investigating figures of professionals – such as physicians, barristers and attorneys – who prepared the way for the detective proper, also in relation to the development of the New Metropolitan Police (1829) and the Detective Police (1842). As Worthington remarks, Samuel Warren's 'Passages from the Diary of a Late Physician' (*Blackwood's Edinburgh Magazine*, 1830–37) inaugurated the 'case structure'[71] that would typify later detective fiction. Although these stories deal with the field of medicine rather than crime, a few years later the 'Experiences of a Barrister' (*Chambers's Edinburgh Journal*, 1849–50), which were also attributed to Warren, explored the world of crime and the legal system, while William Russell's 'Recollections of a Police Officer' (*Chambers's*, 1849–53) definitely focused on the investigating policeman. The sphere of detection was increasingly regarded as the proper domain of professionals who mastered specific disciplines and technical skills, while the theological apparatus that had formerly been utilised to contain crime in the absence of police forces became less and less relevant to the discourses of crime.

The aesthetics of murder

The progressive secularisation of crime implied not only the transition from sin to crime, the deployment of disciplinary figures such as the policeman and the development of the 'professional case' in fiction, but also an aesthetic appreciation of murder as the crime *par excellence*. Thomas De Quincey's seminal essay 'On Murder Considered as One of the Fine Arts' (*Blackwood's*, 1827)[72] proved a ground-breaking work in this respect, for De Quincey claimed the right to consider murder not morally but 'in relation to good taste'.[73] The disruptive and provocative character of De Quincey's satirical text is apparent, since in order to prove his thesis the author referred to the Bible so as to reassess the figure of the archetypal murderer, Cain. 'As the inventor of murder, and the father of the art', Cain was irreverently presented by De Quincey as 'a man of first-rate genius',[74] although his performance – judged by the standards of a later age – 'was but so-so'.[75] With its tongue-in-cheek tone, this subversive essay advocated not only a revision of the Western approach to murder (tracing a historical account of this 'art' which culminated in what the author termed 'the Augustan age of murder'),[76] but also a new appreciation of crime literature.

As Worthington perceptively claims, 'this essay exemplifies the intellectual appropriation of the sensational crime of the broadsides by the literary establishment'.[77] Indeed, Milton and Shakespeare were both identified as amateurs of murder[78] by De Quincey, who thus claimed them as forerunners of a lofty genealogy of crime literature. Due to this strategy, which was aimed at legitimising a literary genre that was perceived as 'low', the Romantic author can be regarded as the precursor of writers such as Edward Bulwer-Lytton and Elizabeth Braddon, whose 'self-ennobling' critical works defend sensationalism against its conservative detractors.

As we have seen, a huge shift from the rhetoric of sin to a disciplinary and aesthetic treatment of crime took place at the beginning of the Victorian period. The paradigm of divine justice, however, survived this generalised interest in legal matters. Indeed, precisely when the detective was acquiring a growing importance as hero, other writers were 'rediscovering' the link between detection and the supernatural. This varied output, straggling across the border between metaphysics and pseudo-sciences, will be the object of chapters 4 and 5, but first let us see how the paradigm of divine omniscience was appropriated by eighteenth-century writers such as Godwin as a subversive tool and was subsequently absorbed into mainstream detective fiction.

3
Persecution and Omniscience

Persecution is a typical gothic theme, a display of evil power associated with dungeons and danger, and with a distorted view of religious or political orthodoxy. Following a tradition which is rooted in Renaissance tragedies, gothic novels are often set in Southern European countries and do not refrain from depicting the stock in trade of anti-Catholic propaganda – depraved monks, corrupted convents, devilish Inquisitors. Alternatively, the agents of persecution may be villainous aristocrats, whose prime motives are incest, money, revenge. It is easy to understand why persecution is central in gothic fiction, but can the same be said of omniscience?

Rather than any gothic connotations, the ideal of universal knowledge seems to evoke the twin icons of the Enlightenment – light and rationality – as well as the *Encyclopédie*, a positive utopia of complete human control over nature. Yet omniscience is originally linked to the idea of God and we should not forget that its closest correlatives are other attributes of the divinity such as omnipresence and omnipotence. This trinity of absolutes defines a distinctly Foucauldian paradigm, since the French scholar claims 'that power and knowledge directly imply one another; that there is no relationship of power without a corresponding field of knowledge nor any relationship of knowledge which does not presuppose and constitute at the same time a relationship of power.'[1] With this in mind, I will explore the gothic import of omniscience and its subsequent metamorphosis within detective fiction.

When, in 1752, Henry Fielding published his pamphlet 'Examples of the Interposition of Providence in the Detection and Punishment of Murder' he could still claim that the primary cause of the recent increase in murders was 'the general neglect [...] of religion'.[2] In order to reassert the existence of 'a being, in whose words we must be assured there is all truth, and in whose right hand is all power'[3] Fielding cited what he regarded as a series of reliable cases – although today one would rather label them as an assortment of legends – taken from disparate sources. The first of them is Cain's murder of Abel, which offers Fielding the opportunity to claim the truth-value of an ancient belief:

> for it was a notion which prevailed among the Jews, as well as all other nations, that the ghosts of those who were murdered, persecuted the Murderers, continually terrifying them, and requiring their punishment at the hands of justice. And of the truth of this opinion, the most authentic histories, as well as the traditions of all ages and countries, afford us very positive assurance.[4]

As is shown by Fielding's text, in early-modern Europe divine omniscience was used as a form of preventive psychological policing, but the religious component of justice was instrumental to secular power in other respects, since the right of the king to judge and punish was constructed as a reflection of the supreme power of God. Thus the deviant behaviour of the criminal set off what we may regard as two parallel forms of 'persecution' – that of divine justice and that of royal justice.

If I might resort to a brief play on words, it could be said that with the transition from *sovereign* power – which according to Foucault is based on the public display of punishment and authority – to *disciplinary* power – which is grounded in specialist knowledge and conversely aims at being invisible – the concept of *persecution* now turned into *prosecution*. During the eighteenth century, torture and the death penalty were either abolished or restricted in various countries and more equitable trials were devised. Cesare Beccaria advocated that someone who had been indicted for a crime had the right to be considered innocent until proved guilty and that the truth-value of clues was to be ascertained in order to give an objective basis to every accusation. Martin Kayman stated this clearly when he wrote that 'the transitional morality of the Bloody Code' was rapidly superseded by 'a new model of authority in which mystery by an organic Providence is replaced by mastery by "police" '.[5]

The enlightened ideal of 'secular omniscience'

In this new ideological climate, the concept of omniscience underwent a fundamental transformation. One of the most intriguing architectural machines for the application of disciplinary power pivots on that idea. I am referring to what Foucault regarded as a utopian dream of perfect surveillance, Jeremy Bentham's *Panopticon* (1791). This multi-functional building – which may be used as a penitentiary, but also as a madhouse or a hospital – is made up of a central tower with windows on all sides, protected by shutters, and a surrounding ring of cells, each of them housing a single individual. The cells are separated by walls which make it impossible for the inmates to communicate with one another, but the inner wall is open so that the light entering the cell through two windows turns it into a stage where every move becomes visible. Punishment is no longer linked to the darkness of the dungeon, but to the light that traverses the cell. Visibility becomes a trap. The prisoner is subject to a virtually uninterrupted surveillance because there is no reciprocity between his eye and that of his jailer. He is seen, but he does not see. He is a pure object of perception. Obviously this structure is based on the principle of omniscience because potentially a single jailer can be watching any prisoner at any time, while he remains invisible to them. While sovereign power relied on *divine* omniscience as an instrument of prevention, disciplinary power considers omniscience as an attribute of *humans*, or rather of *human institutions*, for as Foucault remarks, the panopticon turns power into an automatic mechanism which can temporarily work even without a human eye.[6]

Incidentally, the tendency towards panopticism was already apparent before Bentham created this model. In 1774 the utopian French architect Claude-Nicolas Ledoux started to build the salt-processing plant of Arc-et-Senans, which was commissioned by King Louis XV. According to the architect, inside the establishment 'One must see everything, hear everything, hide nothing. The worker should not be allowed to escape surveillance thanks to a round or square column.'[7] Total visibility is once again appropriated as a human attribute. Jean Starobinski was so impressed by this confident assertion of the architect's claim to absolute knowledge and power that in *The Invention of Freedom* he included Ledoux's drawing of the plant together with his project for the Theatre of Besançon, which is interestingly shown – with a close-up effect – as reflected in the pupil of an eye.[8]

In this rather disquieting image we have a complex apotheosis of visibility insofar as the eye does not only see, but it also reflects what is basically conceived as a machine for seeing – for what else is a theatre? And yet there is no public; the tiers of seats are empty. The architectural structure itself becomes the protagonist, like the panopticon. The eye of the Christian God – traditionally inscribed within the perfect shape of a triangle – has become the eye of a revolutionary lay goddess, reason itself, who tends to be dehumanised by her adepts in order to emphasise her purely geometrical nature. The metamorphosis of the eye of God into the eye of the police seems to be accomplished in 1791 when this emblem of detection is chosen as the symbol of a new police corps – the French *Officiers de paix*.

Another sign of the increasing secularisation of omniscience is the development of probability theory in the second half of the seventeenth century, partly as the result of a new scientific approach, for the concepts of chance and fortune were superseded by a new paradigm of causation, and partly as a response to the early stages of globalisation, which involved risky commercial ventures.[9] Laplace's *Essai philosophique sur les probabilités* (*Philosophical Essay on Probabilities*, 1814) is a fruit of this cultural climate. In this text – an expanded version of a lecture Laplace gave in 1795 – the French astronomer and mathematician asserted his belief in determinism:

> We ought then to consider the present state of the universe as the effect of its previous state and as the cause of that which is to follow. An intelligence that, at a given instant, could comprehend all the forces by which nature is animated and the respective situation of the beings that make it up, if moreover it were vast enough to submit these data to analysis, would encompass in the same formula the movements of the greatest bodies of the universe and those of the lightest atoms. For such an intelligence nothing would be uncertain, and the future, like the past, would be open to its eyes.[10]

We can regard this oft-quoted passage as a declaration of faith in the 'omniscient' character of scientific thought. Laplace famously discarded the idea of God as a conceptual tool that explained everything without enabling one to foresee anything. On the other hand, science endowed human beings with unprecedented power, turning them into modern-day seers, for by following the chain of cause and effect humanity was able to 'travel' in time, comprehending the past and the future in its quest for knowledge.

Moreover, determinism ruled out the traditional superstitious belief in God as the supernatural agent who periodically punished humanity for its sins by means of catastrophes: 'Let us recall that formerly, and indeed not too long ago, torrential rain or severe drought, a comet with a very long tail in train, eclipses, the aurora borealis and generally all extraordinary phenomena were regarded as so many signs of divine anger.' Taking place only at long intervals, these phenomena 'seemed contrary to the order of nature' and 'it was supposed that heaven, incensed by the crimes of the earth, had created them to give warning of its vengeance'.[11]

The dark side of omniscience

While in the years preceding and following the French Revolution the enlightened dream of human omniscience was celebrated under the auspices of reason, the concept of divine omniscience conversely acquired disquieting connotations. Gothic fiction offered a nightmarish view of omniscience as being rooted in the power of a God who was perceived no longer as a source of justice but of terror. To explain this statement, I will focus on the relationship between politics and aesthetics in Edmund Burke's seminal *Philosophical Enquiry into the Origin of our Ideas of the Sublime and the Beautiful* (1757). It is ironic that Burke, who was regarded by many of his contemporaries as a champion of the status quo because of the reactionary tone of his *Reflections on the Revolution in France* (1790), was also the man who elaborated in his *Enquiry* something similar to what two centuries later Foucault would call the 'analytics of power'. I would go so far as to claim that Burke's treatise has a potentially revolutionary import insofar as it deconstructs the aesthetic apparatus of power, reducing its sublime components to a strategy and thereby defusing their emotional impact.

Adam Phillips touches on this point when he asserts that Burke's *sublime* is 'bound up with the idea of authority as a species of mystification',[12] but he does not develop this notion. What he makes clear, however, is that the 'apparently aesthetic category' of the sublime is 'unavoidably politicized' insofar as 'the sublime experience is one of domination. Bulls are sublime, oxen are not.'[13] Burke recognises this political component when he claims: 'I know of nothing sublime which is not some modification of power.'[14] After presenting pain and danger as 'the most powerful of all the passions' – since they are directly linked to that basic instinct, 'the preservation of the individual' – Burke claims that 'Whatever is fitted in any sort to excite the ideas of pain, and danger [...] is a source of the *sublime*' and therefore 'productive of the strongest emotion which the mind is capable of feeling'.[15]

According to Burke, we perceive what may endanger us as a form of power, be it a ferocious animal or 'the power which arises from institution in kings and commanders', but the strongest form of power and correspondingly the strongest source of the sublime is represented by God himself. Burke hesitates before openly asserting that the idea of God is accompanied by an element of terror which links it to natural and cultural icons of power: 'I purposely avoided' – he writes – 'when I first considered this subject, to introduce the idea of that great and tremendous being, as an example in an argument so light as this.'[16] Yet, after hedging for a whole page, he claims that 'though in a just idea of the Deity, perhaps none of his attributes are predominant, yet to our imagination, his power is by far the most striking.'[17]

The pre-modern chain of associations which lead from God to justice via omniscience – and which was appropriated by the *philosophes*, who substituted the divinity with reason – is superseded by a new chain of associations that connects God with power and the sublime. Moreover, Burke deconstructs the sacred texts, uncovering their rhetorical strategy: 'In the scripture, whenever God is represented as appearing or speaking, every thing terrible in nature is called up to heighten the awe and solemnity of the divine presence.'[18] The representation of God in the Bible is analysed as an awe-inducing mechanism.

Does omniscience play a role in the sublime apparatus which surrounds the divinity? Burke is not very interested in visibility and transparency, but he is attracted by the opposite concepts of invisibility and opacity, since 'darkness is more productive of sublime ideas than light',[19] and he expands on this concept in another revealing passage: 'To make any thing very terrible, obscurity seems in general to be necessary. When we know the full extent of any danger, when we can accustom our eyes to it, a great deal of the apprehension vanishes.' Fear is stronger when we cannot assess the real entity of danger and, in his 'anthropological' perspective, Burke associates once again the political and the religious machinery: 'Those despotic governments, which are founded on the passions of fear, keep their chief as much as may be from the public eye. The policy has been the same in many cases of religion.'[20] God is terrible and sublime not because he can see everything but because we cannot see him; his power is felt, but his presence is not to be identified. The two contrasting concepts of omnipresence and absence seem to coincide, as in the panopticon, and they likewise produce a virtual omniscience and a concrete omnipotence.

Preternatural powers

Let us consider how these new ideas filtered into the domain of the novel. In William Godwin's *Caleb Williams* (1794) – which was conceived as a fictional appendix to Godwin's *Enquiry Concerning Political Justice* (1793) – the aristocratic Falkland is endowed with God-like attributes thanks to factors as varied as his steely will, his social position, the help of a thief-taker and the instrumental use of printing, which all together generate a relentless persecution, turning his former secretary and protégé Caleb into an outcast. The opening of Caleb's first-person narrative is given its power because of its straightforward appeal to the reader as the sole confidant, the only outlet of an otherwise frustrated need to denounce the hero's abysmal experience of injustice:

My life has for several years been a theatre of calamity. I have been a mark for the vigilance of tyranny, and I could not escape. My fairest prospects have been blasted. My enemy has shown himself inaccessible to intreaties and untired in persecution. My fame, as well as my happiness, has become his victim. Every one, as far as my story has been known, has refused to assist me in my distress, and has execrated my name. I have not deserved this treatment.[21]

Although the main ingredients of the novel are all detailed in this dense opening paragraph – persecution and tyranny, solitude and innocence – the agent of Caleb's persecution is not mentioned. Suspense is created from the first and the identity of the hero's implacable enemy is shrouded in silence. Falkland is in fact absent not only from the opening of the novel, but from most of the third volume, which focuses on persecution and shows Caleb restlessly fleeing in disguise all over England in pursuit of a new life, although all his attempts are nullified by the thief-taker Gines. In this part of the novel Falkland is kept – like every icon of sublime power – from the eye of the public and is consequently surrounded by a quasi-supernatural aura.

I do not claim that this results from a precise design, for it may be only a side effect of the plot, but what should be regarded as a literary strategy is that Falkland's attributes are modelled on those of God. When, in 1832, Godwin listed the books he had read before writing *Caleb Williams*, he mentioned John Reynolds's *God's Revenge against Murder* – a pamphlet 'where the beam of the eye of Omniscience was represented as perpetually pursuing the guilty, and laying open his most hidden retreats to the light of day'.[22] Godwin thus acknowledged one of the literary sources of Falkland's absolute knowledge and power, which are reiterated throughout the text:

You little suspect the extent of my power. At this moment you are enclosed with the snares of my vengeance, unseen by you [...] You might as well think of escaping from the power of the omnipresent God, as from mine! If you could touch so much as my finger, you should expiate it in hours and months and years of a torment of which as yet you have not the remotest idea![23]

When, towards the end of the novel, Caleb discovers that his real persecutor has been Falkland's half-brother – Mr Forester – this does not change his situation for the better, since Falkland declares: 'You have sought to disclose the select and eternal secret of my soul. Because you have done that, I will never forgive you.'[24] In other words, persecution starts over again and this time Falkland himself is its agent.

Persecution and omniscience closely intertwine in this novel, which may be regarded as an exercise in the sublime. B.J. Tysdahl notes that Godwin knew Burke's *Enquiry* very well and develops what he calls a 'metaphysical reading' of the novel, insisting on the biblical analogy and comparing Caleb's intrusion into Falkland's trunk – a repository of forbidden knowledge – to Adam's theft of the apple.[25] David Punter includes *Caleb Williams* with Robert Maturin's *Melmoth the Wanderer* (1820) and James Hogg's *The Private Memoirs and Confessions of a Justified Sinner* (1824) in a chapter of *The Literature of Terror* that is entitled 'The dialectic of persecution' and he claims that the three novels pursue a common object, which is precisely 'to investigate the extremes of terror'.[26]

Punter also traces Godwin's influence on later novels such as Mary Shelley's *Frankenstein* (1818) and Charles Brockden Brown's *Wieland; or, the Transformation* (1798), where the characters who play the role of villains – due to a series of unfortunate circumstances rather than innate malignity – are similarly endowed with supernatural powers. As we know, one of the first books that Shelley's creature reads is *Paradise Lost*, which contributes to shaping his identity in biblical terms since he identifies himself with Satan and regards Frankenstein as a negligent creator, 'Remember that I am thy creature; I ought to be thy Adam; but I am rather the fallen angel.'[27] Reversing the traditional pattern of domination – and following the typical romantic tendency to Titanism – it is the creature who becomes a persecutor due to his desperate sense of solitude. In this novel Frankenstein and his creature tend more and more to resemble one another – both are condemned to loneliness, both are pursuer and pursued and they are united by a bond of hatred that can end only in mutual annihilation.

The theme of the double is of utmost importance in many gothic texts. Suffice it to say that in the novels by Hogg and Brown cited above one can likewise find elements such as solitude, persecution and preternatural powers. In *The Confessions of a Justified Sinner*, which was conceived as a satire against the religious belief of antinomianism, the ambiguous Gil-Martin – who turns out to be the devil himself – claims that 'by looking at a person attentively, I by degrees assume his likeness, and by assuming his likeness I attain to the possession of his most secret thoughts'.[28] This technique of thought-reading anticipates a famous passage from Poe's 'The Purloined Letter' (1845), where a schoolboy explains to Dupin how he manages to identify with his opponents while playing 'even and odd':

> 'When I wish to find out how wise, or how stupid, or how good, or how wicked is any one, or what are his thoughts at the moment, I fashion the expression of my face, as accurately as possible, in accordance with the expression of his, and then wait to see what thoughts or sentiments arise in my mind or heart, as if to match or correspond with the expression.'[29]

These lines betray the influence of physiognomy and the pseudo-scientific dream of a perfect correspondence between the outward aspect and the inner nature of man. The analogy between Hogg's and Poe's texts is just one example of the many ways in which gothic fiction anticipated detective fiction. Similarly, in *Wieland*, thanks to the gift of ventriloquism, Carwin the Biloquist becomes virtually omnipresent. Not only is he able to fake voices coming from locked rooms, creating enigmas of a truly detective flavour, but also to fake the voice of God, for once again religious belief is of utmost importance in this American tragedy.

What these gothic novels have in common is the fact that a seemingly infinite power is in the hands of a character who is either a true villain or else is perceived as such. Poe's trilogy reverses this situation, since here it is the detective who holds a supreme power that is based on his encyclopaedic knowledge and analytical frame of mind. While the omniscience of the villain is a source of terror, that of the detective is apparently reassuring. Yet Dupin's vision has a paradoxical quality that brings us back to the gothic, since it is not associated with light, but with darkness. Already in 'The Murders in the Rue Morgue' (1841) we discover that Dupin and the narrator live in complete seclusion and in absence of light, since they walk the streets only after the advent of the 'true Darkness'[30] and spend the day behind the closed shutters of their 'time-eaten and grotesque mansion'.[31] Dupin is an uncanny creature of the night, like the predatory vampire, but also a super-hero like Batman, somebody who can pierce the darkness of the city streets as well as of human hearts.

In 'The Purloined Letter' Dupin's affinity with darkness becomes apparent when the prefect pays the detective a visit in order to ask his advice and he remarks, ' "If it is any point requiring reflection […] we shall examine it to better purpose in the dark." '[32] The symbolic chain that in the Enlightenment linked reason, omniscience and light has been superseded by an alternative trinity. We should not forget that the detective praises Minister D—'s mental faculties because he is both a mathematician and a poet, and that in the first story of the trilogy Poe compares the minor talent of ingenuity to the concept of fancy, while drawing a parallel between analytical power and the supreme romantic gift of imagination. Dupin's main attributes are therefore imagination, omniscience and darkness, since his power of abduction has a creative element which enables him to reverse every commonplace and to take into account the unforeseen. Poe acknowledged his romantic belief in imagination also in 'A Chapter of Suggestions' (1845), where this definition of abduction is offered: 'Some of the most profound knowledge – perhaps all *very* profound knowledge – has originated from a highly stimulated imagination. Great intellects *guess* well.'[33]

Probability vs chance

The omniscient status of the detective, however, was not sanctioned once and for all. Before creating the character of Dupin, Poe wrote 'The Man of the Crowd' (1840), an ambivalent story where the narrator's attempt to dissect the London crowd, revealing its social and criminal strata, is successful only up to a point since 'the type and the genius of deep crime'[34] remains unknowable. This text can be considered as an act of exorcism, a tribute Poe paid to the genius loci of the metropolis, which came to be regarded as a labyrinth of intersecting stories and a place of mystery.

Even Dupin's omniscience, resting on the detective's ability to probe the inner dimension of his fellow human beings and to perceive the connections between phenomena along the chain of cause and effect, soon revealed its faultlines. The detective's second adventure is usually considered as the least palatable episode of the trilogy. In 'The Mystery of Marie Rogêt' (1842–43) Poe bravely attempted to fictionalise the recent – and unsolved – murder case of Mary Rogers, setting the story in Paris; but while the text was being serialised a woman confessed on her death-bed that the girl had died because of an attempted abortion. This version of the facts contrasted with the hypothesis Poe was developing and the author, in order to find a way out of this impasse, devised a rather surprising ending for his narrative, exploiting the appeal and authority of the concept of probability.

As early as 'The Murders in the Rue Morgue' Dupin utilises the theory of probability to deconstruct the fake criminal plot which coincidences have traced.[35] This theory also looms large in the detective's second adventure, where he claims that 'We make chance a matter of absolute calculation. We subject the unlooked-for and unimagined to the mathematical *formulæ* of the schools.'[36] As a result of this insistence on probability, one might be tempted to read 'The Mystery of Marie Rogêt' as an apologia of secular omniscience. Yet, when the enquiry of Poe's fictional alter ego collided with the testimony that a witness rendered on the verge of death – ironically, according to a typical providential pattern – the author felt the need to reassert the presence of God as the ultimate agent behind reality, although he carefully avoided reinstating the maker in the role of a 'revenger' who intervenes in human affairs to punish and purge:

> In my own heart there dwells no faith in præter-nature. That Nature and its God are two, no man who thinks will deny. That the latter, creating the former, can, at will, control or modify it, is also unquestionable. I say 'at will'; for the question is of will, and not, as the insanity of logic has assumed, of power. It is not that the Deity *cannot* modify his laws, but that we insult him in imagining a possible necessity for modification. In their origin these laws were fashioned to embrace all contingencies which could lie in the Future. With God all is *Now*.[37]

As Poe wrote in *Eureka*, 'The Plots of God are perfect.'[38] Like other nineteenth-century thinkers Poe believed that God had no need to modify the perfect machine he had set into motion. The supernatural was thus 'limited to God himself and to his original act of creation',[39] while miracles and other forms of divine intervention in mundane affairs were ruled out.

Although Poe's attempt at 'factional' detection failed, instead of declaring himself vanquished the resourceful author drew once again on probability calculus to evade defeat. As Poe claimed in the epilogue, two series of events can be parallel up to a point, but this does not imply that their denouement is the same: 'Nothing, for example, is more difficult than to convince the merely general reader that the fact of sixes having been thrown twice in succession by a player at dice, is sufficient cause for betting the largest odds that sixes will not be thrown in the third attempt.'[40] This unfounded popular belief is described as 'one of an infinite series of mistakes which arise in the path of Reason through her Propensity for seeking truth *in detail*'.[41]

While in the first part of the story Poe had emphasised Dupin's interest in marginal details, since truth often arises 'from the seemingly irrelevant',[42] here details are presented as misleading, since two parallel chains of events can diverge at any time. Chance, rather than causality, rules this story, which is – unsurprisingly – less popular than the other Dupin adventures. Because of its structural incoherence 'The Mystery of Marie Rogêt' is an unsettling tale, which deflates the status of the detective, an epistemological super-hero whose serendipity should be due to his mastery of observation and imaginative genius rather than to fickle luck. Varying doses of discipline and chance, however, accrue to the enquiries of later nineteenth-century fictional detectives. The power of coincidence is a fundamental factor of discovery in Émile Gaboriau's *L'Affaire Lerouge* (*The Lerouge Case*, 1866), where the criminal and the detective live in the same house. As we know, T.S. Eliot contrasted Poe with Collins, praising the latter for creating the first 'fallible' detective, since in *The Moonstone* (1868) 'the mystery is finally solved, not altogether by human ingenuity, but largely by accident'.[43] Moreover, when in R.L. Stevenson's *The Dynamiter* (1885) a young man decides to embrace 'the only profession for a gentleman'[44] – that is to become a detective – he ironically introduces a new principle of omniscience: 'Chance, the blind Madonna of the pagan, rules this terrestrial bustle; and in Chance I place my sole reliance.'[45] Since deduction – according to Poe – is the ability to guess well, the detective may well need a fair dose of chance. After all, if detective fiction does not reflect order, but rather a yearning for order, then a principle of order is needed, be it only a rhetorical strategy, like Burke's sublime god or the myth of the detective's infallibility.

Secret societies, the city and the sublime

As we have seen, the detective's claim to omniscience was the result of a complex process of myth-making. What is more, in nineteenth-century crime fiction this panoptical view of the urban space is associated not only with the valiant knights of modernity, but also with the forces of darkness. While in one of his many adventures Sherlock Holmes is described as somebody who 'loved to lie in the very centre of five millions of people, with his filaments stretching out and running through them, responsive to every little rumour or suspicion of unsolved crime',[46] in another story Moriarty – 'the Napoleon of crime' – is correspondingly described as somebody who 'sits motionless, like a spider in the centre of its web, but that web has a thousand radiations, and he knows well every quiver of each of them'.[47]

The nightmarish quality of gothic persecution is also a basic ingredient of those crime stories where the conspiracy theme recurs, such as the above-mentioned novel by Stevenson. The original title of *The Dynamiter* was *More New Arabian Nights* and like its model the text is made up of interconnected episodes. The 'Story of the Destroying Angel', which is set in Utah, describes the tragic destiny of a family which is persecuted by the evil chiefs of the Mormon community mainly because the man has grown too rich and is regarded as an unbeliever, having only one wife. Not only is the area surrounding Salt Lake City presented as an open-air prison from which the only exit is the grave,[48] but the mystery surrounding the disappearance of every unorthodox inhabitant is made even more sinister by the fact that not a single trace of the bodies is found. The unfortunate family discovers that behind the legend of the Destroying Angel there is an evil scientist who first electrocutes the dissidents and then burns them in his crematorium. The symbol of the Open Eye is omnipresent in the novel, where we find it sculpted over the door of the scientist's house or 'drawn very rudely with charred wood'[49] close to the trail the fugitives have taken.

The elder members of the persecuted family are doomed to die, but in exchange for his services Dr Grierson obtains permission from the Mormons to save the girl and organises her flight to London, where he will join her. Anticipating the mad dream of Dr Jekyll – whose story was published by Stevenson a few months after *The Dynamiter* – the scientist is trying to concoct a philtre that will rejuvenate him and help him to win the heart of the girl. Yet when the scientist arrives in London and tries to drink his elixir, the phial falls down, causing an explosion which enables his reluctant fiancée to escape. In the end we discover that the story was made up by the young female narrator – who is presumably a terrorist – to ensure the protection of a naive young man.

This story closely resembles the American subplot of *A Study in Scarlet* (1887) and both can be seen as Victorian variations on the gothic themes of omniscience and persecution. On the one hand, Stevenson declines the sublime in the singular. He repeatedly uses the symbol of the Open Eye, which stands for inescapable surveillance, and he creates the legend of the Destroying Angel, which shrouds the experiments of Dr Grierson. On the other hand, Doyle insists on the plural nature of 'The Avenging Angels', the secret society which punishes all unorthodox behaviour inside the Mormon community – 'None knew who belonged to this ruthless society. The names of the participators in the deeds of blood and violence done under the name of religion were kept profoundly secret.'[50] Moreover, following a psychological mechanism of cause and effect which is typical of gothic and sensation fiction, evil is rooted in previous evil:

> The victims of persecution had now turned persecutors on their own account, and persecutors of the most terrible description. Not the Inquisition of Seville, nor the German Vehmgericht, nor the Secret Societies of Italy, were ever able to put a more formidable machinery in motion than that which cast a cloud over the State of Utah.

Its invisibility and the mystery which was attached to it, made this organization doubly terrible. It appeared to be omniscient and omnipotent, and yet was neither seen nor heard.[51]

The last sentence nicely sums up Burke's basic intuitions on the sublime. In addition, omniscience and persecution are here linked to a topos of turn-of-the-century crime, anarchist and spy novels – the conspiracy. As we know, the false clue Holmes finds in the room where the murder has been committed is a single word 'scrawled in blood-red letters'[52] – RACHE, which is described by the detective as 'the German for Revenge'.[53] Later, when the newspapers comment on the facts, the *Daily News* observes that 'there was no doubt as to the crime being a political one'.[54] In reality, at the heart of the crime there are neither international anarchist groups nor European secret societies fighting against the autocracy of continental governments, but the revenge of a single individual.

Both the misleading and the correct interpretation of the crime, however, contribute to the neo-gothic atmosphere of the novel by evoking two different kinds of sublime. On the one hand, the theme of terrorism embodies the *fin-de-siècle* European sublime, which is linked to the urban environment, notably that of London. On the other, the story of a religious utopia that turns into dystopia, against the backdrop of 'an arid and repulsive desert',[55] is a form of American sublime not far from the tradition of Hawthorne and Brown. The same combination of European and American neo-gothic is present in *The Dynamiter*, where the theme of terrorism and that of religious persecution also exist side by side, together with the sublime landscapes of London and the American West.

Turn-of-the-century novels repeatedly focused on a repentant terrorist who cannot escape from the surveillance of his ex-comrades, since European secret societies were thought to bind their adepts by an oath of allegiance that could never be undone. What happened in Utah for religious reasons, at least according to anti-Mormon propaganda, could happen in London for political ones, at least according to conservative propaganda. The gothic claustrophobic myth of absolute surveillance and relentless persecution was revived in late nineteenth-century detective and terrorist novels set both in exotic lands and in London. Being the heart of the British Empire, London was itself tinged with exoticism, and I regard it as no mere coincidence that the first line of Stevenson's *The Dynamiter* – a modern version of the *Arabian Nights* – reads: 'In the city of encounters, the Bagdad of the West...'[56] One might even claim that the great protagonist of late nineteenth-century sublime is London, which came to represent a 'heart of darkness' at the core of the empire, as we shall see in Chapter 8.

4
Victorian Ghosts and Revengers

In May 1827 a country girl called Maria Marten mysteriously disappeared. Maria had actually been murdered by her lover, William Corder, but the truth came to light only in March 1828, when her stepmother repeatedly dreamt that the girl had been killed and buried in a barn. After the discovery of the body, the site became the object of a macabre pilgrimage, was pillaged for souvenirs and even reproduced in small scale as a bibelot. The 'Red Barn Murder' inspired a long series of poetic, narrative and theatrical works, such as *The Murder of Maria Marten, or, The Red Barn*, a popular melodrama. Needless to say, these texts capitalised on the sensational appeal of the dream, as is shown by this 1828 ballad, where the case is related by the murderer himself:

Her bleeding, mangled body I buried under the Red Barn floor.
Now all things being silent, her spirit could not rest,
She appeared unto her mother, who suckled her at her breast;
For many a long month or more, her mind being sore oppress'd,
Neither night nor day she could not take any rest.
Her mother's mind, being so disturbed, she dreamt three nights o'er,
Her daughter she lay murdered beneath the Red Barn floor;
She sent the father to the barn when he the ground did thrust,
And there he found his daughter mingling with the dust.[1]

Martin Kayman reminds us (with emphasis) that the passage from tragedy and epic to detective fiction entailed a *'secularization of mystery'*,[2] but this process did not completely rule out a certain amount of interaction between detection and the supernatural in nineteenth-century literature. Throughout the century the paradigm of legal/scientific detection vied for supremacy with that of divine detection, which still survived and also interacted with pseudo-scientific – as well as esoteric – forms of inquiry. In those times of uncertainty, when doubt was being cast on traditional Christian values, powerful forces were fighting positivism, and literature inevitably took part in the conflict.

A 'ghost story' of crime and detection

Julia Briggs sees the Victorian ghost story as rooted precisely in 'The combination of modern scepticism with a nostalgia for an older, more supernatural system of beliefs',[3] but critics have seldom explored the nexus between this genre and the theme of crime and detection. To understand how traditional beliefs filtered into nineteenth-century crime literature, I will analyse a ghost story by the American novelist W.G. Simms – 'Grayling; or, "Murder Will Out"' (1842), whose opening paragraph reads:

> The world has become monstrous matter-of-fact in latter days. We can no longer get a ghost story, either for love or money. The materialists have it all their own way; [...] That cold-blooded demon called Science has taken the place of all the other demons. He has certainly cast out innumerable devils, however he may still spare the principal. Whether we are the better for his intervention is another question. There is reason to apprehend that in disturbing our human faith in shadows, we have lost some of those wholesome moral restraints which might have kept many of us virtuous, where the laws could not.[4]

In presenting the supernatural as a form of psychological policing, Simms was clearly aware of the fact that the ideological frame of his story belonged to a former age and as such would be regarded by most as no longer valid. He therefore not only displayed a self-conscious attitude, immediately revealing the aim of his parable of crime and punishment, but he adopted a narrative filter, having the story told by his grandmother and casting himself – together with his reader – in the role of an expectant grandchild who is ready to suspend his disbelief. This narrative strategy is extremely effective, but precisely when Simm's grandmother has managed to captivate her audience, the supernatural apparatus of the story is deconstructed by Simm's father, who offers a parallel rational explanation of the events. Due to its ambivalence 'Murder Will Out' can be regarded as a manifesto for nineteenth-century crime fiction – a literary territory that lay suspended, like revenge tragedies, between two competing systems of values.

After the War of Independence, young James Grayling is travelling with his family when a stranger approaches the group, a Scotsman whose allegiance during the war was uncertain. Another traveller also joins the camp for the night, Major Sparkman, who was James's superior in the army. The next day the Scotsman and the major leave to pursue their respective journeys, but when the Graylings reach an inn along the road James discovers that only the Scotsman has stopped there. This is followed by a sensational revelation, for while James is wandering in the woods, the voice of Major Sparkman denounces his death at the hand of the Scotsman and asks for justice. Although James repeatedly denies having fallen asleep, his family believe this was only a dream, but the young man decides to pursue his inquiry. The plot develops steadily along increasingly 'procedural' lines, for James informs the local authorities of his suspicions and manages to frame the murderer. Having apprehended the criminal, it becomes necessary to find the body of the victim and in this predicament the role of God as the ultimate agent of justice is reasserted. This leads to the moral message of the story, '"And here," said my grandmother devoutly, "you behold a proof of God's watchfulness to see that murder should not be hidden, and that the murderer should not escape."'[5]

The last part of the tale, however, is told by Simm's father, who deconstructs the supernatural explanation of the events, downgrading the apparition to a dream and 'proving' that young James did not act on the spur of a revelation but followed the train of his deductions, motivated by fears and unconscious perceptions. Simms, however, remarks that his father's theory did not succeed in undermining his youthful belief in ghosts and therefore deconstructs in turn the critical attitude of those who wish to rationalise every aspect of the supernatural, depriving the artists of an inspiring field and their public of a rightful pleasure, for 'the higher orders of poets and painters [...] must have a strong taint of the superstitious in their compositions'.[6] By reasserting the role of the 'romantic' in art, Simms anticipated an important component of mid-century crime fiction.

It may be argued that a new attention towards the link between crime and the supernatural was fostered by the public interest in spiritualism, following the events that supposedly took place in 1848 at the house of John D. Fox, a farmer who lived in the State of New York. Having been repeatedly disturbed at night by unaccountable knocking, one of the farmer's daughters managed at last to establish communication with what turned out to be the spirit of a peddler who had been slain in that building. Since at the origin of the spiritualist vogue for séances and mediums there is a ghost denouncing his own murder, one can surmise that this new belief in communication with the spirits helped to revive the old paradigm of supernatural detection. As Nicholas Rance claims, contrary to the concept of crime as the result of social causes, spiritualism reasserted the responsibility of the individual in the choice between good and evil,[7] thus supporting or replacing a set of Christian values that was in crisis.

The melodramatic imagination also represented a conservative antidote to modernity, whose aesthetic fruit was realism and whose ideological fruit was positivism.[8] Inspired by the theatre, Victorian writers depicted deeply contrasting psychological types, staging an inexorable duel between the incompatible principles of good and evil. Plots were often based on parallelism – showing, for instance, that the sins of the fathers would be visited on their children (a pattern that combined an old biblical formula with the new scientific emphasis on heredity) – while characterisation relied on symmetry and opposition. Coincidences multiplied and plots pivoting on guilty secrets acquired a baroque complexity, supporting a vision of life as ruled by arcane forces, reasserting the presence of meaning in the face of chance and chaos, but also defending ethics against the basic assumption of social Darwinism, that is, the survival of the fittest. The peculiar flavour of much Victorian popular literature is the result of a blend between anti-realistic elements (in terms of character and plot) and a realistic setting. Therefore it comes as no surprise that in the course of the century the supernatural asserted its presence in stories revolving around crime and detection along four major intersecting lines – premonitory/revelatory dreams, ghosts, the revenger as hero and pseudo-scientific crime and detection.

Dreams, dead witnesses and daring women

Premonitory and revelatory dreams recur in some of Collins's major novels, starting from *Basil* (1852), as well as in a variety of short stories. Dreams contribute to the melodramatic impact of Collins's plots by emphasising that his characters are involved in a portentous conflict between good and evil. They also represent a narrative technique employed by the author to create suspense. In fact, by circumventing the limited point of view of his first-person narratives they enabled Collins to hint at sensational elements in the development of the story, titillating the curiosity of readers. In addition, dreams reassert a principle of order, compensating for the epistemological uncertainty of multiple narration, which entails ambiguities and contradictions.

In Collins's fiction, however, dreams themselves are ambiguous and can often be read either as messages from heaven or as the result of inner fears and desires, anticipating the psychoanalytic link between dreams and the unconscious. Having stretched the use of revelatory/premonitory dreams to its utmost possibilities, Collins himself felt the need to write an appendix to *Armadale* (1866), leaving his readers free to interpret the dreams on which the plot pivots 'by the natural or the supernatural theory, as the bent of their own minds may incline them'.[9] Drawing on Tzvetan Todorov's theory of the fantastic,[10] one might argue that the readers' pleasure is often stimulated precisely by their vacillation between these two interpretations of dreams, as can be seen in one of Collins's early short stories.

Right from its outset, 'The Dream Woman' (1855) conflates elements of detection with preternatural coincidences. The inexplicable event that is at the root of Isaac's obsession – a pathological condition of fear that soon infects the readers – takes place in a country inn. Before going to bed Isaac has not extinguished his candle and when he wakes up in the middle of the night, he can see a woman who repeatedly tries to stab him with a knife, until the light of the candle goes out. Falling prey to sheer terror, Isaac cries for help, but he soon realises that both the door and the window of his room are locked from the inside. An enraged landlord dispels Isaac's lingering doubts, explaining that the attempted murder was only a dream.

When Collins wrote his story the mystery of the locked room had already been exploited by authors like Charles Brockden Brown and Edgar Allan Poe, but instead of moving from mystery to rational solution, Collins moved from mystery to dream, opening up a new space of ambiguity. Should we interpret Isaac's dream as a premonition, that is, as a supernatural revelation of a future danger, or as the fruit of a personal obsession linked to his fear of women? Is it a benevolent forewarning or the source of the fatal enmity that opposes Isaac and his mother to his wife? For Isaac marries a woman who in the end re-enacts the scene of the dream. The temporal symmetry of the story (based on the recurrence of Isaac's birthdays) favours the supernatural reading, but Collins – who is never straightforward – provides contrasting clues. Between the lines we may read another story – that of a fallen woman (for this is the status of the lady in question) who is destined to find in her marriage not the redemption from a degrading past, but the definite proof of her deviance, since in nineteenth-century society and literature fallen women were not given a second chance. Needless to say, this subversive reading is implicit in the story only as a subtext, whereas the supernatural interpretation corresponds to mainstream values.

While 'The Dream Woman' is a variation on gothic motifs, 'The Diary of Anne Rodway' (1856) is often cited in the stories of crime/detective fiction as an early example of the genre, mainly due to the presence of a prototypical woman detective; but the story is likewise tinged with the supernatural. Although – given the position of women within the Victorian social order – the heroine lacks the authority to pursue her inquiry, she is confirmed in her role of detective by providence, thanks to a dream testifying to the fact that the clue she has found will lead her to the truth. Replicating the structure of broadsides and *Newgate Calendar* stories, the investigation is ultimately coordinated by God, and the crime itself brings us back to Holy Writ. Like the biblical Noah, the perfidious Noah Truscott is associated with drunkenness and embodies its worst effects. After leading Mary's father to his death by having him fall into the habit of drinking, this reprobate by chance also kills Mary herself, due to his intoxication. The message these criminal symmetries conveyed would not be lost on Victorian readers, who were familiar with Bible stories and used to an allegorical mode of reading.

'The Diary of Anne Rodway' provided Collins with a model for the narrative of Marian Halcombe in *The Woman in White* (1860), which also takes the form of a diary and presents the brave deeds of a woman detective. Yet, while the earlier story reassuringly conforms to the traditional providential pattern, the novel derives its power from the tension between gothic elements and modernity. Collins's choice to exploit the supernatural aura of the gothic, ultimately offering a domesticated version of the genre, is apparent from the beginning of the book, when Anne Catherick appears around midnight at a crossroads in the vicinity of London. The hand of this solitary woman 'in white garments' is 'pointing to the dark cloud over London',[11] a gesture that takes on a symbolic value, framing the whole story within a providential plot. The tension between this gothic character and its urban surroundings becomes apparent when, after Anne has disappeared in a cab, a policeman approaches on his beat, and another carriage stops, inquiring after a woman in white who has escaped from an asylum. Institutions such as the police and the asylum bring us back to the disciplinary character of nineteenth-century society and to the modern face of the novel, while Anne is a residual character uneasily trapped between past and present.

Anne's attempt to forewarn Laura of the dangers inherent in her marriage to Sir Percival Glyde is doomed to fail, not least because of the form her message takes – a letter recounting a dream: '"Do you believe in dreams? I hope, for your own sake, that you do. See what Scripture says about dreams and their fulfilment (Genesis xl. B, xli. 25; Daniel iv. 18–25); and take the warning I send you before it is too late."' What modernity needs are sound clues and lucid statements, instead of Anne's highly symbolic and emotional figurations of evil:

> 'I looked along the two rays of light; and I saw down his inmost heart. It was black as night; and on it were written, in the red flaming letters which are the handwriting of the fallen angel: "Without pity and without remorse. He has strewn with misery the paths of others, and he will live to strew with misery the path of this woman by his side." [...] And I woke with my eyes full of tears and my heart beating – for *I* believe in dreams.'[12]

Not only is the 'prophetic' value of this dream undermined because of Anne's unreliability as a 'madwoman', but in the course of the novel the time-honoured conception of providential detection is further called into question by none other than Count Fosco:

> The machinery [society] has set up for the detection of crime is miserably ineffective – and yet only invent a moral epigram, saying that it works well, and you blind everybody to its blunders, from that moment. Crimes cause their own detection, do they? And murder will out (another moral epigram), will it? Ask Coroners who sit at inquests in large towns if that is true, Lady Glyde. Ask secretaries of life-assurance companies, if that is true, Miss Halcombe. Read your own public journals. [...] The hiding of a crime, or the detection of a crime, what is it? A trial of skill between the police on one side, and the individual on the other.[13]

Collins skilfully detached himself from this materialistic view of detection by having it voiced by an arch-villain. Moreover, the providential paradigm is subsequently reasserted in the course of the novel by means of another premonitory dream, or possibly a form of clairvoyance, which Marian describes as 'a trance, or daydream of my fancy'. Thanks to this vision, the girl is reassured that Walter Hartright will return unhurt from the wilds of Central America to save Laura: '"Wait," he said. "I shall come back. The night, when I met the lost Woman on the highway, was the night which set my life apart to be the instrument of a Design that is yet unseen."'[14]

The simultaneous presence within the novel of providential and detective elements, of gothic and modernity, of biblical rhetoric and untrammelled rationality, testifies not only to the hybrid status of sensation fiction but more generally to the complex nature of Victorian culture, where different approaches to crime and punishment coexisted. Suffice it to say that as late as 1860 – the year *The Woman in White* appeared in book form – Cassell's *Illustrated Family Paper* published an article entitled 'Murder Will Out: Being singular instances of the manner in which concealed crimes have been detected', reasserting traditional beliefs such as the idea that the body of the victim would bleed if touched by its murderer.[15] In the same year the Victorian public could feast on another sensational best-seller, Ellen Wood's *East Lynne*, which was serialised in 1860–61. A revelatory dream also plays a major role in this novel, where Mrs Hare is haunted by a dream concerning the murder of which her son has been unjustly accused.

The literary landscape, however, was changing fast, as is proved by some 1870s crime stories where the supernatural is offered not as an overarching explanation of the plot (that is, as a device framing the story and legitimising it in spite of its crude subject matter), but rather as a transitory explanation – a picturesque and eerie component, a frisson to be enjoyed and eventually refuted. In order to assert a new standard of verisimilitude, the supernatural was marginalised both as an instrument of detection and as a criminal tool, but it re-entered the genre through the back door, so to speak, for writers were unwilling to foresake its powerful grip on the public. Re-enacting the transition from the gothic proper to the rationalised gothic, crime writers resorted to 'staging' the supernatural and deconstructing their own 'plots'.

Anna Katharine Green's *The Leavenworth Case* (1878) is a case in point. Mr Harwell's supposedly premonitory dream – anticipating the scene of the murder and pointing to Mr Clavering as the culprit – is actually a false clue, artfully revealed to the amateur detective in order to focus his suspicion on an innocent person.[16] The revelatory dream, however, plays a marginal role in the investigation and one may argue that even nineteenth-century readers were familiar enough with the dynamics of suspense to understand that the disclosure could not be dependable, coming so early in the story. In fact, in order not to lessen the vibrant expectations of readers, when in sensation novels such as *East Lynne* a revelatory dream points to the real culprit, we are offered just a few hints of his/her identity so as not to dispel the mystery too early. With a melodramatic *coup de théâtre*, at the end of *The Leavenworth Case* we discover not only that Mr Harwell had faked his dream, but that he actually had a different dream,[17] which is less liable to a supernatural interpretation and much closer to his unconscious.

Sensation writers made a subtle use of another element they had inherited from the tradition of supernatural detection – the return of the victim from the netherworld to denounce his/her murder. Poe playfully revisited this element in "'Thou Art the Man'" (1844). After the death of Mr Shuttleworthy, suspicion falls upon his nephew. The narrator, however, comes to the conclusion that the young man has been framed by Mr Goodfellow, who Shuttleworthy regarded as his best friend. To induce Goodfellow to betray himself, the narrator organises a gory mise-en-scène, hiding the decaying body of the victim inside a huge wine-box and having the corpse appear all of a sudden, like a grotesque pop-up toy, before Goodfellow, who confesses to the murder – thanks also to the narrator's ability as a ventriloquist – and falls to the ground dead. While here Poe turned pathos into bathos, without renouncing a final 'quasi-providential' reassertion of justice, sensationalists opted for a more serious treatment of the subject. In 'John Jago's Ghost' (1874),[18] Collins manipulates his readers even in the title, which creates a certain set of expectations that are related to the ghost story genre, only to dispel this supernatural aura by proving in the end that the victim himself, not his ghost, repeatedly appeared near the scene of the presumed crime.[19] Mary Elizabeth Braddon's 'Levison's Victim' (1870) is yet another variation on this highly melodramatic theme. Harbouring the certainty that Michael Levison killed his wife Laura during their honeymoon, Horace Wynward (who was also in love with the girl) plans to frame Levison in spite of his assertion that his wife is in Trinidad. Rejecting a traditional revenge, Wynward confronts his rival by means of an 'experiment', that is, by ushering into the room the dead Laura. On seeing her, Levison is flabbergasted and unwittingly reveals his crime, but a rational explanation of the event soon follows, for the girl is actually Laura's sister. Supernatural agency has thus been superseded by human ingenuity, yet the old pattern of divine justice is deftly reintroduced in the last paragraphs, where we are told that the culprit is dying in prison 'of a heart-disease from which he had suffered for years'.[20]

The return of the revenger

Revenge frequently lies at the heart of the traditional canon of detection. In 'The Purloined Letter' (1845), for example, the intellectual duel between Dupin and Minister D— rests not only on gallantry and loyalty (towards the endangered queen) or money (the price of Dupin's services), but also on a private motive which comes to light only at the end of the story, when Dupin describes the contents of the letter he has left in D—'s study in place of the original. Desiring to repay an 'evil turn' the Minister had done him in Vienna, Dupin writes on the blank sheet a quotation from Crébillon's *Atrée* which leads us back to the world of Seneca's tragedies,

– Un dessein si funeste,
S'il n'est digne d'Atrée, est digne de Thyeste.[21]

In Poe's story the bloody deeds of rival twin brothers Atreus and Thyestes become an ironic metaphor for the conflict between Dupin and the minister, emphasising the uncanny resemblance between these two figures.

While Dupin's revenge has no preternatural import, in Victorian literature this theme is often associated with the power of divine justice. In Doyle's *A Study in Scarlet* (1887), for instance, where revenge plays a major role, a natural and a supernatural interpretation of the story coexist till the very end. After the omniscient retrospective narrative entitled 'The Country of the Saints' – telling the events that took place in Utah and providing the motive for the murders at the heart of the novel – Watson resumes his own narrative of crime and detection. At the heart of this final section is the murderer himself – Jefferson Hope, who revives the ancient role of the revenger. After his capture, Hope – who suffers from heart complaints and is doomed to die in a short time – freely confesses all the details concerning the two murders he has committed in order to fulfil his mission. In spite of the eminently rational atmosphere of the novel, which mirrors Holmes's frame of mind, this section exemplifies a different set of values, since the pre-positivist world of the revenger is ruled by providence.

Like Hamlet and his Renaissance *confrères*, Hope is in touch with the souls of the dead he prepares to avenge. While Hope, who is disguised as a cab driver, is carrying a drunken Enoch Drebber to the house on Brixton Road where he intends to kill him, he has the sensation that the dead approve of his act: '"As I drove, I could see old John Ferrier and sweet Lucy looking at me out of the darkness and smiling at me... one on each side of the horse."'[22] Hope repeatedly emphasises his perception of the presence of the dead at the scene of what is regarded as a ritual and legitimate murder: '"I give you my word that all the way, the father and the daughter were walking in front of us."'[23]

This confession reveals a strong melodramatic component, as does the method Hope chooses to kill the two villains. Hope offers Drebber a box containing two pills – only one of them is poisoned while the other is harmless and it is Drebber who has to choose between them, spectacularly becoming the agent of his own punishment. Thus Hope (whose name itself corresponds to the allegorical tradition of melodrama) runs the risk of dying instead of his intended victim, but he is certain that providence will not allow murder to go unpunished. Drebber makes the wrong choice and dies; but when Stangerson is asked to shape his own destiny in turn he refuses to swallow a pill and tries to stab Hope, who has the better of him and subsequently claims: '"It would have been the same in any case, for Providence would never have allowed his guilty hand to pick out anything but the poison."'[24]

The presence of the two ghosts and the belief in providence can be regarded as the self-delusions of a man who has nurtured his revenge for years with maniacal passion, hunting his victims 'from Salt Lake City to St. Petersburg'.[25] Yet they also create an ambivalence in the text, implying that a superior form of justice operates within the story, which therefore authorises an irrational, providential interpretation, turning the revenger into a righteous instrument of divine justice and a martyr, as is proved by Hope's last words: '"You may consider me to be a murderer; but I hold that I am just as much an officer of justice as you are."'[26] Doyle's respect for the heroic status of the revenger is proved by the fact that he enables him to escape the shame and dishonour of prison through sudden death – 'A higher Judge had taken the matter in hand'[27] writes Watson.

Far from being an isolated case in the Holmes saga, the story of Hope is paralleled by other instances of 'unlawful' but 'legitimate' revenge. In 'The Adventure of Charles Augustus Milverton' the eponymous character is killed by a lady he has blackmailed, causing the death of her husband, and Holmes deems her act as justified. This primeval code of justice also pervades stories like 'The Greek Interpreter', where the death of two shady characters is finally imputed to the revenge of a Greek girl. In 'The Five Orange Pips' Holmes's desire to track down two criminals is frustrated by an unexpected event, since the boat that is carrying them to America wrecks before reaching its goal. God himself has ensured that justice be done. To avoid the monotonous repetition of a formula, Doyle had some of his stories end with a melodramatic event that deprives the detective of his retributive role. By signalling that closure is achieved thanks to a higher principle of justice – an ethical code his public share 'in spite' of the law – Doyle tapped into a powerful source of emotions.

In conclusion, the transition from divine detection, with its supernatural trappings, to scientific detection – depending only on the superior faculties and training of the detective, notably his (or her) ability to decipher clues – involved a long experimental phase, when both patterns did not simply vie for supremacy, but often combined to create effects of tension and surprise, drawing on the expectations of the readers and ministering to their aspiration for an infallible justice, exceeding the powers of the police and even of a 'superhuman' detective like Holmes.

5
Pseudo-Sciences and the Occult

In the course of the nineteenth century the increasing importance of science changed the role that 'mystery' played in the collective imagination. Even before Queen Victoria's reign Thomas Carlyle had reassessed common religious and popular beliefs in a chapter of *Sartor Resartus* (1833–34) entitled 'Natural Supernaturalism'. While acknowledging the value of science, Carlyle questioned its mechanical view of the universe, refusing to renounce either faith or 'mystery', and relocating the supernatural in the inner dimension of the human being:

> Witchcraft, and all manner of Spectre-work, and Demonology, we have now named Madness, and Diseases of the Nerves. Seldom reflecting that still the new question comes upon us: What is Madness, what are Nerves? Ever, as before, does Madness remain a mysterious-terrific, altogether *infernal* boiling up of the Nether Chaotic Deep ...[1]

Victorians were attracted both to the aberrant side and to the 'super-human' powers of the mind. While the ancient abyss of hell seemed to close its doors, previously unfathomed inner abysses opened up their depths in a world whose coordinates of time and space were being traced with increasing exactitude.

We tend to think of positivism as the triumph of the scientific method and a materialist approach to reality, but this cultural phase was ambivalent, involving an interest in the spiritual and in the occult. Victorian culture engaged in a vast debate concerning the supernatural, as is shown by J.N. Radcliffe's *Fiends, Ghosts and Sprites, Including an Account of the Origin and Nature of Belief in the Supernatural* (1854), William Howitt's *The History of the Supernatural* (1863), A.R. Wallace's *The Scientific Aspect of the Supernatural* (1866) and several other works.[2] While some scholars historicised the cultural approach to the supernatural in order to fight against superstition, others had a sympathetic attitude to tradition and hoped that a rational investigation of that domain would ultimately lead to bewildering advances in our knowledge of the universe and the human.

Old beliefs were reassessed in the light of recent discoveries and were often subsumed into the discourses of what today we regard as pseudo-sciences rather than sciences. Mesmerism, for instance, was refashioned as hypnotism by James Braid (*Neurhypnology*, 1843) and William Carpenter, setting the ground for the late nineteenth-century development of psychology and psychoanalysis. We should remember that Jean-Martin Charcot used this technique to treat hysteria at the Paris hospital of La Salpêtrière, where Sigmund Freud came to study in 1885, and that before developing the 'free association' method Freud used hypnotism to explore his patients' unconscious, as is shown by *Studies on Hysteria* (1895). In the meantime, spiritualism was provided with a philosophical basis thanks to Andrew Jackson Davies, while Mme Blavatsky and H.S. Olcott founded the Theosophical Society in New York in 1875.

Towards the end of the century, disciplines that we now regard as the foundations of twentieth-century sciences intertwined with theories that were subsequently largely discredited. Sir Oliver Lodge, for instance, is known both as a physicist who developed wireless telegraphy and for his interest in psychical research – a passion he shared with his friend Sir Arthur Conan Doyle. The discovery of radio waves and the increasing ability to communicate at a distance provided a powerful paradigm for the investigation of the occult. The Society for Psychical Research was founded in London in 1882 by eminent scholars in order to study phenomena such as clairvoyance, telepathy and precognition. Six years later an American branch was created, thanks to the efforts of William James, the father of modern psychology. James's comprehensive theory of mind entailed an interest in what he called 'abnormal mental states', including trance. James's involvement with mediums such as Leonora Piper and Helen Berry is well known and in a series of talks he gave in Boston in 1896 – 'The Exceptional Mental Phenomena' – the philosopher dealt with subjects such as dreams and hypnotism, automatism, hysteria, multiple personality, demonic possession, witchcraft and degeneration.[3]

The Italian Cesare Lombroso, who is mainly remembered as the founder of criminal anthropology, also studied hypnotism and – after meeting the Italian medium Eusapia Paladino in 1891 – converted to spiritualism.[4] Applying a positivist method to the study of the occult, Lombroso argued that certain apparently 'spiritual phenomena' actually pertained to the realm of matter: 'as the laws concerning Hertz's waves largely explain telepathy, so the new discoveries concerning the radioactive properties of certain metals, notably *radium* ... dispel the greatest objection a scientist had to oppose to the mysterious manifestations of spiritualism'.[5] The development of photography contributed to this renewed interest in the connection between body and soul, which was conceptualised in pseudo-scientific terms. In Nathaniel Hawthorne's *The House of the Seven Gables* (1851) ghosts, dreams and mesmerism are evoked together with the daguerrotype, and the daguerrotypist Holgrave describes his art as follows:

> I make pictures out of sunshine ... There is a wonderful insight in heaven's broad and simple sunshine. While we give it credit only for depicting the merest surface, it actually brings out the secret character with a truth that no painter would ever venture upon, even could he detect it.[6]

As the photographer Félix Nadar wrote in his memoirs, Honoré de Balzac was afraid of being photographed lest one of the infinitesimal layers constituting his soul might be stripped away each time his image was captured by the camera. In the nineteenth century the soul was increasingly 'materialised' and photography contributed to this new approach, as is shown by *L'Âme humaine: ses mouvements, ses lumières et l'iconographie de l'invisible* (*The Human Soul: its movements, its lights and the iconography of the invisible*, 1896), where Hippolyte Baraduc claimed that photography could capture the luminous vibrations of the soul. Photography actually enlarged the domain of the visible, showing distant planets, minute things and even the inside of the human body, for W.C. Röntgen developed 'radiography' in the 1890s.

The study of electricity also seemed to deconstruct the opposition between antithetical terms like natural and supernatural or matter and spirit, as is shown by Poe's works. Suffice it to think of the philosophical essay *Eureka* (1848), where Poe wrote:

> To electricity – so, for the present, continuing to call it – we *may* not be wrong in referring the various physical appearances of light, heat and magnetism; but far less shall we be liable to err in attributing to this strictly spiritual principle the more important phenomena of vitality, consciousness and *Thought*.[7]

A few decades later, the mysterious powers of electricity were fictionalised by the French writer Villiers de l'Isle Adam in *L'Ève future*

(*Tomorrow's Eve*, 1886), whose main character is a delicate creature, half android and half spirit. The 'Frankenstein' who brings Hadaly to life is no less than a historical figure, the scientist Edison. Thanks to electricity, this modern wizard has fashioned an underground fairy kingdom whose beauty rivals oriental fantasies: ' "The *Arabian Nights* pale beside your kind of positivism!" exclaimed Lord Ewald. "But indeed, what Scheherazade is electricity!" answered Edison.'[8] Poe himself had already written 'The Thousand-and-Second Tale of Scheherazade' (1845), where he jokingly presented the achievements of science as so many prodigies of magic. Science became a source of wonder and opened up new vistas to the imagination, creating a pattern of expectation.

Satirists, however, were ready to stigmatise any excess. Ambrose Bierce, for instance, ironically defined electricity as 'The power that causes all natural phenomena not known to be caused by something else.'[9] Bierce repeatedly ridiculed pseudo-science in his writings, and in *The Parenticide Club* (1911) he told the grotesque story of a hypnotist whose criminal career starts as a child, when he deprives a schoolmate of her lunch, and reaches its climax when he has his parents kill one another.

Mesmerism, murder and mystery

As we can see, sharing the public interest in the connections between traditional beliefs and the recent advances in science, writers eagerly embraced the fictional opportunities this intellectual climate offered. As Max Nordau – the arch-critic of nineteenth-century culture – claimed in *Entartung* (*Degeneration*, 1892), 'Ghost-stories are very popular, but they must come on in scientific disguise, as hypnotism, telepathy, somnambulism.'[10] This sensational literary field, however, was not universally regarded as acceptable, as is proved by the fact that George Eliot's *The Lifted Veil* – a gruesome tale combining detection, pseudo-science and the supernatural – was published anonymously in *Blackwood's* in July 1859 so as not to impinge on the reputation of the author.[11]

Drawing on the lure of phrenology, mesmerism and clairvoyance, Eliot created a character who is endowed with a preternatural faculty that enables him both to read the soul of his fellow human beings and to foresee his own future. These premises set the ground for a lurid story of crime and detection, since the hero falls in love with the only girl whose heart escapes his scrutiny (or perhaps his vision is hindered by his passion...). As time passes and love fades, the protagonist acquires the power to see into his wife's heart, only to discover that she finds him hateful and repugnant, until at a later stage he is completely freed from the poisonous gift of insight. Events are precipitated when his wife's maid dies and a family friend, a famous physician, manages to revive her, albeit for a short time. As a result, the maid reveals that her mistress intends to kill her husband: ' "You mean to poison your husband ... the poison is in the black cabinet ... I got it for you..." '[12] Since we are led to believe that the lady herself had poisoned her maid to seal her lips, this posthumous revelation can be regarded as a pseudo-scientific variation on the theme of the return of the victim as ghost.

A synergy between the supernatural, mesmerism and detection also marks a ghost story by Charles Dickens – 'The Trial for Murder' (1865) – describing the trial in which the narrator has been called to take part as a juror. Although paranormal phenomena play a major role in this plot, I will focus my attention on a single episode. The narrator is in his bedroom with his valet when a man enters through a door that was nailed up years before, beckons to him and then withdraws. The valet has no inkling of what has happened because he has been standing with his back to the wall, but when the narrator touches him a contact is established and he shares his vision:

> Conscious that my servant stood amazed, I turned round to him, and said, 'Derrick, could you believe that in my cool senses I fancied I saw a...'
> As I there laid my hand upon his breast, with a sudden start he trembled violently, and said, 'Oh, Lord, yes, sir! A dead man beckoning!'[13]

Within the context of Dickens's interest in mesmerism, this scene implies the passage of an invisible fluid. Thanks to the techniques Dickens had learnt from John Elliotson – who used mesmerism to treat patients with nervous diseases and on account of this had been forced to resign from the University College Hospital in 1838 – Dickens himself treated a woman who was troubled by spectral illusions. It is in a letter to this woman that Dickens described mesmerism as 'a philosophical explanation of many Ghost Stories. Though it is hardly less chilling than a ghost story itself.'[14] Like other Victorians, Dickens regarded mesmerism as a means to incorporate the supernatural into the natural, thus distinguishing it from superstition.

Unsurprisingly, William Wilkie Collins shared his friend's interest in pseudo-science and combined it with detection in a classic of sensation, *The Moonstone* (1868). The story pivots on the theft of a diamond, but the criminal act has been committed by a person who at the time was not in full possession of his mental faculties, as he was in a state of trance induced by opium. Due to the 'irrational' character of the mystery to be solved, the police enquiries of Superintendent Seegrave and Sergeant Cuff result in a partial failure, but the case is eventually solved by Ezra Jennings, a physician who has studied the brain and who is able to penetrate those regions of the psyche which are not controlled by 'reason' – what we would now term as the unconscious.

In order to make Jennings's investigation more credible, Collins has him quote as scientific referees two physiologists, the above-mentioned Carpenter and Elliotson, who were both actively interested in phrenology, mesmerism and spiritualism. In *The Moonstone* Collins also exploited the exotic aura that mesmerism/hypnotism had acquired thanks to works such as James Esdaile's *Mesmerism in India* (1866), relating criminal cases connected to an unlawful use of mental suggestion.[15] At the beginning of Collins's novel, three Indian jugglers and an English child are seen in the vicinity of Lady Verinder's country house. Their presence is immediately perceived as dangerous because of the strange ritual they perform:

> Upon that, the Indian took a bottle from his bosom, and poured out of it some black stuff, like ink, into the palm of the boy's hand. The Indian – first touching the boy's head, and making signs over it in the air – then said, 'Look.' The boy became quite stiff, and stood like a statue, looking into the ink in the hollow of his hand.[16]

The Indians ask the boy various questions about the man who is bringing the diamond to Lady Verinder's house and in a trance he answers like a clairvoyant. The Moonstone is subsequently stolen from Rachel Verinder's boudoir, and the theft triggers a complex investigation.

Although at first the Brahmins are depicted as a possible threat, it is Britons – rather than colonials – who are guilty of crime in this novel. As the Prologue makes clear, the gem is in Britain because Colonel John Hearncastle stole it during the storming of Seringapatam, after killing three Indians, whose last words were: ' " The Moonstone will have its vengeance yet on you and yours!" '[17] The Moonstone, however, had been repeatedly stolen before and readers are taken back through the centuries to the time of its primal theft from the Indian temple where it was worshipped as a sacred stone. Since that time, a group of three Brahmins has always followed the diamond, waiting for the right moment to restore it to their god. Legend has it that Vishnu appeared to the first three Brahmins in a dream, ordering them to devote their lives to a mission that involves investigation, even murder if necessary, to recover the gem, and eventually self-sacrifice.

At the end of *The Moonstone*, the Brahmins kill the man who has the diamond, thus ensuring the triumph of divine (and poetical) justice. By accomplishing their mission, however, they have 'forfeited their caste in the service of the god'[18] and are condemned to part, spending the rest of their lives on a penitential pilgrimage – an epilogue which might be read as an exotic variation on the tragic theme of the revenger. In the eyes of a contemporary reviewer, it was precisely this pathetic ending that redeemed 'the somewhat sordid detective element'[19] of the novel!

In this text, then, Collins clearly refused to attribute an absolute value to rational detection, whose agents are policemen and detectives, and he devised two alternative forms of enquiry. Jennings's investigation, on the one hand, is based on disciplines whose scientific status is ambiguous, while on the other, 'divine detection' resurfaces within the context of an extra-European society, where religious beliefs still prevail over scientific modes of knowledge.

Yet another variation on the theme of supernatural detection is provided by Collins's short novel *The Haunted Hotel* (1879), where the final mystery revolves around a case of identity. Indeed, what makes the heroine doubt the revelations she has received by means of a night vision is not their surprising character, but the fact that she had apparently been unacquainted with the victim:

> I can understand the apparition making itself visible to *me*, to claim the mercy of Christian burial, and the vengeance due to a crime. I can even perceive some faint possibility of truth in the explanation which you described as the mesmeric theory ... But what I do *not* understand is, that I should have passed through that dreadful ordeal; having no knowledge of the murdered man in his lifetime...[20]

Needless to say, what further enquiries prove is that a connection between victim and 'witness' actually existed, thus validating the supernatural explanation.

Mesmeric villains

Far from being conceived simply as an instrument at the service of detection and justice, mesmerism was also regarded as a dark power, as is seen in Charles Felix's *The Notting Hill Mystery* (which was serialised in 1862–63), where the villain can poison a woman indirectly by giving antimony to her twin sister, thanks to the mesmeric connection between them. A homicidal technique such as this could only be accepted by the public as long as mesmerism was the object of a collective suspension of disbelief, but as soon as their curiosity waned and incredulity prevailed, stories like *The Notting Hill Mystery* – or like Metta Fuller's *The Dead Letter* (1867), where the detective relies on clairvoyance to further his investigation – became unacceptable.

At the end of the century, however, writers still eagerly embraced the connections between pseudo-science and the occult, which enabled them to experiment with the paradigms of crime and detection along new lines. The best-known 'mesmeric villain' is Svengali, who haunts the pages of George Du Maurier's best-selling *Trilby* (1894). Du Maurier – who had already illustrated *The Notting Hill Mystery* – managed to exploit the sensational appeal of a theme that had enjoyed a certain popularity since the eighteenth century. The power of mesmerism, which promised the complete control of one mind over another, had in fact been repeatedly fictionalised all over Europe, giving writers the opportunity to explore the dreams and fears of sexual dominance it implied.

In his novel Du Maurier combined this sexual subtext with the aesthetic concerns with which he was familiar as an artist, and also with the anti-Semitic undercurrent that marks so much Victorian literature. Thus Du Maurier created Svengali, a Jew who is endowed with extraordinary musical talent and willpower. Thanks to his mesmeric influence, this malignant and repulsive character gains complete control of tone-deaf, simple-minded Trilby, turning her into La Svengali, an accomplished opera singer who enthrals the public of all Europe. Yet Svengali considers Trilby only as a musical instrument in his hands, precipitating her fate. As Daniel Pick claims, the heartless Svengali soon came to embody the prejudices that surrounded the Jews at the end of the century, when they 'were often depicted as contaminating the mind and body of gentiles, as well as controlling everything from the stock market to public taste in art'.[21]

The 1890s also witnessed the publication of Bram Stoker's *Dracula* (1897), yet another gothic fantasy where the superhuman willpower of an 'alien' threatens the stability of human society by attacking the heart of Western civilisation, London. The novel has been repeatedly read as an 'invasion story', but what is less often underlined is the nature of the forces brought to bear by the vampire masters – an array of weapons that reconcile arcane beliefs with modern pseudo-science, as is shown by this dialogue between Professor Van Helsing and Jonathan Harker:

'I suppose now you do not believe in corporeal transference. No? Nor in materialization. No? Nor in astral bodies. No? Nor in the reading of thought. No? Nor in hypnotism –'

'Yes,' I said. 'Charcot has proved that pretty well.' He smiled as he went on: ...
'Then tell me – for I am a student of the brain – how you accept the hypnotism and reject the thought-reading. Let me tell you, my friend, that there are things done today in electrical science which would have been deemed unholy by the very men who discovered electricity – who would themselves not so long before have been burned as wizards.'[22]

Drawing on his contemporaries' faith in the power of science to explain what was once perceived as supernatural, Stoker presented Dracula as a freak of nature and as a criminal rather than as a devil to be 'exorcised'. Like Frankenstein, Dracula is potentially 'the father or furtherer of a new order of Beings', although in his case a reverse evolutionary process (that is, a degenerative path) 'must lead through Death, not Life'.[23]

Not only did Stoker choose to explain Dracula's 'superpowers' (corporeal transference, mind-reading, hypnotism) in pseudo-scientific terms, but he also grounded Van Helsing's process of detection in similar techniques, for it is by hypnotising Mina Harker that the professor manages to discover the whereabouts of Dracula while he is preparing his escape from London.[24] A 'philosopher and a metaphysician' as well as 'one of the most advanced scientists of his day',[25] Professor Van Helsing is an iron-willed and supple-minded detective of the occult who is able to match his opponent's superior strength, foiling his ascent to power in the course of a breathtaking duel.

The extraordinary success of Dracula was due to Stoker's ability to conflate icons of modernity, such as technology and science, with the gothic trappings of distant castles and sinister chapels. Stoker's characters use typewriters and keep their journals in shorthand, they record their thoughts on the phonograph, send telegrams and take trains, but they also have to deal with a danger surfacing from the abyss of time. Interestingly, far from simply belonging to a gothic tradition of vampire stories,[26] *Dracula* was strongly influenced by the sensation school. It is from Collins's *The Woman in White* (1860) that Stoker apparently borrowed the technique of multiple narration he used in his novel,[27] as well as the sensational setting of the asylum. Even minor details seem to betray an influence, for Mina Harker shares the initials and the strong personality of Marian Halcombe, while Lucy Westenra reminds one of Laura Fairlie.

This brings us back to Collins's novel itself. In the course of his long and flamboyant confession, Count Fosco launches into a cynical apotheosis of the immense power of chemistry, which he presents as a tool capable of utterly subjugating his fellow human beings: 'Mind, they say, rules the world. But what rules the mind? The body. The body (follow me closely here) lies at the mercy of the most omnipotent of all potentates – the Chemist.'[28] Chemistry, however, is not the only weapon on which Fosco relies in his quest for absolute power. Indeed, when Fosco is first presented in the novel through Marian's diary we are told that his peculiarity lies entirely 'in the extraordinary expression and extraordinary power of his eyes'.[29] A little later, Marian's first impression is confirmed when Fosco confronts a vicious dog, turning him into a meek puppy thanks to his mental strength, which he exerts through his eyes.[30] Although no direct reference to mesmerism is made, we can regard Fosco as an antecedent of those *fin-de-siècle* villains – from Svengali to Dracula – who use their superior faculties to further their criminal schemes.

The 'other' Doyle

Another story critics often mention as an antecedent of *Dracula* is Doyle's 'The Parasite' (1890). Rather than for its influence on Stoker, however, 'The Parasite' deserves a place in this chapter for the light it sheds on the author's own bewilderment and fascination in the face of the preternatural. Doyle's main character – whose autobiographical dimension is apparent – is Professor Gilroy, who teaches medicine at the university. As a physiologist, he is aware of operating within the safe boundaries of 'a recognized science',[31] 'something positive and objective',[32] but he is both intrigued and irritated by the indefatigable activity of a colleague named Wilson who has enthusiastically thrown himself into psychology. Although Gilroy regards this debatable discipline as unsafe ground, he labels it as 'a science of the future'.[33] Two modes of approach to reality are contrasted at the beginning of the story. Gilroy is a materialist who is interested only in facts and proofs, while Wilson is trying to draw him into a twilight-zone of knowledge where one can meet eerie creatures such as 'some new mesmerist or clairvoyant or medium or trickster'.[34] To make Gilroy's predicament more complex, he is aware of the fact that in spite of his positivist beliefs he is 'a highly psychic man', who in his youth was 'a dreamer, a somnambulist, full of impressions and intuitions'.[35]

It is Wilson who introduces Gilroy to the mysteries of mesmerism, which threaten to wreak havoc in his life. In spite of the 'exact knowledge'[36] Gilroy masters, his sensitive inner nature makes him vulnerable to the power of Miss Penclosa, a mesmerist who agrees to 'convert' the cynical doctor, practising hypnotic suggestion both on him and on his fiancée. Gilroy's devotion to science and his desire to analyse those unseen forces whose very existence he doubted as a physiologist expose him to the influence of the redoubtable mesmerist, who is able to impose her will on him, entering his body like a parasite. When Gilroy discovers he has become dependent on the limping crone, who has fallen in love with him and is slowly teaching him to return her feelings, he gives vent to all his anger and repugnance, turning the woman's attachment into hatred and triggering her terrible revenge, which entails making a criminal of him.

Like much Victorian fiction, this text is far from innocent of racial implications. Not only does the evil Miss Penclosa come from Trinidad (like the wife of Wilson, who is therefore shown as 'tainted'), but the narrator's vulnerability to her pernicious influence is explained by referring to his Celtic origin, while people of 'Saxon temperament'[37] are less liable to be subjugated.

The story of Gilroy's divided self reflects Doyle's own contradictory attitude towards those beliefs that would later play such an important role in his life. While in the Holmes saga any supernatural frisson had simply been aimed at achieving a powerful hold over the readers, from his 'conversion' in 1916 to his death in 1930 Doyle was a fervent advocate of spiritualism, as is shown by *The Land of Mist* (1926), a propaganda text that exploited the appeal of Professor G.E. Challenger, the serial hero Doyle had created to probe into pseudo-scientific matters and whose adventures – such as those of *The Lost World* (1912) and 'The Poison Belt' (1913) – often border on science fiction.

Far from being restricted to 'supernatural' phenomena such as spiritualism and clairvoyance, Doyle's curiosity also embraced 'subhuman forms of life',[38] whose existence he averred in *The Coming of the Fairies* (1922). In 1917, two Yorkshire girls – Elsie Wright (who was 16 at the time) and Frances Griffiths (who was 10) – claimed to have photographed some fairies. Impressed by this evidence, Doyle first published an account of the matter in the 1920 Christmas number of the *Strand* and later collected various writings relating to the case in a volume. To Doyle the progress of technology offered new means to record and understand phenomena that were previously considered as supernatural. Photography, in particular, provided a way in which to catch frequencies of light that cannot be perceived by the naked eye:

> We see objects within the limits which make up our colour spectrum, with infinite vibrations, unused by us, on either side of them. If we could conceive a race of beings which were constructed in material which threw out shorter or longer vibrations, they would be invisible unless we could tune ourselves up or tone them down. It is exactly

that power of tuning up and adapting itself to other vibrations which constitutes a clairvoyant and there is nothing scientifically impossible, so far as I can see, in some people seeing that which is invisible to others.[39]

Doyle even anticipated the invention of 'some sort of psychic spectacles',[40] enabling future generations to perceive those aspects of 'nature' that were still veiled in his time, since 'If high-tension electricity can be converted by a mechanical contrivance into a lower tension, keyed to other uses, then it is hard to see why something analogous might not occur with the vibrations of ether and the waves of light.'[41] As we can see, Doyle regarded clairvoyance and fairies as belonging to the same order of phenomena, considering energy – both in the form of light and electricity – as the principle that unites the solidity of matter to the ethereal quality of spirits:

> First, it must be clearly understood that all that can be photographed must of necessity be physical. Nothing of a subtler order could in the nature of things affect the sensitive plate. So-called spirit photographs, for instance, imply necessarily a certain degree of materialization before the 'form' could come within the range even of the most sensitive of films.[42]

What most commentators underline when they deal with this text is the gullibility of Doyle, a true gentleman whose ethics prevented him from believing that the whole affair might be a hoax, but the case of the Cottingley fairies also shows how strongly the development of science and technology helped foster the resurgence of popular beliefs. Discarded traditions were reassessed within a new system of knowledge that promised surprising revelations. Science would provide society with the means to confront what had previously been deemed as unattainable or doubtful. People felt they were at the dawn of a new era. Therefore it does not come as a surprise that crime, detection and the supernatural coalesced in the *fin-de-siècle* climate of syncretism to form a new variety of detective adventures.

Towards psychic detection

Le Fanu's *In a Glass Darkly* (1872) is a prototypical example of the late nineteenth-century tendency to conflate a mystery involving the occult with an investigating agent and the serial structure of the 'professional case'. To connect the ghost stories he had previously published in mag-azines, Le Fanu utilised the figure of Dr Martin Hesselius as a framing device, presenting each narrative – by means of a prologue written by Hesselius's secretary – as a case he had collected in his files. As a medical man who is also endowed with metaphysical knowledge, Hesselius antici-pated another detective of the occult, Bram Stoker's Van Helsing, and we should not forget that Le Fanu's *Carmilla* – featuring a redoubtable female vampire – was reprinted in this collection.

Yet no real detection occurs in these texts, whose pseudo-scientific pretences are usually restricted to the prologue, hinting at Dr Hesselius's learned essays on arcane subjects and the complex classification of his works ('This reference is to Vol. I. Section 317, Note Z[a]').[43] In his medical practice, Hesselius repeatedly deals with people who are haunted by unexplainable presences and these supernatural encounters are presented in a detached register and an analytical mode that mimic the discourse of science:

> In a rough way, we may reduce all similar cases to three distinct classes. They are founded on the primary distinction between the subjective and the objective. Of those whose senses are alleged to be subject to supernatural impressions – some are simply visionaries, and propagate the illusions of which they complain, from diseased brain or nerves. Others are, unquestionably, infested by, as we term them, spiritual agencies, exterior to themselves. Others, again, owe their sufferings to a mixed condition. The interior sense, it is true, is opened; but it has been and continues open by the action of disease.[44]

To understand this classification we must remember that Le Fanu's depiction of the world of spirits is closely linked to his interest in the doctrines of Swedenborg, who theorised not only a correspondence between the world of humans and that of spirits, but also the possibility of perceiving the latter dimension by means of a special faculty, the inner eye.

While in the well-known 'Green Tea' Reverend Jennings is haunted by a monkey that can be regarded as a metaphor for the man's repressed sexual desire, in other stories the apparitions deal explicitly with crime. In 'The Familiar' Captain Barton is haunted by the sight of a man he brought to death, while in 'Mr Justice Harbottle' a higher tribunal judges a corrupt representative of the law. These stories reassert the existence of a superior justice that works autonomously, without requiring any assist-ance from human agents.

At the end of the century, detection and the supernatural combined to form what Cox and Gilbert called 'the story of psychic detection', with atypical sleuths such as Flaxman Low, John Silence and Carnacki 'pitting their wits against a variety of supernatural opponents'.[45] Because of the mysteries they tackle, these three figures can be regarded as the heirs of Martin Hesselius, but other aspects of their personality point towards another predecessor, Sherlock Holmes. Indeed, not only do they show a dashing indifference to danger, and in some cases enjoy the help of an assistant, but many of their adventures also reveal an underlying imperialist subtext. Moreover, they all show a marked indifference to the paradigm of divine justice and seem to rely on the belief that every aspect of reality would soon be explained thanks to the development of science.

In this respect their closest antecedent is Edward Bulwer-Lytton's enthralling 'The Haunted and the Haunters' (1859), which deserves to be looked into, notably because its hero and narrator enunciates the theoretical premises of 'psychical detection': 'Now, my theory is that the Supernatural is the Impossible, and that what is called supernatural is only a something in the laws of nature of which we have been hitherto ignorant.' To prove his theory, Bulwer's character mentions a whole set of phenomena, including 'the tales of Spirit Manifestation in America'[46] and 'mesmerism or electro-biology'.[47] As a result of this pseudo-scientific creed, the protagonist decides to enquire into the mystery of a haunted house, with the help of his servant and a dog. The night the three spend in the house results in disaster, for the neck of the dog is broken by an obscure entity, and the terrified servant subsequently emigrates to Australia. But what becomes clear is that the supposed haunting is linked to a crime that took place in the building. However, the hero refuses to believe in 'the popular superstition that a person who had been either the perpetrator or the victim of dark crimes in life could revisit, as a restless spirit, the scene in which those crimes had been committed' and thinks instead that at the bottom of the mystery there must be 'a living human agency'.[48] By this, however, the hero does not intend to imply an imposture, but rather 'a power akin to mesmerism, and superior to it – the power that in the old days was called Magic'.[49]

We thus discover that the old house conceals two different layers of mystery – one concerns a murder that was committed about 35 years before, while the other involves magic and takes us back to the eighteenth century. An inquiry into the past enables the hero to understand the nature of the evil that lurks in the house, while the demolition of a room where a horrific event took place suffices to 'cut off the telegraph wires'[50] that link past and present. Although the fate of Bulwer's murderers – in the criminal subplot of the story – still evokes the presence of divine justice, the final section of the tale rests on a different system of beliefs, involving arcane knowledge rather than science or religion. This esoteric plot is clearly linked to Bulwer's lifelong interest in Rosicrucianism and immortality. As Marie Roberts claims, 'Bulwer endorsed a synthetic approach to knowledge', rejecting 'a strict demarcation between magic and science'.[51] This may help us understand the ambivalent conceptual framework of the story, where the events which the hero confronts are the result neither of imposture nor of truly supernatural agencies, but rather of unknown human powers:

> 'These phenomena belong to neither class; my persuasion is, that they originate in some brain now far distant; that that brain had no distinct volition in anything that occurred; that what does occur reflects but its devious, motley, ever-shifting, half-formed thoughts; in short, that it has been but the dreams of such a brain put into action and invested with a semi-substance.'[52]

By extending the realm of the natural so as to include a whole range of phenomena whose causes were unknown and whose actual existence was disputed Bulwer provided a firm basis for the subsequent tales of 'psychic detection'.

Doyle himself responded to this intellectual climate with a number of creepy stories he first published in the *Strand* and then collected in two volumes – *Round the Red Lamp, Being Facts and Fancies of Medical Life* (1894) and *Round the Fire Stories* (1908). As Doyle explained in his preface to the 1894 collection, the red lamp was the sign of a general practitioner and these stories of medical life confront us with a variety of predicaments, mostly of a mundane character, although the subtitle of the book – mingling 'facts' with 'fancies' – should alert us to its hybrid nature. Thus in 'Lot No. 249' a natural and a supernatural interpretation of events coexist until the very end of the tale. Although the whole story rests on the account of a single witness and it is possible to believe that his intellect may have 'some strange flaw in its workings', an alternative view is offered:

> Yet when we think how narrow and how devious this path of Nature is, how dimly we can trace it, for all our lamps of science, and how from the darkness which girds it round great and terrible possibilities loom ever shadowly upwards, it is a bold and confident man who will put a limit to the strange by-paths into which the human spirit may wander.[53]

The three main characters, who study at Oxford and live in the same house, embody the racial and cultural prejudices of the time. The villainous Edward Bellingham is described as 'a man of wide reading, with catholic tastes',[54] while Monkhouse Lee, who seems to be under the influence of Bellingham, is 'olive-skinned and dark-eyed, of a Spanish rather than of an English type, with a Celtic intensity of manner'. These traits contrast with 'the Saxon phlegm'[55] of Abercrombie Smith, the man of action.

Bellingham – who is an expert in Eastern languages and arcane lore – has apparently managed to revive an ancient mummy and is willing to use it against whoever stands in his way. According to Smith, whose reliability is never seriously questioned, Bellingham 'was a murderer at heart, and ... he wielded a weapon such as no man had ever used in all the grim history of crime'.[56] Although Smith has uncovered 'a striking chain of events',[57] he is aware that a police magistrate would simply laugh in his face and decides to prevent further mischief by confronting Bellingham with a gun. While Lee and Smith correspond to the prescribed male identity, which was based on a healthy mixture of athleticism, rationality and Anglicanism, Bellingham has crossed the border between 'us and them' and is condemned to exile, since at the end of the story we are told that this modern enchanter 'was last heard of in the Soudan'.[58]

Although in 'Lot No. 249' the supernatural is associated with crime rather than detection, this text provides us with a useful paradigm through which to interpret the stories of 'psychic detection' that were written in the following years. Let us remember that the setting of Doyle's story is 'so famed a centre of learning and light as the University of Oxford',[59] while the evil forces that are lurking in the Oxford nights are linked to a distant past and distant places. As we know, after Jean-François Champollion had deciphered the hieroglyphs in 1822, Egypt played an increasingly central role in nineteenth-century culture, and even came to occupy the space that Greece had previously held in the collective imagination as the cradle of European civilisation. On the other hand, extra-European societies were regarded by many as a mirror of Europe in the early stages of its development. It is my contention that this story – where modernity fights 'uncanny' forces that it perceives as 'other' although they belong to its own past – exorcised the anxiety that had been engendered by the cultural encounters brought about by the imperial experience.

As we shall see, the interplay between British identity and others, as a result of what today we call 'globalisation', is a recurring subtext in stories of the occult. By specialising in supernatural mysteries, the detective – who had already acquired the status of an 'epistemological superman' – came to grips with a different kind of menace, embodying the collective desire of control not only over crime and the urban space, but also over the exotic, the primitive and, ultimately, the unconscious.

Professionals of the occult

Flaxman Low is the hero of twelve stories that appeared in *Pearson's Monthly Magazine* between 1898 and 1899 and were published in book form later in 1899. The stories, published under the pen names of 'E. and H. Heron', were actually authored by Hesketh Prichard and his mother Katherine. In the first episode, Low is presented as an alias under which 'many are sure to recognise one of the leading scientists of the day, with whose works on Psychology and kindred subjects they are familiar'. He is described as the 'first' researcher who, breaking free from conventional methods, approached 'the elucidation of so-called supernatural problems on the lines of natural law'.[60] Low's adventures rest on the belief that the advancement of rational knowledge will dispel the supernatural aura of many events. To explain ghostly apparitions and related phenomena Low relies on 'psychology', which is defined as 'a lost science of the ancients'.[61] Having thus provided psychology with a suitable pedigree, the author introduces Low's first case as an abstract from a paper he gave at the Psychical Research Society as a contribution to the development of science in the exploration of the unknown.

Low's adventures are often concerned with murder. 'The Story of the Spaniards, Hammersmith', where the hero makes his appearance, pivots on a grotesque supernatural criminal – the ghost of a leper who was originally guilty of killing his own wife and who now haunts a certain room, ready to replicate his evil deed. The entities which Low confronts are usually associated with interiors, and their annihilation is often possible only at the expense of the mansion they haunt.

In a way all these stories capitalise on the latent anxiety that the imperial experience evoked in the Victorian public, on fears of the possible forms of contamination that accompanied the early stages of globalisation. Travelling and living in foreign lands, as well as importing goods or receiving people from non-European territories, were perceived as potentially dangerous. Victorians felt that the national identity of Britain was somehow endangered by the empire. In the 'Story of the Spaniards', the man who built the haunted house also owned sugar plantations in Trinidad. Travelling for leisure can likewise result in dangerous encounters, as in 'The Story of Baelbrow', where the proprietor of a Scottish mansion brings home a bulky souvenir from Egypt for his private museum, precipitating the death of a maid and endangering his own son. Interestingly, however, in this story the nefariousness of an 'illegal immigrant' is the result of local agency, since the house stands 'on a barrow or burying place'.[62]

In 'The Story of Konnor Old House', Low is invited to investigate the mystery of another Scottish house whose last inhabitant – Sir James Mackian – 'had been a merchant of sorts in Sierra Leone'.[63] Was Sir James involved in the slave trade or in other shady business? No answer is provided in the text, but Sir James's daughter apparently killed herself by taking an overdose of sleeping draught, to escape from the persecution of Jake, the black servant Sir James brought with him to England, claiming that he had saved his life. In all these stories the evil that ripens on British soil is rooted in the uncanny practices, rituals or beliefs of faraway lands. Even in 'The Story of Yand Manor House', where no travelling is mentioned, other forms of cultural exchange contribute to the supernatural mystery, for in the past one of the owners of the house 'was deeply read in ancient necromancy, Eastern magic, mesmerism, and subjects of a kindred nature'.[64]

As in mainstream detective fiction, in these stories past events must be reconstructed in order to solve a present mystery, which can be either a murder or a minor disturbance. Unknown agencies are involved in these 'crimes' and the only way to penetrate their misdeeds is through an investigation into the past of the victim(s) and/or the place.

A similar pattern recurs in the collection of stories Algernon Blackwood published in 1908, *John Silence – Physician Extraordinary*.[65] Once again the structure of the professional case is combined with occult phenomena, and Silence, in his role as 'Psychic Doctor', tackles investigations that 'no ordinary professional could deal with'.[66] A Watson-like figure – Mr Hubbard – assists Silence in some of the stories and also narrates them. Thus, as in Holmes's stories, readers cannot enter the doctor's mind, which remains enveloped in a superior aura of mystery. Indeed, Silence is closer to Holmes than either Low or Carnacki, and Julia Briggs rightly claims that 'the shadow of Baker Street seems to fall heavily' over some of his stories.[67]

The mysteries that Silence investigates often concern an individual and a place that are haunted by evil entities. Danger usually resurfaces from the past, but it can also be associated with foreign lands, as in 'The Nemesis of Fire', where ancient Egypt is the source of the malediction that threatens to annihilate Colonel Wragge's manor house and family. Readers are told that the colonel's elder brother, who died mysteriously in the grounds of the house twenty years before, 'was a great traveller, and filled the house with stuff he brought home from all over the world'.[68] Blackwood skilfully refrains from offering us any further explanation concerning the dead man's collections, but we are led to believe that danger may lurk in the house due to the cultural exchanges that travelling unwittingly triggered. The empire also plays an interesting role in this story, for the colonel served as a soldier in exotic lands and the unsystematic knowledge he acquired while he was in touch with 'other' cultures helps him bridge the gap between the rational and the irrational.[69]

Silence's stories often rely on the paradigm of supernatural invasion, which needs to be fought by using the right kind of weapons and knowledge. The colonel's house is described as being 'in a state of siege; as though a concealed enemy were encamped about us'.[70] Red herrings are used to mislead the readers: the little wood where strange events take place conceals 'a sort of mound where there is a circle of large boulders – old Druid stones',[71] but local magic here is not disruptive, while danger comes from abroad.

In 'A Psychical Invasion', on the other hand, the forces that haunt the house of Felix Pender have a more local origin. After taking stock of the powerful and dark entities that roam the place at night, Silence makes the following discovery:

> I have been able to check certain information obtained in the hypnotic trance by a 'sensitive' who helps me in such cases. The former occupant who haunted you appears to have been a woman of singularly atrocious life and character who finally suffered death by hanging, after a series of crimes that appalled the whole of England and only came to light by the merest chance. She came to her end in the year 1798.[72]

The ending of the story reveals its close ties to crime fiction. As if by 'magic', Silence is able to show Pender a pencil drawing of the female figure who haunted him, but there is nothing hocus-pocus about this revelation:

> Dr. Silence then produced from his pocket-book an old-fashioned woodcut of the same person which his secretary had unearthed from the records of the Newgate Calendar. The woodcut and the pencil drawing were two different aspects of the same dreadful visage.[73]

Other aspects of Silence's investigations link him to nineteenth-century detectives. Like Holmes, Silence occasionally alludes to previous cases[74] and also indulges in spectacular demonstrations of mind-reading, although his technique differs from those of his predecessors, ' "It's only that you are thinking very vividly," the doctor said quietly, "and your thoughts form pictures in my mind before you utter them. It's merely a little elementary thought-reading." '[75] Clues are often discussed and the element of adventure is also strong, for Silence is often involved in risky operations whose aim is firstly to reconnoitre the ground and then to face the usually invisible enemies that are preying on their victims. Last but not least, like his two *confrères*, Silence is not moved by money, but by the desire to help people in distress and by his erudite curiosity concerning weird phenomena. In this respect, Silence mirrors Blackwood's genuine interest in the occult, which led him not only to take part in séances and to study Oriental religions, but also to join the Hermetic Order of the Golden Dawn in 1900.

Carnacki's six adventures were originally published by W.H. Hodgson in *The Idler* and *The New Magazine* between 1910 and 1912, and were collected in *Carnacki: the Ghost Finder* in 1913. Unlike the two previous 'psychic detectives' Carnacki does not emphasise the dangers of foreign travel and the imperial adventure. Most of the stories are set in peripheral areas of the British Isles, such as Ireland, where old superstitions are evoked and occasionally a touch of local colour is added, thanks to the language of certain characters.

These formulaic stories are presented within a framing narrative: a group of friends assemble for dinner at Carnacki's and after a good meal he recounts his latest adventure. Most of the mysteries that this 'psychic detective' tackles prove not to be genuinely supernatural, but curiously those cases where a 'ghost play'[76] is staged by human agents – or where natural and supernatural plots intertwine – are the least convincing. Hodgson spends too much energy on evoking an uncanny atmosphere of terror simply to dissipate his spell by referring to a few mechanical tricks or by declaring that certain occurrences remain shrouded in mystery. After grotesque masques of evil have been staged against the sinister backdrop of remote manor houses and castles – or even of ordinary terraced houses – a series of contrived and totally unconvincing rational explanations tend to result in a disappointing anticlimax.

As regards Carnacki's strategies of detection, sources of esoteric knowledge – such as the Sigsand MS. and the Saamaaa Ritual – are often mentioned or employed. Moreover, to ward off evil entities, Carnacki repeatedly draws chalk circles, spreads or wears garlic, or makes use of lighted candles and human hair. Modern technology also plays a major role in his investigations as he avails himself of an 'Electric Pentacle' as a ' "Defence" against certain manifestations'.[77] The neon light of the pentacle feebly illuminates with a blue glare the scene of many a frightful apparition. A camera and a flashlight also prove helpful in detecting a supernatural presence, since 'Sometimes the camera sees things that would seem very strange to normal human eyesight.'[78] In 'The Whistling Room' Carnacki even tries 'to get a phonographic record' of the mysterious whistling that haunts Iastrae Castle, 'but it simply produced no impression on the wax at all'.[79] Magnifying glasses and other instruments are used by Carnacki to inspect the scene of a crime in order to detect any possible clues pointing to a natural or supernatural explanation of the events. Moreover, like John Silence – whose 'A Psychical Invasion' is a masterpiece in this respect – Carnacki occasionally avails himself of animals to detect supernatural agencies, for their sensitivity to these entities far exceeds that of humans. Finally, he is sometimes assisted in his investigation by bewildered representatives of the local police, who act as a foil to the superior knowledge of the 'psychic detective'.

Other stories of supernatural detection were published in the following years, such as those written by Sax Rohmer (the pseudonym of A.H.S. Ward) for *The New Magazine* in 1913–14 and collected in *The Dream-Detective* in 1920. The protagonist of this saga is Moris Klaw, who is assisted by a Watson figure – Mr Searles – and also boasts a beautiful daughter, Isis. Although most of the mysteries Klaw investigates actually reveal a human agent, Klaw's techniques of investigation include uncanny tools, such as an 'odically sterilised'[80] cushion that enables him to intercept the thoughts of criminals or to picture the scene of a crime in the form of dreams.

To understand this prodigy of pseudo-science one should remember that the German chemist Karl Ludwig von Reichenbach (1788–1869), who discovered paraffin and phenol, also developed an interest in 'sensitives' and sleepwalkers. Drawing on (pseudo)-scientific discoveries in the fields of magnetism and electricity, von Reichenbach tried to explain these phenomena in physical terms and claimed to have identified an energy he called 'od' (from the Northern god Odin), which acted as an irritant on particularly sensitive people. Von Reichenbach believed that the 'odic' force could be absorbed by metals and that it could enable certain individuals to perceive other people's thoughts. The scientist created special darkrooms which enabled him to experiment with 'sensitives', who were asked to describe the luminous quality of objects and people, that is, their aura. This luminosity could even be photographed and the resulting image was called an 'odograph'.[81]

These pseudo-scientific theories underlie Rohmer's eccentric stories. In Klaw's first adventure – 'The Case of the Tragedies in the Greek

Room' – the dream-detective asks to be allowed to sleep at the scene of a murder, in order to be permeated by the odic force of the place, so as to imprint it on his mind. Klaw's ultimate objective is that of reproducing a 'psychic photograph'[82] of the criminal, who is – characteristically – a somnambulist. Time after time, Klaw's pseudo-scientific investigations reveal the human agency behind incomprehensible crimes, often pivoting on Egyptian and Indian artefacts, while the last episode of the series – 'The Case of the Veil of Isis' – confronts us with genuinely supernatural events.

These borderline texts, which combine detection with pseudo-science and the occult agencies which are typical of weird tales, defied classification either under the label of gothic or of detective fiction. H.P. Lovecraft included both Carnacki and Silence in his *Supernatural Horror in Literature* (1927), but he regarded their adventures as 'marred by traces of the popular and conventional detective-story atmosphere...'[83] On the other hand, the uncomfortable proximity between these stories of 'impossible crime'[84] and mainstream stories of detection was perceived as a danger by those practitioners and critics of detective fiction who placed increasing emphasis on the strictly rational basis of this genre so as to 'detach' it from the neighbouring forms of sensation fiction and the ghost story. At the end of the 1920s theoreticians of detective fiction such as S.S. Van Dine and Ronald Knox made great efforts to define the conventions of the genre, and Knox's 'Detective Story Decalogue' (1929) includes this literary precept: 'All supernatural or preternatural agencies are ruled out as a matter of course.'[85] The 'golden age' of detective fiction saw the triumph of fair play, where readers should be able to solve the crime themselves, thanks to the clues they have been offered by the text.

Fabricated apparitions

As we have seen, the 'psychic detectives' dealt not only with authentic ghosts, but also with fake ones. We should remember that false apparitions 'legitimately' played a large role in sensation and detective fiction, representing attempts at concealing crime by clothing it with ghostly attributes. Thus even the most rational nineteenth-century detectives – Holmes comes to mind – repeatedly face mysteries of purportedly supernatural import. The extent to which Doyle relied on irrational ingredients to concoct his narrative recipes is demonstrated by *The Hound of the Baskervilles* (1902), where the tension between natural and supernatural is exploited in order to enmesh the readers in mystery, rousing their emotions and setting the ground for a final explanation. In this novel the criminal acts like a sinister conjuror, performing deadly tricks that satisfy the public's aesthetics of evil.

Interestingly, in late nineteenth-century stories fake apparitions are often presented as the result of extreme ingenuity and the deviant use of technology. A case in point is a story from the popular series by L.T. Meade and Clifford Halifax published in the *Strand* – 'Stories from the Diary of a Doctor'. In 'The Horror of Studley Grange' (1894) Lady Studley implores the doctor to pay a visit to the country house where she lives with her husband in order to enquire into the causes of his shattered nerves, but when the physician is introduced to Sir Henry he realises that the man is in turn worried about the health of his wife, who is consumptive. Sir Henry is also troubled by the nightly appearance of a ghost in the bedroom where he sleeps alone, due to his wife's condition:

> In a certain spot of the room, always in the same spot, a bright light suddenly flashes; out of its midst there gleams a preternaturally large eye, which looks fixedly at me with a diabolical expression. As time goes, it does not remain long; but as agony counts, it seems to take years of my life away with it.[86]

Without telling the other inmates of the house, the doctor takes the place of Sir Henry and has the opportunity to witness the apparition, which occurs just in front of the blue glass doors of a large wardrobe. The next day, the doctor takes a closer look at the quaint piece of furniture – which is inset in a mullion – and realises that it harbours a secret passage, leading to Lady Studley's adjoining room. Setting a trap, the doctor is able to frame the culprit, the dying Lady Studley, whose motive is jealousy. Fearing that her husband might remarry after her death, she has tried to disrupt his health in the hope that he may follow or even anticipate her destiny. The technological innovation on which this plan is based is explained as follows:

> I attached the mirror of a laryngoscope to my forehead in such a manner as to enable it to throw a strong reflection into one of my eyes. In the centre of the bright side of the laryngoscope a small electric lamp was fitted. This was connected with a battery which I carried in my hand. The battery was similar to those used by the ballet girls in Drury Lane Theatre, and could be brought into force by a touch and extinguished by the removal of the pressure. The eye which was then brilliantly illuminated looked through a lens of some power. All the rest of the face and figure was completely covered by the black cloak.

Thus the brightest possible light was thrown on the magnified eye, while there was corresponding increased gloom around.[87]

It is technology – coupled with ingenuity – that makes it possible to stage this sinister show, which also relies on the symbolic power the eye of God has within Western culture, as discussed in the previous chapters. Moreover, in spite of the rational framework of the story and the presence of a medical man as the torch-bearer of science, the events retain their preternatural aura in the eyes of Sir Henry, for the compassionate doctor fulfils the Lady's dying wish that her husband might not know of her design. Thus after his wife's death Sir Henry still believes that the apparition was a message sent from heaven to announce his imminent bereavement.

To conclude, in the Victorian period religion lost part of its power to shape collective expectations concerning justice and the afterlife. This ideological gap was replaced not only by a positivist approach that denied the supernatural in favour of a materialistic view of the world, but also by pseudo-scientific paradigms that combined with past beliefs. Nineteenth-century literature mirrors this complex cultural phase, revealing a wide spectrum of interactions between crime, detection and the supernatural. While in Dickens's 'The Trial for Murder' and in Collins's 'The Haunted Hotel' mesmerism is still functional to a providential narrative, in most of the cases that Low, Silence and Carnacki investigate both the mystery and the inquiry rest on pseudo-scientific and/or esoteric conceptual frameworks.

I regard it as no coincidence that at the turn of the century the outdated belief in dreams as supernatural messages was supplanted by two diverging paradigms. On the one hand, in 1900 Freud's *The Interpretation of Dreams* related dreams to the waking life of the subject, describing them as wish-fulfilment mechanisms. On the other, writers revived pseudo-scientific theories of dreams, as is shown both by Rohmer's 'dream detective' and by 'The Leather Funnel' (*Round the Fire Stories*, 1908), a sensational story where Doyle capitalised on the idea that sleep may be influenced by the proximity of objects that are charged with particular energies, taking us back to the seventeenth-century trial of a notorious poisoner, the Marquise de Brinvilliers.

Finally, we should not underestimate the role of the imperial adventure in this significant change; as U.P. Mukherjee reminds us, the discourses of crime and those of the empire often intertwined in Victorian fiction.[88] This is shown not only by *The Moonstone*, where the supernatural is associated with a basically open attitude towards 'other' cultures and identities, but also by Doyle's minor works and by the above-mentioned stories of 'psychic detection', which often became the vehicle of racial fears and prejudices. As Steven Connor claims, 'the Other Worlds of Victorian speculation were no mere fantasy retreats',[89] but they reflect the tensions and aspirations of their time and therefore offer a privileged viewpoint from which to study the Victorian age itself.

Part II
Sensational

6
The Language of Auguste Dupin

What is the language of Auguste Dupin?

Is it the American English of Edgar Allan Poe? Is it French, supposedly the hero's mother tongue? Or does the Chevalier speak English as well? For instance when he addresses the narrator of the story – a character contemporary readers presumably tended to identify with Poe himself. These questions provide a humorous pretext to introduce a less idle matter, since the nineteenth-century development of crime fiction can be regarded as the product of a network of exchanges between French, British and American cultures.

In recent years, British scholars have denounced the traditional clear-cut view of the genesis of detective fiction as a myth. According to Martin Kayman, for instance, twentieth-century critics saw Poe as the creator of detective fiction because they read his work through the eyes of Conan Doyle, although in Great Britain this genre developed a precise identity only in the late 1880s.[1] Stephen Knight likewise acknowledges that the sources of crime fiction are varied and underlines that in England the pattern initiated by Poe did not spread 'until, in the late 1880s, Doyle saw how to both dilute and localise Dupin's power in the semi-respectable form of Sherlock Holmes …'[2] Starting from the assumption that the 1840s were an eventful decade in the development of crime fiction, in terms both of production and of reception, I will examine some trans-cultural dynamics that contributed to the definition and diffusion of the genre in the second half of the century.

Narrative metamorphoses

First of all, crime stories tended to metamorphosise through various forms with their already ambivalent status further blurring the boundaries between fact and fiction. Reviews like *Blackwood's* played a major role in these exchanges, publishing factional texts that were characterised by great suspense and grotesque incidents. *Blackwood's* stories not only paved the way for the subsequent development of English sensation fiction *à la* Collins, but they were also imported to the United States by Poe – as we shall see in the next chapter – and exported to the continent. The anonymous 'Le Revenant', which was published in the Edinburgh periodical in 1827 is a case in point. In spite of its French title, the story was set in London. This breathtakingly realistic first-person narration – describing the sensational experiences of a man who survived hanging – was plundered by British printers, who turned its first pages into a broadside,[3] but this process of 'recycling' also had a transnational dimension, for in 1838 part of the story was reprinted in the French *Magasin pittoresque*. The story – now set in the States – was entitled 'Sensations d'un Américain pendu' ('Sensations of an American Who Was Hanged') and it was introduced by the following editorial note, hinting at a previous French version:

> An American who had been condemned to death happened not to be entirely deprived of his life when he was detached from the scaffold. He was taken care of, he regained his health, and, having been solicited by several people, he tried to describe all he had thought and suffered while he was waiting to be executed. His account was translated and published in France, under the Restoration, by a literary journal: it made a vivid impression on the public, and it soon triggered some remarkable imitations that little by little cancelled its memory. We are reproducing it now ...[4]

Editors and publishers freely appropriated texts whose authorship was of marginal consideration, since they were frequently published anonymously and/or were regarded as devoid of 'literary' value.

On a different plane, the act of adapting and borrowing from foreign fiction or drama was a common literary practice. The plot of Elizabeth Braddon's *The Trail of the Serpent* (1861) – possibly the first English detective novel – has strong similarities with Charles Reade's adaptation of the French play *Le Courier de Lyons* (*The Courier of Lyons*, 1850), which is mentioned in the novel.[5] The detective Hawkshaw, who appeared in Tom Taylor's *The Ticket-of-leave Man* in 1863, is often referenced as the first English detective in drama, but we are less frequently reminded that the play was in itself an adaptation from Brisebarre and Nus's *Le Retour de Melun* (*The Return from Melun*), which was published in 1860 and performed in Paris in 1862.[6] We also know that Doyle borrowed the bipartite structure of his first Sherlock Holmes novels – exploring the motives for a crime by means of a long retrospective narrative – from Émile Gaboriau.

Indeed, although the American subplot of *A Study in Scarlet* (1887) is a replica of Stevenson's 'Story of the Destroying Angel' in *The Dynamiter* (1885),[7] the time-scheme of the novel – including a long flashback to the period in which the London murder mystery is rooted – actually derived from a novel by Gaboriau, as Doyle implicitly acknowledged, with a touch of irony. We are often reminded that in his first adventure Holmes ungracefully labels Lecoq as 'a miserable bungler', adding: 'That book made me positively ill. The question was how to identify an unknown prisoner. I could have done it in twenty-four hours. Lecoq took six months or so.'[8] The book Holmes is referring to is not *L'Affaire Lerouge* (*The Lerouge Case*, 1866), where Lecoq made his appearance on the literary scene, but *Monsieur Lecoq* (1869), whose first part describes the failure of the detective to ascertain the identity of a murderer, who is even allowed to escape from prison – and followed – in the hope that he betrays his secret. Only after a long flashback to 1815 do readers get to know the truth. In spite of Holmes's disparaging remarks on Lecoq, Doyle actually appropriated the narrative structure of *Monsieur Lecoq* so as to combine the story of the investigation with the story of the crime. The result is not a seamless structure, but Doyle's technique improved in his following novels.

As we know, Doyle was not the first crime writer to hint at foreign antecedents for his work, implicitly acknowledging a debt, although these references were usually spiced up with a bit of chauvinism. Poe had famously mentioned Vidocq in 'The Murders of the Rue Morgue' (1841), while Gaboriau's Père Tabaret had described his flair for detection – a power he would hand down to the younger Lecoq – as rooted in books:

> Reading the memories of celebrated policemen, as enticing as the best plotted fairy tales, I became an enthusiast of those men with a subtle scent, more elastic than silk, flexible like steel, penetrating and sly, rich in unexpected resources, who follow crime on its track, with the code in their hand, through the bushes of the law, like Cooper's savages pursuing their enemies amidst the American forests.[9]

As Messac reminds us, Cooper was also labelled 'the American Walter Scott'[10] by Eugène Sue in *Les Mystères de Paris* (*The Mysteries of Paris*, 1842–43) and critics have underlined his influence on the French *feuilleton*, where the parallel between the American wilderness and the European urban space is repeatedly drawn. Paris was increasingly perceived at the time as a savage place, where criminals adopted the exotic names of *mohicans* and *apaches* (Alexandre Dumas *père* authored a novel entitled *Les Mohicans de Paris* – *The Mohicans of Paris* – in 1845) while detectives focused their attention on minute environmental details, like hunters pursuing their prey.

Citizens of Cosmopolis

We should also remember that nineteenth-century detectives often speak franglais and claim a cosmopolitan status. In Britain, this phenomenon was probably rooted in the reception of Vidocq's *Mémoires* (1828–29), which were immediately translated into English and also became the subject of various plays that were staged in London. Moreover, soon after its serialisation in France, *Les Mystères de Paris* was also translated into English (the 1844 American edition was followed by an English edition in 1845), Spanish, German and Russian. It was thanks to the widespread celebrity of this novel that the vogue of 'urban mysteries' spread like wildfire all over continental Europe and in Great Britain, where it inspired G.W.M. Reynolds to write *The Mysteries of London* and *The Mysteries of the Court of London* (1844–56).

In the following decades, French criminals and detectives enjoyed vast popularity in Britain. In 'Recollections of a Police Officer' (serialised in 1849–52 by 'Waters', the pseudonym of William Russell) French characters often appear in Britain and the detective relies on his knowledge of their language.[11] The 'Recollections' were not only published in book form both in the United States (*Recollections of a Policeman*, 1852) and in Great Britain (*Recollections of a Detective Police-officer*, 1856), but due to their success and to their French dimension, which aroused the interest of Alexandre Dumas, they were also translated into French by Victor Perceval (*Mémoires d'un policier*, 1859).[12] The transnational character of mid-century crime fiction is also demonstrated by *The Experiences of a French Detective Officer* (1861), supposedly authored by Theodore Duhamel, but attributed to Russell himself, and the *Autobiography of a French Detective from 1818 to 1858* (1862), which was adapted from Louis Canler's *Mémoires*.[13]

Given this background, it comes as no surprise that even Holmes (a champion of Britishness) has a touch of the French in him. When the detective is asked about the origin of his faculties of observation, he refers to the laws of heredity, explaining that although his ancestors were country squires, his talent may have come with his grandmother, 'who was the sister of Vernet, the French artist'.[14] The aesthetic tendency that coexists in Holmes with his penchant for science would thus be a legacy of his French blood.

Perhaps it was under the influence of Holmes's mixed ancestry that Robert Barr, a friend of Doyle and a Scottish-Canadian, decided to create a detective hero who united the attributes of Britons and Frenchmen – Eugène Valmont. The Valmont stories were serialised in Great Britain as well as in the United States and published in book form in both countries in 1906. Set on both sides of the Channel, these stories involve many French and British characters, together with an assortment of other nationalities. The hero himself has a cosmopolitan status insofar as he is a former member of the French police who was unjustly dismissed and now secretly works as a private detective in London. Valmont's situation between two worlds provides the background for a set of stories that enable him to make the most of his multifarious experiences:

> my worldly affairs are now much more prosperous than they were in Paris, my intimate knowledge of that city and the country of which it is the capital bringing to me many cases with which I have dealt more or less successfully since I established myself in London.[15]

American millionaires and British aristocrats, French workmen and Italian anarchists move freely in the world of Valmont, who knows how to deal with each and every one.

A few years later, Baroness Orczy chose a mixed lineage for her female detective, Lady Molly of Scotland Yard. As we learn at the end of her adventures, which also bring her to France and Italy, Lady Molly is actually the daughter of the Earl of Flintshire and a French actress, and the misfortunes which led her to embrace the career of a detective in order to clear the reputation of the man she loves can be ascribed to an 'original sin' consequent on her mother's profession.

Criminals proved no less proficient than detectives in switching into different idioms and assuming different national identities. In Ponson du Terrail's *Les Exploits de Rocambole* (*The Exploits of Rocambole*, 1859) we meet a young son of Albion on board a ferry. His English is almost imperceptibly tinged with a foreign accent; but what thoughts are whirling in his mind?

> Have I really become an Englishman? A pure blooded gentleman who is interested in Epsom's races or in a novel by Charles Dickens, who writes small verse in the journal of his county and dreams of marrying an airy young lady, with red arms, blue eyes and carrot coloured hair – somebody who has just returned from his third journey around the world? No, not at all. My heart beats because tomorrow I will be at Havre and because Le Havre is only five hours from Paris ...

And Sir Arthur pronounced this word with all the emotion of a son who is whispering the name of his mother.[16]

Needless to say, Sir Arthur is Rocambole himself, who regards identity as little more than a set of clothes to put on and off according to his needs, 'Luckily Sir Arthur has remembered that he was once called the Vicomte de Cambolh, then the Marquess Don Inigo de los Montes, that he had presided over the Club of the Knaves of Hearts, and that his unfortunate master, Sir Williams, had foretold him a great destiny.'[17]

Within the saga a seemingly endless cycle of reincarnations enables characters to transcend national and even racial barriers. At the end of *Le Club des Valets de cœur* (*The Club of the Jack of Hearts*) the Irish Baron Sir Williams (actually Andréa) is punished for his misdeeds by being blinded and having his tongue cut out. Then he is set on board a vessel heading for the Pacific, but in *Les Exploits de Rocambole* the devilish ruffian reappears, covered with tattoos, as an Australian Aboriginal who is exhibited as a phenomenon in a circus!

The mutability of these heroes is an apt symbol for the transnational character of sensation and detective fiction from around the 1840s, when texts reappeared in new languages, often by means of free translations involving the reinvention of characters and settings. It is too complex a phenomenon to tackle in the space of a few pages, so this chapter will tentatively focus on three authors – Poe, Collins and Gaboriau – in order to deal with three of its aspects, that is, the choice of a foreign setting, critical reception in a foreign country and the quality of translations.

An American and Paris

Sensational themes and atmospheres migrated from Great Britain towards France and the United States, where Poe famously contributed to the development of this international literary trend. Let us focus on the Dupin trilogy, the mini-saga that was canonised by twentieth-century critics as the beginning of a new genre, in order to analyse its cosmopolitan status. Why is it that these stories are set neither in the United States nor in London, where 'The Man of the Crowd' (1840) – the first story by Poe featuring a *flâneur* – takes place? According to Priestman, Poe was induced to set his hero's adventures in the French capital by the need to contrast the investigative talent of Dupin with the blundering efforts of the police.[18] In 1841, when Poe published 'The Murders in the Rue Morgue', a police force had not yet been created either in New York – where the Day and Night Police was founded in 1844, after the sensational murder of Mary Rogers – or in London (where the Detective Police was formed in 1842).

The influence of Vidocq's *Mémoires* should also be taken into account, but Stephen Knight and Heather Worthington point to another possible source, a story entitled 'Murder and Mystery', which appeared in *Fraser's Magazine* – a journal with which Poe was familiar – shortly before 'The Murders in the Rue Morgue' was published. 'Murder and Mystery' is set in Paris and its main character is an Englishman whose morbid solitude anticipated the condition of Dupin:

> With a rashness that partook of recent fever's wild delirium, I rushed from the scene which had closed upon my happiness; for I had a pride in grief that urged me to shun the observation of those who were the authors of it, and my wounded spirit longed to 'flee away and be at rest.' But where might rest be found to a heart pierced and lacerated like mine? … I found myself for the first time in Paris; alone – socially alone – with a body worn and debilitated by suffering, and a mind utterly incompetent to any healthful exercise. It followed that, as soon as the haste and excitement of my journey were past, I became prostrate in spirit, passive in action, and so abjectly wedded to my melancholy, as to render all the gay surroundings I had sought, indifferent – nay, hateful – to my feeling.[19]

Finally, one should remember that Paris is the background of E.T.A. Hoffmann's *Das Fräulein von Scuderi* (*Mademoiselle de Scudéry*, 1818), where the seventeenth-century novelist Mademoiselle de Scudéry is portrayed in her old age and faced with a case of theft and murder. Hoffmann's crime story – whose gothic elements include what looks like a case of demonic possession and a secret passage in a Paris house – might also have contributed to Poe's choice of a foreign setting.

In 1845 an important edition of Poe's *Tales* was printed in the United States[20] and various stories were soon translated into French, usually without acknowledging their authorship. 'The Purloined Letter' was published anonymously in the *Magasin pittoresque* in August 1845 as 'Une Lettre volée'. One year later, two translations of 'The Murders in the Rue Morgue' followed suit. 'Un Meurtre sans exemple dans les fastes de la Justice (Histoire retrouvée dans les papiers d'un Américain)' ('A Murder without Equals in the Annals of Justice: a story that was found in the papers of an American') was printed between 11 and 13 June 1846 in *La Quotidienne* and signed G.B. (perhaps Gustave Brunet) while 'Une Sanglante énigme' ('A Bloody Enigma') was published on 12 October 1846 in *Le Commerce* and signed O.N., that is to say Old Nick, the devil, a pseudonym of Paul-Émile Daurand, alias Émile Forgues. While Brunet turned Dupin into an American called Henry Bernier, who lives in Paris in rue de Clichy, Forgues set the story in Baltimore, Poe's home town, exchanging the identity of Dupin for that of an American called Jones. The affinity between the two French versions of 'The Murders in the Rue Morgue' came to light thanks to an article that appeared on 14 October 1846 in the daily paper *La Presse*, and Forgues was publicly denounced as a plagiarist. The following day Forgues – who was the editor of the *Revue des deux mondes* – published a long essay entitled 'Études sur le roman anglais et américain. Les contes d'Edgar A. Poe' ('Studies on the English and the American Novel: the tales of E.A. Poe') which analysed 'The Murders in the Rue Morgue'. Comparison of the essay with the two stories that had been published in France, allowed the public to recognise both as plagiarism, as *L'Entr'acte* acknowledged on 20 October. This scandal contributed to the celebrity of Poe in France and the author himself soon came to learn of it.[21]

Whatever might have motivated Forgues's contradictory strategy of careless appropriation and critical celebration, his essay is of great interest. The author of the so-called *Tales of Ratiocination* is described as obsessed with the 'power of reasoning',[22] Dupin's exploits are compared to Zadig's power of divination[23] and Poe is related to a literary genealogy that is founded on mystery – 'Clothed with the fantastic livery of Hoffmann, or with the grave and masterful costume of Godwin, renewed by Washington Irving or by Dickens, it is always the same combination confronting Oedipus with the Sphynx.'[24] Forgues did not forget Charles Brockden Brown, describing him as being as talented as Poe in depicting 'those inner tortures, those obsessions of the soul, those illnesses of the spirit that offer such a wide field to observation'.[25]

However, Forgues's major criticism concerns Poe's decision to set the story in a city he did not know, for the French were surprised to discover that the topography of their capital had been oddly redesigned. Nor could the critic forgive Poe for a social blunder such as having a prefect of police seek the help of a private citizen (Dupin), and he accused the American author of naively applying the mores of his egalitarian country to France.[26] Yet Forgues acknowledged the value of this act of distancing with regard to the American public insofar as 'The marvellous, and even the extraordinary, need perspective.'[27] This perhaps explains why Forgues set his translation for the French public in the United States.

In order to neutralise the incongruities of the trilogy the translators of Poe in the 1840s used a series of techniques that are apparent in the above-mentioned 'Une lettre volée', where the French coordinates of Poe's story are systematically redefined. Not only is the detective renamed as Armand

Verdier (a name which echoes that of Vidocq),[28] but the action is ante-dated to the 1780s to recreate an *Ancien Régime* ambience. This appears more in accordance with the story of a theft from the queen, although in the new text the august personage prudently becomes a princess. Was the original version of the story too risky in terms of censorship?

The detective's lodgings are also moved to Rue Saint-Honoré, in con-cordance with the plan de Paris, and it is not the prefect who visits Verdier, but a more modest 'secretary of the chief inspector of the police', who is moreover a relative of his. In Poe's text, we know only the initial of Minister D—, but in the 'Duke of G...'[29] we no longer recognise a malig-nant double of Dupin. Even the place the hero mentions as the site of his previous encounter with the minister – Vienna – is revised as Dresden, although the function of these minor changes is less easy to explain.

A clearer strategy informs other aspects of the translation. Most of Poe's ponderous digressions concerning Dupin's method – often based on a comparison with games or optics – disappear; but while Dupin's inquiry originally rests on a pecuniary motive, in the translation the money he earns goes to a needy widow.[30] Instead of the pantheon of authors that Poe invoked to magnify Dupin's talent for detection – including La Rochefoucauld and the imaginary La Bougive – readers are offered a more familiar literary reference: 'There was something in him [Verdier] of Beaumarchais: he loved intrigue in itself and because it allowed him to exercise his imagination and his spirit.'[31]

These changes reduced the cultural scope of the text, normalising its more eccentric and speculative aspects and bringing it into conformity with the common denominator of popular literature. In addition to the most sophisticated passages, the translator also modified those scenes that lacked verisimilitude, such as Dupin's visit to the minister, when behind a protective pair of green glasses the detective's eyes are free to roam around the room, searching it for the letter. In the French version, which is more aware of social differences, Verdier is provided with a rea-son for breaching the minister's privacy. Perhaps in order to make this scene more credible, the translator split it into two parts, having the let-ter retrieved by a policeman instead of Dupin. Last but not least, the story does not end with a quotation from Crébillon's *Atrée*, linking it to the classical tradition of revenge, but with a moralising paragraph.[32]

Poe's reception in France and Great Britain in turn influenced his for-tune in America. At the end of 1846 Poe asked a journalist to publish an article to enhance his popularity and the strategy is apparent right from the title, 'An Author in Europe and America' (9 January 1847). Here the attitude of the American public is contrasted with that of the Europeans, notably of the French, due to the wealth of translations and essays that had recently appeared across the ocean. Poe is presented as a writer who is 'quite unique and apart from the rest of the literary race',[33] following in the footsteps of an article dated October 1845 (likewise influenced, if not actually written, by Poe) where the author is described as an inveterate experimenter, who is able to escape from the clutches of tradition and is for that reason appreciated by English critics.[34]

Meanwhile, in France the cultural assimilation of Poe was reaching its climax. 'L'Assassinat de la Rue Morgue', translated by Isabelle Meunier, appeared on 31 January 1847 in *La Démocratie pacifique*, and the anonymous 'La Lettre soustraite' was serialised on 20–22 May in *Le Mémorial Bordelais*, though no early translations of 'The Mystery of Marie Rogêt' have been detected.[35] Baudelaire's first canonical translations – 'Facultés divinatoires d'Auguste Dupin I. Double assassinat dans la Rue Morgue' and 'Facultés divinatoires d'Auguste Dupin II. La lettre volée' – were published in *Le Pays* between February and March 1855, while 'Le Mystère de Marie Roget', which had less appeal to the market, appeared only in the 1865 edition of the *Histoires grotesques et sérieuses*.[36]

Baudelaire's translations were themselves cannibalised and in August 1864 he complained: 'What is this *Double assassinat dans la Rue Morgue* that appeared two or three months ago in the *Petit Journal*, without naming the translator, signed by *Edgar Poe* and under the column "*Chronique judiciaire*"?'[37] As this further example of unlawful appropriation shows, Poe was linked by some to the ambivalent field of faction, where *chronique* and *littérature judiciaire* mingled, but we should not forget that 'The Mystery of Marie Rogêt' was actually based on a real case. Baudelaire, however, was more interested in asserting the universal status of Poe as a romantic genius, without associating him to a specific genre, as is shown by the essays he wrote on the American author. Baudelaire's role in the French and European reception of Poe was immense and his mediation contributed to the vogue Poe enjoyed in Great Britain at the end of the century, when the aesthetic movement regarded both writers as illustrious antecedents.

Meanwhile, on the English shore of the Channel, Poe's 'The Purloined Letter' had been recast by Collins as a story that was first included in the 1854 Christmas number of *Household Words* and then republished as 'The Lawyer's Story of a Stolen Letter' in *After Dark* (1856). Interestingly, at the end of the text the narrator aggressively claims that what he has related is fact, not fiction: 'Observe the expression, will you? I said it was a Statement before I began; and I say it's a Statement now I've done. I defy you to prove it's a Story!'[38] One might be tempted to believe that here Collins (more or less unconsciously) was exorcising the ghost of plagiarism that haunted his tale of detection, but biters are often bit and the American magazine *Harper's* pirated this story, presenting it as the work of the better known Charles Dickens.

The strange case of Wilkie Collins and M. Forgues

British writers often turned to France in their search for new plots. Although Edward Bulwer-Lytton based his *Lucretia; or, the Children of the Night* (1846) on the life of the British serial killer Thomas Griffiths Wainewright, he refashioned him as a villain of French origin – Gabriel Honoré Varney. The ghost of the French Revolution hovers over this Newgate novel, whose prologue is set in Paris during the Reign of Terror. To prepare readers for the excesses of Varney, Bulwer depicted an episode from his character's childhood. In this climactic scene the perfidious Dalibard is taking his son Gabriel to see a public execution. The wretched victim is an English dancer whose only fault was being the mistress of a French *proscrit*. When the child realises that the woman is his mother he starts to cry, but his father's hand grasps his arm and a voice hisses in his hear 'Learn how they perish who betray me!'[39]

The sensational turmoil of the French Revolution was subsequently chosen by Collins as the background of powerful short stories such as 'Nine o'clock!' (1852), 'Gabriel's Marriage' (1853) and 'Sister Rose', which appeared in *After Dark* in 1856. It was in the same year that, travelling in Paris with his friend Dickens, Collins bought a collection of criminal cases – Maurice Méjan's *Recueil des causes célèbres* (1808–14), one of which is the source of Collins's *The Woman in White* (1860). The story of the dastardly Sir Percival Glyde, who decides to lay his hands on the patrimony of his wife by having her confined to an asylum and pretending she is dead, replicates an eighteenth-century criminal case – 'l'Affaire de madame de Douhault', in which a rich widow was drugged and imprisoned in the Salpêtrière under the name of Blainville at the beginning of 1788, while another person was buried under her name, so that her relatives could inherit from her. With the help of a loyal friend Madame de Douhault gained her freedom in June 1789, but none of her relatives would recognise her. Her struggle to regain a position in society took place against the backdrop of the French Revolution.

Méjan's text did not simply provide Collins with the sensational story of a woman of rank who has lost her identity due to a criminal plot and strives to reclaim it, but it also anticipated many other aspects of *The Woman in White*. Méjan's emphasis on documents arguably was an inspiration to Collins's polyphonic narrative technique. Moreover, Madame de Douhault provided a model for the psychological profile of Lady Glyde, enabling Collins to create a new kind of 'damsel in distress' – a woman whose mental balance is endangered by means of chemistry and confinement. Collins stressed Lady Glyde's inability to remember what she had done after her arrival in London, that is, before she was drugged by Count Fosco: 'At this point in her sad story there was a total blank.'[40] Méjan's treatment of Madame de Douhault's abduction is correspondingly marked by an ellipsis. After inhaling a pinch of tobacco, the woman feels dizzy and soon falls asleep, but this is the last clear memory she has:

> Here the series of the notable facts which have been faithfully preserved in Madame de Douhault's memory ends. Her intellectual faculties, having been altered by a forced illness, do not enable her to shed any further light on the events that took place in Orléans.[41]

Méjan devoted several pages to Madame de Douhault's psychological state. Her amnesia is associated with a series of false beliefs, deriving from her plans and preoccupations: 'Her memory vainly represents to her a visit to her brother, a dinner with Mme de Polastron, and an arrest at Fontainebleau: these misty souvenirs are linked to the intentions she actually had before her illness, *to see her brother, to visit Mad. de Polastron, etc.*'[42] Following in Méjan's footsteps, Collins also had his protagonist assert that after arriving in London she had spent the night under Mrs Vesey's roof and that Mrs Rubelle had helped her to undress, while these 'memories' are only the fruit of her intentions and worries.[43] Many other parallels could be drawn between the two texts. Suffice it to say that when she is imprisoned Madame de Douhault is dressed all in white, and that Méjan took great pains to show how the time that she spent in the asylum compromised her mental balance and her subsequent ability to prove her case.

Collins's novel was translated into French in 1861, but the author had long been known in France thanks to Émile Forgues, who published a long essay on him in the *Revue des deux mondes* in November 1855, and who had also translated *The Dead Secret* (1857) as *Le Secret* (1858), under the usual pseudonym of Old Nick. Collins was so enthusiastic about the translation that he dedicated *The Queen of Hearts* (1859) to Forgues with these words: 'I was by no means surprised to find my fortunate work of fiction [*The Dead Secret*] – not translated, in the mechanical sense of the word – but transformed from a novel that I had written in my language,

to a novel that you might have written in yours.'[44] The close relationship between Collins and his French public is demonstrated by the preface
the author wrote for the 1861 edition of *La Femme en blanc*, which had also
been translated by Forgues. Collins flatteringly addressed the compatri-
ots of Balzac, Hugo, Sand, Soulié, Sue and Dumas, hoping that the translation of his novel might partly repay the debt he had incurred 'both as a
reader and as a writer, towards French novelists'.[45]

In his 1855 essay Forgues was writing about a thirty-one-year-old author
of solid novels such as *Basil* (1852) and *Hide and Seek* (1854). Forgues's
admiration of Collins rested on his disregard of moral conformity rather
than on his ability as a plot-maker, and while discussing the last pages of
Basil the critic claimed: 'Unfortunately, they remind us of a number of
second-class works and of techniques which the feuilleton-novel has too
frequently abused, so that a real writer can only lose by using them.'[46]
Forgues disliked the melodramatic element in Collins's work, while he
relished his descriptive, almost pictorial, talent – a quality he related to
the author's background as the son of the painter William Collins.

A few years later Forgues returned to sensation fiction – first in
'Littérature anglaise. Dégénérescence du roman' ('English literature:
decay of the novel', 1862), an article in which he briefly discussed Ellen
Wood's *East Lynne* (1861);[47] then more extensively in 'Le roman anglais
contemporain. Miss M.E. Braddon et le roman à sensation' ('The English
Contemporary Novel: Miss M.E. Braddon and the sensation novel',
1863). The latter essay focuses on twenty-six-year-old Elizabeth Braddon,
whose *Lady Audley's Secret* (1862) and *Aurora Floyd* (1863) pivot on the
theme of bigamy, as does Charlotte Brontë's *Jane Eyre* (1847), although
Braddon – to make this theme even more sensational – had the fault lie
with the heroine. Forgues was fiercely critical of Braddon's plots, which
he regarded as teeming with incongruities and vulgar coincidences,
briefly with 'all the elements of the drama they manufacture for the
masses'. The contrast between these shortcomings and Braddon's talent
at characterisation produced in her books the effect of 'a bad play interpreted by intelligent actors'.[48]

Setting Braddon against the backdrop of the sensation vogue, Forgues
claimed that her success was 'of the same order of that of *Woman in
White* and *No Name*',[49] although he regarded Collins as a superior author
and did not include him in this disparaging verdict:

> With the compatriots of Ann Radcliffe, a returning vogue has made
> the fortune of the *sensation novel*, as they say – the novel with a secret,
> the riddle novel, whose main element of interest, whose invariable

means of seduction is an *imbroglio* that is already obscure in itself and that is made even darker, so complex that readers are kept in suspense till the very end, for the ending is unpredictable. Miserable in every other respect, these narratives should be approached from the end, since by reading the last page you would be luckily dispensed from going through the previous ones.[50]

Forgues regarded sensation fiction as a byproduct of a democratic society that addressed the lowest stratum of the reading public – 'simple-minded readers, easy to please, whose credulity is boundless, whose leniency admits no exceptions'.[51]

M. Gaboriau and the 'unknown public'

In 1858 Collins had devoted an essay to what he had defined as 'The Unknown Public', the numerous readers of 'penny-novel-journals',[52] cheap illustrated periodicals in small print, featuring a miscellany of serialised novels, short stories, curiosities and poetry. Collins remarked that a valuable work would never be accepted in these magazines, whose standard – in obedience to the principles of mass production – was homogenised to the extent of offering 'A combination of fierce melo-drama and meek domestic sentiment.'[53] With a streak of didacticism, Collins wondered whether it would not be possible to educate this 'monster audience'[54] – which he estimated including three million read-ers. The attempts to publish Dumas's and Sue's *feuilletons* in these infer-ior British magazines had been unsuccessful precisely because of the inability of readers to locate these works in their cultural context:

The mere references in 'Monte Christo,' 'The Mysteries of Paris,' and 'White Lies' (the scene of this last English fiction having been laid on French ground), to foreign names, titles, manners, and customs, puz-zled the Unknown Public on the threshold. Look back at the answers to correspondents, and they say, out of fifty subscribers to a penny journal, how many are likely to know, for example, that mademois-elle means miss?[55]

Collins's remarks shed an interesting light on the difficulty of translating popular culture in the nineteenth century, that of the problems its read-ership had in grasping the cultural references implicit in foreign texts. This helps us understand the unashamed creative freedom – bordering on betrayal and appropriation – of many nineteenth-century translations.

The *romans judiciaires* of the French writer Émile Gaboriau are a case in point, for shortly after publication they appeared in the Sunday supplements of American newspapers with captivating, often alliterative, titles such as *Crimson Crime* (*L'Affaire Lerouge*, 1866) and *Dark Deeds* (*Le crime d'Orcival*, 1867). However, we should regard these texts as acts of plagiarism rather than translations, since the originals were shortened, the action was set in the United States and the names of author and detective were changed. Thus *Les Esclaves de Paris* (1868) became *Manhattan Unmasked* and *Le dossier No. 113* (1867) was restyled as *The Steel Safe; or the stains and splendours of New York Life* (1868). The author of this rewriting was indicated as Henry L. Williams, while Lecoq was renamed Clayton Newlife and the book was refashioned right from the beginning:

> Whoever read the New York evening papers on the 28th of February, 186–, would have found the following item under big-type heading that any night-editor would have envied:

> IMMENSE ROBBERY
> Upward of $100,000 Stolen.
> Arrest of a clerk.

> 'There was great excitement in Wall Street, and everywhere in the shadow of Trinity to-day, in consequence of a most gigantic burglary having been committed in the banking establishment of Mr. Andrew Van Kieft, lately located in the splendid new "Prince Albert stone" building on Broadway near Liberty street.'[56]

The first official American translation of Gaboriau appeared in Boston in 1870, while in Great Britain in 1881 the publisher Henry Vizetelly launched a series of translations entitled *Gaboriau's Sensational Novels*, a definition which was regarded as the closest equivalent of the French *roman judiciaire*. It was probably the Vizetelly edition of Gaboriau that inspired the Melbourne writer Fergus Hume to write his best-selling *The Mystery of a Hansom Cab. A Sensational Novel* (1886), which in turn contributed to inducing Doyle to invest his time in Sherlock Holmes.[57]

A metropolitan genesis

In conclusion, my contention is that translation and other transnational forms of intertextuality played a major role in the nineteenth-century development of crime fiction, although they often amounted to acts of appropriation. To understand this phenomenon, we should regard popular literature not as a uniform territory, but as including a wide range of social and cultural layers, where trite commercial formulas coexisted with works that were far from devoid of value. The translations that appeared in popular magazines often applied all too literally the principle Poe himself advocated – with a very different intent – while discussing C.H. Town's inferior translation of *Les Mystères de Paris*, 'We should so render the original that *The version should impress the people for whom it was intended, just as the original impresses the people for whom it (the original) is intended.*'[58] While in the best translation this implied (and still implies) extreme accuracy in choice of words as well as a deep knowledge of the cultural background of the source text, it allows for flexibility in popular translations which sometimes simply obliterated most or all references to foreign settings and cultures, catering to the needs of an audience that apparently proved incapable of projecting itself imaginatively into different places and ways of life. Of course, this technique also made it easier for magazines to eschew the problem of copyright.

Leaving aside the most unscrupulous acts of plagiarism, foreign literatures were perceived by mid-century crime writers as a reservoir of stories and settings that could foster inspiration. These fertile acts of hybridisation not only enabled various literary traditions to interact, but also laid the ground for the literary representation of the new – and mainly urban – experience of cosmopolitanism. With few exceptions – the most notable are Melbourne (where *The Mystery of a Hansom Cab* is set and was first published),[59] Philadelphia, Dublin and Edinburgh – it was mainly Paris, London and New York that participated in the formation of the new genre, both as literary backdrops and as centres of production/diffusion. While Great Britain, the United States and France were involved in this process of cross-fertilisation, other countries were simply receptive, without actively contributing to the evolution of these new forms.

In Italy, for instance, detective and sensation novels, as well as the French *romans judiciaires*, were widely published in translation at the end of the nineteenth century, but a true body of local crime writing developed only at a later stage and did not achieve any immediate popularity abroad. Domenico Giuriati's *Memorie di un vecchio avvocato* (*Memories of an Old Lawyer*, 1888) can be regarded as one of the earliest Italian examples of what Heather Worthington terms 'professional anecdote' – a kind of fiction that had already achieved popularity in Great Britain thanks to works like 'The Experiences of a Barrister' (1849–50) and 'The Confessions of an Attorney' (1850–52). Interestingly, one of the cases that features in Giuriati's book is entitled 'Un pagamento a Londra' ('A Payment in London').[60] The story exploits both the attraction of the London metropolitan background, which had recently been explored by the Italian writer Edmondo De Amicis in his popular travelogue *Ricordi di Londra* (*Memories of London*, 1874), and the efficiency of the London police, which was regarded as a model in the newly created Kingdom of Italy.

As we can see, the nineteenth-century growth of crime fiction was closely associated with increasing urbanisation and the perceived need for social control, as well as the image of the city as an unending spectacle. After all, this was the century of the *flâneur*, half artist and half surveillant, a by-product of the metropolis, as Pierre Larousse acknowledged in his *Grand Dictionnaire universel du XIXe siècle* (1866–76), where he classified this human type, claiming that 'It is only in Paris that we find flâneurs.'[61]

Crime fiction capitalised on hidden threats, the colourful ambience and the wealth of clues the urban space provided. As G.K. Chesterton famously wrote in 1902, the detective story was the only form of popular literature which expressed 'the poetry of modern life'. By combining the main elements of *romance* – the hero and adventure – with an urban setting, the detective story turned this background into a huge hieroglyph: 'there is no stone in the street and no brick in the wall that is not actually a deliberate symbol – a message from some man, as much as if it were a telegram or a post-card'.[62]

Although we can claim that the urban environment – where social anomie coexisted with the omnipresence of human artefacts and traces – strongly contributed to the development of crime fiction, it was thanks to its ability to adapt, like a literary virus, to different climates and cultures that this genre subsequently acquired such an aggressive vitality, disseminating all over the world.

7
On the Sensational in Literature

One can hardly study the development of nineteenth-century crime fiction without giving sensation fiction its due. After reaching its climax in the 1860s and 1870s, the sensation vogue lost momentum at the end of the century, precisely when detective fiction was asserting itself as a literary phenomenon. At its peak, however, sensationalism not only enjoyed a vast success in terms of sales, enthralling the reading public, but was also at the heart of a heated critical debate, which included several long essays in literary magazines such as *Blackwood's*, *The Argosy* and *Belgravia* where the aesthetic and ethical import of the movement as a whole was placed under discussion. As Lyn Pykett claims, 'the sensation genre was a journalistic construct, a label attached by reviewers to novels whose plots centred on criminal deeds, or social transgressions and illicit passions'.[1] What makes the case of sensation fiction so interesting is precisely the close interaction between literary and critical works, that is to say the battle engaged in by opposite factions either in favour of or against a literary movement that thrived on scandal.

Between romance and journalism

As early as 1800 William Wordsworth complained that a 'multitude of causes unknown to former times' were contributing 'to blunt the discriminating powers of the mind'. As an example of this cultural regression, Wordsworth mentioned his contemporaries' appetite for lurid news and stories, describing it as a side-effect of both historical factors (the aftermath of the French Revolution) and social factors, such as 'the encreasing accumulation of men in cities, where the uniformity of their occupation produces a craving for extraordinary incident which the rapid communication of intelligence hourly gratifies'. As a result of these changes, the

British poetical tradition was endangered by the growth of a new gothic sub-culture: 'The invaluable works of our eldest writers, I had almost said the works of Shakespear and Milton, are driven into neglect by frantic novels, sickly and stupid German Tragedies, and deluges of idle and extravagant stories in verse.'[2] This controversial cultural transition can be regarded as the prelude to the growth of sensationalism, a phenomenon that was related – as Wordsworth insightfully acknowledged, despite his misgivings – to modernity, journalism and the urban environment.

Sensation fiction inherited from the gothic the theme of the double (twins and impersonators abound in these novels), the ambiguous presence of supernatural elements (which either were ultimately rationalised or coexisted with a rational approach) and paradigmatic figures such as the persecuted heroine and the villain, while the sly and redoubtable villainess is a typical product of the age of sensation, with its new emphasis on women as the agents of crime. Yet to understand the origins of this literary phenomenon one cannot simply revert to the uncanny mysteries of Udolpho, where Ann Radcliffe's Emily is immured by the devilish Montoni. In reality sensationalism was rooted in a wide range of discourses, both literary and non-literary, including the gothic, melodrama, the Newgate novels, the street literature of broadsides and the nascent mass medium of journalism.

In the first half of the century, newspapers paid close attention to the supposed increase in crime and the development of police methods; rationally enough in view of the many changes that accompanied the creation of the Metropolitan Police in 1829 and of the Detective Police in 1842. Such reports had a seminal role in the evolutionary process of crime fiction around the middle of the century. According to G.K. Craik, writing in 1843 'A police reporter, indeed (or penny-a-liner, as he is sometimes, with too much levity, styled), is the truest historian of his age', and his province is 'the most important as well as attractive department of modern literature'.[3]

The development of journalism fostered a first wave of sensationalism, which was indebted to criminal reports and marked by a morbid interest in catastrophe as well as the nightmarish aspects of modern urban life:

> My greatest pleasure, through life, has been the perusal of any extraordinary narrative of fact. An account of a shipwreck in which hundreds have perished; of a plague which has depopulated towns or cities; anecdotes and inquiries connected with the regulation of prisons, hospitals, or lunatic receptacles; nay, the very police reports of a common newspaper – as relative to matters of reality; have always excited a

degree of interest in my mind which cannot be produced by the best invented tale of fiction.[4]

This passage from Henry Thomson's 'Le Revenant' (*Blackwood's*, 1827) could be chosen as a manifesto for the late gothic tales that were published in the Edinburgh review between 1817 and 1832. Its narrative formula was imported to the United States by Poe, a master of extreme sensations, a conjuror of morbid and hallucinatory states where madness and degeneration combine to evoke sinister patterns of heredity. The stories in which Poe explored the theme of premature burial are a case in point, for they were inspired by John Galt's 'The Buried Alive' (*Blackwood's*, 1821). The American author openly acknowledged his debt to the review in a parody he entitled 'How to Write a Blackwood Article' (1838), where an aspiring female novelist is offered this precious advice: 'Sensations are the great things after all. Should you ever be drowned or hung, be sure and make a note of your sensations – they will be worth to you ten guineas a sheet.'[5] In the 1830s, sensations – be they claustrophobic or dynamic – had already gained value in the publishing market as capable of inducing accelerated heartbeats and women novelists had become particularly associated with this mode of writing. This was the beginning of a phenomenon that attained its full scope in the 1860s and 1870s – the sensational decades *par excellence*.

A fundamental ingredient in the recipe for sensation is the ambiguity of stories that are presented as real, but stretch the boundaries of what we might call reality to the utmost, so as to make room for the deepest terrors of the public. *Blackwood's* tales achieved their sensational effect through their confessional form, which triggered the reader's emotional identification with the first-person narrator, justifying the melodramatic quality of his/her memoirs. Poe, on the other hand, chose to present notorious hoaxes under the guise of scientific reports, introducing an observer and stressing reliability through detachment. 'The Facts in the Case of M. Valdemar' (1845) – the story of a man who is mesmerised on the verge of death and is suspended in that condition for six months, until he decomposes in a few instants – provoked an international controversy since, due to the pseudo-scientific halo of mesmerism, the text was read in Great Britain as a serious report.

Newgate novelists likewise took advantage of the appeal of faction – a blend of fact and fiction that enabled them to capitalise on widespread fears and curiosity, uncannily combining gruesome details from the chronicles of crime and melodrama. When in 1846 Edward Bulwer-Lytton published his *Lucretia; or, the Children of the Night* the author underlined the documentary 'truth' of the novel, 'Incredible as it may seem, the crimes herein related took place within the last seventeen years. There has been no exaggeration as to their extent, no great departure from their details.'[6] Bulwer-Lytton was the first in a long series of writers who helped turn the 'exemplary life' of the serial killer Thomas Griffiths Wainewright into an icon of evil – a process of criminal 'canonisation' that culminated in Oscar Wilde's famous essay 'Pen, Pencil and Poison' (1889).

A renowned artist and dandy, Wainewright, who turned out to be a forger as well as a poisoner, was arrested in 1837 and transported to Van Diemen's Land, where he died in 1847.[7] As proof of the lasting impact of Wainewright on the imaginary of crime novelists, he can be regarded as the source of several of Dickens's poisoners, from Jonas Chuzzlewit in *Martin Chuzzlewit* (1843–44) to Rigaud in *Little Dorrit* (1855–57)[8] and Julius Slinkton in 'Hunted Down' (1859). This short story, which was commissioned by the American periodical *New York Ledger* for the enormous sum of £1000, also owes part of its sinister charm to the sensational case of William Palmer, the so-called 'prince of poisoners', a doctor who used his medical knowledge to murder his wife and children, among others, and was executed in 1856. Both murderers were motivated by money and hoped to gain from insurance policies taken out on the lives of family members and/or friends.

In his proto-sensational *Lucretia*, Bulwer-Lytton relied on the sensational resonance of a real criminal case, magnifying it so as to exploit all its melodramatic potential. The poisoner whose deeds are the subject of this epic of crime is called Gabriel Honoré Varney and recalls a preternaturally evil literary figure, the eponymous hero of *Varney the Vampyre; or, the Feast of Blood*, which was published in penny instalments between 1845 and 1847. Following a literary recipe that was unashamedly based on excess, Bulwer-Lytton chose to create a female counterpart of Varney – Lucretia Clavering, a villainess whose main instrument of death is also poison and who is aptly named after the she-devil of the Italian Renaissance, Lucrezia Borgia. To increase the horror of readers even further, Bulwer-Lytton's two young villains are at one and the same time the adepts, the victims and the murderers of the arch-villain Dalibard, a man of French origin, 'with some Italian blood in his veins',[9] who is the father of Varney and the tutor of Lucretia. Dalibard – who at the time of the French Revolution sympathised with Jacobins but who is ready to betray any cause for power and money – acts as a foil to his two pupils, showing their evil bent as a consequence of his nefarious influence on their early life.

Although *Lucretia* embodied many aspects which were to become seen as typical of sensation, another novel from the 1840s was more usually regarded by sensation novelists and critics as the main antecedent of the movement – Charlotte Brontë's *Jane Eyre* (1847). The dark mysteries of

Thornfield, the country house where Jane Eyre works as a governess, provided a perfect transition from the world of the gothic to that of sensation, inaugurating a tradition that H.L. Mansel described as 'Bigamy Novels'.[10] Several critics have pointed out the seminal role that *Jane Eyre* played in the development of the sensation vogue, but G.A. Sala interestingly contrasted it with both the early nineteenth-century sentimental tradition and the romantic character of most Newgate novels:

> Do I intend to maintain that the modern, the contemporary novel of life and character and adventure – the outspoken, realistic, moving, breathing fiction, which mirrors the passions of the age for which it is written, is preferable to the silly sentimentalities of Lady Blessington and Mrs. Gore, to the aristocratic highwaymen and intellectual assassins of *Paul Clifford* and *Eugene Aram*, – or to the dead thieves, bullies, doxies, and turnkeys who were galvanised by Mr. Harrison Ainsworth? Unhesitatingly I say that I do. *Jane Eyre* was to all intents and purposes a 'sensational' novel, and some fastidious parents might forbid their daughters to read a book in which there is a deliberate attempt at bigamy; in which there is a mad wife who tries to burn her husband's house; in which the flogging of a girl at school is minutely described; and in which an impulsive little governess sits on a blind gentleman's knee, and pulls his beautiful dark hair about – likening it to the hair of Samson.[11]

Sala dismissed the Newgate novel as an antecedent of sensation fiction because of Bulwer-Lytton's and Ainsworth's romanticised vision of the villain and their historical interest in eighteenth-century crime, while perceiving that it was in the female tradition of the Brontës – bringing mystery, crime and madness into the contemporary age, and incorporating the right blend of realism and romanticism – that sensation writers mirrored themselves.

The sensation recipe

The innovative character of sensation fiction – resulting from the juxtaposition of everyday reality and the horrors that gothic fiction used to set against the exotic backgrounds of faraway countries and times – was perceived in 1865 by Henry James, who credited Collins with 'having introduced into fiction those most mysterious of mysteries, the mysteries which are at our own doors'.[12] Sinister and impregnable castles in the Apennines as well as ruined abbeys surrounded by labyrinthine forests – those improbable icons of fear – were superseded as scenes of crime by the orderly Victorian country house and the modern London lodgings. Topicality is a fundamental attribute of sensation fiction, as Mansel had noted in 1863:

> Proximity is, indeed, one great element of sensation. It is necessary to be near a mine to be blown up by its explosion; and a tale which aims at electrifying the nerves of the reader is never thoroughly effective unless the scene be laid in our own days and among the people we are in the habit of meeting.[13]

Mansel also regarded personality as a sensational correlative of proximity, claiming that 'If a scandal of more than usual piquancy occurs in high life, or a crime of extraordinary horror figures among our *causes célèbres*, the sensationalist is immediately at hand to weave the incident into a thrilling tale.'[14] The Glasgow Poisoning (the story of Madeleine Smith, who was accused to murdering her lover, Emile L'Angelier, in 1857) and the Road Murder (the story of Constance Kent, who killed her four-year-old half-brother in 1860) attracted the attention of journalists and novelists alike. Both cases were fictionalised in *Such Things Are* (1862) – a novel Mansel analysed in his article, while Collins's use of the Road Murder in *The Moonstone* is further proof of the sensationalists' readiness to translate real crime into fiction in their relentless hunt for a good plot.

Although Mansel – who was a clergyman and taught moral philosophy at Oxford – openly condemned the writers who gathered 'fresh stimulants from the last assizes', he defended those who recognised the 'romantic interest' of a 'memorable crime of bygone days'. The critic regarded the relation between 'the criminal variety of the Newspaper Novel' and 'the genuine historical novel'[15] as no closer than that which opposes the police reports of *The Times* to the pages of Thucydides, but his criticism was not focused exclusively on the link between sensation novels and the vilest aspects of reality (a reproach that was commonly directed at naturalist writers). On the one hand, Mansel stigmatised the commercial motives of sensation writers, who were spurred by 'the market-law of demand and supply'.[16] On the other he observed that this fiction engendered a pernicious variety of reading, which was aimed at arousing 'Excitement, and excitement alone'.[17]

This accusation is far from groundless, for sensationalists usually wrote with serialisation in mind, employing a technique which is similar to the devices which soap opera screenwriters utilise today. To engender addiction in their readers, to induce them to subscribe to a review or to buy the monthly instalments of a book, authors elaborated narrative strategies that pivoted on suspense, creating cliff-hangers at the end of each episode – final moments of unexplained mystery or imminent danger. The titillation of curiosity, the postponement and the pleasure of revelation are the three stages in the reading of a serial. Interweaving 'circuits of knowledge' are opened and closed one after the other with a chain-like effect in order to set the story to the right rhythm, to create a powerful machine for producing intense and ephemeral thrills, to engulf readers in the twists of the plot.

In his study of 'popular reading', Clive Bloom remarks that 'Novelty dominated Victorian literature; the literary arts were firmly rooted in, indeed one *condition of*, the Victorian entrepreneurial business spirit.'[18] Used as we nowadays are to taking the economic and social role of commercial literature for granted, we find it difficult to understand the scope of the battle Mansel and other critics fought against sensation fiction. We should keep in mind that the success of this popular genre was due to an efficient network of distribution, involving serialisation in magazines, publication in multi-volume book form to serve the needs of the circulating libraries and production of cheap editions to be sold in the kiosks of railway stations, since 'passengers could now read in a train compartment whereas before the coach was simply too shaky'.[19] Nor should we forget the entrepreneurial genius of women writers such as Elizabeth Braddon and Ellen Wood, who respectively edited the sensational magazines *Belgravia* and *Argosy*.

Writing in 1865, William Fraser Rae complained that Braddon 'had temporarily succeeded in making the literature of the Kitchen the favourite reading of the Drawing room'. While in the past 'stories of blood and lust, of atrocious crimes and hardened criminals' excited the interest of readers of low social status and education, thanks to the literary efforts of writers like Braddon these stories were now 'published in three volumes in place of issuing them in penny numbers'.[20] Sensationalists had subverted the rules of the literary market, breaking the boundaries between low and high literature and creating a new public for crime literature, which now spoke a respectable English and enjoyed the privilege of hard bindings.

Women as sensation writers and readers

Readers of the August 1863 issue of *Blackwood's* were treated to the following comment: 'Out of the mild female undergrowth, variety demands the frequent production of a sensational monster to stimulate the languid life.'[21] This decade indeed saw an unprecedented output of sensation novels by women – Wood's *East Lynne* was published in 1861, while in 1862 Braddon explored the scandal of bigamy in *Lady Audley's Secret*, which was followed one year later by *Aurora Floyd*, yet another variation on the theme of the double menage. It is, therefore, no surprise that in the 1860s this genre was identified as feminine, often in a condescending tone.

Sensation novels did not abide by the tacit agreement whereby British authors abstained from dealing with subjects regarded as unsuitable for the young. This voluntary form of preventive censorship – a pact James was to describe as 'the convention'[22] – had allowed novels to circulate freely in every respectable household, but sensation fiction put the Victorians in mind of licentious French novels. Public opinion was particularly disturbed by the role of young women within this literary circuit of production and consumption, given the important function that novels had traditionally had in their education:

> To a French girl fresh from her convent the novels of her own language are rigorously tabooed; whereas we are all aware that they are the favourite reading of her contemporary in this country, and are not unfrequently even the production, with all their unseemly references and exhibitions of forbidden knowledge, of young women ...[23]

Sensation fiction was deemed capable of having nefarious effects both on the nerves – due to the physical condition of quivering tension it induced – and on the character. These alluring novels were seen as repositories of corruption, confronting female readers with villains and villainesses who were capable of any mischief – from bigamy to blackmail and murder – and yet who presented an appearance of beauty, dignity and goodness. In spite of their inevitable punishment, the consummate duplicity of these characters, their ability to penetrate every layer of society and to gain the confidence of honest unsuspecting people, offered insidious role models and ventured into areas of knowledge that were precluded to young women, whose 'innocence' was a fundamental pre-marital requisite. The world of crime, madness and passion entered Victorian houses unhindered and threatened to pervert the young, causing them to stray from the righteous path.

Sensationalism, degeneration and modernity

The climate of suspicion surrounding sensationalist writing fostered repeated attacks against it and also evoked the spectre of degeneration. In his famous 'Fiction, Fair and Foul' (1880), John Ruskin examined works such as Dickens's *Bleak House* (1852–53), Collins's *Poor Miss Finch* (1871–72), Sue's *Les Mystères de Paris* and Gaboriau's *Le Crime d'Orcival* (1866–67), including them under the heading of 'literature of the

Prison-house'. By this term Ruskin meant 'not only the cell of Newgate, but also and even more definitely the cell of the Hôtel-Dieu, the Hôpital des Fous, and the great corridor with the dripping slabs of the Morgue'.[24] Half a century earlier, Thomson had regarded the prison, the hospital, the asylum and the mortuary as capable of producing a degree of interest exceeding that of fiction. A century later, the same institutions were to attract the attention of the French philosopher Michel Foucault (*Folie et déraison* [*Madness and Civilisation*], 1961; *Naissance de la clinique* [*The Birth of the Clinic*], 1963; *Surveiller et punir* [*Discipline and Punish*], 1975) as the tools of disciplinary power. For Ruskin they were the settings of literary works that revealed a morbid fascination with death, as is shown by his analysis of *Bleak House*, highlighting the violent deaths of the majority of the characters.

To Ruskin, such literature was the expression of a debased urban environment, where the individual, deprived of a beneficent contact with nature and art, turned to sensationalism to revive his/her emotional life:

> The monotony of life in the central streets of any great modern city, but especially in those of London, where every emotion intended to be derived by men from the sight of nature, or the sense of art, is forbidden forever, leaves the craving of the heart for a sincere, yet changeful, interest, to be fed from one source only.[25]

As we know, at the turn of the century the concept of *degeneration* – the obverse of Darwin's evolutionism – exerted a strong fascination on thinkers, who regarded urbanisation not as a road to progress but as a regression, for which evidence could be adduced in the appalling conditions of life in London's East End.

Sensational canons

In order to counteract the repeated attempts to undermine the literary status of the genre, sensationalists wrote critical essays that reveal a high degree of self-awareness, reasserting their dignity by means of a genealogy of sensation that includes the greatest authors of the past. This strategy of appropriation and legitimisation is already apparent in 'A Word to the Public', an essay Bulwer-Lytton published in January 1847 to reassert the moral value of his much discussed *Lucretia* – a novel that can be regarded as proto-sensational due to its domestic criminal plot, its attraction towards the horrors of the French Revolution and the theme of female madness, which anticipates the destiny of Lady Audley.

Twenty years after De Quincey's seminal essay on the aesthetics of murder, 'A Word to the Public' offered a genealogy of crime literature that included Greek classics, French theatre and even Shakespeare, for crime was regarded by Bulwer-Lytton as 'the essential material of the Tragic Drama'.[26] Ready to claim for the novelist the rights of the playwright, the author asserted that 'What is free to the imagination, if put into five acts, does not become reprehensible, if employed in three volumes.' After offering Shakespeare as the ancestor of the genre, Bulwer-Lytton presented a list of works that conformed to the literary tradition of 'the tragic prose romance',[27] among them Fielding's *Jonathan Wild*, Richardson's *Clarissa Harlowe*, Mackenzie's *Julia de Roubigné* (involving murder by poison and a suicide), Moore's *Zeluco*, Godwin's *Caleb Williams* and Scott's *The Bride of Lammermoor*.

Reverting to the sources of inspiration of contemporary writers, Bulwer-Lytton also refuted the notion that modern crime did not lend itself to literary treatment:

> All crimes now, if detected, must obtain the notoriety of the Old Bailey, or reap their desert in Newgate; and to contend that Newgate and the Old Bailey unfit them for the uses of the writer of fiction, is virtually to deprive him of the use of all crimes punished by modern law and enacted in the modern day ... as if there were no terror in the condemned cell, no tragedy at the foot of the gallows![28]

Crime is part and parcel of life and authors are therefore entitled to represent it. Moreover this element is present in the imaginative works of every epoch and in order to 'exclude from the mind the dark certainties of guilt' you must 'silence the long succession of poets' from Shakespeare to the present.[29] Furthermore, unlike the graphic descriptions of crime and punishment offered by newspapers, fiction analyses the criminal's psychology, thus providing a deep moral lesson. Bulwer-Lytton even called upon Burke to testify in his favour, quoting various passages from his *Enquiry* to assert that 'the association of power with destruction is one of the most obvious sources of the sublime'.[30]

Bulwer-Lytton's defence of crime fiction anticipated many aspects of the critical debate that was to take place in the 1860s, as is apparent in the review James devoted in 1865 to Collins and Braddon, where the terms of the problem are ironically reversed:

> Crime, indeed, has always been a theme for dramatic poets; but with the old poets its dramatic interest lay in the fact that it compromised the criminal's moral repose. Whence else is the interest of *Orestes* and

Macbeth? With Mr. Collins and Miss Braddon (our modern Euripides and Shakespeare) the interest of crime is in the fact that it compromises the criminal's personal safety.[31]

With a benevolent smile, James drove home his poisoned arrows, hinting at the fact that the torment of guilt, rather than the fear of detection, had been at the heart of ancient tragedies (in 1866 Dostoevski's *Crime and Punishment* was to achieve a similar effect), but similar attacks did not prevent sensation writers from using genealogy as a means to legitimate their ultimately commercial motives, although even the official organs of the movement published ambiguous accounts of its origin.

A case in point is an unsigned review entitled 'Past "Sensationalists" ' that appeared in *The Argosy* in December 1867. Lamenting the fact that nobody had written a history of the English novel, in spite of its growing importance, the author defended the importance of the novelist, who 'has generally proved himself the social historian of his times'.[32] Starting from Fielding and Smollett, the essay touches upon gothic authors like Walpole, Beckford, Radcliffe, Godwin, Shelley, Lewis and Maturin. Introducing a distinction which is still regarded as primary, the critic underlined the difference between Lewis's novels – which are marked by 'supernatural, libidinous, and impious components' – and the rationalised gothic of Radcliffe, who attains her goal by means of 'certain apparent supernatural agencies, which she subsequently falsifies'.[33] While Maturin is regarded as the only disciple of Lewis's outdated school of romance, Radcliffe is defined as 'the first poetess of romantic fiction' and considered as a figure playing an important role within a nobler tradition of melodrama:

> The various elements that interpenetrate her conceptions, indeed, of which her conceptions are composed, render her, as they render Shakespeare, Scott, Lytton, Hugo, intensely melodramatic. A wide survey of life invariably entails the melodramatic spirit. Life itself is a melodrama. The common-place yields to the romantic, the romantic to the ridiculous, the ridiculous to the sublime.[34]

In the critic's eyes, eclecticism is the key to understanding this attitude to life. Godwin also deserves a place among the melodramatists and the critic perceptively highlighted the strange fate of *Caleb Williams*, which had been intended as a 'vehicle for the expression of particular opinions'[35] and survived because of its narrative merits, over and above the ideas it conveyed. The article ends with a discussion of the controversial role of melodrama in contemporary literature, contrasting its most 'vulgar, improbable, or foolish' dimension with its 'genuine spirit', and extending this criticism to sensationalists, who 'still copiously colour; still freely exaggerate; still travestie human nature'.[36]

A few months later – in the February 1868 issue of *Belgravia* – G.A. Sala published 'On the "Sensational" in Literature and Art', which adopted a different strategy and drew a parallel between the current debate on sensationalism and that on romanticism in early nineteenth-century France. Sala regarded Dickens as the greatest sensationalist of his time, but he located the origin of the movement right at the heart of the English canon:

> The late Mr. William Shakespeare was an arrant sensational writer. He wrote the play of 'Macbeth,' which is founded mainly on murder and witchcraft. He wrote 'Hamlet,' in which there are many murders, a suicide, a suspicion of madness, and a ghost.[37]

Sala's extended analysis of Shakespeare's plays is part of his aim to present sensationalism as a multifaceted cultural phenomenon that had illustrious precedents in every art and science, as well as in history. He includes in his genealogy painters like Millais and Holman Hunt, art critics like Ruskin, scientists like Darwin, patriots like Garibaldi and soldiers like General Grant. With a powerful rhetorical strategy, those who criticise sensationalism are ridiculed as blindly opposed to modernity:

> no more sensation novels, no more sensation leading-articles, no more sensation pictures ... Let the Bishop of London, in a wig like a bird's nest, preach a sermon in St. Paul's against photography and the Electric Telegraph. Don't let us move, don't let us travel, don't let us hear or see anything; but let us write sonnets to Chloe, and play madrigals on the spinet, and dance minuets, and pray to Heaven against Sensationalism, the Pope, the Devil, and the Pretender; and then let Dulness reign triumphant, and Universal Darkness cover all.[38]

Sala's vigorous defence of the sensational as the emblem of the nineteenth century, however, did not suffice to quench the debate and in the August 1874 issue of *The Argosy*, Braddon dealt again with the status of this genre in 'The Sensation Novel'. By describing the public's thirst for sensations as a healthy compensation for the ever increasing time Victorians devoted to intellectual exertion, she legitimated this source of entertainment, acknowledging its important social function:

> It cannot be denied, I think ... that the present is an age of sensation. It is at the same time an age of reading desks and writing desks: this

implies that it is also an age of thought ... Perhaps it may be the very thoughtfulness of the age which leads people to seek relaxation in what appears light and almost childish amusements.[39]

To dignify the sensational, Braddon underlined its genealogical link to romance, defining Walpole's *The Castle of Otranto* as 'the first sensation novel', studying the works of Radcliffe, highlighting the importance of *Jane Eyre* as a model for the latest generation of sensationalists and coming to the conclusion that 'What gives success to the novelist to-day is the same as brings audiences to the theatre – sensation.'[40]

In their attempts to ennoble the genre of which they regarded themselves as practitioners, sensationalists pursued a double strategy, claiming to be the descendants of a literary lineage they proudly described as rooted in Shakespeare and pronouncing the blatantly sensational character of the nineteenth century in all its artistic and social facets, tracing an equivalence between sensationalism and modernity. Critics thus provided historical and theoretical foundations for the poetics of sensation that Collins had already expounded in his pioneering 1852 'Dedication' to *Basil*, where he described the novel and the play as 'twin sisters in the Family of fiction', declaring that 'all the strong and deep emotions which the Playwriter is privileged to excite, the Novel-writer is privileged to excite also'. The charm of sensationalism resides precisely in its hybrid character, combining realism with melodrama, detection with the designs of providence, according to a pattern that ultimately locates conflict in the opposition between the absolute principles of good and evil. The fortune of sensation fiction, however, rested on a transitional cultural phase.

A prophecy

As we have seen, due to the indifference – if not hostility – of some sectors of public opinion, sensationalists developed a self-reflexive interest in their writing at a time when popular fiction was not regarded as worthy of much critical effort. They also tended to see sensationalism as the aesthetic paradigm of the nineteenth century. As early as 1863 an anonymous critic referred to crime and detection as ingredients that were fundamental not only to the sensational recipe, but to all the literature of the time:

We turn with a national instinct rather to the brutalities than to the subtleties of crime. Murder is our *cheval de bataille* ... Sometimes the entire story is conceived in the spirit of circumstantial evidence, and the detective officer, more or less skilfully disguised, is the hero of the piece; and in most cases the plot culminates in a trial where somebody is finally brought to justice, and some other innocent person vindicated. Murder, conspiracy, robbery, fraud, are the strong colours upon the national palette ... The charm of killing somebody, of bringing an innocent person under suspicion of the deed, and gradually, by elaborate processes of detectivism, hunting out the real criminal, seems to possess an attraction which scarcely any English novelist can resist.[41]

To justify the British attraction to crime, and to counter the inevitable accusation of bloodthirstiness, the critic observed that this curiosity sprang

from a lively appreciation of the advantages of a good police, mingled with certain conceptions of the picturesque, as exemplified in the conduct and position of a man who finds himself or his friend unjustly suspected, and who makes it the object of his life to bring the criminal to justice.[42]

Thanks to the freedom of the British press, which provided the forum for an outspoken debate on public institutions, police forces were regarded from the outset as two-sided – on the one hand a reliable tool of law and order, on the other a potential source of individual wrongs, because of the possibility that evidence could be manipulated so as to frame the innocent and save the criminal. The accusation in fiction that unjustly weighs on an innocent person, threatening to stain his/her reputation for ever, could not fail to involve readers in the main characters' plight. What is at stake in *The Moonstone* is Franklin Blake's reputation – and the outcome of his love for Rachel Verinder – rather than the diamond in itself. Similarly in *The Law and the Lady* (1875) the heroine undertakes her investigation to prove the innocence of her husband. Incidentally, 'the woman-saves-her-man formula'[43] – as Patricia Craig and Mary Cadogan label it – is the main reason for women becoming detectives in crime fiction at the turn of the century.

In this unsigned 1863 article, however, the fictional resources deployed by sensationalists to bring the real culprits to justice are condemned as immoral because they entail a biased view of the modern police system: 'Murder has become, with a quaint realisation of De Quincey's brilliant maunderings, a fine art; and the science of the detective – which is by no means founded on truth-telling – one of the most largely appreciated of modern sciences.'[44] Clues, not witnesses, are the main element in modern detection, as various nineteenth-century novelists well understood, and this element above all others would come to characterise detective fiction. Even when the plots of sensation novelists did not hinge on the sorrowful predicament of a fallen woman or on female madness, but rather on a genuinely criminal case, they often entertained an ambiguous relationship with the supernatural, as discussed in chapters 4 and 5. Let us remember the importance of premonitory dreams in *The Woman in White* and *Armadale*, or the non-scientific forms of enquiry that compete with 'detectivism' in *The Moonstone*, where the Brahmins repeatedly rely on clairvoyance to locate the diamond. These choices certainly did not represent modernity and in May 1862 Margaret Oliphant recognised that a great realism would reassert itself with the imminent confluence of sensation into detective fiction: 'We have already had specimens, as many as are desirable, of what the detective policeman can do for the enlivenment of literature: and it is into the hands of the literary Detective that this school of story-telling must inevitably fall at last.'[45]

From amateur to professional detective

This transition towards detective fiction resulted from the sensation novelists' attempts to adjust to the changing demands of the market, but the increasing importance that professional detectives and clues acquired in the world of sensation – to the detriment of amateur investigation and preternatural coincidences – was a far from linear process, as can be seen in the literary career of Mary Elizabeth Braddon, whose works have recently been reassessed thanks to a wealth of new editions and critical studies. Focusing on the relationship between the class element of Braddon's novels and her use of the detective, Jennifer Carnell claims that after relying on professional investigating agents in her early works, which were aimed at a lower-class audience, Braddon 'became reluctant to introduce policemen as central characters in middle-class fiction'.[46]

To understand Carnell's argument we should keep in mind that in Collins's foundational *The Woman in White* the mystery is solved through the acumen and efforts of the amateur detective Walter Hartright. Collins utilised this formula over and over again – sometimes with gender variations, as in *The Law and the Lady* – while his few professional detectives play subordinate roles. Thus in *The Moonstone* Superintendent Seegrave embodies the inefficient methods of the local police, while Sergeant Cuff – in spite of his superior intellect – is still unable to solve a mystery that rests on a psychological paradox, that is, a case of split personality.

Braddon's best-known novels – *Lady Audley's Secret* (1862) and *Aurora Floyd* (1863) – follow the same pattern. In the former the investigation is carried out by a young barrister – Robert Audley, who is part of the family – while in the latter Scotland Yard detective Joseph Grimstone is privately hired to investigate a case that involves, among other suspects, the mistress of the house. As in *The Moonstone* – where Sergeant Cuff is disempowered by his dependence on the authority of Lady Verinder, who has employed him to inquire into the loss of the diamond – Grimstone has no freedom to act. The social element plays a major role in both novels, where the position of police officers acting in a private capacity is ambiguous. A higher-class detective would be required to pry into the secrets of the rich and noble, while these police agents are perceived as intruders in the world of their betters.

As Carnell points out, however, Braddon's earlier *The Trail of the Serpent* (1861) – originally published in penny parts as *Three Times Dead* (1860) 'and aimed at a lower class audience'[47] – features an unusual detective in the person of Joe Peters, a working-class policeman who is also dumb. While Peters capitalises on his dumbness – people also think him deaf and therefore speak freely before him – his marginal corporeal status also reflects his marginality in the social order. The police suspect the wrong person of murder and it is thanks only to this atypical detective – who reminds us of Collins's physically handicapped characters, like the dumb heroine of *Hide and Seek* (1854) – that justice is done. The police likewise play a major role in Braddon's *The Black Band; or, The Mysteries of Midnight* (1861–62), which appeared anonymously in a lower-class magazine.

Professional detectives feature in many of Braddon's subsequent novels, although their degree of importance varies according to the social milieu of the story, but to understand the growing relevance of the professional investigating agent in Braddon's works, I will concentrate on her later creation, the detective John Faunce, who is at the heart of both *Rough Justice* (1898) and *His Darling Sin* (1899). To appreciate the nature of these texts, we should keep in mind two elements. First, that unlike Braddon's own early sensation novels each was published in a single volume. Instead of an imposing three-decker, readers were offered more compact stories. Second, that they were the fruit of Braddon's untiring versatility, although in her effort to keep up with changing literary vogues Braddon sometimes ran the risk of self-parody.

The stories which Braddon created in this late stage of her career still feature melodramatic elements such as murder, blackmail, revenge, doubles, aliases and a tendency to rely on coincidences, but they also point to detection as a new science and demonstrate the author's growing interest in the professional detective and his expertise. Yet, in her effort to be 'modern', Braddon relied more on the detective element of sensation fiction (as well as the *roman judiciaire*) than on Doyle's works, as is shown by the kind of books Faunce mentions as his favourite reading:

> It is only natural, perhaps, that a man of my calling should take a keener interest in stories of crime than in any other form of fiction; and I am not ashamed to confess a liking for those novels in which some mystery of guilt is woven and unravelled by the romancer. I have read, I believe, all the criminal stories of Gaboriau and Boisgobey. I have hung spell-bound over Bulwer's 'Lucretia,' over 'Armadale,' and 'The Woman in White,' over 'Martin Chuzzlewit,' 'Bleak House,' and the unsolved problem of 'Edwin Drood' ...[48]

The absence of *The Moonstone* from this list is probably due to the fact that Sergeant Cuff is the closest antecedent of Faunce, since both of them focus their suspicions on the wrong person and retire from the police in the course of the story. Braddon goes so far as to parody Cuff's passion for roses, for after his retirement Faunce is warmly invited by his wife to tend his garden; however, the still active detective does not intend to restrict his view of the world to the domestic precincts and the garden imagery recurs in the novel as a metaphor for boredom.

His Darling Sin testifies to the growing status of the policeman and also acknowledges Braddon's debt to *The Moonstone*. Having been introduced to Faunce, Susan Rodney – who is the bosom friend of the heroine, Lady Perival – exclaims, 'I have always wanted to know a detective, like Bucket, the beloved of my childhood; or Mr. Cuff, the idol of my riper years. You must invite Mr. Faunce to a quiet little luncheon some day. There is no question of class distinction with a clever man like that.'[49] Because of his talent for detection, Faunce is even regarded by a female criminal with a form of preternatural awe, as the agent of a superior justice, 'She looked at him as if a spirit of supernatural omniscience, a Nemesis in human form, were before her.'[50]

Allusions to contemporary literature (from Zola to France and D'Annunzio), social phenomena (the New Woman, Fenians and socialists), and technology (typewriters, electric light and photography) contribute to the sense of topicality that Braddon wished to achieve. Yet, these constant references to cultural icons of every sort are responsible for a slightly artificial tone, as if Braddon were a twentieth-century author writing a pastiche of *fin-de-siècle* literature. Furthermore, although the question of personal identity – a mainstay of sensation fiction – remains at the core of the plot, much emphasis is placed on clues, often of a rather predictable form – photographs, sheets of blotting paper, newspaper cuttings – and these are used by Braddon in a rather trite way.

The rise of forensic science is the subject of a recent study in which Ronald R. Thomas examines the new techniques or technologies used by nineteenth- and twentieth-century literary detectives to discover the truth and define identity. Thanks to this know-how the body of criminal and victim alike becomes a text, but this act of interpretation also has a political dimension,[51] which is apparent in Braddon's novels, where deviancy is regarded by Faunce as an inborn trait: 'There are born murderers as well as born poets; indeed, I incline to believe that the murderer is born, not made. He is not the victim of circumstances, the creature of environment, that we are disposed to think him.'[52] Over and over again, characters are described on the ground of their family history, or rather of their 'race'. This is how the nature of Colonel Rannock – a gentleman of doubtful conduct – is discussed in *His Darling Sin*: 'Who said he was ill-born? Surely, you know that there are good races and bad. Who can tell when the bad blood came in, and the character of the race began to degenerate? Under the Plantagenets perhaps ... A man's family history is the man.'[53] In her late novels Braddon utilised the increasingly popular pseudo-scientific concepts of race and degeneration as causal models, presenting them as sufficient to explain the behaviour of people.

By conflating different formulas, Braddon created hybrid texts whose status is atypical, as is apparent in *Rough Justice*, where the tension of the inquiry is broken by a long digression devoted to the murderer's biography and inner life, revealing the author's interest in the dynamics of motive and guilt. This section of the novel reminds one of Dostoevski rather than Doyle, because of the tragic status of Braddon's criminal – a philanthropist, who killed what he regarded as a social nonentity in order to inherit a large amount of money that would enable him to implement his enlightened schemes for social improvement. In conclusion, Braddon's late works offer an interesting blend of sensation and detective elements and although one should not peruse these books hoping to find innovative ideas concerning the detection of crime, they represent a sort of litmus test, a sign of the times, pointing to the growing importance of clues and detectives, but also to the persistent power of sensational ingredients.

Parodies and adaptations

The rise and fall of sensation fiction covered less than half a century, but by the 1860s this hugely popular genre had already attained a solid literary identity in the eyes of the public. This was due not only to the sales figures that sensation novels achieved and the critical debate that they triggered, but also to the wide range of parodies and adaptations they fostered. The early 'Mokeanna; Or, The White Witness' – which was serialised in *Punch* in 1863, following the success of Collins's *The Woman in White* (1860)[54] – testifies to the immediate and resounding cultural impact of sensationalism. Combining a vertiginous sequence of incidents with pretentious and incongruous details, an awkward rhetoric and blatant errors in the rendering of reality, this concise and rather contrived parody gleefully explores the comic potential of textual elements such as titles, quotations and footnotes.

Moreover, each episode was accompanied by a large illustration so as to underline the importance of pictures in popular literature. Renowned visual artists were asked to contribute pastiches of their previous works and George Du Maurier decided to create an ironic version of the engravings he had made to accompany *The Notting Hill Mystery*, which had been serialised in *Once a Week* in 1862–63.[55] The sensational character of Du Maurier's earlier images is caricatured in this self-parody, which underlines the stereotypical ingredients of the genre. The raven hair of the female figure becomes impossibly long, the contrast between darkness and light is polarised thanks to the moonlight and a flash of lightning. The clock predictably strikes midnight and a curtain is waving as if a gust of wind had just swept into the room. The hub of this infernal turmoil is poor Mokeanna, the donkey that can be seen through the window and whose prosaic presence deflates the whole visual construction, turning melodrama into bathos.

Parody joins hands with satire in the pages of *The Doctor's Wife* (1864), where Braddon – adopting a self-reflexive strategy – created a fictional alter ego to give vent to her ideas on sensation literature:

> Mr. Sigismund Smith was a sensation author. That bitter term of reproach, 'sensation,' had not been invented for the terror of romancers in the fifty-second year of this present century; but the thing existed nevertheless in divers forms, and people wrote sensation novels as unconsciously as Monsieur Jourdain talked prose. Sigismund Smith was the author of about half a dozen highly-spiced fictions, which enjoyed an immense popularity amongst the classes who like their literature as they like their tobacco – very strong.[56]

Smith's prosaic lifestyle openly contrasts with his wild imagination and his rhetorical flourishes. Catering for a public 'that bought its literature in the same manner as its pudding – in penny slices',[57] he is an indefatigable weaver of murky stories whose basic ingredients he describes as follows: 'What the penny public want is plot, and plenty of it; surprises, and plenty of' em; mystery, as thick as a November fog.'[58] To underline the interplay between high and low literature, Braddon has her sensation author appropriate every sort of literary material. The playful Smith even plans to rewrite *The Vicar of Wakefield* 'in the detective pre-Raphaelite style',[59] spicing it up with a murder and its inevitable detection.

Braddon's tongue-in-cheek account of Smith's authorial pragmatism, resulting in commercial success rather than in posthumous fame, simultaneously celebrated and criticised the sensation formula, which was becoming popular on both shores of the Atlantic, as is shown by Louisa May Alcott's sensational output. 'A Whisper in the Dark' was published anonymously in 1863, while *A Modern Mephistopheles* followed – also anonymously – in 1877. Even the American writer Bret Harte paid tribute to this genre in a series of parodies he first published in *The Californian* (the weekly newspaper he edited from 1864 to 1865) and later collected in *Condensed Novels* (1867), an assortment of tasty appetizers where one can read 'Miss Mix' by Ch-l-tte Br-nte, 'No Title' by W-lk-e C-ll-ns as well as 'Selina Sedilia' by Miss M.E. B-dd-n and Mrs. H-n-y W-d – two writers whose profiles were closely connected in the eyes of the public.[60]

Meanwhile, in Great Britain, Reverend Frederick Paget published *Lucretia, or the Heroine of the Nineteenth Century* (1868), a delightful epistolary novel with a moralising afterword. The story of Lucretia Beverley – an orphaned girl whose real but unfashionable name is Lucky Frummage – recalls Charlotte Lennox's *The Female Quixote* and Jane Austen's *Northanger Abbey*. Like the misguided heroines of those novels, Lucretia 'rewrites' her surrounding world according to the books she has read, consequently getting herself into an endless series of scrapes. After marrying her uncle's cowman, who claims to be an aristocrat called Marmion de Mowbray living under an assumed name in order to escape the persecution of his evil stepmother, Lucretia discovers that he is actually a cracksman and a bigamist whose many aliases fill half a page. When her uncle locks her in a garret, hoping that in solitude she may recover her reason, Lucretia feels like the imprisoned heroine of a sensation novel, feigns madness (a virtuoso piece!) and finally manages to escape, although her walk on the roof ends with a broken leg. Dissatisfied with her lot, Lucretia all but falls into the snares of a fortune hunter and is saved once again by her cousin John Benbow, an attorney who champions the causes of common sense, honesty and propriety.

Fast-paced and hilarious, the novel is a catalogue of sensation characters and accidents, which are despoiled of their charm and shown as vulgar, shallow or grotesque, instead of being 'aristocratically sensational and elegantly embarrassing, as is universally the case in the novels that are most read, and therefore, of course, the truest to nature'.[61] Yet, the continuous references betray a deep knowledge of the genre and – what is more – great relish in portraying its conventions. No short excerpt from this text can render either its brisk and witty tone or Paget's ability in building up the heroine's sensational expectations and in deflating them. By contrast, the afterword gives vent to the author's indignation and tragic foreboding; for a country that relies on sensation novels for the education of its young women and lower classes is doomed: 'If our humbler classes only read in order to be sensualized, there is only one possible result. France is not the only country in the annals of the world in which a reign of lust has been followed by a reign of terror.'[62]

While *Lucretia* was aimed at showing the unprofitable character of sensation fiction, genuine entertainment is the goal pursued by *A Sensation Novel* (1871). This comic opera was the joint effort of the writer W.S. Gilbert and the musician German Reed (Gilbert's collaboration with Sullivan started later that year). At the beginning of the opera a hack writer of sensation fiction is stuck in the middle of a three-decker novel, the ebullient sources of his inspiration having momentarily dried up, and in order to fulfil the terms of the contract that binds him to his publisher ('50 three-volumed novels per annum'), he evokes the Demon of Romance. The enchantment is wrought by throwing into a cauldron these basic ingredients of sensation fiction:

> Take of best quill pens a score,
> Take of ink a pint or more,
> Take of foolscap half a ream,
> Take, oh take, a convict's dream,
> Lynch pin, fallen from a carriage,
> Forged certificate of marriage,
> Money wrongly won at whist,
> Finger of a bigamist,
> Cobweb from mysterious vaults,
> Arsenic sold as Epsom Salts,
> Pocket-knife with blood-stained blade,
> Telegram, some weeks delayed,
> Parliamentary committee,
> Joint stock panic in the city,
> Trial at Old Bailey bar,
> Take a Newgate Calendar,
> Take a common jury's finding,
> Take a most attractive binding,
> Hold the saucepan by the handle,
> Boil it on a penny candle.[63]

What the author discovers after securing the spirit's help is that the characters featuring in his novel are real people, who have been punished in the afterlife by compelling them to personate 'those stock characters of the sensation novelist which are most opposed to their individual tastes and inclinations'.[64] Thus we learn that the hero, a Sunday school teacher, is not in love with the heroine, but with Rockalda, a villainess whose main guilt was her over-indulgence as a mother. On the other hand the heroine is in love with the villain, Sir Ruthven. These characters come to life at the end of each volume to discuss the development of the novel, which predictably does not correspond to their desires. The conventions of sensation fiction are ridiculed by means of this strategy, which contrasts the expectations of the public with the inner feelings of the characters, creating a comic counterpoint.

Gilbert's opera was written at the height of the sensation vogue and arguably contributed to the dissemination/regeneration of the sensation formula, but even at a later stage – when the phenomenon had lost its creative drive – parodies kept flowering, signalling the enduring popularity of the genre. An exchange of letters between Monsieur Lecoq, Inspector Bucket, Count Fosco and Mr Pickwick is included in Andrew Lang's *Old Friends: Essays in Epistolary Parody* (1890).[65] In this delightful apocryphal piece, the French policeman asks his British colleague to help him arrest the dangerous Italian count, who appears to be involved in an international plot, but the count manages to have poor Pickwick apprehended in his stead.

Yet another symptom of the immense popularity that sensation novels achieved is their migration from the shelf to the stage. Given the great success of *The Woman in White*, it comes as no surprise that by November 1860 an unauthorised version was already on stage in London. However, Collins did not write his own adaptation of the novel until 1871. The play was produced at the Olympic Theatre in October that year, had a run of nineteen weeks and was followed by an extended run in the provinces. The success of the play probably induced Collins to strengthen his links with the theatre, but we must remember that Collins had started work on theatrical versions of *Man and Wife* and *The New Magdalen* before writing these novels. While *Man and Wife* was published in book form in 1870 and performed as a play at the Prince of Wales Theatre only in April 1873, *The New Magdalen* was published and performed as a play at the Olympic Theatre at the same time, in May 1873.[66] Interestingly, after the success of this theatrical season Collins decided to embark for the States on a lecture tour (September 1873–March 1874), following in the footsteps of Dickens. On this occasion, Collins revised stories such as 'The Dream Woman', expanding them so as to take up two hours of public reading.[67]

Collins's interest in stage melodrama, however, should not be simplistically regarded as parasitical on his fiction, for his inspiration was triggered both by prose and by drama. His first play – *The Lighthouse* – is a case in point. Originally performed by Dickens's theatrical company in 1855, *The Lighthouse* was produced at the Olympic Theatre (and printed) in 1866. It was subsequently used by the author during his American tour and it was finally 'novelised' as *The Frozen Deep* in October 1874.[68] Even Collins's stage version of *The Woman in White* differs substantially from the novel and in a note the writer explained that he had 'endeavoured to produce a work which shall appeal the audience purely on its own merits as a play'.[69] Not only was the action moved forward from the 1840s to March 1862, but the plot was substantially altered and the most celebrated scene of the novel – the encounter between Walter and Anne at a moonlit crossroads – was completely reshaped.

While the theatre held a strong appeal for Collins, whose talent repeatedly crossed the border between page and stage, his interest was not exceptional. Braddon had a short career as an actress under the name of Mary Seaton and it was this that underpinned her knowledge and conception of literature. In her novels, Braddon both thematised the theatre and utilised it as a source of inspiration. Unsurprisingly, *Lady Audley's Secret* (1862) was repeatedly dramatised in the years following its publication and four film versions were made before 1915. The melodramatic impact of the play, however, elicited mixed responses and the London stage adaptation of 1863 was stigmatised by a contemporary reviewer as 'an appeal to that low taste for criminal horrors which is sufficiently catered for by the Old Bailey reports, without enlisting the arts of the novelist or the dramatist for its prurient gratification'.[70]

Other sensation novelists had a less direct involvement with the theatre, but one should not forget that Wood's *East Lynne* (1861) generated – well into the twentieth century – a long sequence of pirated and authorised melodramatic versions, both serious and farcical, including T.A. Palmer's celebrated *East Lynne* (1874), Ned Albert's *East Lynne* (1941) – a comic adaptation of what is described as 'the daddy of all the old-fashioned meller drammers, the most talked of play ever written'[71] – and a musical by Brian Burton, *East Lynne, or Never Called Me Mother!* (1984). The vitality of these novels in their transmogrified forms is a sign of the communicative power which sensation novelists were able to achieve by combining the ingredients of popular literature and theatre with a new conception of the plot.

8
London as a 'Heart of Darkness'

The archetypal opposition between holy city and sin city is rooted in the Bible, where Jerusalem, the seat of the Temple, is contrasted with nests of wickedness such as Babel, whose punishment for the erection of its tower – an emblem of impious pride – is a relapse into a primordial chaos of languages, or Sodom and Gomorrah, which are destroyed by 'brimstone and fire' (Genesis, 19: 24). Western culture is imbued with this rhetoric of the urban space, pivoting on the contrast between holiness and sin or between the metaphors of light and darkness. London has often been described as embodying these contradictory terms, that is to say as a beacon of civilisation and a harbour of vice, two dimensions that have also been regarded as coinciding with the diurnal and nocturnal faces of the city.

As early as 1608 Thomas Dekker published *The Belman of London. Bringing to light the most notorious villainies that are now practised in the KINGDOME*,[1] whose title page included an engraving featuring a watchman carrying a pole, a lamp and a bell. Here, the darkness of the night and of the London underworld are conflated and contrasted with two kinds of surveillance. On a practical level, the London streets are policed by the watchman on his beat, while on a literary level the text itself anatomises the mysteries of crime, 'bringing them to light' and thereby preventing further mischief.[2]

In the second half of the nineteenth century a wide range of texts highlighted the contrast between the West End and the East End, focusing on the dark face of London, an unexplored and virtually impenetrable world of crime and poverty, that coexisted side by side with the throbbing heart of modernity. Unsurprisingly, given the positivist climate of Victorian culture, the metaphors of light and darkness were no longer restricted to the moral sphere, but also became the emblem of a different and no less powerful struggle – that between civilisation and the primitive, which paradoxically came into conflict along an urban frontier at the very heart of the empire.

This binary view of London is already apparent in G.W.M. Reynolds's prologue to his seminal urban saga *The Mysteries of London* (1844–48). According to Reynolds, 'There are but two words in the moral alphabet of this great city; for all virtues are summed up in the one, and all vices in the other: and those words are WEALTH/POVERTY.'[3] After claiming that civilisation and vice 'go hand-in-hand',[4] Reynolds observed that the criminal side of London materialised in the darkness of its polluted sky, another side-effect of urban life: 'And, as if to hide all its infamy from the face of heaven, this city wears upon its brow an everlasting cloud, which even the fresh fan of the morning fails to disperse for a single hour each day!'[5]

Setting aside Friedrich Engels's *The Condition of the Working Class in England* (which was published in Germany in 1845 and translated into English in 1887), a long list of titles bridges the temporal span between Reynolds's imposing gothic saga and George Sims's *The Mysteries of Modern London* (1906), a belated version of the 'urban mystery' cycle. These publications, which simultaneously denounced the degradation of London's East End and drew on its picturesque qualities, present a variety of rhetorical strategies. Contrast is often the keynote of these works right from the title – be it the contrast between darkness and light that marks J.E. Ritchie's *The Night Side of London* (1857) and G.A. Sala's *Gaslight and Daylight* (1859) or that between 'haves' and 'have nots', as in D.J. Kirwan's *Palace and Hovel* (1870) and Helen Bosanquet's *Rich and Poor* (1896). 'Estrangement' is another common strategy, as is demonstrated by James Greenwood's *The Wilds of London* (1874) and Mrs. H.M. Stanley's *London Street Arabs* (1890), which emphasise the savage and exotic character of London, while a more homely (if less than wholeheartedly human) metaphor is at the heart of Thomas Beames's *The Rookeries of London* (1850), for the term 'rookeries' was commonly used to indicate those slums where a huge population crowded in a narrow urban space:

> Other birds are broken up into separate families – occupy separate nests; rooks seem to know no such distinction. So it is with the class whose dwellings we are to describe. We must speak of the dwellings of the poor in crowded cities, where large masses of men are brought together; where, by the unwritten laws of competition, rents rise and room is economised in proportion ... Are not these colonies Rookeries, if the description given by the naturalist be correct?[6]

Although most of these works cannot be included even under the widest definition of crime literature – being rather the outcome of recent

disciplines such as anthropology and sociology or the reports of journalists and 'missionaries' – their sensational character is apparent, insofar
as they represented virtual guided tours of those realms of horror that were
unfamiliar to the middle and upper classes. We can regard this type of literature as the result of various forces, such as a frivolous curiosity as to the
sensational details of underclass life or a philanthropic desire to regenerate the poorest sections of society, but we can hardly deny that it helped
arouse the public interest in crime, also drawing attention to the link
between crime and empire that marks so much late nineteenth-century
crime fiction, notably the Sherlock Holmes saga.

Exotic colonies

In a wide range of nineteenth-century texts – variously combining a sensational and an ethnographic approach to low-life – the London slums
are depicted in turn as primitive, barbaric and exotic, both catering for the
taste of the public and revealing imperialist ideological assumptions. And
such discourses were by no means limited to Britain. In his *Della polizia
in Inghilterra, in Francia e in Italia* (*Of Police in England, in France and in Italy*),
a volume that was published in Italy in 1868, Augusto Aglebert suggested
that some areas of London 'form, so to speak, exotic colonies',[7] as is argued
in the following passage:

> There are neighbourhoods that, compared to others, may seem foreign.
> Whoever, for instance, travels from Haymarket to the picturesque
> regions of Wapping and Bethnal Green passes in certain respects from
> civilisation to barbarism. Above all, there is a narrow district that is
> feared by passengers in night time and that was given by the English
> themselves the sinister name of Tiger-Bay, for it is the Bengal of London,
> but a humid and frightening Bengal, where men take the place of tigers.[8]

According to the description of 'Tiger Bay' that Thomas Archer offered
in *The Pauper, the Thief and the Convict* (1865), the real danger of this dis-
trict lay in the presence of brothels rather than of murderers and thieves:
'The tigers are, for the most part, quiet in their lairs; slinking, watchful,
crouching, cruel beasts, who wait there, sharpening their claws, and
looking with hungry eyes for the prey that their treacherous she-cats
bring down.'[9] Interestingly, after claiming that here 'poverty and crime
lie cheek by jowl', Archer went on to describe the hybrid population of
this neighbourhood, where one could meet not only Lascars and
Chinese, who are stereotypically presented as stupefied by drugs, but also

'dark-skinned, snakelike Hindoos (beggars and tract-sellers by day) [who] live with English and Irish women as their wives'.[10] Ethnic and cultural borders were easily crossed in the East End, a medley of races where even 'miscegenation' was far from exceptional. Joseph Salter's *The East in the West, or, Work among the Asiatics and Africans in London* (1896) is another case in point, for in this book distant geographic and cultural coordinates intertwine so as to create a 'dis-orienting' amalgam of peoples and customs.[11]

Local colour and exoticism also mingle in *London. A Pilgrimage* (1872), where the texts of Blanchard Jerrold and the illustrations of Gustave Doré depict the East End in terms that forcefully underline its 'otherness': 'We dismiss our cab: it would be useless in the strange, dark byeways: byeways the natives of which will look upon us as the Japanese looked upon the first European travellers in the streets of Jeddo.'[12] Only thanks to their police escort could the two visitors penetrate that labyrinth of alleys, whose material and moral darkness was provisionally lightened by the 'bull's eye' lantern policemen used to patrol the area.[13] The exotic element also marks Jerrold and Doré's visit to an opium den in Whitechapel, where a Lascar is lost in the artificial paradise of drugs. Curiously enough, on this occasion reality and fiction nonchalantly intermingle both in the text and in the accompanying illustration, for the intensity of the urban travellers' impressions is spiced up by a literary reference to Dickens's unfinished *The Mystery of Edwin Drood* (1870), which famously opens in an opium den. Indeed, we should not forget how often in Victorian works – such as Doyle's 'The Man with the Twisted Lip' – the East End is presented as a domesticated replica of the Orient in an attempt to evoke a flight from reality into the alluring and dangerous realm of dreams and sensual orgies.

The very use of the term 'city Arabs' or 'street Arabs', which recurs in the Sherlock Holmes saga to define the street children of Victorian London (the urchins Holmes employs as the 'Baker Street Irregulars'), chauvinistically evokes an exotic scenery, drawing a parallel between the lowest social strata of the metropolis and non-European populations. To many Victorians, although city Arabs lived in an urban environment, they shared the characteristics of members of more primitive societies; they were thought able to resist hunger and cold, and to be indolent and intolerant of any constriction related to education or work, as an 1852 enquiry on juvenile delinquency claimed.[14]

To understand the full import of this, one should remember the major role that the pseudo-scientific concepts of atavism and degeneration played in the late nineteenth-century, when 'deviant' behaviour (such as crime, prostitution and madness) was often explained either as regression to or a resurfacing of the primitive. For example, in Cesare Lombroso's *L'uomo delinquente* (*Criminal Man*, 1876), the criminal anthropologist drew a parallel between European delinquents and the 'savages' that peopled other continents in a manner that today would be interpreted as an intensely distorted usage of anthropological categories as ideological tools in the service of racist thought. However, while the paradigms of atavism and degeneration will be analysed in Chapter 8, let us now focus on the ways in which external observers related to the East End. Of the many texts that constitute my field of enquiry, I have singled out three different approaches to the poorer districts of London. They are embodied respectively by the *explorer*, the *ethnologist* and the *missionary*.

The explorer

The first approach I intend to highlight is the journey of exploration, which entails confrontation with the unknown and a (real or imagined) degree of danger. In the second half of the nineteenth century various writers, journalists and artists decided to see with their own eyes the conditions of life in the East End in order to expose the painful – and highly sensational – conditions they expected to find. The London slums were often visited under the protection of the police, as we see in Dickens's 'On Duty with Inspector Field' (1851). Instead of focusing directly on his journey into the night, Dickens devoted the first part of his article to the figure of Field, whose character is developed through his association with both the Great Exhibition of 1851 (where he spoke 'French all day to foreigners') and the British Museum, of which he is depicted as the 'guardian genius'.[15] The two faces of London – the imperial capital and the urban inferno – are thus implicitly contrasted and the ability of the police to cross the border between them is stressed. Thanks to his broad cultural associations, Field takes on a quasi-mythological status, for when readers first meet him at the police station they are told that

> [He] has come fast from the ores and metals of the deep mines of the earth, and from the Parrot Gods of the South Sea Islands, and from the birds and beetles of the tropics, and from the Arts of Greece and Rome, and from the Sculptures of Nineveh, and from the traces of an elder world, when these were not.[16]

As a result of this rhetorical strategy, the commercial, globalised and highly cultured face of the metropolis – whose apt symbol is Paxton's Crystal

Palace, with its huge sheets of transparent glass enabling light to pour freely into the temple of universal knowledge and peace – is contrasted with its murky heart.

Another Great Exhibition – that of 1862 – attracted the French traveller Louis Laurent Simonin to London. The result of this visit, however, is not a eulogy to progress, but the account of his excursion into the poorest neighbourhoods of the city. The pictures that accompany this volume highlight a stark contrast between light and darkness. Once again, it is thanks to a policeman's lantern that the squalor of the slums and the degradation of their inhabitants is made visible. Incidentally, the visit to the East End was by definition nocturnal, whether in search of forbidden pleasures – as is often the case in Victorian fiction – or in pursuit of painful knowledge. Characteristically, when Simonin and his travelling companions ventured – in full day – into Seven Dials they discovered that the streets were deserted and were told that the local people worked at night and slept during the day.[17]

The curious inversion of night and day that marked certain places and social strata of London was also underlined by other writers. In *How the Poor Live* (1883)[18] George R. Sims depicts a neighbourhood inhabited by 'thieves and highway cheats' as a 'colony' whose inhabitants sleep in full daylight for 'they reap their harvest in the hours of darkness'.[19] Sims's entire 'exploration' of the East End rests on an extended analogy between this area – which he labelled as 'a dark continent' – and the primitive, as is shown by the following passage:

> This continent will, I hope, be found as interesting as any of those newly-explored lands which engage the attention of the Royal Geographical Society – the wild races who inhabit it will, I trust, gain public sympathy as easily as those savage tribes for whose benefit the Missionary Societies never cease to appeal for funds.[20]

Interestingly, Sims pointed to the 'theory of the survival of the fittest'[21] – in other words, to social Darwinism – as well as to progress, which widened the gap between rich and poor, as the causes of the degradation of the poor.

Political engagement also plays a major role in *The People of the Abyss*, the volume the American writer Jack London published in 1903, after spending a period of around seven weeks in the East End, often sleeping, eating and working – in appalling conditions – in the London workhouses.[22] London, whose humanitarianism rested on his socialist creed, refused to avail himself of the mediation of the police, and to organise his journey to the East End he approached the famous travel agency that

Thomas Cook had created in mid-century. Cook's refusal to help the writer organise his journey takes on a symbolic value, enabling London to emphasise the incommensurable distance that separated the East End from the rest of the capital:

> But O Cook, O Thomas Cook & Son, pathfinders and trail-clearers, living sign-posts to all the world, and bestowers of first aid to bewildered travellers – unhesitatingly and instantly, with ease and celerity, could you send me to Darkest Africa or Innermost Thibet, but to the East End of London, barely a stone's throw distant from Ludgate Circus, you know not the way![23]

While the central section of the volume depicts London's descent into the 'abyss', according to the metaphor he used right from the title, the last chapter of his enquiry opens with a harshly provocative question: *'Has Civilization bettered the lot of the average man?'*[24] To provide his readers with an answer, the American writer compared the East Enders with the Innuits, a primitive population of Alaska, whose living conditions he claimed to be better than those of the metropolitan underclass.

The ethnologist

As we have seen, the aim of 'metropolitan explorers' was to obtain a knowledge they could share with the public. In order to penetrate the darkness of the East End a light was necessary. This light could be provided by the police, with their 'disciplinary' knowledge, but also by other figures. Sims, for instance, availed himself of a 'local' guide, while London finally sought the assistance of a private detective who had been active in the East End for thirty years.[25] Yet, the explorer, the policeman and the detective are not the only late nineteenth-century figures who were vested with the power to sound the unknown and to map a 'foreign' territory. We should not forget that the Ethnological Society was founded in London in 1842. And it is significant that the notion that ethnologists should work in the field – basing their activity on a disciplinary method – instead of relying on the accounts of travellers and missionaries became common in the second half of the century.

A scientific paradigm underlies some important Victorian texts that aimed at classifying the population of the East End, whose ways of life were practically unknown to the luckier inhabitants of the other half of London. Henry Mayhew's *London Labour and the London Poor* (1851–62) is a case in point. In this monumental four-volume work, the many categories of sellers, beggars and criminals who crowded the London streets were classified with meticulous attention. The goal of this encyclopaedic enterprise was avowedly ethnological, that is, to provide information 'concerning a large body of persons, of whom the public had less knowledge than of the most distant tribes of the earth'.[26]

While the approach of the 'urban explorers' that we have seen so far was impressionistic, Mayhew's theoretical premises derived from the new disciplines. Characteristically, the author divided humanity into 'two distinct and broadly marked races, viz. the wanderers and the settlers – the vagabond and the citizen, the nomadic and the civilized tribes',[27] acknowledging the existence of a third social group, standing half-way between the *hunters* and *manufacturers*, that is to say the *herdsmen*. According to Mayhew, each of these social groups is marked by particular physical traits. Thus while hunters have prognathous (that is, protruding) jaws, civilised peoples tend to develop their skull, due to the growth of their brain. Starting from this debatable premise, Mayhew presented his 'discovery', that is to say the idea that nomad and civil social groups are not necessarily confined to distant territories, but often live only a short distance apart, the former preying parasitically on the latter. Thus in London beggars and criminals – the metropolitan wanderers – lived off the more industrious share of the population and were recognisable not only thanks to the shape of their jaws, but also by their use of a jargon, their indifference to pain and deprivation, their revengeful disposition, their immorality and other similar traits.

Needless to say, not all contemporary thinkers explained the condition of the London poor by referring to the presumed 'laws' of physical anthropology; with more insight, some of them studied the environmental factors that helped shape the behaviour and appearance of the socially disadvantaged. Nonetheless, despite its questionable pseudo-scientific basis, Mayhew's study had a noble target, for this 'traveller in the undiscovered country of the poor'[28] believed that only a scientific presentation of his findings could convince the public that action should be taken to remedy what he described as 'a national disgrace'.[29]

The missionary

Given the fact that in 1903 Jack London still felt the need to denounce the conditions of life in the East End, we can surmise that there was a lack of either willingness or ability to take the step from the knowledge these works provided to the action they were supposed to inspire. However, the period was not one of total inactivity. In 1865 the Salvation Army began working in the poorest areas of London, and in 1890 the founder of the movement – General William Booth – authored his influential *In Darkest England*. The book opens with a reflection on its title, which echoes that of *In Darkest Africa* (1890), the account that Henry Morton Stanley had published a few months earlier:

> As there is a darkest Africa is there not a darkest England? Civilisation, which can breed its own barbarians, does it not also breed its own pygmies? May we not find a parallel at our own doors and discover within a stone's throw of our cathedrals and palaces similar horrors to those which Stanley had found existing in the great Equatorial forest?[30]

The metaphor of darkness (and that of the abyss) enabled Booth to expose the illness of the social body more convincingly, denouncing the extreme poverty from which three million people – as much as a tenth of the country's population – suffered in the British slums. Other metaphors enabled him to propose a cure. The Salvation Army, for instance, is clearly structured as a military organisation with the aim of fighting social evils rather than foreign powers. Likewise, the economic solution that Booth devised to solve the problems of unemployment and criminality is based on the logic of colonialism, for Booth aimed to create three kinds of social structures,

1. The City Colony.
2. The Farm Colony.
3. The Over-Sea Colony.[31]

The city colony would provide the homeless with a necessary refuge, answering their immediate needs and preparing them to relocate provisionally to a farm colony, so as to reverse the increasing urbanisation that was the source of so many problems in Britain. The last stage of this regenerative process entailed the creation of overseas colonies to enable this sector of the population to earn their own living without external support. This scheme clearly implied a rejection of industrial progress and the return to a rural economy.

The city disease

To understand Booth's position one should bear in mind the fact that in the late nineteenth century urban life was regarded by several physicians, scientists and thinkers as a hotbed of physical and mental degeneration, as a lecture Sir James Cantlie gave at the Parkes Museum of Hygiene in January 1885 – 'Degeneration amongst Londoners' – makes clear. Being conscious of the increasing tendency of Britons to gather in towns and cities, Cantlie focused his attention on a phenomenon he chose to call ' "*urbomorbus*" or "city disease" ',[32] that is, a gradual degeneration of the population – notably of the poorer classes – due mainly to want of exercise and the poor quality of the air. The East End was indeed teeming with infection from open sewers and inadequate urban graveyards and was also polluted by the coal smoke from factories and houses. London was described by Cantlie as 'the region where sunburning is unknown', because of both the lack of ozone and the coal smoke that darkened the sky.[33]

The presence of smog in the London sky helps us understand the relevance that the metaphor of darkness gained in works such as 'The Storm-Cloud of the Nineteenth Century' (1884), where John Ruskin stigmatised smog as the symbol of the moral degeneracy of a country that was enslaved to the materialist cult of money. Similar concerns were also voiced by Ruskin in his celebrated 'Fiction, Fair and Foul' (1880), an essay in which the art critic focused on a cultural, rather than physiological, form of degeneration, describing the thirst of the Victorian public for sensational plots – pivoting on murder, illness and madness – as the result of a life devoid of the healthy stimuli of nature. According to Ruskin, the 'hot fermentation and unwholesome secrecy of the population crowded into large cities' came to produce a 'smoking mass of decay'.[34]

In the second half of the nineteenth century the city was repeatedly likened to a rubbish dump or a dung heap (rubbish, for instance, plays a major role in *Our Mutual Friend*, 1864–65) and the moral/social problems connected to urbanisation were often described through metaphors that referred back to the significant hygiene problems of London, such as the inadequacy of the sewage system. In *A Study in Scarlet* (1887) London was famously depicted as 'that great cesspool into which all the loungers and idlers of the Empire are irresistibly drained'.[35] An article of 1862 adopted similar figurative language:

> It is clear that we have not yet found out what to do with our criminals. We neither reform them, nor hang them, nor keep them under lock and key, nor ship them off to the Antipodes. Our moral sewage is neither deodorised nor floated out to sea, but remains in the midst of us polluting and poisoning our air.[36]

Before the apocalypse

This itinerary testifies to the disquieting contradictions of the Victorian age, when London was characterised not only as a place of darkness but also as a modern Babylon or Babel, a confusion of languages and the expression of a venal man-made might that defied divine justice. The sense of imminent apocalypse was strong at the end of the century, as is shown by the penultimate image of *London: a Pilgrimage*, where a New Zealander is portrayed on the shore of the Thames, in the act of painting the ruins of London on the opposite shore.[37] This view of the imperial capital can be regarded as both a warning and an act of exorcism, but more interestingly the spectator who observes a metropolis that has fallen back into a primitive obscurity comes from the remotest British colony, New Zealand – a territory that is at the farthest margin of the empire, but that is also at the antipodes of Great Britain and can therefore be regarded as its double.

Similarly, an uncanny parallel between the River Congo and the Thames is drawn by Joseph Conrad right from the start of *Heart of Darkness* (1899), whose central metaphor is associated not only with the depths of 'darkest Africa', but also with the core of the British Empire. In the novella, Marlow is introduced while talking with some friends on board a small boat in the vicinity of London, against the backdrop of a sunset whose symbolic value is apparent: 'The air was dark above Gravesend, and farther back still seemed condensed into a mournful gloom, brooding motionless over the biggest, and the greatest, town of earth.'[38] Inspired by this landscape, Marlow meditates that even London ' "has been one of the dark places of the earth" ',[39] that is to say a 'wilderness' and a colony of faraway Rome, but in Conrad's eyes a primitive darkness still reigned over the powerful metropolis, and in his preface to *The Secret Agent* (1907) London is described as follows: 'There was room enough there to place any story ... darkness enough to bury five millions of lives.'[40]

In his seminal volume on the late nineteenth-century urban imagination – *Writing the Urban Jungle* (2000) – Joseph McLaughlin comes to the conclusion that 'metropolitan London and Londoners, far from being the antithesis of those colonial and imperial places and peoples that comprised the British Empire, were actually their curious doubles'.[41] This is certainly true for the East End, which was made into the object of the discourses of empire, like the remotest colonial territories. The result was what the critic labels as 'the rhetoric of the urban jungle'.[42] This rhetoric rested on categories such as obscurity, savagery and mystery, inviting efforts at classification, colonisation and mission so as to reclaim those who had fallen into the abyss of a new primitive age, a shameful anachronism at the core of the empire. Thus London took on the paradoxical position of centre and frontier of the empire – the seat of an economic and political power that played a major role in the process of globalisation, subjugating its 'others' and commodifying the exotic, but also a 'contact zone',[43] a place of uncanny hybridisation, where modernity was haunted by the ghost of the primitive.

9
The Rhetoric of Atavism and Degeneration

The dream of being able to read the mind through the body – thus making 'evil' legible – has a long history. Physiognomy boasts an ancient lineage that can be traced back to Aristotle, but it was in the eighteenth century that the belief in the correspondence between the outer and inner nature of human beings acquired the status of a pseudo-science and came to play a major role in the European imagination. When the Swiss pastor and theologian Johann Kaspar Lavater authored the influential *Physiognomische Fragmente* (*Essays on Physiognomy*, 1775–78), physiognomy was regarded by many as a benign fruit of the Enlightenment despite its racist and anti-Semitic implications. Georg Christoph Lichtenberg, however, reacted against Lavater's attempt to force the Jewish philosopher Moses Mendelssohn to convert to Christianity and he also spoke out against Lavater's conviction that the fixed features of the face may be read as a mirror of the soul. In a pamphlet published in 1778 Lichtenberg famously wrote: 'If physiognomy becomes what Lavater expects it to become then children will be hanged before they have committed the deeds which deserve the gallows.'[1] Physiognomists, in fact, claimed to be able to detect evil tendencies before they had been translated into crime, and this preventive universal judgement – as Lavater and others understood all too well – did not bode well for the future of civilisation.

Another attempt at establishing a correspondence between the physical appearance and the psychological profile of an individual was made in the following decades by the Viennese doctor Franz-Joseph Gall, the founder of phrenology. This discipline focused its attention on the shape of the skull, which was believed to reveal the underlying structure of the brain. According to a simplistic view of human physiology, Gall aimed at circumscribing those areas of the brain – he called these the 'organs' – that corresponded to the various 'faculties' of a person. In particular, strong emphasis was put on identifying the 'organs' (or rather the bumps) that presided over murder and theft, research Gall and his followers pursued by studying the inmates of prisons and asylums. Both physiognomy and phrenology turned the body into a signifier of crime and posited the possibility of preventing deviant behaviour on the basis of purely physical clues. Although the status of physiognomy was soon contested, both disciplines contributed to the misty amalgam of pseudo-scientific beliefs that marked the second half of the nineteenth century, when – and in relation to the development of anthropology – positivism also offered new models for explaining and stigmatising deviance in terms of biological inheritance. By postulating the continuity between animals and humans, Darwinism, which was mainly interested in evolution, opened up the disquieting possibility of regression, and this biological paradigm came to be regarded as a powerful instrument of social analysis.

The Victorian faith in progress coexisted with a widespread fear of decline, which fostered a climate of anxiety and helped engender a culture of decadence. *Fin-de-siècle* fiction was haunted by the resurfacing of primeval instincts that had been exorcised thanks to the long march of civilisation. Victorian gothic, in particular, readily absorbed the new rhetoric of atavism and degeneration. Sinister creations such as Mr Hyde and Count Dracula embody the dark side of positivism. Hyde is presented as a 'pale and dwarfish' creature, who gave 'an impression of deformity without any nameable malformation',[2] he is the diminutive simian double of Dr Jekyll. On the other hand Dracula is described as 'a criminal and of criminal type. Nordau and Lombroso would so classify him, and *qua* criminal is of an imperfectly formed mind.'[3] Far from pertaining to a separate and timeless realm of gothic horrors, these preternatural villains are the object of pseudo-scientific scrutiny, as Oscar Wilde pithily acknowledged when he wrote that 'the transformation of Dr. Jekyll reads dangerously like an experiment out of the *Lancet*'.[4] This should not come as a surprise, since late nineteenth-century culture obsessively investigated the borderlines between natural and preter/supernatural, sanity and insanity, or even animal and human. Suffice it to think of H.G. Wells's *The Island of Dr. Moreau* (1896), whose terrified hero, after many conjectures, awakes to this awful truth: 'The creatures I had seen were not men, had never been men. They were animals – humanized animals – triumphs of vivisection.'[5]

As Charles Baudelaire wrote, 'although it is not uncommon to see the same cause engender two contrary effects, I am always intrigued and alarmed by this'.[6] This poetic intuition provides us with a key to understanding the pseudo-scientific discourses that flourished around atavism and degeneration, which soon came to be regarded as all-encompassing hermeneutic paradigms and were utilised to explain apparently opposed phenomena by tracing them to a common root. Criminal anthropologists suprisingly dealt at one and the same time with forms of behaviour as different as anarchism and mysticism, crime and artistic talent, presenting them as related forms of 'deviance'.

To analyse this controversial conceptual field let us first briefly focus on the definitions of *atavism* – which is associated with Cesare Lombroso, the founder of criminal anthropology – and *degeneration*, the pivot of Max Nordau's thought. Lombroso studied the presence in some individuals of latent physiological characteristics which resurface when the psychic centres are affected by what he called an arrest of development. Nordau, on the other hand, described degeneration in terms of heredity, insofar as the debilitating effect of cigarettes, alcohol, drugs, unhealthy food, illnesses or simply a degraded metropolitan environment is passed on to one's offspring and increases until it causes the disappearance of the sub-species.[7]

Using atavism as an interpretative category Lombroso drew a dangerous parallel between those who are affected by epilepsy and hysteria (two nervous diseases the scholar often detected at the root of criminal identity) and uncivilised people: 'We have seen that many of the characters of savages, of coloured races, recur very often in born delinquents too.'[8] Thus, the paradigm of atavism accounts both for those deviant groups who are marginalised within Western society and for those populations who belong to non-European undeveloped territories.

To grasp the complexity of this conceptual area, one should recall that Lombroso – who aimed at a global classification of human phenomena – freely combined the analysis of physical, psychological and socio-cultural factors, as is shown in the following passage describing the atavistic analogies between criminals and savages:

> The paucity of body hair, the small capacity of the skull, the receding forehead, the well developed breasts ... the darker skin, the thicker and curlier hair, the big ears ... the great agility, the tactile numbness and the indifference to pain, the acute sight ... the scarce propensity to affections, the precocious tendency to venereal pleasures and wine, and the exaggerated passion for the aforementioned ... the passion for gambling, alcohol and its surrogates ... the custom of tattooing, the often cruel games ... even a special literature which reminds one of those heroic times, as Vico used to call them, when murder was praised.[9]

Lombroso's anarchists and saints

In the specific study that Lombroso devoted to anarchists, *Gli anarchici* (*The Anarchists*, 1894), the ideological foundation of anarchism is regarded precisely as the symptom of a relapse into the primitive: 'Nowadays, when the machine of government tends to become more and more complex, one cannot but consider a theory such as anarchism, which hints at a return to prehistory, before the emergence of the *paterfamilias*, like an enormous regression.'[10] Refusing the principle of authority which is embodied in the father – the pivot of the family from the beginning of civilisation – is uncompromisingly seen as a reversion to a pre-historical condition.

After ambiguously defining the regressive character of the anarchist ideal, Lombroso studied the atavism of anarchists themselves – a category of people he regarded as 'mostly either criminals or mad, or sometimes both'.[11] Yet while to Lombroso regicides, Fenians and anarchists constituted 'a complete criminal type', true revolutionaries (like Charlotte Corday) and many nihilists (like Vera Zassoulich, the anti-tsarist muse who inspired Oscar Wilde's *Vera, or the Nihilists*, 1883) presented 'a perfectly normal type, even more beautiful than the average'.[12] While Lombroso implicitly described the Fenian cause for the liberation of Ireland from British rule as a criminal enterprise, he dignified revolutions as 'the historical expression of evolution'[13] and classified nihilists as offenders whose actions were rooted in a rightful passion.

To provide his theory of anarchism with a scientific basis, Lombroso relied on the method he had already applied to the definition of a criminal type in *L'uomo delinquente* (*Criminal Man*, 1876),[14] in other words he drew on categories pertaining both to physical and cultural anthropology. Thus he analysed the anarchists' use of a criminal jargon similar to the French *argot*; their custom of tattooing (in Lombroso's eyes a definite mark of regression, being popular not only among criminals and anarchists, but also among 'savages');[15] their lack of ethical sense, since anarchists do not abstain from stealing and murdering; and finally their habit of composing jargon songs.

Although *Gli anarchici* opens with an unconvincing and at times grotesque set of arguments, in the last part of the volume Lombroso abandoned his more or less ingenuous explanations of the anarchist phenomenon to tackle its social components, with the result that the monster turns into a martyr:

> But here the psychiatrist and the socialist are faced with a strange problem. Why is it that in these people, who are almost all mad,

criminal and neurotic, and also prey to passions, one discovers such a great altruism? Why is it that this faculty in them is much more developed than in common people and even more so than in madmen and criminals, who are afflicted by the saddest form of egoism?[16]

The following pages contain a wealth of episodes proving the quasi-sanctity of anarchists, although elsewhere Lombroso did not hesitate to describe sanctity as a pathology in itself: 'Moral insanity can be found even in those rare instances of altruism who are the geniuses of goodness and who are called saints.'[17] This comment highlights a major characteristic not only of Lombroso's thought, in whose classification of pathologies opposites often coincide, but also of criminal anthropology more widely. In the same period, Ettore Sernicoli remarked that anarchist theories 'get easily rooted in souls that are inclined to mysticism',[18] and Nordau himself declared that mystical thought, emotional eroticism, fraternal love and a mania for regenerating the world are present in all degenerates at a latent stage.[19]

Between genius and madness

As a symptom of this attitude, one may cite *Genio e follia* (*Genius and Insanity*), which was first published in 1864 and was repeatedly revised until its reissue in 1888 as *L'uomo di genio* (*The Man of Genius*, 1891).[20] While the former title emphasised the ambivalent relationship between genius and madness in Lombroso's thought, the latter can be seen as the counterpart of another study which he published in 1876 and likewise repeatedly revised – *L'uomo delinquente* (*Criminal Man*). Interestingly, the title of *The Man of Genius* changed once more to *Genio e degenerazione* (*Genius and Degeneration*) in 1897, so as to include a term which had become a keyword in the scientific debate after the publication of Max Nordau's *Entartung* (*Degeneration*, 1892), which begins with a long dedication to Cesare Lombroso. The artist and the insane, the genius and the criminal, the saint and the anarchist are all included in Lombroso's geometry of pathologies and can be combined in various polar couples as well as in aggregates of the same sign (artist + genius + saint versus criminal + insane + anarchist).

Following the typical Lombrosian method, *The Man of Genius* is marked by an encyclopaedic and experimental attitude in an attempt to infer a human type from the observation of a certain number of actual people, by analysing their physical aspect, their hereditary and formative influences, their life, works, anecdotes, aphorisms and so forth. The underlying model of Lombroso's enquiries is biography, but he did not refrain from employing potentially unreliable sources.[21] Moreover, although where possible Lombroso drew directly on confessional writings such as diaries and letters, novels and essays, his approach to literary self-revelation cannot be described as very subtle.

Lombroso's view of the relationship between art and atavism is fairly complex. First, however, one should remark that in his enquiry Lombroso dealt mainly with poets and writers, musicians and philosophers, scientists and politicians (suffice it to mention Baudelaire, Schumann, Schopenhauer and Cavour), but not with painters. Some of the most interesting pages that he devoted to the figurative arts are to be found not in his chapters on the pathology of genius, but in those on the artistic expression of madness.

Yet, as a criminal anthropologist, Lombroso did not regard the link between genius and madness as an ideological instrument to deprive the artist of a social role, as is shown by his ambivalent response to Nordau's thought. In 1894 Lombroso devoted a chapter of *The Man of Genius* to Nordau, defining him as 'one of the most beautiful minds of our time',[22] but also accusing him of carrying his theories to extremes. In particular, Nordau was guilty of deconstructing the concept of genius, which should conversely preserve its exceptional value. Lombroso pursued his polemic against Nordau both in a book review he published in the United States in 1895, when the English and American editions of *Degeneration* appeared,[23] and in *Genius and Degeneration*, where he described Nordau as 'an enemy of art'.[24]

The shady apostle of degeneration

Indeed, *Degeneration* was conceived as a massive attack against contemporary art, as Nordau stated right from the dedication of the volume to Lombroso:

> Degenerates are not always criminals, prostitutes, anarchists, and pronounced lunatics; they are often authors and artists. These, however, manifest the same mental characteristics, and for the most part the same somatic features, as the members of the above-mentioned anthropological family, who satisfy their unhealthy impulses with the knife of the assassin or the bomb of the dynamiter, instead of with pen and pencil.[25]

This disquieting book groups under the heading of degenerates the Pre-Raphaelite movement, Symbolism, Tolstoy, Wagner, Parnassian and diabolist poets, decadents and aesthetes, Ibsen and Nietzsche, Zola and

Naturalism. Even the idea that artists may gather in 'schools' is regarded by Nordau as a sign of degeneration in itself and reminds the anthropologist of despicable parties such as criminal gangs and religious sects, since in his eyes artists are individualists by definition.[26] As a matter of fact, at the core of Nordau's distrust is a deep aversion for all art, considered as an expression of the emotional and instinctual dimension and contrasted with the rational world of science, which is conceived of by Nordau as the utmost attainment of humankind – 'The aberrations of art have no future. They will disappear when civilised humanity shall have triumphed over its exhausted condition.'[27]

After describing *fin-de-siècle* culture as a symptom of degeneration and hysteria so serious as to endanger the future of civilisation itself, Nordau proposed the advent of a society where every form of art that betrays 'anti-social' elements (in other words that does not conform to his standard of normality) must be regarded as a criminal act: 'When such a society … should after serious investigation and in the consciousness of a heavy responsibility, say of a man, "He is a criminal!" and of a work, "It is a disgrace to our nation!" work and man would be annihilated.'[28]

Using a rhetorical strategy which is indifferent to logic but which exerts – at least at first sight – a strong emotional appeal, Nordau linked the world of art to that of organised violence by attacking the thematic and ideological choices of novelists and poets: 'they extol crime, deny morality, raise altars to instinct, scoff at science, and hold up loafing aestheticism as the sole aim of life'.[29] These words reveal Nordau's strong fear of the 'other' within us and within society, as well as the inflexibility of the argumentative instruments he used to demonise artists, turning them into 'public enemies' simply to be annihilated. As an example of this degenerate attitude Nordau arbitrarily showed Count Mouffat – in Zola's novel *Nana* – in the act of miming a dog and bringing back the handkerchief of his mistress, the redoubtable Nana herself. Without contextualising this scene or studying the authorial perspective, Nordau designated this literary character as the emblem of *fin-de-siècle* artists, associating the artists with the degenerate genus of anarchists:

That is the liberty of one who is 'emancipated' in the sense of the degenerates! He may be a dog, if his crazed instinct commands him to be a dog! And if the 'emancipated' one is named Ravachol, and his instinct commands him to perpetrate the crime of blowing up a house with dynamite, the peaceable citizen sleeping in this house is free to fly into air, and fall again to the ground in a bloody rain of shreds of flesh and splinters of bone.[30]

Decadent detectives

The stories that M.P. Shiel published in *Prince Zaleski* (1895) offer an example of the bizarre literary fruits this cultural climate engendered. Degeneration provides the typical conceptual frame of the enigmas which Zaleski is called upon to solve, in spite of the fact that the Prince himself could be regarded as a degenerate according to the standards of the time. He is certainly the epitome of the decadent detective, a 'creature of death', as is shown by his ruined abode, a grotesque version of Poe's wildest gothic fancies:

> I could not but wonder at the saturnine fancy that had led this wayward man to select a brooding-place so desolate for the passage of his days. I regarded it as a vast tomb of Mausolus in which lay deep sepulchered how much genius, culture, brilliancy, power! The hall was constructed in the manner of a Roman *atrium*, and from the oblong pool of turgid water in the center a troop of fat and otiose rats fled weakly squealing at my approach.[31]

Exoticism and eclecticism *à la* Huysmans mingle with every form of excess in the long description of the crumbling but luxurious mansion which provides this idle genius of detection with an appropriate setting.

The mysteries which Zaleski unravels reflect the late nineteenth-century obsession with hereditary insanity, suicide and degeneration. In 'The Race of Orven', for instance, the death of Lord Pharanx is related to the dark history of his family – the House of Orven, whose members die suddenly before reaching the age of fifty. What Zaleski discovers is that through the centuries a bloody compact has united the Orvens. Each firstborn son of the Orven family is required to kill his own father in order to prevent 'the heritage of madness' from becoming apparent. Hereditary insanity is 'the guilty secret' behind a series of 'ritual' murders whose ultimate motives were 'the pride and the selfishness of *race*'.[32] These words acquire a clearer meaning if we focus on the term Zaleski uses to define Lord Pharanx's syndrome, for the '*General Paralysis of the Insane*'[33] is caused by syphilis.

In 'The S.S.', whose title sets the tone for anticipation of an ominous future, Zaleski investigates an apparent epidemic of suicides that turns out to be a series of murders orchestrated by a secret society whose aim is to prevent the decay of European peoples due to an excess of medical care. The Society of Sparta fulfils the debatable mission of acting as a scourge, eliminating those degenerate individuals whose very existence and ability to procreate are seen as a threat to the future of society as a whole. The tone of the story is increasingly sinister and one is tempted to imagine the author approving the founding principles of the society he has invented. They certainly coincide with Zaleski's views, as he openly claims, in spite of the fact that he thinks their methods 'too rash, too harsh, too premature'.[34] This proviso is no less disquieting than the statement it is meant to soften.

Degeneration also plays a major role in 'The Siamese Twin of a Bomb Thrower', a lurid story included by Robert Barr in *The Triumphs of Eugène Valmont* (1906). Adolphe Simard, who was unfairly dismissed by the French government after working as a policeman, has embraced the anarchist creed and has also sunk into an addiction to absinthe, which has turned him into a sort of Jekyll and Hyde figure. The parallel is apparent in a scene where the detective Valmont – in disguise – observes his former subordinate while he drinks four glasses of absinthe one after the other, triggering a transformation in which, paradoxically, the civilised and rational nature of the former policeman prevails over the brute instincts of the terrorist:

> Here before my eyes was enacted a more wonderful change than the gradual transformation of transparent absinthe into an opaque opalescent liquid. Simard, under the influence of the drink, was slowly becoming the Simard I had known ten years before. Remarkable! Absinthe having in earlier years made a beast of the man was now forming a man out of the beast.[35]

At the end of the story, thanks to Valmont, Simard is redeemed; he rejects the two 'A's which have marked his transitory ruin – 'anarchy and absinthe';[36] but there is something sinister in this supposedly happy ending. As Valmont proudly remarks, 'Simard will need no purgatory in the next world. I kept him on bread and water for a month in my strong room.'[37] Valmont's London flat hides a prison with no windows that the detective had built to correct the excessive mildness of the British system: 'I have brought many a scoundrel to reason within the impregnable walls of that small room.'[38] Here the word degeneration fits the detective rather than the anarchist, since Valmont is desirous to bring the law back to a former evolutionary stage and regards the respect of the criminal's rights as a contemptible sign of weakness:

> When I began to succeed as a private detective in London, and had accumulated money enough for my project, I determined not to be

hampered by this unexplainable softness of the English toward an accused person. I therefore reconstructed my flat, and placed in the centre of it a dark room strong as any Bastille cell.[39]

New forms of degeneration lay in wait at the turn of the century, ready to strike at the apparatus of power. World War I and Nazi-Fascism were rooted in those years and as Daniel Pick makes clear: 'it is perhaps now impossible to read nineteenth-century texts on racial degeneration without an implicit teleology'.[40]

As the turn-of-the-century debate on atavism and degeneration – and its fictional echoes – show, conceptualising a social phenomenon implies an interpretative strategy which partly constructs the phenomenon itself and influences the institutional response to it. In *L'anarchia e gli anarchici* (*Anarchy and Anarchists*, 1894) Sernicoli initiated a polemic against Lombroso, who opposed the death penalty for anarchists and argued in favour of their imprisonment in lunatic asylums because their underlying altruism offered the promise of their eventual reinstatement in civil society. Sernicoli disapproved of this stance since in his eyes anarchists had to be suppressed – 'to prevent them from committing new crimes and in homage to that principle of selection which should not applied only to thoroughbred horses and to silkworms'.[41]

These lines seem to be inspired by eugenics, the new science created by Francis Galton at the end of the century in order to turn the scientific control of heredity into the cornerstone of a healthier society. Galton himself took part in the debate on criminal anthropology and in a review of Havelock Ellis's *The Criminal* (1890) he wrote:

> The hope of the criminal anthropologist is to increase the power of discriminating between the natural and accidental criminal. He aims at being able to say with well-founded confidence of certain men that it is impossible to make them safe members of a safe society by any reasonable amount of discipline, instruction, and watchfulness, and that they must be locked up wholly out of the way.[42]

As physiognomists and phrenologists had done before, criminal anthropologists dreamt of reinstating a pattern of omniscience. In the course of the modern age, the eye of God had been progressively superseded by the 'unfailing' power of science, but dangerous prejudices now came to be regarded as scientific truths. Physiology – rather than psychology – was considered as the key to the human mystery, and the body was invested with the status of a stable locus of meaning, which could therefore be deciphered. The new belief in biological predestination promised to offer a much more efficient tool for the prevention of crime than the ancient threat of eternal punishment, even though it rested on shaky theoretical and empirical foundations. The time was not yet ripe for the horrors of racial cleansing and genocide, but the mentality that was to make these obscure attainments possible had already found its voice. By a bitter irony of history, the idea that society was degenerate actually contributed to its degeneration, although in an unforeseen direction.

Conclusion: the Age of Formula Fiction

In my attempt to write a counter-history of crime fiction I have touched on a variety of sub-genres, including the ghost story, adventures of psychic detection, sensation fiction, the 'literature' of London and anarchist fiction, so as to shed light on the variety of discourses that intertwined in nineteenth-century 'criminography'. To conclude my survey, I need to focus on the important changes that took place within crime fiction itself at the turn of the century, for it was these changes that set the ground for the formation of a detective canon. Thus I will first consider the relevance that the Sherlock Holmes saga acquired as a complex cultural phenomenon and the ideological framework underlying the Father Brown stories. Then I will briefly sketch the early development of the new subgenre of spy fiction, and finally I will go on to explain why the burgeoning comprehensive tradition of crime criticism discussed in Chapter 1 was progressively marginalised and a more restrictive tradition of detective criticism became dominant.

The Sherlock Holmes 'myth'

As we have seen, while in the second half of the nineteenth century sensation fiction was undergoing a complex process of self-fashioning, it took longer for detective fiction to be recognised as a genre. In the 1840s, Poe's *Tales of Ratiocination* – as he called the Dupin trilogy and 'The Gold Bug' – were regarded as an isolated phenomenon and were not associated with the crime and detective stories that were being published in British, American and Australian magazines at the time.[1] Contemporary critics traced some connections between Poe and Godwin, Brown or Vidocq, but these references did not build up the sense of any real continuity.[2]

Half a century later, however, parody became a symptom of the growing popularity that detective fiction had acquired thanks to the mythical figure of Sherlock Holmes. The first novel of the Holmes saga – *A Study in Scarlet* – appeared in 1887 and by 1892 Robert Barr had published 'The Adventures of Sherlaw Kombs'.[3] In 1893 J.M. Barrie wrote two other parodies – 'The Adventure of the Two Collaborators' and 'The Late Sherlock Holmes'[4] – while in 1899 the American Bret Harte included in his *Condensed Novels* a celebrated Holmesian parody, 'The Stolen Cigar Case'.[5]

The process of adaptation for the theatre also contributed to the canonisation of Holmes. In 1897 Doyle had contemplated the idea of writing a play about the detective, but nothing came of it. This led, however, to repeated contacts between Doyle and the American actor William Gillette, who eventually wrote a play himself, basing it on 'A Scandal in Bohemia' and 'The Final Problem'. *Sherlock Holmes: a Drama in Four Acts* opened in Buffalo in October 1899, and then ran in New York from November 1899 to June 1900. After a tour in the United States, Gillette sailed for Great Britain in 1901, where the play was staged in Liverpool and London.[6] It was Gillette who made some basic elements of the Holmes icon popular, such as the deerstalker cap (originally introduced by Sidney Paget in the 1890s), the cloak and the curved pipe.[7] Actually, 'Gillette did become the living embodiment of Sherlock Holmes',[8] at least for the American public, since when Frederic Dorr Steele was asked to illustrate *The Return of Sherlock Holmes* for *Collier's Weekly* – one of the largest selling magazines in the United States – he chose Gillette as his model.[9]

One can safely claim that this widespread interest in Holmes contributed to Doyle's decision to revive his hero after his presumed death on the Reichenbach Falls. The publication of *The Hound of the Baskervilles* (1901–02) and of Holmes's following adventures made the sleuth even more popular and this sweeping cultural phenomenon, revolving around a single literary figure, helped to consolidate the formulaic character of detective fiction.

Moreover, by the dawn of the century Holmes was the subject of various critical works, the best-known of which is Monsignor Ronald A. Knox's 'Studies in the Literature of Sherlock Holmes' (1911).[10] Mixing irony with the keen eye of a biblical scholar, Knox compared all the Holmes stories that had been written at that date, punctiliously pointing out their inconsistencies. Yet, by refusing to believe that Doyle was the real author of the Holmes cycle, he ascribed these inconsistencies to Watson himself, hypothesising that Holmes's faithful companion, who was notoriously short of money, had been obliged to add some invented cases to the genuine ones he had witnessed. This interpretation ironically subverted the fictional status of the saga, reducing Doyle to the role of Watson's literary agent and playfully acknowledging the 'real-life' quality Holmes had achieved in the eyes of the public. Knox's essay inaugurated the 'higher criticism' tradition, which is at the origin of the 'Grand Game' that Holmesian/Sherlockian associations (the adjective varies depending on their British or American origin) continue to play – with great relish and imagination – all over the world.

What I wish to emphasise is the pseudo-religious dimension of this phenomenon. In itself, the term higher criticism corresponds to a branch of biblical criticism. Moreover, the Holmes saga is defined by Holmesians/ Sherlockians as the *canon* or the *sacred writings*, while the huge number of Holmes stories that have been written after the death of Doyle are labelled as *apocrypha*. It is my contention that religion had much to do with the development of the detective canon, which somehow came to replace the traditional biblical canon within a society that was increasingly secularised. At a time when traditional values – concerning both metaphysics and the human being – were questioned, detective fiction reinstated truth and justice as the basic coordinates of its system of meaning.

I regard it as no coincidence that in the first decades of the twentieth century various religious-minded people took a strong interest in this genre. Monsignor Knox combined his activity as a detective novelist and critic (in 1929 he authored the famous 'ten commandments' of detection) with his religious calling. Having been ordained an Anglican priest, he then converted and became a Catholic priest in 1919. In 1936 he even served as domestic prelate to the Pope and in the last years of his life he worked on a new translation of the Vulgate.

Another case in point is that of G.K. Chesterton, who was a fervent apologist of religion, converted to Catholicism in 1922 and also played a rather ambivalent role in the canonisation of detective fiction, for in the atypical saga of Father Brown he both curbed the irrational tendencies of late nineteenth-century crime fiction and exalted its imaginative freedom. In the first part of his life Chesterton wrote primarily works of social and literary criticism, while after his conversion he authored books such as *St Francis of Assisi* (1923), *The Catholic Church and Conversion* (1926) and *St Thomas Aquinas* (1933).

Similarly, Dorothy Sayers was not only a detective novelist and critic, but also a medieval scholar and a noted Christian writer.[11] In addition to her translation of Dante's *Divine Comedy* (a work she left unfinished), Sayers authored various religious plays, including *The Zeal of Thy House* (1937), *The Devil to Pay* (1939), *In the Mind of the Maker* (1941) and *The Man Born to Be King*, a cycle of radio plays on the life of Jesus that was broadcast in 1941–42. Incidentally, the London Detection Club was founded in 1928 precisely by Knox, Chesterton (who was its first president) and Sayers, together with Anthony Berkeley Cox and Agatha Christie.

Nightmares and orthodoxy

In 'A Defence of Detective Stories' (1902) Chesterton identified the sensational components of detective fiction as the source of the prejudice that surrounded it, pointing out the social stigma that was still attached to the representation of crime, since 'To write a story about a burglary is' – in the eyes of many – 'a sort of spiritual manner of committing it.'[12] According to Chesterton, however, detective fiction should be regarded as the modern equivalent of epic literature and the detective as knight-errant actually embodies a principle of order.

In Chesterton's 'heroic poems in prose' detectives and policemen form a benevolent conspiracy to support civilisation against the disruptive activities of criminals, who subscribe to a primitive code of behaviour. The 'romance of police activity' – as Chesterton wrote – 'tends to remind us that we live in an armed camp, making war with a chaotic world, and that the criminals, the children of chaos, are nothing but the traitors within our gates.'[13] To understand the full import of these words, we should keep in mind the author's own terror of chaos, as is demonstrated in the disturbingly comic *The Man Who Was Thursday: a Nightmare* (1908), a fantasy of crime, anarchy and detection where the agents of 'good' and 'evil' swap roles with disquieting nonchalance. As Chesterton explained in his dedication to E.C. Bentley, the novel was actually written in response to the cultural climate of the *fin de siècle* – a time that was precariously suspended between the opposite poles of decadence and positivism:

> When we were boys together,
> Science announced nonentity
> And art admired decay; ...
> This is a tale of those old fears,
> Even of those emptied hells ...[14]

In 1936 the author reiterated his message by claiming that the book 'was intended to describe the world of wild doubt and despair which the pessimists were generally describing at that date'.[15] *The Man Who Was Thursday* can therefore be interpreted as a paradoxical act of exorcism, ritualising the death of the old century and announcing – at the very end of the story – the dawn of a new age.[16]

Consistent with this world-view, Chesterton's saga of Father Brown helped 'normalise' detective fiction by severing its links with the super-natural. In spite of their apparent emphasis on the metaphysical, Father Brown's stories actually combine detection with an orthodox view of religion, refuting every 'irrational' approach to reality as a form of supersti-tion. Drawing inspiration from Poe's Dupin, Chesterton endowed his hero with a flair for paradoxes, but the author of *Orthodoxy* (1908) knew all too well where to draw the line between licit and illicit knowledge. Thus although Father Brown claims: 'The most incredible thing about miracles is that they happen', the word miracle should be taken to indicate 'an elem-ent of elfin coincidence which people reckoning on the prosaic may per-petually miss'[17] – that is to say an event that contradicts the laws of probability rather than those of science. Likewise when Chesterton started a crusade to defend *magic*,[18] he was actually fighting to preserve a tension towards transcendence and the claims of imagination against the levelling action of materialism.

On the other hand, in Father Brown's stories crime is typically presented at first as the result of supernatural agencies, but this transitory explanation is soon deconstructed by the humble religious hero. Far from pursuing the nineteenth-century tradition of melodrama (with its emphasis on premon-itory/revelatory dreams) or 'psychic detection' (which was grounded on pseudo-sciences and/or the occult), Chesterton's stories actually decon-struct it, for they present bizarre cases which are solved by means of an utterly rational investigation. They border on fantasy and the grotesque, but always keep on the safe side. Having exorcised the twin demons of super-stition and anarchy, thanks to miraculous intuitions that could be better described as *abductions*, Father Brown can re-establish the realm of reason.

Reason itself, however, can become a tool of destruction in these stories when, instead of being subservient to faith, it becomes an all-explaining principle. This is apparent right from the beginning of the saga. In 'The Blue Cross' – the first episode of *The Innocence of Father Brown* (1911) – Father Brown actually faces two opponents: the international criminal Flambeau and the head of the Paris police, Valentin, who is presented not only as a famous investigator, but also as a sceptic. Father Brown's victory over Flambeau – who is won over to the cause of good and will eventually become Father Brown's assistant – is complete and it also coincides with the victory of 'Christian reason' over Flambeau's heretical claim that 'there may well be wonderful universes above us where reason is utterly unreasonable'.[19]

On the other hand, Father Brown's victory over Valentin becomes appar-ent in the second episode of the saga – 'The Secret Garden' – where the policeman turns criminal for ideological motives, that is to prevent a rich man from leaving all his money to the Church of France. The obsessively anti-clerical Valentin embodies the dangers inherent in atheism. His fate also sheds a sinister light on positivist detection, which is elsewhere described by Chesterton as follows:

> Science is a grand thing ... But what do these men mean, nine times out of ten, when they use it nowadays? When they say detection is a science? They mean getting outside a man and studying him as if he were a gigantic insect: in what they would call a dry impartial light, in what I should call a dead and dehumanized light. They mean getting a long way off him, as if he were a distant prehistoric monster; staring at the shape of his 'criminal skull' as if it were a sort of eerie growth, like the horn on a rhinoceros's nose ... I don't try to get outside the man. I try to get inside the murderer.[20]

Chesterton's suspicion of positivist detection (with its potentially atheistic connotations) led him to bypass the tradition of Holmes and revert to Dupin's more psychological method, through which he solved the case of the purloined letter by identifying with the mind of his opponent.

Britain under threat

As we have seen, in early twentieth-century Britain the detective story provided authors and their public with a discursive space that enabled them to share a common fund of certainties. Chesterton put the problem in a nutshell when in an essay on Sherlock Holmes he claimed: 'I would rather have the man who devotes a short story to saying that he can solve the problem of a murder in Margate than the man who devotes a whole book to saying that he cannot solve the problem of things in general.'[21] In the age of Nietzsche and Freud, philosophy and psychoanalysis were undermining the certainties of Western societies. Disquieting vistas and frightening abysses were opening up in the perception of the absolute and of the psyche. Even the possibility of grasping external reality in its concrete consistency seemed to become more remote after Walter Pater – the arch-priest of aestheticism – had written that experience 'is ringed round for each one of us by that thick wall of personality through which no real voice has ever pierced on its way to us, or from us to that which we can only conjecture to be without'.[22]

To obtain a better understanding of the cultural climate in which the detective story acquired its canonical status we must plunge into this world of crumbling certainties and of increasing complexity. The last decades of the nineteenth century had seen widespread terrorist campaigns take place all over Europe. In Britain this phenomenon was due mainly to the activity of Fenians, who were fighting to achieve the independence of Ireland, but those novelists who chose to deal with terrorism often obscured its Fenian matrix by vaguely referring to anarchist or nihilist plots which deflected the attention of the public from the real causes of the bombings, reshaping the terrorist conflict as an episode in the endless fight between the opposing principles of order and chaos, civilisation and anarchy. Chesterton's nightmarish vision of God – the ultimate source of power and knowledge – as an entity who presides at one and the same time over the anarchist and the police organisations speaks volumes about the anxieties of the British public at the time.

The development of the spy novel can be regarded as another side effect of this climate of fear, which was due both to the internal threat of social unrest and to the external threat of military conflict. People became increasingly conscious of the fragility of the enormous British empire, notably of the vulnerability of the British Isles to a foreign invasion, due to factors as diverse as the development of naval technology, the shifting European alliances and a series of international crises. In the late Victorian and Edwardian ages, Britain was still a world power, but public confidence was rapidly declining and this condition of uncertainty fostered the development of the so-called 'invasion novel', starting with George Chesney's *The Battle of Dorking* (1871), a formula that was successfully exploited by William Le Queux, the author of best-selling invasion novels such as *The Great War in England in 1897* (1894), dramatising the dangers of a Franco-Russian alliance. Novelists, of course, responded quickly to changing geopolitical conditions and after the signing of the *entente cordiale* between France and Britain in 1904 Germany became the number-one enemy, as is shown by Le Queux's *The Invasion of 1910* (1906) and *Spies of the Kaiser* (1909).

While some novels dealt specifically with the act of invasion, others alerted the public to the dangers inherent in those spy networks that represented a prerequisite to any invasion. E. Phillips Oppenheim's *The Mysterious Mr Sabin* (1898) is a case in point, together with Headon Hill's *The Spies of the Wight* (1899). In these thrillers we typically meet shady cosmopolitan characters whose mysterious political allegiance is the source of much suspense and foul play, while international secret societies occasionally play a role in the unravelling of the action (Collins had used that strategy to punish Count Fosco in *The Woman in White*). Needless to say, turn-of-the-century spy novels betray a barely disguised xenophobia, which is directed both towards foreign powers and towards foreign individuals living on British soil, the 'aliens'.

While early spy novels depicted cosmopolitans – often of Jewish origin – as hybrid and/or dangerous, the writers' patriotic enthusiasm supported a Manichean distinction between the honourable defenders of Britain and its dastardly opponents, which led to the dichotomy *secret agents* vs *spies*. Although espionage was a rough and dirty game, Britons could take part in it without forgetting the rules of fair play. What is more, the spying game could help regenerate a society that was betraying signs of decline, as is shown by the immensely popular novel Erskine Childers wrote in 1903, *The Riddle of the Sands*, whose first lines clearly evoke the stagnant atmosphere of *fin-de-siècle* London:

> I have read of men who, when forced by their calling to live for long periods in utter solitude – save for a few black faces – have made it a rule to dress regularly for dinner in order to maintain their self-respect and prevent a relapse into barbarism. It was in some such spirit, with an added touch of self-consciousness, that, at seven o'clock in the evening of September 23 in a recent year, I was making my evening toilet in my chambers in Pall Mall. I thought the date and the place justified the parallel; to my advantage even; for the obscure Burmese administrator might well be a man of blunted sensibilities and coarse fibre, and at least he is alone with nature, while I – well, a young man of condition and fashion, who knows the right people, belongs to the right clubs, has a safe, possibly a brilliant, future in the Foreign Office – may be excused for a sense of complacent martyrdom, when, with his keen appreciation of the social calendar, he is doomed to the outer solitude of London in September.[23]

Although these words – which are spoken by Carruthers, the protagonist and first-person narrator of the story – have, right from the beginning, an ironic undertone, the novel is presented as an antidote to the danger of 'going native', to the condition of 'degeneration' Conrad chose to stigmatise in Kurtz in *Heart of Darkness* (1899). However, the setting of the protagonist's meditation is not the jungle, but rather the heart of the civilised world. Carruthers's life in the London clubs is presented as a series of sterile social rituals, while his yachting holiday with his friend Davies will be conducive to a personal regeneration, as well as to the defusing of a German invasion. The safety and future of Britain lie in the power and initiative of the individual, who must escape the unhealthy influence of city life and recover his thirst for adventure.

A disparaging view of London also marks the beginning of another celebrated spy novel – John Buchan's *The Thirty-nine Steps* (1915), whose hero, like Carruthers, turns secret agent by chance:

> I returned from the City about three o'clock on that May afternoon pretty well disgusted with life. I had been three months in the Old Country and was fed up with it ... The weather made me liverish, the talk of the ordinary Englishman made me sick, I couldn't get enough exercise, and the amusements of London seemed as flat as soda-water that has been standing in the sun.[24]

Thus speaks Richard Hannay (another protagonist and first-person narrator), who – after spending most of his life in South Africa – finds England exceedingly disappointing. Like Carruthers, he is *the* individual the British nation/empire needs to safeguard its borders and to ensure its survival: 'Here was I, a very ordinary fellow, with no particular brains, and yet I was convinced that somehow I was needed to help this business through – that without me it would all go to blazes.'[25]

Hannay is regarded by critics as the typical 'clubland hero',[26] whose potential for daring exploits can be fully revealed under the appropriate conditions of danger. Although Carruthers declares: 'I'm not cut out for a Sherlock Holmes',[27] secret agents and detectives actually share many characteristics – from their powers of observation to their physical prowess and mastery of foreign languages. Moreover, both detectives and secret agents tend to become serial heroes. Hannay, for instance, features also in *Greenmantle* (1916), *Mr Standfast* (1919) and other adventures. On the other hand, Sherlock Holmes deals with state secrets and spies in stories such as 'The Naval Treaty' and 'The Bruce-Partington Plans'.

Of course, tracing a history of spy fiction exceeds the scope of this book, but I wish to underline that spy fiction variously intertwined with detective fiction. The gothic theme of persecution that had already filtered into crime fiction by the end of the eighteenth century, thanks to Godwin's *Caleb Williams*, is at the heart of detective, terrorist and spy novels alike. We are all familiar with the predicament of the literary character who finds him/herself falsely accused of a crime and has to prove his/her innocence, while evading the police. Likewise, in terrorist novels the main character is often persecuted by the mysterious underground anarchist organisations to which he had recklessly vowed allegiance, and in spy novels the hero is usually pursued by the omnipresent and invisible spy network he threatens with disclosure. *The Thirty-nine Steps* owes its swift-paced rhythm and its thrilling appeal precisely to this gothic theme of flight and pursuit. As the narrator remarks, 'I reckoned that two sets of people would be looking for me – Scudder's enemies to put me out of existence, and the police who would want me for Scudder's murder.'[28] Secret agents typically experience the condition of living in a 'no man's land' where their identity becomes a source of mortal danger and survival depends on concealment or disguise.

Spy and detective novels thrived on the same market laws, responded to similar kinds of anxiety and promoted analogous ideological stances. Many spy novels were conceived as mass products and contributed to the growth of formula fiction: Oppenheim is credited with having written 115 novels and 39 collections of short stories, while Le Queux was scarcely less prolific.[29] Moreover, both genres reflected social, political and institutional changes, although the development of detective fiction followed the creation of the police, while that of spy fiction partly anticipated the creation of secret services.[30] Like much detective fiction, the spy-thriller formula was based on the claims of faction: maps, faked photographs and documents were repeatedly included in these novels to simulate their truth-value. On the other hand, while the nineteenth-century tradition of crime fiction embraced complexity (consider *The Moonstone*, where a diamond is stolen by a man in an unconscious state), the 'clubland' tradition – with its nationalist emphasis on heroism and a good cause – supported a black-and-white contrast between 'us and them' or the agents of order and chaos, mirroring the parallel development of detective fiction.

Towards a conservative view of detection

Having summarily mapped the development of spy fiction at the turn of the century, let us focus once again on mainstream detective fiction and criticism, which were becoming increasingly 'conservative' in those years. Critics were also developing a sharper interest in form, as is proved by the importance that the term 'mystery' acquired in their vocabulary. Carolyn Wells's *The Technique of the Mystery Story* was published in 1913, only two years after *The Innocence of Father Brown*. As we saw in Chapter 1, the range of sub-genres analysed by Wells, with the aim of shedding light on their interrelation, does not include forms of 'criminography' such as picaresque novels or criminal biographies. On the other hand, Wells's umbrella definition of *Mystery Story* comprises ghost stories, riddle stories and detective stories – three fictional types that imply a question and an answer, for Wells identified the foundational elements of the genre as mystery and its correlative, that is, curiosity or inquisitiveness. The inclusion of ghost stories within the scope of Wells's analysis testifies to the fact that detective fiction had not yet asserted its identity as a separate genre, but was still regarded as part of a larger cluster of popular genres. It was the search for form – to the detriment of other concerns, such as subject matter and ideological assumptions – that progressively helped foster a narrow critical perspective, which restrictively identified the new genre, tracing its borders with increasing fastidiousness. Characteristically, while the first chapters of Wells's study offer a classification of related sub-genres and a historical account of their respective developments, the bulk of the volume focuses on the structural elements of detective fiction proper.

The apex of this normative trend coincided with works such as 'The Professor and the Detective' (1929), by the American scholar Marjorie Nicholson. As this semi-humourous essay shows, the identity of the new genre was being contrasted not only with popular literature, but also with the latest developments of 'high' literature. Nicholson regarded the academics' interest in detective fiction as an antidote to the subjectivity of modernist novels and to 'the "stream of consciousness" which threatens to engulf us in its Lethean monotony'.[31] Being the product of lucid ratiocination, a process akin to the method philosophers and scientists apply to their fields of scholarship, detective fiction gives readers an intellectual pleasure that is reassuringly unemotional:

> We seek our chamber of horrors with no adolescent or morbid desire to be shocked, startled, horrified. We handle the instruments of the crime with scientific detachment. It is for us an enthralling game, which must be played with skill and science, in which the pieces possess no more real personality than do the knights and bishops and pawns of chess, the kings and queens of bridge.[32]

A stern advocate of 'fair play',[33] Nicholson regarded with suspicion both popular literature and modernist works, and contrasted the selectivity of detective fiction – where every element is functional to the denouement – with the 'all-inclusiveness' of *Ulysses*.[34] Giving vent to her reactionary spirit, Nicholson described detective fiction as a form of 'neo-Calvinistic justice',[35] reasserting the value of moral choice and human agency against 'a smart and easy pessimism, which interprets the universe in terms of relativity and purposelessness'.[36]

Nicholson's position – which reminds us of Chesterton's emphasis on Catholic orthodoxy – was both anti-melodramatic and anti-modernist, although not all the theorists of the 1920s were affected by these prejudices. Perhaps as a reaction to the increasing tendency of 'golden-age' authors and scholars to disparage every 'irrational' element, T.S. Eliot felt the need to tackle the opium-related mystery that is at the heart of Collins's *The Moonstone*, reassessing its melodramatic impact and its importance as an antecedent of modern detective fiction. 'Wilkie Collins and Dickens' (1927) opens with the hope that 'a critic of the present generation may be inspired to write a book on the history and aesthetics of melodrama'.[37] In Eliot's eyes, while in the early twentieth century highbrow fiction was regarded as opposed to thrillers and detective fiction, the intellectual and the sensational dimensions had actually coexisted in the best novels of the nineteenth century, *The Moonstone* being a case in point. Due to its reliance on 'the intangible human element', Collins's book was described by Eliot as 'the first and greatest of English detective novels', in contrast with the American tradition inaugurated by Poe's trilogy, which offers 'a *pure* detective interest'.[38] Of course, Eliot's attempt to identify two intertwining national traditions of detection did not correspond to the mainstream historical accounts of the genre, which normatively highlighted only the Poe tradition, but Eliot was evidently aware of the possibility of writing a counter-history of crime fiction.

The role of anthologies

A central role in the canonisation of detective fiction was also played by the anthologies that were published in the late 1920s, both in Great Britain and in the United States. Anthologies helped shape the public view of the genre not only through the selection of representative texts but also by means of the editor's introductory essay. E.M. Wrong's *Crime and Detection* (1926) is a case in point. Voicing a common prejudice, Wrong traced the history of a genre that – in his eyes – had appeared at an embryonic stage in ancient times, had hibernated for centuries and had been resurrected thanks to the catalysing genius of Poe. According to the critic, the apex of this phenomenon coincided with Doyle's creation of Sherlock Holmes – such a powerful figure that we 'tend to think of the pre-*Holmes* detectives as of the pre-Shakespearian drama; to call them precursors only'.[39] Most of the texts Wrong collected are grouped under the heading 'Crime and detection', while he significantly decided to offer only one example of 'Crime without detection' and two of 'Detection without crime'.

It was in 1927 that Willard Huntington Wright (Van Dine's real name) edited *The Great Detective Stories*. The literary territory that Wright mapped in his introductory essay is the so-called 'popular' or 'light' novel, which he divided into four areas – the romantic novel, the novel of adventures, the mystery novel and the detective novel.[40] Like most of his predecessors, Wright defined the specificity of this genre by underlining the active role readers play in unravelling 'a complicated and extended puzzle cast in fictional form',[41] but his words indicate that by now detective fiction had achieved a clear consciousness of its own status:

> Because of this singularity of appeal the detective novel has gone its own way irrespective of the *progressus* of all other fictional types. It has set its own standards, drawn up its own rules, adhered to its own heritages, advanced along its own narrow-gage track, and created its own ingredients as well as its own form and technic.[42]

A sense of verisimilitude, a rather neutral characterisation, a plain style and a 'unity of mood'[43] – since no emotional interference should be allowed to distract readers from their intellectual pursuit – are the elements that comprise this literary recipe. In his attempt to establish the genre on a purely intellectual basis, Wright even claimed that the detective story 'is the only type of fiction that cannot be filmed', unless one chooses to reduce 'the actual detective elements to a minimum', emphasising 'all manner of irrelevant dramatic and adventurous factors'.[44]

Significantly, while normative critics refused to recognise the variety of ingredients that contributed to the detective fiction recipe, the entertainment industry was fast appropriating the character of Holmes. The first silent film featuring Holmes – *Sherlock Holmes Baffled* – dates back to the year 1900.[45] In the following decades dozens of films about Holmes were made both in France and in Great Britain by various companies. In September 1921 a dinner was organised by Stoll Film Productions to celebrate the release of their sixteenth Holmes film, *The Hound of the Baskervilles*. In the speech he gave at the convention dinner, Doyle acknowledged the debt he owed to 'those gentlemen who have, apart from myself, associated themselves with [Holmes]'.[46] The list included Sidney Paget, who created the Holmes type with his illustrations, and three actors – William Gillette, H.A. Saintsbury and Eille Norwood – who had played Holmes in the Stoll films. Of course this speech had been written for a particular occasion and Doyle certainly wished to be polite, but seemingly he was also highly aware of the multifaceted character of the cultural process that had ensured the celebrity of Holmes – a process involving serial publication in the *Strand* and *Collier's*, publication in book form, accompanying illustrations, not to mention the theatrical and film versions of the Holmes stories.

This survey of the main detective fiction anthologies that were published in the 1920s would not be complete without a mention of Dorothy Sayers's celebrated *Great Short Stories of Detection, Mystery and Horror* (1928).

Although the book appeared in the United States as *The Omnibus of Crime* (1929), the original title is better suited to the contents, for Sayers – following Wells's approach – actually detached detection from the sphere of crime and related it to other kinds of 'mystery fiction'. As the table of contents of the book shows, Sayers identified two intertwining macro-categories – 'Detection and Mystery' and 'Mystery and Horror' – which she divided into a number of categories and sub-categories. This complex scheme represents a brave attempt to map both the historical development of detective fiction and its present wealth of forms, so as to underline its proximity to the twin genre of supernatural fiction within the overarching category of 'mystery'.

Sayers's introduction supports this canonical vision of the detective story, tracing its origin to 'the Jewish Apocrypha, Herodotus, and the Æneid', and claiming that after 'a spasmodic history' the genre 'suddenly burst into magnificent flower in the middle of the last century'.[47] Sayers also offered an original interpretation of Poe's role as the ancestor of a legitimate and illegitimate progeny. In Sayers's eyes the least celebrated story of the Dupin trilogy – 'The Mystery of Marie Rogêt' (1842–43) – is the prototype of the intellectual (or classic) branch of detective fiction, while 'The Gold Bug' (1843) is at the root of the sensational (or romantic) branch. Although the theme of the two stories (the brutal murder of a young girl on the one hand, the interpretation of a cryptogram on the other) might lead to opposite conclusions, Sayers convincingly argued that in the first case the newspaper accounts of the murder offer all the elements we need to inquire by ourselves, while in the second text 'the reader is led on from bewilderment to bewilderment till everything is explained in a lump in the last chapter'.[48] It is therefore the role of the reader which determines the character of a story, creating a polarity of genres that was still alive in the 1920s, when the sensational had been replaced by the thriller, while detective fiction had fully developed its intellectual calling thanks to the fair play principle.

I will conclude this survey by mentioning *The Mystery Book*, an anthology H. Douglas Thomson edited in 1934, a few years after publishing a book-length study of the genre – *Masters of Mystery: a Study of the Detective Story* (1931). In 1946 Howard Haycraft would not only include a large section of this volume in his seminal collection *The Art of the Mystery Story* (1946), but he would even describe Thomson as 'the first major historian anywhere of the contemporary police romance as living literature'.[49] In *Masters of Mystery* Thomson took time to meditate on the nature of criticism, which he regarded as based at bottom on personal feelings. In his opinion, to avoid this subjective element, a critic should develop 'a code of rules to which the work under consideration must in general conform'. The following conclusion – relating specifically to detective fiction – follows from this general premise:

> Now it is a fair submission that the stricter the rules and the more stringently they are enforced, the higher will be the standard of the play. If we admit this – as presumably we must – it will not be difficult to show that the detective story has a just claim to be a work of art.[50]

When Thomson wrote this passage, normative criticism dominated the cultural arena and the label of 'mystery' was the umbrella term which mainstream critics commonly adopted in analysis of detective fiction and its neighbouring genres. Coherent with this view, Thomson's anthology *The Mystery Book* includes fifty stories under three sections: 'Stories of Mystery and Adventure', 'Stories of Crime and Detection' and 'Stories of the Supernatural'. As Thomson explained, in the first group of stories, 'the mystery lies for the most part in the unexpected train of events recorded', the second group of stories contains 'the statement and solution of a problem', and in the third group the explanations of supernatural phenomena 'are left to the readers' imagination'.[51]

Like Wrong, Wright and Sayers before him, Thomson combined a theoretical and a historical approach, simultaneously drawing the boundaries of detective fiction as a genre (within the larger territory of 'mystery') and grounding this view of the genre on a genealogical enquiry which leads back to ancient literature.[52] Needless to say, in their quest for the origin of a form they conceived as pivoting on a riddle, these scholars were oblivious to what Chandler had already described as the family tree of detective fiction – revenge tragedies, the picaresque, criminal biographies and gothic novels.

Detection and modernism

As Sayers wrote, 'In its severest form, the mystery-story is a pure analytical exercise, and, as such, may be a highly finished work of art, within its highly artificial limits.'[53] Although she was conscious of the psychological shortcomings of a genre that was constitutionally forbidden from entering into the mind of the criminal, Sayers was also proud of the technical skill involved in writing a detective story, with its 'Aristotelian perfection of beginning, middle, and end'.[54]

The normative character that mainstream detective criticism acquired in the 1920s mirrored the formalist concerns of modernist literature, with its emphasis on technique and on the rendering of time. The modernists' interest in detective fiction was likewise linked to its formal aspects and therefore helped confirm a clear-cut profile which focused on the core of the enquiry. Ford Madox Ford, for example, repeatedly drew convincing parallels between detective and impressionist novels, claiming that 'The best technical work that is being done in the novel to-day is, perforce, being put into the romance of mystery.'[55] Not only did Ford compare the structural coherency of detective fiction to the *progression d'effet* of the impressionist novel, but he also likened the flashbacks in detective fiction (insofar as it actually tells two stories – that of murder and that of investigation) to the modernist time-shift.[56]

Detective fiction – with its emphasis on plot and narrative technique – came to be considered as a sign of the times. High literature was experiencing a similar tension between experimentation and systematisation, and several theoretical studies on the novel – from Percy Lubbock's *The Craft of Fiction* (1921) to E.M. Forster's *Aspects of the Novel* (1927) – were published in the 1920s. Incidentally, although Forster claimed to be too priggish to enjoy Doyle, he also stated that 'Mystery is essential to a plot'[57] and devoted several pages of his volume to the relation between a story, curiosity, memory and intelligence.

Acknowledging this special connection between detective and modernist fiction, Clive Bloom regards the detective story as 'a very special link in the emergence of the full theoretically based modernism of the early years of the twentieth century', since 'Its self-absorption abolished subject matter in favour of form.'[58] We should not forget that the cultural phase in which detective fiction acquired a sense of its own identity was also marked by the advent of structuralism in the Soviet Union. Interestingly, Victor Šklovskij's *O teorii prozy* (*Theory of Prose*, 1925) includes an essay on detective fiction where the critic dissects Doyle's stories in order to identify the elements which contributed to their serial success. Šklovskij goes on to trace a genealogy, showing that Doyle's formula represents the evolution of the scheme Poe had created in his stories, particularly in 'The Gold Bug'.[59]

While impressionist and modernist writers – ranging from James and Ford to Mansfield, Woolf and Joyce – were experimenting with narrative techniques, detective novelists were working in the same direction, as is shown by Agatha Christie's *The Murder of Roger Ackroyd* (1926), a book that stirred a scandal. Choosing to tell her story of crime and detection by means of an 'unreliable narrator' (who is moreover a physician, that is, the quintessentially reliable figure of Victorian literature), Christie broke the traditional alliance between the Watson-type narrator (another doctor!)

and its readers.[60] After acknowledging his double crime – that is to say, his actual crime and his narrative dissembling of it – Dr Sheppard may be ashamed of his failure as a murderer but he actually calls the readers' attention to the passages where he deliberately misled them, commenting: 'I am rather pleased with myself as a writer.'[61] Christie's deft use of the point of view in *The Murder of Roger Ackroyd* highlights the occasionally subversive quality of her fundamentally conservative novels.

Moreover, although the canonical tradition of detective fiction that Christie came to embody as the 'queen of crime' emphatically relied on rational investigation, it never completely detached itself from the super-natural dimension that characterised the counter-canon of crime fiction. Like Doyle and Chesterton before her, Christie reduced the supernatural to the subsidiary role of transitory explanation, but at the same time she also exploited it to conjure up an ominous atmosphere of mystery that lures the public into reading and is progressively cleared away by the investigation.

As Charles Osborne claims, Christie 'was interested in the supernatural, and indeed was to write some of her finest short stories on supernatural subjects'.[62] *The Sittaford Mystery* (1931) opens with a séance, during the course of which the table dutifully begins to rock, informing those present that Captain Trevelyan has been murdered. Only the Captain lives six miles away and all the roads are blocked because of the snow... In *Endless Night* (1967) Michael Rogers falls in love with Ellie Goodman, who turns out to be a rich American heiress, and they decide to have their house built on a piece of land called Gypsy's Acre, in spite of the fact that the land is believed to be cursed and that a local gypsy even urges them to leave the place for she foresees death in their futures. The mystery at the heart of *Sleeping Murder* (1976), the last Christie novel featuring Miss Marple, also revolves around a house. A newlywed couple from New Zealand settles in a Victorian villa, but due to a series of déjà vu experi-ences the girl starts to believe that the house is haunted. The discovery that the protagonist had actually lived in the villa as a child is far from reassuring, for the place is linked to the disquieting memory of a murder that took place eighteen years before. As we can see, Christie brilliantly condensed the two strands of crime and detective fiction in her appar-ently rational but actually gothic mysteries.

Reading in the age of Cultural Studies

Only in the second half of the twentieth century did scholars defini-tively widen their field of inquiry, reassessing the relationship between detective fiction proper and crime literature, and thus breaking down all those generic boundaries that had been carefully erected in the previous decades. Aiming to recover those hybrid aspects of detective fiction that the 'golden age' had removed, Julian Symons refreshingly wrote in 1972:

> The detective story pure and complex, the book that has no interest whatever except the solution of a puzzle, does not exist, and if it did exist would be unreadable. The truth is that the detective story, along with the police story, the spy story and the thriller, all of them immensely popular in the past twenty years, makes up part of the hybrid creature we call sensational literature.[63]

While half a century earlier the genre was asserting its own literary status against its sensational antecedents, since the 1970s the canon of detection has come under scrutiny in an attempt to circumvent precisely the defensive attitude that influenced its formation. This deconstructive approach mirrors the contemporary tendency to regard genre as a set of rules that are productive as long as they are transgressed. It also mirrors the theoretical framework that marks the age of Cultural Studies, when literature is no longer regarded as an independent domain of words, a 'power-free' zone which is ruled by the laws of aesthetics, but rather as part of a wider network of cultural phenomena that unceasingly interact with market laws and ideological issues.

Following these trends in contemporary theory, the present book has tried to reassess the development of detective fiction as part of a larger and more complex 'plot'. Instead of choosing intellectual enigmas and rational detection as my guiding lights, I have followed some of those circuitous and at times unkempt paths that early twentieth-century normative criticism either overlooked or stigmatised as 'deviant'. Along those dark lanes I have met exotic figures, faced bizarre mysteries, seen extreme poverty and pondered over discarded beliefs and (pseudo)scientific theories – the 'waste-products' of the nineteenth-century collective imagination.

As Michel Foucault claimed in the 1970s: 'our critical discourses of the last fifteen years have in effect discovered their essential force in this association between the buried knowledges of erudition and those disqualified from the hierarchy of knowledges and sciences'.[64] This theoretical framework has been conducive to new critical and historical approaches in our collective effort to revitalise our perception of culture. It certainly helped inspire my work. Following in the footsteps of Foucault and other scholars I deeply admire – ranging from Julian Symons and Stephen Knight to Clive Bloom, Martin Priestman and Martin Kayman – I realised that a prodigious amount of material was waiting to be analysed from an alternative viewpoint, so as to trace a counter-history of crime fiction, with a comparative and 'cultural' emphasis on market forces, translation, adaptation, criticism and ideology.

The present book is the result of this critical intention. Its aim – needless to say – is not to supersede, but rather to integrate the traditional view of the genre so as to pave the road for other critical interpretations that may enable us to reconsider our perception of this genre in the light of works and issues that had been previously overlooked. A parting question takes shape as I tap these last few words into my computer. In my effort to reassess the profile of this genre have I played the role of a detective or that of a criminal? I am afraid there is no time for an answer. The clues are all in the text and then, probably, there is a shade of both sides in each of us...

Notes

Introduction

1. 'Preface', in *Science, Pseudo-Science and Society*, eds M.P. Hanen, M.J. Osler and R.G. Weyant (Waterloo, Ontario: Wilfrid Laurier University Press, 1980), p. viii.
2. See Michel Foucault, *L'ordre du discours* (Paris: Gallimard, 1971), pp. 16–23.
3. Rosemary Jackson, *Fantasy: the Literature of Subversion* (London and New York: Routledge, 1981), p. 20.
4. Ibid., pp. 25–6.
5. Clive Bloom, 'Introduction', in *Gothic Horror: a Reader's Guide from Poe to King and Beyond*, ed. Clive Bloom (Basingstoke and London: Macmillan, 1998), p. 2.
6. Ibid.
7. Clive Bloom, *The 'Occult' Experience and the New Criticism: Daemonism, Sexuality and the Hidden in Literature* (Sussex: Harvester Press, 1986), p. 80.
8. Ibid., p. 81.
9. Linda Hutcheon, *A Poetics of Postmodernism: History, Theory, Fiction* (New York and London: Routledge, 1988), p. 9.
10. Bloom, 'Introduction', in *Gothic Horror*, p. 16.

1. Revising the canon of crime and detection

1. Hayden White, *Metahistory: the Historical Imagination in Nineteenth-Century Europe* (Baltimore and London: The Johns Hopkins University Press, 1973), p. ix.
2. See Joseph Bell, Review of *The Adventures of Sherlock Holmes* (*Bookman*, December 1892), in *The Uncollected Sherlock Holmes*, ed. Richard Lancelyn Green (Harmondsworth: Penguin, 1983), p. 362.
3. A.C. Doyle, 'The Adventure of the Cardboard Box', in *Sherlock Holmes: the Complete Illustrated Short Stories* (London: Chancellor Press, 1985), p. 257.
4. A.C. Doyle, 'Preface to *The Adventures of Sherlock Holmes*', in *The Uncollected Sherlock Holmes*, p. 270.
5. Carolyn Wells, *The Technique of the Mystery Story* (Springfield, MA: The Home Correspondence School, 1913), p. 63.
6. Howard Haycraft, 'Foreword', in *The Art of the Mystery Story: a Collection of Critical Essays*, ed. Howard Haycraft (New York: Simon and Schuster, 1946), p. v.
7. Howard Haycraft, *Murder for Pleasure: the Life and Times of the Detective Story* (New York: Carroll and Graf, 1984), p. 6.
8. Ibid., p. 1.
9. Ibid., p. 2.
10. Ibid.
11. Haycraft (ed.), *The Art of the Mystery Story*, p. 128. This definition also embraced Friedrich Depken's *Sherlock Holmes, Raffles, und Ihre Vorbilder: Ein Beitrag zur Entwicklungsgeschichte und Technik der Kriminalerzählung* (Heidelberg: C. Winter, 1914). The book was translated into English by Jay Finlay as *Sherlock Holmes, Raffles, and their Prototypes* (Chicago: Fanlight House, 1949).

12. F.W. Chandler, *The Literature of Roguery* (New York: Burt Franklin, 1958), p. 1.
13. Ibid., p. 406.
14. Ibid., p. 524.
15. Ibid., pp. 532–3.
16. Ibid., p. 547.
17. Régis Messac, *Le 'Detective Novel' et l'influence de la pensée scientifique* [*The Detective Novel and the Influence of Scientific Thought*] (Paris: Champion, 1929), p. 99. All unsigned translations from Italian and French into English are mine.
18. See Michel Foucault, *Power/Knowledge: Selected Interviews and Other Writings 1972–1977*, ed. Colin Gordon (New York: Pantheon Books, 1980).
19. Julian Symons, *Bloody Murder: from the Detective Story to the Crime Novel: a History* (New York: Viking, 1985 [1972]), p. 13.
20. Stephen Knight, *Form and Ideology in Crime Fiction* (London: Macmillan, 1980), p. 8.
21. Martin Kayman, *From Bow Street to Baker Street: Mystery, Detection and Narrative* (London: Macmillan, 1992), p. 105.
22. Martin Priestman, *Detective Fiction and Literature: the Figure on the Carpet* (London: Macmillan, 1990), p. xi.
23. Martin Priestman, 'Introduction', in *The Cambridge Companion to Crime Fiction*, ed. Martin Priestman (Cambridge: Cambridge University Press, 2003), p. 6.
24. Stephen Knight, *Crime Fiction, 1800–2000: Detection, Death, Diversity* (London: Macmillan, 2004), p. xii.
25. Alastair Fowler, *Kinds of Literature: an Introduction to the Theory of Genres and Modes* (Cambridge, MA: Harvard University Press, 1982), p. 154.
26. Ibid., p. 56.
27. Ibid., p. 38.
28. Ibid., p. 37.
29. Stephen Knight, 'Enter the Detective: Early Patterns of Crime Fiction', in *The Art of Murder. New Essays on Detective Fiction*, eds H.G. Klaus and Stephen Knight (Tübingen: Stauffenburg Verlag, 1998), p. 11.
30. See Stephen Knight, 'Radical Thrillers', in *Watching the Detectives: Essays on Crime Fiction*, eds Ian A. Bell and Graham Daldry (Basingstoke and London: Macmillan, 1990), p. 173.
31. Kayman, *From Bow Street to Baker Street*, p. 62.
32. Caleb Carr, *The Italian Secretary: a Further Adventure of Sherlock Holmes* (London: Little, Brown, 2005), p. 260.
33. See Umberto Eco, 'Postille a *Il nome della rosa*' (Milano: Bompiani, 1984). The text had previously appeared in *Alfabeta*, 49 (June 1983).
34. Michael Holquist, 'Whodunit and Other Questions: Metaphysical Detective Stories in Post-war Fiction', *New Literary History*, 3(1) (Autumn 1971): 135–56; reprinted in *Two Centuries of Detective Fiction: a New Comparative Approach*, ed. Maurizio Ascari (Bologna: COTEPRA, 2000), p. 176.
35. P.D. James, *The Murder Room* (London: Faber and Faber, 2003), p. 7.
36. Ibid., p. 286.

2.   Detection before detection

1. Quoted in Barry Cunliffe, *Roman Bath Discovered* (Stroud, Gloucestershire: Tempus, 2000), p. 64.

2. *Everyman*, in *Everyman and Medieval Miracle Plays*, ed. A.C. Cawley (London and Melbourne: Dent, 1977), p. 210.

3. Michel Foucault, 'Truth and Power', in *Power/Knowledge*, p. 119.

4. Ibid., p. 118.

5. Suffice it to think of Artemidorus Daldianus's *Oneirocritica* – a treatise on the interpretation of dreams.

6. In the Book of Genesis, Joseph, who is a prisoner in Egypt, interprets the dreams of two fellow convicts – Pharaoh's cupbearer and baker. After predicting the former's freedom and the latter's death, Joseph professes the sacred origin of his divinatory power: 'Do not interpretations belong to God?' (40:8; quotations are from the New International Version). Two years later Joseph is summoned by the cupbearer to interpret a dream of Pharaoh, who has already consulted wise men and fortune tellers in vain; the young Hebrew reasserts his role as a messenger of God: 'The dreams of Pharaoh are one and the same. God has revealed to Pharaoh what he is about to do' (41:25). This scenario recurs later in the Bible when Chaldean magicians, enchanters, astrologers and diviners fail to interpret the dream of Nebuchadnezzar, and Daniel decodes this secret because 'the spirit of the holy gods is in him' (Daniel 4:8).

7. The story is based on a classic source – Cicero's *De Divinatione* (I, 27).

8. Geoffrey Chaucer, *The Canterbury Tales*, a verse translation with an introduction and notes by David Wright (Oxford and New York: Oxford University Press, 1985), p. 208.

9. See *The Wakefield Second Shepherds' Pageant*, in *Everyman and Medieval Miracle Plays*, pp. 79–108.

10. See Jeremiah 27: 9–10; 28: 8–9.

11. This is what happens to Joseph when in a dream he first sees the haystacks erected by his brothers prostrating before him, and then sees the sun, the moon and eleven stars paying homage to him – two images which prefigure his ascent (Genesis 37:5–11).

12. Christopher Marlowe, *The Jew of Malta*, ed. Richard W. Van Fossen (London: Edward Arnold, 1965), pp. 8–9.

13. Francis Bacon, *Essays* (London: Oxford University Press, n.d.), p. 18.

14. Thomas Kyd, *The Spanish Tragedy*, ed. J.R. Mulryne (London: A. & C. Black, New York: W.W. Norton & Company, 1989), p. 9.

15. Virgil, *The Aenaeid*, Book VI, vv. 893–6. Translated by John Dryden.

16. Kyd, *The Spanish Tragedy*, p. 85.

17. Here Saint Paul is quoting in turn Deuteronomy 32:35.

18. William Shakespeare, *Hamlet*, in *The Norton Shakespeare*, general ed. Stephen Greenblatt (New York and London: W.W. Norton & Company, 1997), pp. 1703–4.

19. Ibid., p. 1715.

20. Cyril Tourneur, *The Atheist's Tragedy*, eds Brian Morris and Roma Gill (London: Ernest Benn, New York: W.W. Norton & Company, 1976), p. 51.

21. Ibid., p. 52.

22. Ibid., p. 103.

23. *The Murder of John Brewen*, p. 15, in *Illustrations of Early English Popular Literature*, ed. J. Payne Collier, 2 vols (New York: Benjamin Blom, 1966), Vol. I.

24. Thomas Nashe, *The Unfortunate Traveller*, in *An Anthology of Elizabethan Prose Fiction*, ed. Paul Salzman (Oxford and New York: Oxford University Press, 1987), p. 303.

25. Ibid., p. 302.
26. Ibid., pp. 303–4.
27. Ibid., pp. 307–8.
28. Ibid., p. 308.
29. Ibid., p. 305.
30. The six books were published in the following order: Book 1 (1621), Book 2 (1622), Book 3 (1623), Books 4–6 (1635).
31. John Reynolds, *The Triumphs of Gods Revenge*, Book I (London: Felix Kyngston, 1621), p. 1
32. Albert Borowitz, *An International Guide to Fact-based Crime Literature*, Note by Jacques Barzun, Foreword by Jonathan Goodman (Kent, OH: Kent State University Press, 2002), p. 5.
33. Reynolds, 'Historie I', in *The Triumphs of Gods Revenge*, Book I, p. 47.
34. Reynolds, 'Historie V', in *The Triumphs of Gods Revenge*, Book I, p. 197.
35. Reynolds, 'Historie VII', in *The Triumphs of Gods Revenge*, Book II (London: Felix Kyngston, 1622), p. 93.
36. Reynolds, 'Historie IV', in *The Triumphs of Gods Revenge*, Book I, p. 165.
37. Reynolds, 'Historie I', in *The Triumphs of Gods Revenge*, Book I, p. 55.
38. John Reynolds, 'Historie XII', in *The Triumphs of Gods Revenge*, Book III (London: Felix Kyngston, 1623), p. 108.
39. See F.W. Chandler, *The Literature of Roguery*, 2 vols (New York: Burt Franklin, 1907), Vol. I, p. 4.
40. Hal Gladfelder, *Criminality and Narrative in Eighteenth-century England: Beyond the Law* (Baltimore: Johns Hopkins University Press, 2001), p. 33.
41. Ibid., p. 297.
42. Thomas Middleton, *The Last Will and Testament of Laurence Lucifer*, in *The Elizabethan Underworld*, ed. A.V. Judges (London and New York: Routledge, 2002), p. 302.
43. Due to the success of Richard Head's 1665 book, in 1668 Francis Kirkman, the bookseller, supplied a second part, while in 1671 a third and fourth part were jointly authored by Head and Kirkman.
44. Richard Head and Francis Kirkman, *The English Rogue* (London and New York: Routledge, 2002), p. 233.
45. Daniel Defoe, *Roxana. The Fortunate Mistress*, ed. David Blewett (Harmondsworth: Penguin, 1982), p. 379.
46. Daniel Defoe, *The Life, Adventures, and Pyracies of Captain Singleton*, ed. Shiv K. Kumar (London: Oxford University Press, 1969), p. 195.
47. See Stephen Knight, *Robin Hood: a Mythical Biography* (Ithaca and London: Cornell University Press, 2003).
48. The edition I consulted is a reprint of the 5th edition, published in 1719 (see note 50).
49. See also Christopher Hibbert, *Highwaymen* (New York: Delacorte Press, 1967).
50. Captain Alexander Smith, 'Whitney, A Highwayman', in *A Complete History of the Lives and Robberies of the Most Notorious Highwaymen, Footpads, Shoplifts and Cheats of Both Sexes*, ed. Arthur L. Hayward (London and New York: Routledge, 2002), p. 42.
51. Ibid., p. 44.
52. Captain Alexander Smith, 'Captain James Hind, Murderer and Highwayman', in *A Complete History of the Lives and Robberies of the Most Notorious Highwaymen, Footpads, Shoplifts and Cheats of Both Sexes*, pp. 136–40.

53. Gladfelder, *Criminality and Narrative in Eighteenth-century England*, p. 50.
54. Ibid., p. 49.
55. Knight, *Crime Fiction 1800–2000: Detection, Death, Diversity* (Basingstoke and New York: Palgrave Macmillan, 2004, p. 8.
56. *The Malefactor's Register; or, the Newgate and Tyburn Calendar*, 5 vols (London: Alexander Hogg, 1779), Vol. I, title page.
57. 'Singular Case of JOHN SMITH, called HALF-HANGED SMITH, who was convicted, but escaped Death in a most remarkable manner', in *The Malefactor's Register*, Vol. 1, pp. 89–92.
58. *The Malefactor's Register*, title page.
59. Ibid.
60. *The Malefactor's Register*, frontispiece.
61. 'A Narrative of the very singular Case of ROBERT FULLER, who was convicted on the Black Act, for shooting Francis Bailey; but recommended to Mercy', in *The Malefactor's Register*, Vol. III, pp. 53–5.
62. See *Dei delitti e delle pene*, Introduzione di Arturo Carlo Jemolo, Premessa al testo e note di Giulio Carnazzi (Milano: Rizzoli, 1981), p. 59.
63. Ibid.
64. William Godwin, *Enquiry Concerning Political Justice* (Harmondsworth: Penguin, 1976).
65. Gladfelder, *Criminality and Narrative in Eighteenth-century England*, pp. 5–6.
66. Ibid., p. 9.
67. 'THOMAS PICTON, ESQ. Late Governor of Trinidad. Convicted 24th of February, 1806, of applying Torture, in order to extort Confession from a Girl', in *The New Newgate Calendar* (1826), eds Andrew Knapp and William Baldwin. Online source: http://www.exclassics.com/newgate/ngintro.htm (visited 30.06.06).
68. 'Appendix IX. Torture', in *The New Newgate Calendar*.
69. 'Appendix XIII. Pretended Ghosts', in *The New Newgate Calendar*.
70. Pierre-Simon Laplace, *Philosophical Essay on Probabilities*, ed. Andrew I. Dale (New York and Berlin: Springer-Verlag, 1995), p. 78.
71. Heather Worthington, *The Rise of the Detective in Early Nineteenth-century Popular Fiction* (Basingstoke: Palgrave Macmillan, 2005), p. 46.
72. De Quincey subsequently integrated the essay with two other sections – a 'Supplementary Paper' (1839) and a 'Postscript' (1854).
73. Thomas De Quincey, *On Murder Considered as One of the Fine Arts*, in *The Complete Works*, 13 vols, Vol. IV (Edinburgh: Adam and Charles Black, 1862), p. 5.
74. Ibid., p. 8.
75. Ibid., p. 9.
76. Ibid., p. 26.
77. Worthington, *The Rise of the Detective in Early Nineteenth-century Popular Fiction*, p. 24.
78. See De Quincey, *On Murder Considered as one of the Fine Arts*, p. 9.

3 Persecution and omniscience

1. Michel Foucault, *Surveiller et punir: Naissance de la prison* (Paris: Gallimard, 1975), p. 32.

2. Henry Fielding, 'Examples of the Interposition of Providence in the Detection and Punishment of Murder', in *An Enquiry into the Causes of the late Increase of Robbers and Related Writings*, ed. Malvin R. Zirker (Oxford: Clarendon Press, 1988), p. 179.

3. Ibid., p. 180.

4. Ibid., p. 181.

5. Martin Kayman, *From Bow Street to Baker Street: Mystery, Detection and Narrative* (London: Macmillan, 1992), p. 63.

6. See Foucault, *Surveiller et punir*, p. 203.

7. Cited in Georges Jean, *Voyages en Utopie* (Paris: Gallimard, 1994), p. 73.

8. See Jean Starobinsky, *L'invention de la liberté* (Genève: Skira, 1964), p. 198.

9. See Ian Hacking, *The Emergence of Probability* (Cambridge: Cambridge University Press, 2006 [1975]).

10. Pierre-Simon Laplace, *Philosophical Essay on Probabilities* [1814–25], ed. Andrew I. Dale (New York and Berlin: Springer-Verlag, 1995), p. 2.

11. Ibid., p. 3.

12. Adam Phillips, 'Introduction', in Edmund Burke, *A Philosophical Enquiry into the Origin of our Ideas of the Sublime and Beautiful*, ed. Adam Phillips (Oxford and New York: Oxford University Press, 1990), p. xv.

13. Ibid., p. xxii.

14. Ibid., p. 59.

15. Ibid., p. 36.

16. Ibid., p. 62.

17. Ibid.

18. Ibid., pp. 63–4.

19. Ibid., p. 73.

20. Ibid., p. 54.

21. William Godwin, *Caleb Williams*, ed. David McCracken (Oxford and New York: Oxford University Press, 1970), p. 3.

22. Ibid., p. 340.

23. Ibid., p. 144.

24. Ibid., p. 281.

25. See B.J. Tysdahl, *William Godwin as Novelist* (London: Ahtlone, 1981), pp. 47–58.

26. David Punter, *The Literature of Terror: a History of Gothic Fictions from 1765 to the Present Day*, 2 vols (London and New York: Longman, 1996), Vol. I, p. 117.

27. Mary Shelley, *Frankenstein; or, The Modern Prometheus*, eds James Kinsley and M.K. Joseph (Oxford and New York: Oxford University Press, 1969), p. 100.

28. James Hogg, *The Private Memoirs and Confessions of a Justified Sinner*, ed. John Carey (Oxford: Oxford University Press, 1990), p. 89.

29. E.A. Poe, 'The Purloined Letter', in *The Complete Illustrated Stories and Poems* (London: Chancellor Press, 1994), pp. 326–7.

30. E.A. Poe, 'The Murders in the Rue Morgue', in *The Complete Illustrated Stories and Poems*, p. 78.

31. Ibid., p. 77.

32. Poe, 'The Purloined Letter', p. 320.

33. E.A. Poe, 'A Chapter of Suggestions', in *The Complete Works*, ed. James A. Harrison, 17 vols (New York: AMS Press, 1965), Vol. XIV, p. 187.

34. E.A. Poe, 'The Man of the Crowd', in *The Complete Illustrated Stories and Poems*, p. 217.

35. See Poe, 'The Murders in the Rue Morgue', pp. 92–3.
36. E.A. Poe, 'The Mystery of Marie Rogêt', in *The Complete Illustrated Stories and Poems*, p. 506.
37. Ibid., pp. 521–2.
38. E.A. Poe, *Eureka*, in *The Complete Works*, ed. James A. Harrison, 17 vols (New York: AMS Press, 1965), Vol. XVI, p. 292.
39. Nicola Bown, Carolyn Burdett and Pamela Thurschwell, 'Introduction', in *The Victorian Supernatural*, eds Bown, Burdett and Thurschwell (Cambridge: Cambridge University Press, 2004), p. 5.
40. Poe, 'The Mystery of Marie Rogêt', p. 522.
41. Ibid.
42. Ibid. p. 506.
43. T.S. Eliot, 'Wilkie Collins and Dickens', in *Selected Essays* (London: Faber and Faber, 1932), p. 464.
44. R.L. Stevenson, *The Dynamiter* (Phoenix Mill, Stroud, Gloucestershire: Alan Sutton, 1984), p. 5.
45. Ibid., p. 6.
46. A.C. Doyle, 'The Adventure of the Cardboard Box', in *Sherlock Holmes: the Complete Illustrated Short Stories* (London: Chancellor Press, 1985), p. 257.
47. A.C. Doyle, 'The Adventure of the Final Problem', in *Sherlock Holmes: the Complete Illustrated Short Stories*, p. 423.
48. Stevenson, *The Dynamiter*, p. 25.
49. Ibid., p. 26.
50. A.C. Doyle, *A Study in Scarlet*, in *Sherlock Holmes: the Complete Illustrated Novels* (London: Chancellor Press, 1987), p. 74.
51. Ibid., p. 73.
52. Ibid., p. 24.
53. Ibid., p. 27.
54. Ibid., p. 41.
55. Ibid., p. 58.
56. Stevenson, *The Dynamiter*, p. 1.

4. Victorian ghosts and revengers

1. 'A ballad about William Corder (1828)'; online at http://gaslight.mtroyal.ab.ca/martbald.htm (visited 14.6.06).
2. Martin Kayman, *From Bow Street to Baker Street: Mystery, Detection and Narrative* (London: Macmillan, 1992), p. 5.
3. Julia Briggs, *Night Visitors: the Rise and Fall of the English Ghost Story* (London: Faber and Faber, 1977), p. 19.
4. W.G. Simms, 'Grayling; or, "Murder Will Out" ', online at http://arthurwendover.com/arthur/simms/wigwam10.html (visited 01.05.05), p. 1.
5. Ibid., p. 18.
6. Ibid., p. 1.
7. See Nicholas Rance, *Wilkie Collins and Other Sensation Novelists* (Basingstoke: Macmillan, 1991), pp. 60–3.
8. See Peter Brooks, *The Melodramatic Imagination: Balzac, Henry James, Melodrama and the Mode of Excess* (New Haven and London: Yale University Press, 1976), pp. 14–15.

9. William Wilkie Collins, *Armadale*, ed. Catherine Peters (Oxford and New York: Oxford University Press, 1989), p. 662.

10. See Tzvetan Todorov, *Introduction à la littérature fantastique* (Paris: Seuil, 1970).

11. William Wilkie Collins, *The Woman in White*, ed. John Sutherland (Oxford: Oxford University Press, 1996), p. 20.

12. Ibid., p. 79.

13. Ibid., p. 236.

14. Ibid., p. 278.

15. See 'Murder Will Out: Being singular instances of the manner in which concealed crimes have been detected' (*Cassell's Illustrated Family Papers*, 160, 22 December 1860), cited in Beth Kalikoff, *Murder and Moral Decay in Victorian Popular Literature* (Ann Arbor, Michigan: UMI Research Press, 1986), p. 74.

16. Anna Katharine Green, *The Leavenworth Case: a Lawyer's Story*, ed. Michele Slung (New York: Dover, 1981), pp. 146–8.

17. Ibid., p. 315.

18. The story simultaneously appeared in the States as 'The Dead Alive'.

19. See William Wilkie Collins, 'John Jago's Ghost', in *The Complete Shorter Fiction*, ed. Julian Thompson (New York: Carroll & Graf, 1995), pp. 435–74.

20. Mary Elizabeth Braddon, 'Levison's Victim', in *Victorian Detective Stories: an Oxford Anthology*, ed. Michael Cox (Oxford and New York: Oxford University Press, 1993), p. 83.

21. E.A. Poe, 'The Purloined Letter', in *The Complete Illustrated Stories and Poems* (London: Chancellor Press, 1994), p. 333.

22. A.C. Doyle, *A Study in Scarlet*, in *Sherlock Holmes: the Complete Illustrated Novels* (London: Chancellor Press, 1987), p. 99.

23. Ibid., p. 99.

24. Ibid., p. 102.

25. Ibid., p. 99.

26. Ibid., p. 103.

27. Ibid.

5. Pseudo-sciences and the occult

1. Thomas Carlyle, *Sartor Resartus*, eds Kerry McSweeney and Peter Sabor (Oxford: Oxford University Press, 1987), p. 199.

2. See 'Introduction', in *The Victorian Supernatural*, eds Nicola Bown, Carolyn Burdett and Pamela Thurschwell (Cambridge: Cambridge University Press, 2004), pp. 1–19.

3. See Patrizia Guarnieri, *Introduzione a James* (Roma and Bari: Laterza, 1985), p. 40.

4. *Studi sull'ipnotismo* (*Studies on Hypnotism*, 1886); *Ricerche sui fenomeni ipnotici e spiritici* (*Researches on Hypnotic and Spiritual Phenomena*, 1909).

5. *Delitto, genio, follia: Scritti scelti*, a cura di Delia Frigessi, Ferruccio Giacanelli, Luisa Mangoni (Torino: Bollati Boringhieri, 1995), p. 315.

6. Nathaniel Hawthorne, *The House of the Seven Gables*, ed. Milton R. Stern (Harmondsworth: Penguin, 1981), p. 91.

7. E.A. Poe, *Eureka*, in *The Complete Works*, 17 vols., Vol. XVI, p. 213.

8. Villiers De l'Isle-Adam, *L'Ève future*, Édition établie par Nadien Satiat (Paris: Flammarion, 1992), p. 240.

9. Ambrose Bierce, *The Devil's Dictionary* (New York: Dover, 1993), p. 29.
10. Max Nordau, *Degeneration* (London: Heinemann, 1895), pp. 13–4.
11. See Beryl Gray, 'Afterword', in George Eliot, *The Lifted Veil*, ed. Beryl Gray (London: Virago Press, 1985), p. 69.
12. Eliot, *The Lifted Veil*, p. 65.
13. Charles Dickens, 'The Trial for Murder', in *The Complete Ghost Stories*, ed. Peter Haining (New York and Toronto: Franklin Watts, 1983), p. 292.
14. Charles Dickens, Letter to Émile de la Rue (10 February 1845), cited in Louise Henson, 'Investigations and Fictions: Charles Dickens and Ghosts', in *The Victorian Supernatural*, p. 51.
15. See James Esdaile, From *Mesmerism in India*, in *Literature and Science in the Nineteenth Century: an Anthology*, ed. Laura Otis (Oxford: Oxford University Press, 2002), pp. 410–14.
16. William Wilkie Collins, *The Moonstone*, ed. Anthea Trodd (Oxford and New York: Oxford University Press, 1982), p. 19.
17. Ibid., p. 5.
18. Ibid., p. 521.
19. Geraldine Jewsbury, unsigned review (*Athenaeum*, 106, 25 July 1868), in *Wilkie Collins: the Critical Heritage*, ed. Norman Page (London and Boston: Routledge and Kegan Paul, 1974), p. 170.
20. William Wilkie Collins, *The Haunted Hotel: a Mystery of Modern Venice* (New York: Dover, 1982), pp. 107–8.
21. Daniel Pick, *Svengali's Web: the Alien Enchanter in Modern Culture* (New Haven and London: Yale University Press, 2000), p. 4.
22. Bram Stoker, *Dracula*, ed. Maurice Hindle (Harmondsworth: Penguin, 1993), pp. 246–7.
23. Ibid., p. 389.
24. See Ibid., p. 401.
25. Ibid., p. 147.
26. See *The Penguin Book of Vampire Stories*, ed. Alan Ryan (Harmondsworth: Penguin, 1987).
27. See Maurice Hindle, 'Introduction', in Stoker, *Dracula*, p. xxv.
28. Collins, *The Woman in White*, p. 617.
29. Ibid., p. 221.
30. See Ibid., pp. 223–4.
31. A.C. Doyle, *The Parasite* (New York: Harper & Brothers, 1895), p. 3.
32. Ibid., p. 4.
33. Ibid., pp. 3–4.
34. Ibid., p. 7.
35. Ibid., p. 5.
36. Ibid., p. 6.
37. Ibid., p. 72.
38. A.C. Doyle, *The Coming of the Fairies* (London: Pavilion Books, 1996), p. 3.
39. Ibid., p. 7.
40. Ibid.
41. Ibid., p. 8.
42. Ibid., p. 100. Doyle dealt with 'spirit photography' also in Chapter V of *The History of Spiritualism* (1926), Vol. II, online at http://www.horrormasters. com/Text/a0014.pdf (visited 05.09.06), p. 2.

43. Sheridan Le Fanu, 'Mr Justice Harbottle', in *In a Glass Darkly*, ed. Robert Tracy (Oxford and New York: Oxford University Press, 1993), p. 83.
44. Sheridan Le Fanu, 'The Familiar', in *In a Glass Darkly*, p. 40.
45. Michael Cox and R.A. Gilbert, 'Introduction', in *Victorian Ghost Stories: an Oxford Anthology*, eds Michael Cox and R.A. Gilbert (Oxford: Oxford University Press, 1991), p. xviii.
46. Edward Bulwer-Lytton, 'The Haunted and the Haunters', in *The Mystery Book*, ed. H. Douglas Thomson (London: Odhams Press, 1934), p. 917.
47. Ibid., p. 918.
48. Ibid., p. 924.
49. Ibid., p. 925.
50. Ibid., p. 927.
51. Marie Roberts, *Gothic Immortals: the Fiction of the Brotherhood of the Rosy Cross* (London and New York: Routledge, 1990), p. 193.
52. Bulwer-Lytton, 'The Haunted and the Haunters', p. 927.
53. A.C. Doyle, *Round the Red Lamp, Being Facts and Fancies of Medical Life* (Freeport, New York: Books for Libraries Press, 1969), pp. 205–6, online at http://etext.lib.virginia.edu/toc/modeng/public/DoyLamp.html (visited 10.10.06).
54. Ibid., p. 224.
55. Ibid., p. 216.
56. Ibid., p. 246.
57. Ibid., p. 254.
58. Ibid., p. 262.
59. Ibid., p. 205.
60. Hesketh and Katherine Prichard, 'The Story of the Spaniards, Hammersmith', in *The Experiences of Flaxman Low*, ed. Jack Adrian (Ashcroft, British Columbia: Ash-Tree Press, 2003), p. 1.
61. Ibid., p. 4.
62. Hesketh and Katherine Prichard, 'The Story of Baelbrow', in *The Experiences of Flaxman Low*, p. 3.
63. Hesketh and Katherine Prichard, 'The Story of Konnor Old House', in *The Experiences of Flaxman Low*, p. 2.
64. Hesketh and Katherine Prichard, in 'The Story of Yand Manor House', in *The Experiences of Flaxman Low*, p. 9.
65. The volume included only five stories, while 'A Victim of Higher Space', also featuring Silence, was first published in *Day and Night Stories* (1917).
66. Algernon Blackwood, 'A Psychical Invasion', in *The Complete John Silence Stories*, ed. S.T. Joshi (Mineola, NY: Dover, 1997), p. 1.
67. Briggs, *Night Visitors*, p. 63.
68. Blackwood, 'The Nemesis of Fire', p. 92.
69. See Ibid., p. 119.
70. Ibid., p. 101.
71. Ibid., p. 95.
72. Blackwood, 'A Psychical Invasion', p. 42.
73. Ibid., p. 43.
74. See Blackwood, 'The Nemesis of Fire', p. 84.
75. Ibid., p. 99.
76. W.H. Hodgson, 'The Searcher of the End House', in *Carnacki: the Ghost Finder* (Doulestown, Penn.: Wildside Press, 2000), p. 136.

77. W.H. Hodgson, 'The Gateway of the Monster', in *Carnacki*, p. 17.
78. W.H. Hodgson, 'The Horse of the Invisible', in *Carnacki*, p. 93.
79. W.H. Hodgson, 'The Whistling Room', in *Carnacki*, p. 69.
80. Sax Rohmer, 'Case of the Tragedies in the Greek Room', in *The Dream-Detective. Being some account of the methods of Moris Klaw* (London: Jarrolds, 1920), p. 21.
81. See Gerry Vassilatos, *Lost Science* (Kempton, IL.: Adventures Unlimited, 1999).
82. Rohmer, 'The Case of the Tragedies in the Greek Room', p. 23.
83. H.P. Lovecraft, *Supernatural Horror in Literature* (New York: Dover, 1973), p. 97.
84. See 'Supernatural Detectives', at http://members.aol.com/MG4273/weirdmen. htm (visited 02.11.04).
85. Haycraft, *The Art of the Mystery Story*, p. 194.
86. L.T. Meade and Robert Eustace, 'The Horror of Studley Grange' ('Stories from the Diary of a Doctor', VII), *The Strand Magazine*, 7 (January-June 1894), p. 8.
87. Ibid., p. 16.
88. See Upamanyu Pablo Mukherjee, *Crime and Empire: the Colony in Nineteenth-century Fictions of Crime* (Oxford: Oxford University Press, 2003).
89. Steven Connor, 'Afterword', in *The Victorian Supernatural*, eds. Bown, Burdett and Thurschwell, p. 258.

6. The language of Auguste Dupin

1. See Martin Kayman, *From Bow Street to Baker Street: Mystery, Detection and Narrative* (London: Macmillan, 1992), p. 105.
2. See Stephen Knight, 'General Introduction', in *Two Centuries of Detective Fiction: a New Comparative Approach*, ed. Maurizio Ascari (Bologna: COTEPRA, 2000), p. 8.
3. See Stephen Knight, *Crime Fiction 1800–2000: Dectection, Death, Diversity* (Basingstoke and New York: Palgrave Macmillan 2004), p. 17.
4. 'Sensations d'un Américain pendu', *Le magasin pittoresque* (1838), p. 178. See Henry Thomson, 'Le revenant', in *Tales of Terror from Blackwood's Magazine*, eds Robert Morrison and Chris Baldick (Oxford: Oxford University Press, 1995), p. 80.
5. See Chris Willis, 'Afterword', in Mary Elizabeth Braddon, *The Trail of the Serpent*, ed. Chris Willis, Introduction by Sarah Waters (New York: The Modern Library, 2003), p. 409. See also: Anon. [Charles Reade], *The Courier of Lyons; or, the attack upon the mail. A Drama. In four acts. Translated from the French of Messieurs Moreau, Siraudin, & Delacour* (London: Lacy, 1850), online at http://www.worc.ac.uk/victorian/victorianplays/Vol15xCourier.pdf (visited 21.09.06).
6. The texts of the two plays are compared in the following website: http://www.hull.ac.uk/cpt/transla/trans1.html (visited 21.09.06).
7. See R.L. Stevenson, *The Dynamiter* (1885); reprint (Phoenix Mill, Stroud, Gloucester: Allan Sutton, 1984), pp. 16–44.
8. A.C. Doyle, *A Study in Scarlet* (1887); reprint, in *Sherlock Holmes: the Complete Illustrated Novels* (London: Chancellor Press, 1987), p. 17.
9. Émile Gaboriau, *L'affaire Lerouge* (Paris: Liana Levi, 1991), p. 39.
10. Régis Messac, *Le 'detective novel' et l'influence de la pensée scientifique* (Paris: Champion, 1929), p. 425.

11. See William Russell, *Recollections of a Detective Police-officer* (London: Covent Garden Press, 1972).
12. (Paris: A. Cadot, 1859), 2 vols.
13. *Autobiography of a French Detective from 1818 to 1858* (New York: Arno Press 1976); Louis Canler, *Mémoires* (Paris: Mercure de France, 1986).
14. A.C. Doyle, 'The Adventure of the Greek Interpreter', in *Sherlock Holmes: the Complete Illustrated Short Stories* (London: Chancellor Press, 1985), p. 379.
15. Robert Barr, *The Triumphs of Eugène Valmont*, ed. Stephen Knight (Oxford and New York: Oxford University Press, 1997), p. 3.
16. Ponson du Terrail, *Les exploits de Rocambole*, édition prèsentée et établie par Laurent Bazin (Paris: Laffont, 1992), p. 8.
17. Ibid., p. 9.
18. See Martin Priestman, *Crime Fiction from Poe to the Present* (Plymouth: Northcote House, 1998), p. 10.
19. Anon., 'Murder and Mystery' (*Fraser's Magazine*, 1841, pp. 547–59), in *Murder and Mystery: Nineteenth-century Short Crime Stories*, eds Stephen Knight and Heather Worthington (Cardiff Papers in English Literature No. 5, 2001).
20. *Tales by Edgar A. Poe* (New York: Wiley and Putnam, 1845).
21. See Daniel Compère, 'Poe traduit et introduit en France', *Le Rocambole*, ns 11 (summer 2000), p. 12; and I.M. Walker, 'Introduction', in *Edgar Allan Poe: the Critical Heritage* (London and New York: Routledge and Kegan Paul, 1986), pp. 34–5.
22. Émile Forgues, 'Études sur le roman anglais et américain. Les contes d Edgar A. Poe', *Revue des deux mondes*, 16 (Octobre-Décembre 1846), p. 341.
23. Ibid., p. 343.
24. Ibid., p. 342.
25. Ibid., p. 365.
26. See Ibid., pp. 353–54.
27. Ibid., p. 353.
28. See Arnaud Huftier, 'Poe dans le *Magasin pittoresque* (1845): L Esprit de la *Lettre volée*', *Le Rocambole*, ns 11 (summer 2000), p. 164.
29. E.A. Poe, 'Une lettre volée', *Le Rocambole*, ns 11 (summer 2000), p. 168.
30. See Compère, 'Poe traduit et introduit en France', p. 12.
31. Poe, 'Une lettre volée', p. 173.
32. See Ibid., p. 176.
33. E.A. Duyckinck, 'An Author in Europe and America' (*Home Journal*, 9 January 1847), in *Edgar Allan Poe: the Critical Heritage*, p. 267.
34. See T.D. English/E.A. Poe, 'Review in the *Aristidean*' (October 1845), in *Edgar Allan Poe: the Critical Heritage*, p. 193.
35. See E.A. Poe, *Oeuvres en prose*, traduites par Charles Baudelaire, texte établi et annoté par Y.-G. Le Dantec (Paris: Gallimard, 1951), p. 1149.
36. In addition to Baudelaire's translations, in 1854–55 'La lettre dérobée' and 'L'Assassinat de la Rue Morgue' were published in *Le Mousquetaire*.
37. Cited in Poe, *Oeuvres en prose*, p. 1069.
38. William Wilkie Collins, 'A Stolen Letter', in *The Complete Shorter Fiction*, ed. Julian Thompson (New York: Carroll & Graf, 1995), p. 142.
39. Sir Edward Bulwer-Lytton, *Lucretia; or, the Children of the Night*, in *Cult Criminals: the Newgate Novels 1830–1847*, 6 vols, ed. Juliet John (London and New York: Routledge, 1998), Vol. III, p. 4.

40. W.W. Collins, *The Woman in White* (1860), ed. Harvey Peter Sucksmith (Oxford and New York: Oxford University Press, 1973), p. 436.

41. Maurice Méjan, 'Affaire de madame de Douhault', in *Recueil des causes célèbres et des arrêts qui les ont décidées*, tome III (Paris: Plisson, 1808), p. 15, online at http://gallica.bnf.fr/ark:/12148/bpt6k49870b (visited 23.03.07).

42. Ibid., p. 17.

43. See Collins, *The Woman in White*, p. 435.

44. William Wilkie Collins, *The Queen of Hearts*, in *The Works*, 30 vols (New York: AMS Press, 1970), Vol. XIV, pp. 5–6.

45. William Wilkie Collins, *La Femme en blanc* (Paris: Hetzel, 1861), pp. vi–vii, online at http://www.deadline.demon.co.uk/wilkie/WiW/frtxt.htm (visited 10.12.04).

46. Émile Forgues, 'Études sur le roman anglais. William Wilkie Collins', *Revue des deux mondes*, 12 (Octobre-Décembre 1855), p. 835.

47. See Émile Forgues, 'Littérature anglaise. Dégénérescence du roman', *Revue des deux mondes*, 40 (1 August 1862), p. 703.

48. Émile Forgues, 'Le roman anglais contemporain. Miss M.E. Braddon et le roman à sensation', *Revue des deux mondes*, 45 (1 May 1863), p. 964.

49. Ibid., p. 974.

50. Ibid., p. 975.

51. Ibid., p. 977.

52. William Wilkie Collins, *My Miscellanies*, in *The Works*, Vol. XX, p. 159.

53. Ibid., p. 172.

54. Ibid., p. 174.

55. Ibid., p. 176.

56. Henry L. Williams, Jr, *The Steel Safe; or, The stains and splendors of New York Life. A story of our day and night* (New York: Robert M. De Witt, 1868), p. 3.

57. See Stephen Knight, *Continent of Mystery: a Thematic History of Australian Crime Fiction* (Victoria: Melbourne University Press, 1997), pp. 69–71.

58. E.A. Poe, *Marginalia*, in *The Complete Works*, Vol. XVI, p. 105 (emphasis in original).

59. See Knight, *Crime Fiction 1800–2000*, pp. 25, 37.

60. See Domenico Giuriati, 'Un pagamento a Londra', in *Memorie di un vecchio avvocato* (Milano: F.lli Treves, 1888), pp. 109–37.

61. See entry 'Flâneur', in Pierre Larousse, *Grand Dictionnaire universel du XIX siècle* (Paris: 1866–76).

62. G.K. Chesterton, 'A Defence of Detective Stories', in *The Art of the Mystery Story a Collection of Critical Essays*, ed. Howard Haycraft (New York: Simon and Schuster, 1946), p. 4.

7. On the sensational in literature

1. Lyn Pykett, 'The Newgate Novel and Sensation Fiction, 1830–1868', in *The Cambridge Companion to Crime Fiction*, ed. Martin Priestman (Cambridge: Cambridge University Press, 2003), p. 33.

2. William Wordsworth, 'Preface to Lyrical Ballads (1800)', in *The Prose Works*, 3 vols, eds W.J.B. Owen and Jane Worthington Smyser (Oxford: Clarendon Press, 1974), Vol. I, p. 128.

3. G.K. Craik, 'Old London Rogueries', in *London*, ed. Charles Knight, 6 vols, Vol. IV (London: Charles Knight, 1843), p. 146.

4. Henry Thomson, 'Le Revenant' (1827), in *Tales of Terror from Blackwood's Magazine*, eds Robert Morrison and Chris Baldick (Oxford: Oxford University Press, 1995), pp. 73–4.

5. E.A. Poe, 'How to Write a Blackwood's Article', in *The Complete Illustrated Stories and Poems* (London: Chancellor Press, 1994), p. 652.

6. Edward Bulwer-Lytton, *Lucretia; or, The Children of the Night*, in *Cult Criminals: the Newgate Novels 1830–1847*, ed. Juliet John, 6 vols (London and New York: Routledge, 1998), III, p. x.

7. See Andrew Motion, *Wainewright the Poisoner* (New York: Alfred A. Knopf, 2000).

8. See Charles Swann, 'Wainewright the Poisoner: a Source for Blandois/Rigaud?', *Notes and Queries*, 35 (233) (3 September 1988): 321–2.

9. Bulwer-Lytton, *Lucretia*, p. 8.

10. H.L. Mansel, 'Sensation Novels', *Quarterly Review*, 113:226 (April 1863), p. 490.

11. G.A. Sala, 'The Cant of Modern Criticism' (*Belgravia*, November 1867), in M.E. Braddon, *Aurora Floyd*, eds Richard Nemesvari and Lisa Surridge (Peterborough, Ont.: Broadview, 1998), Appendix B. Reviews and responses, p. 614.

12. Henry James, 'Miss Braddon' (*Nation*, 9 November 1865), in *Wilkie Collins: the Critical Heritage*, ed. Norman Page (London and Boston: Routledge and Kegan Paul, 1974), p. 122.

13. Mansel, 'Sensation Novels', pp. 488–9.

14. Ibid., p. 489.

15. Ibid., p. 501.

16. Ibid., p. 483.

17. Ibid., p. 482.

18. Clive Bloom, *Cult Fiction: Popular Reading and Pulp Theory* (London: Macmillan, 1996), p. 50.

19. Ibid., p. 51.

20. Unsigned Review [W. Fraser Rae], 'Sensation Novelists: Miss Braddon' (*North British Review*, September 1865), in M.E. Braddon, *Aurora Floyd*, p. 592.

21. Unsigned Review, 'Novels', *Blackwood's Edinburgh Magazine*, 94:574 (August 1863): 168.

22. See Henry James, 'Matilde Serao', in *Notes on Novelists: With Some Other Notes* (New York: Biblo and Tannen, 1969), pp. 294–313.

23. Unsigned Review, 'Novels', *Blackwood's Edinburgh Magazine*, 102:623 (September 1867): 258.

24. John Ruskin, 'Fiction, Fair and Foul I', in *The Complete Works*, 30 vols (New York: Thomas Y Crowell & Co, s.d.), Vol. 28, pp. 187–8.

25. Ibid., p. 179.

26. Edward Bulwer-Lytton, 'A Word to the Public', in *Cult Criminals*, ed. Juliet John, Vol. III, p. 306.

27. Ibid., p. 309.

28. Ibid., p. 313.

29. Ibid., p. 314.

30. Ibid., p. 307.

31. James, 'Miss Braddon', p. 123.

32. Unsigned Review, 'Past "Sensationalists"', *The Argosy*, 5 (December 1867): 49.

33. Ibid., p. 51.

34. Ibid., p. 53.
35. Ibid., p. 55.
36. Ibid., p. 56.
37. G.A. Sala, 'On the "Sensational" in Literature and Art', *Belgravia*, 4 (February 1868): 456.
38. Ibid., pp. 457–8.
39. M.E. Braddon, 'The Sensation Novel', *The Argosy*, 18 (July-December 1874): 142.
40. Ibid., p. 143.
41. Unsigned review, 'Novels', *Blackwood's Edinburgh Magazine*, 94:574 (August 1863): 168–9.
42. Ibid., p. 169.
43. Patricia Craig and Mary Cadogan, *The Lady Investigates: Women Detectives and Spies in Fiction* (Oxford and New York: Oxford University Press, 1986), p. 30.
44. Unsigned review, 'Novels': 169–70.
45. Unsigned review [Margaret Oliphant], 'Sensation Novels', *Blackwood's Edinburgh Magazine*, 91:559 (May 1862): 568.
46. Jennifer Carnell, *The Literary Lives of Mary Elizabeth Braddon: a Study of Her Life and Work* (Hastings: The Sensation Press, 2000), p. 239.
47. Ibid.
48. M.E. Braddon, *Rough Justice*, 2 vols (Leipzig: Tauchnitz, 1898), Vol. I, p. 154.
49. M.E. Braddon, *His Darling Sin* (Hastings: The Sensation Press, 2001), p. 44.
50. Ibid., p. 120.
51. Ronald R. Thomas, *Detective Fiction and the Rise of Forensic Science* (Cambridge: Cambridge University Press, 1999), p. 3.
52. Braddon, *Rough Justice*, Vol. I, p. 165.
53. Braddon, *His Darling Sin*, p. 8.
54. F.C. Burnand's 'Mokeanna; Or, The White Witness' was serialised in *Punch* from 21 February to 21 March 1863. It was also republished a few years later in book form as *Mokeanna! A treble temptation. &c., &c., &c.* (London: Bradbury, Agnew, & Co., 1873).
55. Leonée Ormond, *George Du Maurier* (London: Routledge and Kegan Paul, 1969), pp. 145–8.
56. M.E. Braddon, *The Doctor's Wife*, ed. Lyn Pykett (Oxford: Oxford University Press, 1998), p. 11.
57. Ibid., p. 12.
58. Ibid., p. 45.
59. Ibid., p. 48.
60. See Bret Harte, *Condensed Novels* (New York: P.F. Collier & Son, 1902), pp. 57–73, 163–83.
61. Frederick Paget, *Lucretia; or, The Heroine of the Nineteenth Century: a Correspondence, Sensational and Sentimental* (London: Joseph Masters, 1868), p. 112.
62. Ibid., p. 303.
63. W.S. Gilbert, *A Sensation Novel*, online at http://diamond.ibdsu.edu/GaS/other_gilbert/sensation/sensation_novel.html (visited 04.07.04).
64. Ibid.
65. See Andrew Lang, *Old Friends: Essays in Epistolary Parody* (London: Longmans, Green, and Co., 1913), pp. 146–54.
66. See William M. Clarke, *The Secret Life of Wilkie Collins* (London: Allison & Busby, 1988), pp. 134–9.

67. See Julian Thompson, Note on 'The Dream Woman', in *Wilkie Collins. The Complete Shorter Fiction*, ed. Julian Thompson (New York: Carroll and Graf, 1995), p. 143.
68. See Julian Thompson, Note on 'The Frozen Deep', in *Wilkie Collins. The Complete Shorter Fiction*, p. 475.
69. The note is included in 'Appendix A', in Collins, *The Woman in White*, p. 635.
70. ' "Lady Audley". On the stage' (*London Review*, 7 March 1863), in *Varieties of Women's Sensation Fiction: 1855–1890*, general ed. Andrew Maunder, 6 vols (London: Pickering & Chatto, 2004), Vol. I, *Sensationalism and the Sensation Debate*, ed. Andrew Maunder, p. 30.
71. Ned Albert, *East Lynne: Mrs. Henry Wood's Celebrated Novel Made into a Spirited and Powerful Mellow Drammer in Three Acts* (New York and London: Samuel French, 1941), p. 3.

8.   London as a 'heart of darkness'

1. See Thomas Dekker, 'An Episode taken from The Bellman of London', in *The Elizabethan Underworld*, ed. A.V. Judges (London and New York: Routledge, 2002), pp. 303–11.
2. A second volume was published by Dekker in the same year, 'Lantern and Candlelight, or The Bellman's Second Night's Walk', in *The Elizabethan Underworld*, pp. 312–65.
3. G.W.M. Reynolds, *The Mysteries of London*, ed. Trefor Thomas (Keele, Staffordshire: Keele University Press, 1996), p. 4.
4. Ibid., p. 3.
5. Ibid., p. 4.
6. Thomas Beames, *The Rookeries of London* (London: Thomas Bosworth, 1852), pp. 2–3. online at http://www.victorianlondon.org/publications5/rookeries.htm (visited 15.10.05).
7. Augusto Aglebert, *Della Polizia in Inghilterra, in Francia e in Italia* (Bologna: Monti, 1868), p. 26.
8. Ibid., pp. 25–6.
9. Thomas Archer, *The Pauper, The Thief and The Convict*, p. 128, online at http://www.perseus.tufts.edu/cache/perscoll_Bolles.html (visited 18.10.05).
10. Ibid., p. 133.
11. See Joseph Salter, Extracts from *The East in the West*, in *The Metropolitan Poor: Semifactual Accounts, 1795–1910*, eds John Marriott and Masaie Matsumura, 6 vols (London: Pickering and Chatto, 1999), Vol. VI, pp. 373–99.
12. Gustave Doré and Blanchard Jerrold, *London. A Pilgrimage* (New York: Dover Publications, 1970), p. 144.
13. *The Policeman's Lantern* (1888) is the apt title Joseph Greenwood chose for a collection of London crime stories. Part of the text is included in *The Metropolitan Poor: Semifactual Accounts, 1795–1910*, eds John Marriott and Masaie Matsumura, 6 vols (London: Pickering and Chatto, 1999), II, pp. 416–40.
14. See 'Reports of the Select Committee of the House of Commons on Criminal and Destitute Juveniles' (1852), in *Human Documents of the Victorian Golden Age (1850–1875)*, ed. E. Royston Pike (London: George Allen & Unwin, 1967), p. 147.

15. Charles Dickens, 'On Duty with Inspector Field', in *Selected Journalism 1850–1870*, ed. David Pascoe (Harmondsworth: Penguin, 1997), p. 306.
16. Ibid., p. 307.
17. See Louis Laurent Simonin, 'Un'escursione ai quartieri poveri di Londra', in Edmondo De Amicis, *Ricordi di Londra*, prefazione di Natalia Milazzo (Milano: Messaggerie Pontremolesi, 1989), p. 70.
18. Like Jerrold and Doré, Sims was also travelling with a painter (Mr Frederick Barnard), who produced the many engravings that accompany the 1883 original edition of *How the Poor Live*. This edition is available on the website http://nils.lib.tufts.edu/cgi-bin/perscoll?collection=Perseus:collection:Bolles& type=text (visited 05.10.05).
19. George R. Sims, *How the Poor Live and Horrible London* (New York and London: Garland, 1984), pp. 10–11.
20. Ibid., p. 1.
21. Ibid., p. 3.
22. Jack London, *The People of the Abyss* (Miami: Synergy International of the Americas, 2000), p. 51.
23. Ibid., p. 11.
24. Ibid., p. 124.
25. See respectively Sims, *How the Poor Live*, p. 5 and London, *The People of the Abyss*, pp. 16–18.
26. Mayhew, Henry, *London Labour and the London Poor*, ed. John D. Rosenberg, 4 vols (New York: Dover, 1968), Vol. I, p. xv.
27. Ibid., Vol. I, p. 1.
28. Ibid., Vol. I, p. xv.
29. Ibid., Vol. I, p. xvi.
30. William Booth, *In Darkest England and the Way Out*, with an Introduction by General Erik Wickberg (London: Charles Knight & Co., 1970), pp. 11–12.
31. Ibid., p. 92.
32. Sir James Cantlie, *Degeneration amongst Londoners. A Lecture delivered at the Parkes Museum of Hygiene, January 27, 1885* (London: Field and Tuer, 1885), p. 24, online at http://www.perseus.tufts.edu/cache/perscoll_Bolles.html (visited 05.10.05).
33. See ibid., p. 16.
34. John Ruskin, 'Fiction, Fair and Foul I' (1880), in *The Complete Works*, 30 vols (New York: Thomas Y. Crowell & Co., n.d.), xxviii, p. 178.
35. A.C. Doyle, *A Study in Scarlet* (1887), in *Sherlock Holmes: the Complete Illustrated Novels* (London: Chancellor Press, 1987), p. 4.
36. Anonymous article (*Saturday Review*, 1862), cited in Daniel Pick, *Faces of Degeneration. A European Disorder, c. 1848–c. 1918* (Cambridge: Cambridge University Press, 1989), p. 178.
37. This image is analysed by Lynda Nead in *Victorian Babylon: People, Streets and Images in Nineteenth-century London* (New Haven and London: Yale University Press, 2000), pp. 212–25.
38. Joseph Conrad, *Heart of Darkness*, in *'Heart of Darkness' and Other Tales*, ed. Cedric Watts (Oxford and New York: Oxford University Press, 1990), p. 135.
39. Ibid., p. 138.
40. Joseph Conrad, 'Author's Note', in *The Secret Agent*, ed. Martin Seymour-Smith (Harmondsworth: Penguin, 1984), p. 41.

41. Joseph McLaughlin, *Writing the Urban Jungle: Reading Empire in London from Doyle to Eliot* (Charlottsville and London: University Press of Virginia, 2000), p. 5.
42. Ibid., p. 14.
43. See Mary Louise Pratt, *Imperial Eyes: Travel Writing and Transculturation* (London and New York: Routledge, 1992), pp. 4–7.

9. The rhetoric of atavism and degeneration

1. Georg Christoph Lichtenberg, *Über Physiognomik wider die Physiognomen* (1778), cited in Steven Decaroli, 'The Greek Profile: Hegel's Aesthetics and the Implications of a Pseudo-Science', in *The Philosophical Forum*, 2006, p. 124; online at http://www.blackwell-synergy.com/doi/pdf/10.1111/j.1467-9191.2006.00234.x (visited 01.10.06).
2. R.L. Stevenson, *The Strange Case of Dr Jekyll and Mr Hyde*, ed. Emma Letley (Oxford and New York: Oxford University Press, 1987), p. 19.
3. Bram Stoker, *Dracula* (1897), ed. Maurice Hindle (Harmondsworth: Penguin, 1993), p. 439.
4. Oscar Wilde, 'The Decay of Lying', in *The Complete Works*, Introduction by Vyvyan Holland (London and Glasgow: Collins, 1966), p. 973.
5. H.G. Wells, *The Island of Dr. Moreau*, afterword by Brian Aldiss (New York: Signet, 1988), p. 71.
6. Charles Baudelaire, 'Le crépuscule du soir' (from *Le Spleen de Paris: Petits Poèmes en Prose*), in *Oeuvres complètes*, texte établi et annoté par Y.G. Le Dantec (Paris: Gallimard, 1951), p. 307.
7. See Max Nordau, *Degeneration* (London: Heinemann, 1985), p. 16, p. 34 and ff.
8. Ibid., p. 435.
9. Ibid., pp. 435–36.
10. Cesare Lombroso, *Gli anarchici: Psicopatologia criminale d'un ideale politico*, commento di Francesco Novelli, con una testimonianza di Pietro Valpreda (Milano: Gallone, 1998), p. 7.
11. Lombroso, *Gli anarchici*, p. 23.
12. Ibid.
13. Ibid., p. 21.
14. *Criminal Man: According to the classification of Cesare Lombroso*, briefly summarised by Gina Lombroso Ferrero (New York and London: G. P. Putnam, The Knickerbocker Press, 1911).
15. See Cesare Lombroso, 'Sul tatuaggio in Italia, in ispecie fra i delinquenti' (1874), in *Delitto, Genio, Follia. Scritti scelti*, a cura di Delia Frigessi, Ferruccio Giacanelli, Luisa Mangoni (Torino: Bollati Boringhieri, 1995), pp. 426–9.
16. Ibid., p. 71.
17. Cesare Lombroso, *L'uomo di genio in rapporto alla psichiatria, alla storia ed all'estetica*, 2 vols (Roma: Napoleone editore, 1971), Vol. II, p. 354.
18. Ettore Sernicoli, *L'anarchia e gli anarchici* (Milano: Fratelli Treves, 1894), p. 19.
19. See Nordau, *Degeneration*, p. 241.
20. The book was published in London by W. Scott and in New York by C. Scribner's and Sons.
21. A case in point is Maxime Du Camp's questionable *Souvenirs littéraires* (*Literary Recollections*, 1882–83), which are repeatedly used to obtain information on French writers.

22. Lombroso, *L'uomo di genio in rapporto alla psichiatria, alla storia ed all'estetica* (1891); reprint, 2 vols (Roma: Napoleone editore, 1971), I, p. 15.
23. See Linda L. Maik, 'Nordau's *Degeneration*: the American Controversy', *Journal of the History of Ideas*, 50:4 (October–December 1989): 614.
24. Cesare Lombroso, *Genio e degenerazione* (Palermo: Sandron, 1907), p. 286.
25. Nordau, *Degeneration*, p. vii.
26. See Ibid., p. 29.
27. Ibid., p. 550.
28. Ibid., p. 559.
29. Ibid., p. 554.
30. Ibid.
31. M.P. Shiel, 'The Race of Orven', in *Prince Zaleski and Cummings King Monk* (Sauk City, Wisconsin: Mycroft & Moran, 1977), p. 4.
32. Ibid., p. 37.
33. Ibid., p. 38.
34. M.P. Shiel, 'The S.S.', in *Prince Zaleski and Cummings King Monk*, p. 107.
35. Robert Barr, 'The Siamese Twin of a Bomb-Thrower', in *The Triumphs of Eugène Valmont* (1906), ed. Stephen Knight (Oxford and New York: Oxford University Press, 1997), p. 56.
36. Ibid., p. 64.
37. Ibid.
38. Ibid., p. 33.
39. Ibid.
40. Pick, *Faces of Degeneration*, p. 27.
41. Ettore Sernicoli, *L'anarchia e gli anarchici*, 2 vols (Milano: Fratelli Treves, 1894), p. 52.
42. Francis Galton, Review of Havelock Ellis, *The Criminal* (1890) (*Nature*, 22 May 1890), p. 76, online at http://galton.org/bib/JournalItem.aspx_action=view_id=205 (visited 05.04.06).

Conclusion: the age of formula fiction

1. See Stephen Knight, 'Enter the Detective: Early Patterns of Crime Fiction', in Gustav S. Klaus and Stephen Knight (eds), *The Art of Murder: New Essays on Detective Fiction* (Tübingen: Stauffenberg Verlag, 1998), pp. 10–25.
2. See *Edgar Allan Poe. The Critical Heritage*, ed. I.M. Walker, (London and New York. Routledge and Kegan Paul, 1986)$$.
3. The story, which was reissued as 'The Great Pegram Case' in 1895, was followed by 'The Adventure of the Second Swag' in 1904. See Stephen Knight, 'Introduction', in Robert Barr, *The Triumphs of Eugène Valmont*, ed. Stephen Knight (Oxford and New York: Oxford University Press, 1997), pp. x–xi. The two parodies are included in this text (pp. 204–20).
4. The former appeared only ten years later in Doyle's autobiography, while the latter was published in a magazine in 1893. Both are included in *The Uncollected Sherlock Holmes*, ed. Richard Lancelyn Green (Harmondsworth Penguin, 1983), pp. 367–78.
5. See Bret Harte, *Condensed Novels* (1867); reprint (New York: P.F. Collies & Son, 1874), pp. 39–61.
6. A parody of Gillette's play was published as early as 1901. See M. Watson and E. La Serre, *Sheerluck Jones: a Dramatic Criticism in Four Paragraphs and as many Headlines* (London and New York: Peter Schoffer, 1982).

7. See http://en.wilkipedia.org/wiki/William_Gillette (visited 07.04.06).
8. Richard Lancelyn Green, 'Introduction', in *The Uncollected Sherlock Holmes*, ed. Richard Lancelyn Green, p. 83.
9. Gillette's farewell Holmes tour took place in 1929–30, thirty years after his first appearance in that role. He had played Holmes over 1300 times on stage and in 1916 he had even made a silent film version of the play.
10. Knox's essay was presented to the Gryphon Club in 1911, published in *The Blue Book Magazine* in 1912 and included in *Essays in Satire* in 1928. An e.text version of the essay is available on the website http://www.diogenes-club.com/studies.htm (visited 10.04.06).
11. Moreover she was the daughter of the Revd Henry Sayers, the director of the Christ Church Cathedral Choir School in Oxford.
12. G.K. Chesterton, 'A Defence of Detective Stories' (1902), in *The Art of the Mystery Story: a collection of Critical Essays*, ed. Howard Haycraft (New York: Simon and Schuster, 1946), pp. 3–4.
13. Ibid., p. 6.
14. G.K. Chesterton, 'Dedication', in *The Man Who Was Thursday: a Nightmare*, Introduction by Kingsley Amis (London: Penguin, 1986), pp. 5–6.
15. G.K. Chesterton, 'Extract from an article published in the *Illustrated London News* 13 June 1936', in *The Man Who Was Thursday*, p. 186.
16. For an insightful reading of this ambiguous novel see Heather Worthington, 'Anarchy in G.K. Chesterton's *The Man Who Was Thursday*', in *'To Hell with Culture': Anarchism and Twentieth Century British Literature*, eds H. Gustav Klaus and Stephen Knight (Cardiff: University of Wales Press, 2005), pp. 21–34.
17. G.K. Chesterton, 'The Blue Cross', in *The Complete Father Brown* (Harmondsworth: Penguin, 1981), p. 11.
18. See 'The Ethics of Elfland', the fourth chapter of *Orthodoxy* (London: Bodley Head, 1908) and the play *Magic: a Fantastic Comedy* (London: M. Secker, 1913).
19. Chesterton, 'The Blue Cross', p. 20.
20. G.K. Chesterton, 'The Secret of Father Brown', in *The Complete Father Brown*, pp. 465–6.
21. G.K. Chesterton, 'Sherlock Holmes', in *A Handful of Authors: Essays on Books and Writers*, ed. Dorothy Collins (London and New York: Sheed and Ward, 1953), p. 171.
22. Walter Pater, 'Conclusion', in *The Renaissance: Studies in Art and Poetry*, ed. Adam Phillips (Oxford and New York: Oxford University Press, 1986), p. 151.
23. Erskine Childers, *The Riddle of the Sands: a Record of Secret Service*, ed. David Trotter (Oxford and New York: Oxford University Press, 1998), p. 11.
24. John Buchan, *The Thirty-nine Steps*, ed. Christopher Harvie (Oxford and New York: Oxford University Press, 1993), p. 7.
25. Ibid., p. 86.
26. See Richard Usborne, *Clubland Heroes: a Nostalgic Study of the Recurrent Characters in the Romantic Fiction of Dornford Yates, John Buchan and 'Sapper'* (London: Constable, 1953).
27. Childers, *The Riddle of the Sands*, p. 71.
28. Buchan, *The Thirty-nine Steps*, p. 20.
29. See Wesley K. Wark, 'The Spy Thriller', in *Mystery and Suspense Writers: the Literature of Crime, Detection and Espionage I–II*, eds Robin W. Winks and Maureen Corrigan (New York: Charles Scribner's, 1998), p. 1201.

30. The Naval Intelligence Board was created in 1887 and the first Official Secrets Act was passed in 1889. The second Official Secrets Act (1911) led in turn to the creation of a counter-intelligence service, MI5, and of a secret intelligence service, MI6. See David A. Stafford, 'Spies and Gentlemen: the Birth of the British Spy Novel. 1893–1914', *Victorian Studies*, 24 (Summer 1981): 493–4.

31. Marjorie Nicholson, 'The Professor and the Detective', in *The Art of the Mystery Story*, ed. Howard Haycraft, p. 114.

32. Ibid., p. 118.

33. Ibid., p. 121.

34. Ibid., p. 122.

35. Ibid., p. 125.

36. Ibid., p. 124.

37. T.S. Eliot, 'Wilkie Collins and Dickens', in *Selected Essays* (London: Faber and Faber, 1932), p. 460.

38. Ibid., p. 464.

39. E.M. Wrong, 'Introduction', in *Crime and Detection* (Oxford: Oxford University Press, 1926), p. xiv.

40. See Willard Huntington Wright, 'Introduction', in *The Great Detective Stories: a Chronological Anthology* (New York: Charles Scribner's Sons, 1927), p. 4.

41. Ibid., p. 5.

42. Ibid., p. 6.

43. Ibid., p. 10.

44. Ibid., p. 11.

45. See 'Sherlock Holmes on Film', in *Sherlock Holmes: the Major Stories with Contemporary Critical Essays*, ed. John A. Hodgson (Boston and New York: Bedford Books of St. Martin's Press, 1994), pp. 437–41.

46. 'Conan Doyle's Speech at the Stoll Convention Dinner', in *The Uncollected Sherlock Holmes*, ed. Richard Lancelyn Green (Harmondsworth: Penguin, 1983), p. 299.

47. Dorothy Sayers, 'Introduction', in *Great Short Stories of Detection, Mystery and Horror* (London: Gollancz, 1928), p. 9.

48. Ibid., p. 19.

49. Haycraft, *The Art of the Mystery Story*, p. 128.

50. H.D. Thomson, *Masters of Mystery: a Study of the Detective Story* (London: Collins, 1931), p. 52.

51. Thomson, 'Introduction', in *The Mystery Book*, pp. 9–10.

52. Thomson underlined the 'time-honoured antiquity' of the detective story, dating its origin back to the times of Solomon. Ibid., p. 8.

53. Dorothy Sayers, 'Introduction', in *Great Short Stories of Detection, Mystery and Horror*, p. 37.

54. Ibid., p. 31.

55. Ford Madox Ford, 'Conrad and the Sea', in *Mightier than the Sword: Memories and Criticisms* (London: George Allen & Unwin, 1938), p. 95.

56. See Ford Madox Ford, *The March of Literature: from Confucius' Day to Our Own* (Normal: The Dalkey Archive Press, 1994), pp. 845–6.

57. E.M. Forster, *Aspects of the Novel* (London: Edward Arnold, 1927), p. 88.

58. Clive Bloom, *The Occult Experience and the New Criticism* (Sussex: Harvester Press, 1986), pp. 80–1.

59. An Italian translation of the essay, 'La novella dei misteri' is included in *La trama del delitto*, eds Renzo Cremante and Loris Rambelli (Parma: Pratiche, 1980), pp. 23–41.
60. See Stephen Knight, *Form and Ideology in Crime Fiction* (London: Macmillan, 1980), pp. 112–15.
61. Agatha Christie, *The Murder of Roger Ackroyd* (London: HarperCollins, 1957), p. 234.
62. Charles Osborne, *The Life and Crimes of Agatha Christie* (London: Collins, 1982), p. 63.
63. Julian Symons, *Bloody Murder: from the Detective Story to the Crime Novel: a History* (New York: Viking, 1985 [1972]), p. 15.
64. Michel Foucault, 'Two Lectures', in *Power/Knowledge: Selected Interviews and Other Writings 1972–1977*, ed. Colin Gordon (New York: Pantheon Books, 1980), p. 82.

Bibliography

Primary sources

Aglebert, Augusto, *Della Polizia in Inghilterra, in Francia e in Italia* (Bologna: Monti, 1868).

Albert, Ned, *East Lynne: Mrs. Henry Wood's Celebrated Novel Made into a Spirited and Powerful Mellow Drammer in Three Acts* (New York and London: Samuel French, 1941).

Anon. [Charles Reade], *The Courier of Lyons; or, the attack upon the mail. A Drama. In four acts. Translated from the French of Messieurs Moreau, Siraudin, & Delacour* (London: Lacy, 1850); online at http://www.worc.ac.uk/victorian/victorianplays/Vol15xCourier.pdf (visited 21.09.06).

Anon., *Everyman* (1495); reprint, *Everyman and Medieval Miracle Plays*, ed. A.C. Cawley (London and Melbourne: Dent, 1988).

Anon., *The Malefactor's Register; or, the Newgate and Tyburn Calendar*, 5 vols (London: Alexander Hogg, 1779).

Anon., *The Newgate Calendar*, ed. B. Laurie (London: T. Werner Laurie, 1932).

Anon., *The Wakefield Second Shepherds' Pageant*; reprint *Everyman and Medieval Miracle Plays*, ed. A.C. Cawley (London and Melbourne: Dent, 1988).

Archer, Thomas, *The Pauper, The Thief and The Convict* (1865); online at http://www.perseus.tufts.edu/cache/perscoll_Bolles.html (visited 18.10.05).

Bacon, Francis, *Essays* (1601); reprint (London: Oxford University Press, no date).

'A ballad about William Corder (1828)'; online at http://gaslight.mtroyal.ab.ca/martbald.htm (visited 14.06.06).

Barr, Robert, *The Triumphs of Eugène Valmont* (1906); reprint, ed. Stephen Knight (Oxford and New York: Oxford University Press, 1997).

Baudelaire Charles, *Le Spleen de Paris: Petits Poèmes en Prose* (1869); reprint in *Oeuvres complètes*, texte établi et annoté par Y.G. Le Dantec (Paris: Gallimard, 1951).

Beames, Thomas, *The Rookeries of London* (1850); reprint (London: Thomas Bosworth, 1852); online at http://www.victorianlondon.org/publications5/rookeries.htm (visited 15.10.05).

Beccaria, Cesare, *Dei delitti e delle pene* (1764); reprint, Introduzione di Arturo Carlo Jemolo, Premessa al testo e note di Giulio Carnazzi (Milano: Rizzoli, 1981).

Bierce, Ambrose, *The Devil's Dictionary* (New York: Dover, 1993).

——, 'The Hypnotist', in *The Parenticide Club* (1911); online at http://www.gutenberg.org/etext/3715 (visited 01.09.06).

Blackwood, Algernon, *John Silence – Physician Extraordinary* (1908); reprint, *The Complete John Silence Stories*, ed. S.T. Joshi (Mineola, New York: Dover, 1997).

Booth, Charles, *Life and Labour of the People in London*, 4 vols (London: Macmillan, 1902–04); online at http://nils.lib.tufts.edu/cgi-bin/perscoll?collection=Perseus:collection:Bolles&type=text (visited 15.10.05).

Booth, William, *In Darkest England* (1890); reprint, *In Darkest England and The Way Out*, Introduction by Erik Wickberg (London: Charles Knight & Co., 1970).

Braddon, Mary Elizabeth, *Aurora Floyd* (1863); reprint, ed. Richard Nemesvari and Lisa Surridge (Peterborough, Ont.: Broadview Press, 1998).

——, *His Darling Sin* (1899); reprint (Hastings: The Sensation Press, 2001).

——, *The Doctor's Wife* (1864); reprint, ed. Lyn Pykett (Oxford: Oxford University Press, 1998).

——, *Lady Audley's Secret* (1862); reprint, Introduction by Norman Donaldson (New York: Dover, 1974).

——, 'Levison's Victim' (1870); reprint, in *Victorian Detective Stories: an Oxford Anthology*, ed. Michael Cox (Oxford and New York: Oxford University Press, 1993).

——, *Rough Justice*, 2 vols (Leipzig: Tauchnitz, 1898).

——, *The Trail of the Serpent* (1861); reprint, ed. Chris Willis, Introduction by Sarah Waters (New York: The Modern Library, 2003).

Brisebarre, Édouard and Eugène Nus, *Le Courier de Lyons*, in *Drames de la vie* (Paris: Bourdilliat et Cie, 1860); online at http://www.hull.ac.uk/cpt/transla/noframes/txt1a.html (visited 21.09.06).

Brown, Charles Brockden, *Wieland; or, the Transformation* (1798); reprint, in *Wieland and Memoirs of Carwin the Biloquist*, ed. Jay Fliegelman (Harmondsworth: Penguin, 1991).

Brown, Dan, *The Da Vinci Code: a Novel* (2003); reprint (New York and London: Doubleday, 2004).

Buchan, John, *The Thirty-Nine Steps* (1915); reprint, ed. Christopher Harvis (Oxford and New York: Oxford University Press, 1993).

Bulwer-Lytton, Edward, 'The Haunted and the Haunters' (1859); reprint, in *The Mystery Book*, ed. H. Douglas Thomson (London: Odhams Press,1934).

——, *Lucretia; or, The Children of the Night* (1846); reprint, in *Cult Criminals: the Newgate Novels 1830–1847*, ed. Juliet John, 6 vols (London and New York: Routledge, 1998), Vol. III.

——, *Pelham, Or Adventures of a Gentleman* (1828); reprint (Kessinger Publishings, n.d.).

Burke, Edmund, *A Philosophical Enquiry into the Origin of our Ideas of the Sublime and the Beautiful* (1757); reprint, ed. Adam Phillips (Oxford and New York: Oxford University Press, 1990).

Burnand, F.C., 'Mokeanna; Or, The White Witness', *Punch* (21 February–21 March 1863).

Camden Pratt, A.T., *Unknown London: Its romance and tragedy* (London: Neville Beeman, 1896).

Canler, Louis, *Mémoires* (1862); reprint (Paris: Mercure de France, 1986).

Cantlie, James, *Degeneration amongst Londoners* (London: Field and Tuer, 1885); online at http://www.perseus.tufts.edu/cache/perscoll_Bolles.html (visited 05.10.05).

Carlyle, Thomas, *Sartor Resartus* (1833–34); reprint, eds Kerry McSweeney and Peter Sabor (Oxford: Oxford University Press, 1987).

Carr, Caleb, *The Italian Secretary: a Further Adventure of Sherlock Holmes* (London: Little, Brown, 2005).

Chaucer, Geoffrey, *The Canterbury Tales*, a verse translation, Introduction and Notes by David Wright (Oxford and New York, Oxford University Press, 1985.

Chesterton, G.K., 'A Defence of Detective Stories' (1902); reprint, in *The Art of the Mystery Story: a Collection of Critical Essays*, ed. Howard Haycraft (New York: Simon and Schuster, 1946).

——, *A Handful of Authors: Essays on Books and Writers*, ed. Dorothy Collins (London and New York: Sheed and Ward, 1953).

——, *The Innocence of Father Brown* (1911); reprint, in *The Complete Father Brown* (Harmondsworth: Penguin, 1981).

——, *Magic: a Fantastic Comedy* (London: M. Secker, 1913).

——, *The Man Who Was Thursday: a Nightmare* (1908); reprint, Introduction by Kingsley Amis (London: Penguin, 1986).

——, *Orthodoxy* (London: Bodley Head, 1908).

——, *The Secret of Father Brown* (1927); reprint, in *The Complete Father Brown* (Harmondsworth: Penguin, 1981).

Childers, Erskine, *The Riddle of the Sands: a Record of Secret Service* (1903); reprint, ed. David Trotter (Oxford and New York: Oxford University Press, 1998).

Christie, Agatha, *Endless Night* (1967); reprint (London: Fontana, 1970).

——, *The Murder of Roger Ackroyd* (1926); reprint (London: Fontana, 1957).

——, *The Sittaford Mystery* (1931); reprint (London: Fontana, 1994).

——, *Sleeping Murder* (London: Fontana, 1976).

Collins, William Wilkie, *Armadale* (1866); reprint, ed. Catherine Peters (Oxford and New York: Oxford University Press, 1989).

——, *La Femme En Blanc* (Paris: Hetzel, 1861).

——, *Basil* (1852); reprint, ed. Dorothy Goldman (Oxford and New York: Oxford University Press, 1990).

——, 'The Diary of Anne Rodway' (1856); reprint, in *The Complete Shorter Fiction*, ed. Julian Thompson (New York: Carroll & Graf, 1995).

——, 'The Dream Woman' (1855); reprint, in *The Complete Shorter Fiction*.

——, *The Haunted Hotel: a Mystery of Modern Venice* (1879); reprint (New York: Dover, 1982).

——, *Hide and Seek* (1854); reprint, ed. Catherine Peters (Oxford: Oxford University Press, 1993).

——, 'John Jago's Ghost' (1874) ; reprint, in *The Complete Shorter Fiction*.

——, *The Law and the Lady* (1875); reprint, ed. Jenny Bourne Taylor (Oxford and New York: Oxford University Press, 1992).

——, 'The Lawyer's Story of a Stolen Letter' (1854); reprint, in *The Complete Shorter Fiction*.

——, 'The Unknown Public' (1858); reprint, in *The Works*, 30 vols (New York: AMS Press, 1970) Vol. XX.

——, *The Moonstone* (1868); reprint, ed. Anthea Trodd (Oxford and New York: Oxford University Press, 1982).

——, *The Queen of Hearts* (1859); reprint, in *The Works*, Vol. XIV.

——, *Le secret. Roman anglais traduit avec l'autorisation de l'auteur par Old Nick* (Paris: Hachette, 1889).

——, *The Woman in White* (1860), ed. Harvey Peter Sucksmith (Oxford and New York: Oxford University Press, 1973).

——, *The Woman in White* (1860), ed. John Sutherland (Oxford: Oxford University Press, 1996).

Conrad, Joseph, *The Secret Agent* (1907); reprint, ed. Martin Seymour-Smith (Harmondsworth: Penguin, 1984).

——, *Heart of Darkness* (1899); reprint, in *Heart of Darkness and Other Tales*, ed. Cedric Watts (Oxford and New York: Oxford University Press, 1990).

Dangerfield, Thomas, *Don Tomazo* (1680); reprint, in *An Anthology of Seventeenth-Century Fiction*, ed. Paul Salzman (Oxford and New York: Oxford University Press, 1991).

Defoe, Daniel, *The Fortunes and Misfortunes of the Famous Moll Flanders* (1722); reprint, ed. David Blewett (Harmondsworth; Penguin, 1989).

——, *Roxana. The Fortunate Mistress* (1724); reprint, ed. David Blewett (Harmondsworth: Penguin, 1982).

——, *The Life, Adventures, and Pyracies of Captain Singleton* (1720); reprint, ed. Shiv K. Kumar (London: Oxford University Press, 1969).

De l'Isle-Adam, Villiers, *L'Éve future* (1886); reprint, Édition établie par Nadien Satiat (Paris: Flammarion, 1992).

De Quincey, Thomas, *On Murder Considered as One of the Fine Arts* (1827–54); reprint, in *The Complete Works*, Vol. IV (Edinburgh: Adam and Charles Black, 1862).

Dickens, Charles, *Martin Chuzzlewit* (1844); reprint, ed. Margaret Cardwell (Oxford and New York: Oxford University Press, 1984).

——, 'On Duty with Inspector Field' (1851); reprint, in *Selected Journalism 1850–1870*, ed. David Pascoe (Harmondsworth: Penguin, 1997).

——, 'The Trial for Murder' (1865); reprint, in *The Complete Ghost Stories*, ed. Peter Haining (New York and Toronto: Franklin Watts, 1983).

Doré, Gustave and Blanchard Jerrold, *London: a Pilgrimage* (1872); reprint (New York: Dover, 1970).

Doyle, Arthur Conan, 'The Adventure of Charles Augustus Milverton', in *Sherlock Holmes: the Complete Illustrated Short Stories* (London: Chancellor Press, 1985).

——, *The Coming of the Fairies* (1922); reprint (London: Pavilion Books, 1996).

——, 'The Five Orange Pips', in *Sherlock Holmes: the Complete Illustrated Short Stories*.

——, 'The Greek Interpreter', in *Sherlock Holmes: the Complete Illustrated Short Stories*.

——, *The History of Spiritualism* (2 vols, 1926); online at Vol. I: http://gutenberg. net.au/ebooks03/0301051.txt; Vol. II: http://gutenberg.net.au/ebooks03/ 0301061.txt (visited 05.09.06).

——, *The Hound of the Baskervilles* (1902); reprint, in *Sherlock Holmes: the Complete Illustrated Novels* (London: Chancellor Press, 1987).

——, *The Lost World* (1912); reprint, in *The Lost World and Other Thrilling Tales*, ed. Philip Gooden (Harmondsworth: Penguin, 2001).

——, 'The Man with the Twisted Lip', in *Sherlock Holmes: the Complete Illustrated Short Stories*.

——, *The Parasite* (1890); reprint (New York: Harper & Brothers, 1895).

——, 'The Poisoned Belt' (1913); reprint, in *The Lost World and Other Thrilling Tales*.

——, *Round the Fire Stories* (1908); online at http://www.horrormasters.com/ Collections/SS_Col_Doyle2.htm (10.10.06).

——, *Round the Red Lamp, Being Facts and Fancies of Medical Life* (1894); reprint (Freeport, New York: Books for Libraries Press, 1969); online at http://etext.lib. virginia.edu/toc/modeng/public/DoyLamp.html (10.10.06).

——, *A Study in Scarlet* (1887); reprint, in *Sherlock Holmes: the Complete Illustrated Novels*.

Du Camp, Maxime, *Souvenirs littéraires* (1882–83); reprint, 2 vols (Paris: Hachette, 1906).

Du Maurier, George, *Trilby* (1894); reprint, ed. Elaine Showalter (Oxford and New York: Oxford University Press, 1998).

Du Terrail, Ponson, *Les exploits de Rocambole* (1859); reprint, édition prèsentée et établie par Laurent Bazin (Paris: Laffont, 1992).

Duhamel, Theodore [William Russell?], *Autobiography of a French Detective from 1818 to 1858* (1862); reprint (New York: Arno Press, 1976).

Eco, Umberto, *Il nome della rosa* (Milano: Bompiani, 1980).

——, *Il pendolo di Foucault* (1988); reprint (Milano: Bompiani, 2001).

Eliot, George, *The Lifted Veil* (1859); reprint, ed. Beryl Gray (London: Virago Press, 1985).

Engels, Friedrich, *The Condition of the Working Class in England* (1845); reprint, trans. and ed. by W.O. Henderson and W. H. Chaloner (Oxford: Basil Blackwell, 1971).

Felix, Charles, *The Notting Hill Mystery* (London: Saunders Otley and Co., 1865).

Fielding, Henry, 'Examples of the Interposition of Providence in the Detection and Punishment of Murder' (1752); reprint, in *An Enquiry into the Causes of the late Increase of Robbers and Related Writings*, ed. Malvin R. Zirker (Oxford: Clarendon Press, 1988).

Fuller, Metta Victoria [as Seeley Register], *The Dead Letter: an American Romance* (New York: Beadle and Co., 1867).

Gaboriau, Émile, *L'Affaire Lerouge* (1866); reprint (Paris: Liana Levi, 1991).

Galt, John, 'The Buried Alive' (1821); reprint, in *Tales of Terror from Blackwood's Magazine*, eds Robert Morrison and Chris Baldick (Oxford: Oxford University Press, 1995).

Galton, Francis, Review of Havelock Ellis, *The Criminal* (1890) (*Nature*, 22 May 1890, pp. 75–6); online at http://galton.org/bib/JournalItem.aspx_action=view_id= 205 (visited 05.04.06).

Garwood, Revd John, *The Million Peopled City, or One-Half of the People of London Made Known to the Other Half* (London: Wertheim and Macintosh, 1853); online at http://nils.lib.tufts.edu/cgi-bin/perscoll?collection=Perseus:collection:Bolles& type=text (visited 11.10.05).

Giuriati, Domenico, *Memorie di un vecchio avvocato* (Milano: F.lli Treves, 1888).

Godwin, William, *Enquiry Concerning Political Justice and Its Influence on Modern Morals and Happiness* (1793); reprint, ed. Isaac Kramnick (Harmondsworth: Penguin, 1976).

——, *Caleb Williams* (1794); reprint, ed. David McCracken (Oxford and New York: Oxford University Press, 1970).

Green, Anna Katharine, *The Leavenworth Case: a Lawyer's Story* (1878); reprint, ed. Michele Slung (New York: Dover, 1981).

Greenwood, James, *Low-Life Deeps: an account of the strange fish to be found there* (1875); reprint (London: Chatto and Windus, 1881); online at http://www. victorianlondon.org/publications4/low.htm (visited 11.10.05).

——, *Unsentimental Journeys; or Byways of the Modern Babylon* (London: Ward, Lock, & Tyler, 1867); online at http://nils.lib.tufts.edu/cgi-bin/perscoll?collection= Perseus:collection:Bolles&type=text (visited 09.10.05)

——, *The Wilds of London* (London: Chatto & Windus, 1874).

Harte, Bret, *Condensed Novels* (1867); reprint (New York: P.F. Collier & Son, 1902).

Hawthorne, Nathaniel, *The House of the Seven Gables*, ed. Milton R. Stern (Harmondsworth: Penguin, 1981).

Head, Richard and Francis Kirkman, *The English Rogue, Described in the Life of Meriton Latroon, A Witty Extravagant, Being a Complete History of the Most Eminent Cheats of Both Sexes* (1665); reprint (London and New York: Routledge, 2002). [*Key Writings on Subcultures 1535–1727. Classics from the Underworld.* Vol. II.]

Hodgson, William Hope, *Carnacki: the Ghost Finder* (1913); reprint (Doulestown, Penn., Wildside Press, 2000).

Hoffmann, E.T.A., *Mademoiselle de Scudéry* (1818); reprint, Traduction de Loéve-Veimars, Présentation et notes de Erika Tunner (Paris: Librarire Générale Française, 1995).

Hogg, James, *The Private Memoirs and Confessions of a Justified Sinner* (1824); reprint, ed. John Cary (Oxford: Oxford University Press, 1990).

Hollingshead, John, *Ragged London in 1861* (London: Smith, Elder and Co, 1861); online at http://www.perseus.tufts.edu/cache/perscoll_Bolles.html (visited 10.10.05).

Hosier, Sydney, *Elementary, Mrs. Hudson* (New York: Avon, 1996).

Hume, Fergus, *The Mystery of a Hansom Cab* (Melbourne: Kemp and Boyce, 1886).

James, P.D., *An Unsuitable Job for a Woman* (1977); reprint (New York: Warner Bross, 1982).

——, *Death in Holy Orders* (London: Faber and Faber, 2001).

——, *The Murder Room* (London: Faber and Faber, 2003).

Johnson, Captain Charles, *A General History of the Robberies and Murders of the Most Notorious Pirates, from Their First Settlement in the Island of Providence to the Present Year* (1724); reprint, ed. Arthur L. Hayward (London and New York: Routledge, 2002). [*Key Writings on Subcultures 1535–1727. Classics from the Underworld.* Vol. IV.]

Knapp, Andrew and William Baldwin (eds), *The New Newgate Calendar* (5 vols, 1826); online at http://www.exclassics.com/newgate/ngintro.htm (visited 30.06.06).

Knight, Charles (ed.), *London*, 6 vols (London: Charles Knight & Co., 1841–44); online at http://www.perseus.tufts.edu/cache/perscoll_Bolles.html (visited 20.10.05).

Kyd, Thomas, *The Spanish Tragedy* (c. 1587); reprint, ed. J.R. Mulryne (London: A. & C. Black, New York: W.W. Norton & Company, 1989).

Lang, Andrew, *Old Friends: Essays in Epistolary Parody* (London: Longmans, Green, and Co., 1913).

Laplace, Pierre-Simon, *Philosophical Essay on Probabilities* (1814–25); reprint, ed. Andrew I. Dale (New York and Berlin: Springer-Verlag, 1995).

Larousse, Pierre, *Grand Dictionnaire universel du XIX siècle* (Paris: Larousse, 1866–76).

Le Fanu, Sheridan, *In a Glass Darkly* (1872); reprint, ed. Robert Tracy (Oxford and New York: Oxford University Press, 1993).

——, *Uncle Silas* (1864); reprint, eds W.J. Mc Cormack and Andrew Swarbrick (Oxford and New York: Oxford University Press, 1981).

Lombroso, Cesare, *After Death – What? Spiritistic phenomena and their interpretation*, rendered into English by William Sloane Kennedy (London: T. Fisher Unwin, 1909).

——, *Gli anarchici: Psicopatologia criminale d'un ideale politico* (1894); reprint, commento di Francesco Novelli, con una testimonianza di Pietro Valpreda (Milano: Gallone, 1998).

——, *Delitto, genio, follia: Scritti scelti*, a cura di Delia Frigessi, Ferruccio Giancanelli, Luisa Mangoni (Torino: Bollati Boringhieri, 1995).

——, *Genio e degenerazione: nuovi studi e nuove battaglie* (1897); reprint (Milano, Palermo, Napoli: Sandron, 1907).

——, *L'uomo di genio in rapporto alla psichiatria, alla storia ed all'estetica* (1891); reprint, 2 vols (Roma: Napoleone editore, 1971).

——, *L'uomo delinquente in rapporto all'antropologia, alla giurisprudenza ed alle discipline carcerarie* (1876); reprint (Roma: Napoleone editore, 1971).

——, *Ricerche sui fenomeni ipnotici e spiritici* (Torino: Utet, 1909).

——, *Studi sull'ipnotismo, con ricerche oftalmoscopiche del prof. Reymond e dei prof. Bianchi e Sommer* (Torino: Bocca, 1886).

——, 'What I think of Psychical Research: a Report on Eusapia Paladino, most famous of all mediums', *Hampton's Magazine* (July 1909), pp. 85–96.

—— and Guglielmo Ferrero, *La donna delinquente, la prostituta e la donna normale* (Torino and Roma: Roux, 1893).

London, Jack, *The People of the Abyss* (1903); reprint (Miami: Synergy International of the Americas, 2000).

Marlowe, Christopher, *The Jew of Malta* (*c.* 1590); reprint, ed. Richard W. Van Fossen (London: Edward Arnold, 1965).

Mayhew, Henry, *London Labour and the London Poor* (4 vols, 1861); reprint, ed. John D. Rosenberg (New York: Dover, 1968).

Mearns, Andrew, *The Bitter Cry of Outcast London* (1883); reprint (New York: Augustus M. Kelley, 1970).

Meade, L.T. and Robert Eustace, 'The Horror of Studley Grange' (1894), *The Strand Magazine*, 7 (January–June 1894).

Méjan, Maurice, 'Affaire de madame de Douhault', in *Recueil des causes célèbres et des arrêts qui les ont décidées*, tome III (Paris: Plisson, 1808); online at http://gallica.bnf.fr/ark:/12148/bpt6k49870b (visited 23.03.07).

Middleton, Thomas, *The Last Will and Testament of Laurence Lucifer, The Old Bachelor of Limbo* (1604); reprint, in *The Elizabethan Underworld*, ed. A.V. Judges (London and New York: Routledge, 2002). [*Key Writings on Subcultures 1535–1727. Classics from the Underworld.* Vol. I.]

——, and William Rowley, *The Changeling* (1622); reprint, in Thomas Middleton, *Five Plays*, eds Bryan Loughrey and Neil Taylor (Harmondsworth: Penguin, 1988).

Morrison, Arthur, *Martin Hewitt: Investigator* (1894); reprint (Westport, CT: Hyperion Press, 1975).

The Murder of John Brewen, Goldsmith of London, who through the entisement of John Parker, was poysoned by his owne wife in eating a measse of Sugersops (1592); reprint, in *Illustrations of Early English Popular Literature*, ed. J. Payne Collier, 2 vols (New York: Benjamin Blom, 1966), Vol. I.

Nashe, Thomas, *The Unfortunate Traveller; or, The Life of Jack Wilton* (1594); reprint, in *An Anthology of Elizabethan Prose Fiction*, ed. Paul Salzman (Oxford and New York: Oxford University Press, 1987).

Nordau, Max, *Entartung* (1892); trans. as *Degeneration* (London, Heinemann, 1895).

Orczy, Baroness, *Lady Molly of Scotland Yard* (1910); reprint, ed. Alice Thomas Ellis (Pleasantville, New York: The Akadine Press, 1999).

Paget, Frederick, *Lucretia; or, The Heroine of the Nineteenth Century. A Correspondence, Sensational and Sentimental* (London: Joseph Masters, 1868).

Pater, Walter, *The Renaissance: Studies in Art and Poetry* (1873); reprint, ed. Adam Phillips (Oxford and New York: Oxford University Press, 1986).

The Penguin Book of Vampire Stories, ed. Alan Ryan (Harmondsworth: Penguin, 1987).

Poe, E.A., *Eureka* (1848); reprint, in *The Complete Works*, ed. James A. Harrison, 17 vols (New York: AMS Press, 1965), Vol. XVI.

——, 'The Facts in the Case of M. Valdemar' (1844); reprint, in *The Complete Illustrated Stories and Poems* (London: Chancellor Press, 1994).

——, 'How to Write a Blackwood Article' (1838); reprint, in *The Complete Illustrated Stories and Poems*.

——, *The Letters*, ed. John Ward Ostrom (New York: Gordian Press, 1966).

——, *Marginalia*; reprint, in *The Complete Works*, Vol. XVI.

——, 'Mesmeric Revelation' (1845); reprint, in *The Complete Illustrated Stories and Poems*.

——, 'The Murders in the Rue Morgue' (1841); reprint, in *The Complete Illustrated Stories and Poems*.

——, 'The Mystery of Marie Rogêt' (1842–3); reprint, in *The Complete Illustrated Stories and Poems*.

——, *Oeuvres en prose*, traduites par Charles Baudelaire, texte établi et annoté par Y.G.-Le Dantec (Paris: Gallimard, 1951).

——, 'The Purloined Letter' (1845); reprint, in *The Complete Illustrated Stories and Poems*.

——, '"Thou Art the man"' (1844); reprint, in *The Complete Illustrated Stories and Poems*.

——, 'Une lettre volée', in *Le Rocambole*, n.s. 11 (été 2000): 168–76.

Prichard, Kate and Hesketh, *The Experiences of Flaxman Low* (1899); reprint, ed. Jack Adrian (Ashcroft, British Columbia: Ash-Tree Press, 2003).

Reynolds, G.W.M., *The Mysteries of London* (6 vols, 1846–50); reprint, ed. Trefor Thomas (Keele, Staffordshire: Keele University Press, 1996).

Reynolds, John, *The Triumphs of Gods Revenege against the crying, and execrable Sinne of Murther: or His Miraculous discoveries and severe punishments thereof*, 6 vols (London: Felix Kyngston, 1621–35).

Rohmer, Sax, *The Dream-Detective. Being some account of the methods of Moris Klaw* (London: Jarrolds, 1920).

Ruskin, John, 'Fiction, Fair and Foul I' (1880); reprint, in *The Complete Works*, 30 vols (New York: Thomas Y. Crowell & Co., n.d.), Vol. XXVIII.

——, 'The Storm-Cloud of the Nineteenth Century' (1884); reprint, in *The Complete Works*, Vol. XXIV.

Russell, William, *Recollections of a Detective Police-Officer* (1856); reprint (London: Covent Garden Press, 1972).

Sernicoli, Ettore, *L'anarchia e gli anarchici*, 2 vols (Milano: Fratelli Treves, 1894).

——, *Gli attentati contro sovrani, principi, presidenti e primi ministri* (Milano: no publisher, 1894).

Shakespeare, William, *Hamlet* (c. 1600); reprint, in *The Norton Shakespeare*, general ed. Stephen Greenblatt (New York and London: W.W. Norton & Company, 1997).

Shelley, Mary, *Frankenstein; or, The Modern Prometheus* (1818), reprint, eds James Kinsley and M.K. Joseph (Oxford and New York: Oxford University Press, 1969).

Shiel, M.P., *Prince Zaleski* (1895); reprint, *Prince Zaleski and Cummings King Monk* (Sauk City, Wisconsin: Mycroft & Moran, 1977).

Simms, W.G., 'Grayling; or, "Murder Will Out"' (1842); online at http://arthurwendover.com/arthur/simms/wigwam10.html (visited 01.05.05).

Simonin, Louis Laurent, 'Un'escursione ai quartieri poveri di Londra'; reprint, in Edmondo De Amicis, *Ricordi di Londra*, prefazione di Natalia Milazzo (Milano: Messaggerie Pontremolesi, 1989).

Sims, George R., *How the Poor Live* (London: Chatto and Windus, 1883); online at http://nils.lib.tufts.edu/cgi-bin/perscoll?collection=Perseus:collection: Bolles& type=text (visited 05.10.05).

——, *How the Poor Live and Horrible London* (1889); reprint (New York and London: Garland, 1984).

Smith, Captain Alexander, *A Complete History of the Lives and Robberies of the Most Notorious Highwaymen, Footpads, Shoplifts and Cheats of Both Sexes* (1714); reprint, ed. Arthur L. Hayward (London and New York: Routledge, 2002). [*Key Writings on Subcultures 1535–1727. Classics from the Underworld.* Vol. III.]

Stevenson, R.L., *The Dynamiter* (1885); reprint (Phoenix Mill, Stroud, Gloucestershire: Alan Sutton, 1984).

——, *The Strange Case of Dr Jekyll and Mr Hyde* (1886); reprint, ed. Emma Letley (Oxford and New York: Oxford. University Press, 1987).

Stoker, Bram, *Dracula* (1897); reprint, ed. Maurice Hindle (Harmondsworth: Penguin, 1993).

Taylor, Tom, *The Ticket-of-Leave Man* (London: Lacy, 1863); online at http://www.hull.ac.uk/cpt/transla/noframes/txt1b.html (visited 21.09.06).

Thomson, Henry, 'Le Revenant' (1827); reprint, in *Tales of Terror from Blackwood's Magazine*, eds Robert Morrison and Chris Baldick (Oxford: Oxford University Press, 1995).

Tourneur, Cyril, *The Atheist's Tragedy* (c. 1611); reprint, eds Brian Morris and Roma Gill (London: Ernest Benn, New York: W.W. Norton & Company, 1976).

Verri, Pietro, *Osservazioni sulla tortura* (1804); reprint, a cura di Giulio Carnazzi (Milano: Rizzoli, 1981).

Watson, M. and E. La Serre, *Sheerluck Jones. A Dramatic Criticism in Four Paragraphs and as many Headlines* (1901); reprint (London and New York: Peter Schoffer, 1982).

Wilde, Oscar, 'The Decay of Lying' (1889); reprint, in *The Complete Works*, Introduction by Vyvyan Holland (London and Glasgow: Collins, 1966).

Williams, Henry L., Jr, *The Steel Safe; or, The stains and splendors of New York Life. A story of our day and night* (New York: Robert M. De Witt, 1868).

Wood, Ellen, *East Lynne* (1861); reprint, ed. Andrew Maunder (Peterborough, Ont.: Broadview, 2000).

Wordsworth, William, '*Preface* to Lyrical Ballads (1800)'; reprint, in *The Prose Works*, eds W.J.B. Owen and Jane Worthington Smyser, 3 vols (Oxford: Clarendon Press, 1974), Vol. I.

Critical sources

Arnett Melchiori, Barbara, *Terrorism in the Late Victorian Novel* (London: Croom Helm, 1985).

Ascari, Maurizio, *La leggibilità del male: Genealogia del romanzo poliziesco e del romanzo anarchico inglese* (Bologna: Patron, 1998).

——, 'Più di una penna, più di un testimone: tecniche narrative in *The Woman in White*', *Paragone*, 32–34 (February–April 1992): 9–27.

—— (ed.), *Two Centuries of Detective Fiction: a New Comparative Approach* (Bologna: COTEPRA, 2000).

Bayuk Rosenman, Ellen, 'Spectacular Women: *The Mysteries of London* and the Female Body', *Victorian Studies*, 40:1 (Autumn 1996): 31–64.

Bell, Ian A., *Literature and Crime in Augustan England* (London and New York: Routledge, 1991).

Bell, Ian A. and Graham Daldry (eds), *Watching the Detectives: Essays on Crime Fiction* (Basingstoke and London: Macmillan, 1990).

Bender, John, *Imagining the Penitentiary* (Chicago and London: University of Chicago Press, 1987).

Binyon, T.J., *'Murder Will Out': the Detective in Fiction* (Oxford and New York: Oxford University Press, 1989).

Bloom, Clive, *Bestsellers: Popular Fiction since 1900* (Basingstoke and New York: Palgrave Macmillan, 2002).

—— (ed.), *Creepers: British Horror and Fantasy in the Twentieth Century* (London: Pluto Press, 1993).

——, *Cult Fiction: Popular Reading and Pulp Theory* (Basingstoke: Macmillan, New York: St Martin's Press, 1996).

—— (ed.), *Gothic Horror: a Reader's Guide from Poe to King and Beyond* (Basingstoke and London: Macmillan, New York: St Martin Press, 1998).

—— (ed.), *Literature and Culture in Modern Britain: Volume One: 1900–1929* (London and New York: Longman, 1993).

——, *The 'Occult' Experience and the New Criticism: Daemonism, Sexuality and the Hidden in Literature* (Sussex: Harvester Press, New Jersey: Barnes & Noble Books, 1986).

Bloom, Clive, Brian Docherty, Jane Gibb and Keith Shand (eds), *Nineteenth-Century Suspense: from Poe to Conan Doyle* (Basingstoke and London: Macmillan, 1988).

Bollettieri Bosinelli, Rosa Maria and Franca Ruggieri (eds), *The Benstock Library as a Mirror of Joyce (Joyce Studies in Italy, 7)* (Roma: Bulzoni, 2002).

Bonniot, Roger, *Emile Gaboriau ou la naissance du roman policier*, Préface de Roger Borniche (Paris: Vrin, 1985).

Borowitz, Albert, *An International Guide to Fact-Based Crime Literature*, Note by Jacques Barzun, Foreword by Jonathan Goodman (Kent, OH: Kent State University Press, 2002).

Botting, Fred, *Gothic* (London and New York: Routledge, 1996).

Bowers, Fredson Thayer, *Elizabethan Revenge Tragedy 1587–1642* (Princeton, NJ: Princeton University Press, 1940).

Bown, Nicola, Carolyn Burdett and Pamela Thurschwell, *The Victorian Supernatural* (Cambridge: Cambridge University Press, 2004).

Braddon, Elizabeth, 'The Sensation Novel', *The Argosy*, 18 (July–December 1874): 137–43.

Brand, Dana, *The Spectator and the City in Nineteenth-Century American Literature* (Cambridge and New York: Cambridge University Press, 1991).

Brantlinger, Patrick, *Rule of Darkness: British Literature and Imperialism, 1830–1914* (Ithaca and London: Cornell University Press, 1988).

Briggs, Julia, *Night Visitors: the Rise and Fall of the English Ghost Story* (London: Faber, 1977).

Brooks, Peter, *The Melodramatic Imagination: Balzac, Henry James, Melodrama and the Mode of Excess* (New Haven and London: Yale University Press, 1976).

Brunt, Lodewijk, 'The Ethnography of "Babylon": the Rhetoric of Fear and the Study of London', *City & Society*, 4:1 (June 1990): 77–87.

Cantor, Paul A., *Hamlet* (Cambridge: Cambridge University Press, 1989).

Caquot, André, *Les songes et leur interprétation* (Paris: Seuil, 1959).

Carnell, Jennifer, *The Literary Lives of Mary Elizabeth Braddon: a Study of Her Life and Work* (Hastings: The Sensation Press, 2000).

Cawelti, John G., *Adventure, Mystery, and Romance: Formula Stories as Art and Popular Culture* (Chicago and London: University of Chicago Press, 1976).

Chamberlin, Edward J. and Sander L. Gilman, *Degeneration: the Dark Side of Progress* (New York: Columbia University Press, 1985).

Chandler, F.W., *The Literature of Roguery*, 2 vols (New York: Burt Franklin, 1907).

Chandler, Raymond, *The Simple Art of Murder* (London: Hamish Hamilton, 1950).

Clarke, William M., *The Secret Life of Wilkie Collins* (London: Allison & Busby, 1988).

Collins, Philip, *Dickens and Crime* (London: Macmillan, 1962).

Compère, Daniel, 'Poe traduit et introduit en France', *Le Rocambole*, n.s. 11 (été 2000): 11–22.

Cox, Michael and R.A. Gilbert, Introduction to *Victorian Ghost Stories. An Oxford Anthology* (Oxford and New York: Oxford University Press, 1991).

Craig, Patricia and Mary Cadogan, *The Lady Investigates: Women Detectives and Spies in Fiction* (Oxford and New York: Oxford University Press, 1986).

Cremante, Renzo (ed.), *Le figure del delitto: Il libro poliziesco in Italia dalle origini a oggi* (Bologna: Grafis, 1989).

Cremante, Renzo and Loris Rambelli (eds), *La trama del delitto* (Parma: Pratiche, 1980).

Cunliffe, Barry, *Roman Bath Discovered* (Stroud, Gloucestershire: Tempus, 2000).

Cvetkovich, Ann, *Mixed Feelings: Feminism, Mass Culture, and Victorian Sensationalism* (New Brunswick, NJ: Rutgers University Press, 1992).

Decaroli, Steven, 'The Greek Profile: Hegel's Aesthetics and the Implications of a Pseudo-Science', in *The Philosophical Forum* (2006); online at http://www.blackwell-synergy.com/doi/pdf/10.1111/j.1467-9191.2006.00234.x (visited 01.10.06).

Dubois, Jacques, *Le roman policier ou la modernité* (Paris: Nathan, 1992).

During, Simon, *Foucault and Literature: Towards a Genealogy of Writing* (London and New York: Routledge, 1992).

Eco, Umberto, 'Postille a *Il nome della rosa*' (Milano: Bompiani, 1984).

—— and Thomas A. Sebeok (eds), *Il segno dei tre* (Milano: Bompiani, 1983).

Edwards, Philip D., *Some Mid-Victorian Thrillers: the Sensation Novel, its Friends and Foes* (St Lucia: Queensland, 1971)

Eliot, T.S., 'Wilkie Collins and Dickens', in *Selected Essays* (London: Faber and Faber, 1932).

Ford, Ford Madox, *The March of Literature: from Confucius' Day to Our Own* (Normal: The Dalkey Archive Press, 1994).

——, *Mightier than the Sword: Memories and Criticisms* (London: George Allen & Unwin, 1938).

Forgues, Émile, 'Études sur le roman anglais et américain. Les contes d'Edgar A. Poe', *Revue des deux mondes*, 16 (Octobre–Décembre 1846): 341–66.

——, 'Études sur le roman anglais. William Wilkie Collins', *Revue des deux mondes*, 12 (Octobre–Décembre 1855): 815–48.

——, 'Littérature anglaise. Dégénérescence du roman', *Revue des deux mondes*, 40 (1 Août 1862): 688–706.

——, 'Le roman anglais contemporain. Miss M.E. Braddon et le roman à sensation', *Revue des deux mondes*, 45 (1 Mai 1863): 953–77.

Forster, E.M., *Aspects of the Novel* (London: Edward Arnold, 1927).

Foucault, Michel, *L'ordre du discours: Leçon inaugurale au Collège de France prononcée le 2 décembre 1970* (Paris: Gallimard, 1971).

——, *Power/Knowledge: Selected Interviews and Other Writings 1972–1977*, ed. Colin Gordon (New York: Pantheon Books, 1980).

——, *Surveiller et punir: Naissance de la prison* (Paris: Gallimard, 1975).

Fowler, Alastair, *Kinds of Literature: an Introduction to the Theory of Genres and Modes* (Cambridge, Mass.: Harvard University Press, 1982).

Frank, Lawrence, *Victorian Detective Fiction and the Nature of Evidence: the Scientific Investigations of Poe, Dickens, and Doyle* (Basingstoke: Palgrave Macmillan, 2003).

Freeling, Nicholas, *Criminal Convictions: Errant Essays on Perpetrators of Literary Licence* (Boston: David R. Godine Publisher, 1994).

Frizot, Michel (ed.), *A New History of Photography* (Köln, Könemann, 1998 [French edition 1994]).

Gladfelder, Hal, *Criminality and Narrative in Eighteenth-Century England: Beyond the Law* (Baltimore: Johns Hopkins University Press, 2001).

Gould, Alan, *A History of Hypnotism* (Cambridge: Cambridge University Press, 1995).

Green, Richard Lancelyn (ed.), *The Uncollected Sherlock Holmes* (Harmondsworth: Penguin, 1983).

Guarnieri, Patrizia, *Introduzione a James* (Roma and Bari: Laterza, 1985).

Hacking, Ian, *The Emergence of Probability* (Cambridge: Cambridge University Press, 2006 [1975]).

Hanen, M.P., M.J. Osler and R.G. Weyant (eds), *Science, Pseudo-Science and Society* (Waterloo, Ontario: Wilfrid Laurier University Press, 1980).

Haycraft, Howard, *The Art of the Mystery Story: a Collection of Critical Essays* (New York: Simon and Schuster, 1946).

——, *Murder for Pleasure: the Life and Times of the Detective Story* (New York: Carroll & Graf, 1984, [1941]).

Hibbert, Christopher, *Highwaymen* (New York: Delacorte Press, 1967).

Hilfer, Tony, *The Crime Novel: a Deviant Genre* (Austin: University of Texas Press, 1990).

Hodgson, John A. (ed.), *Sherlock Holmes: the Major Stories with Contemporary Critical Essays* (Boston and New York: Bedford Books of St Martin's Press, 1994).

Hollingsworth, Keith, *The Newgate Novel 1830–1847* (Detroit: Wayne State University Press, 1963).

Howe, Irving, *Politics and the Novel* (New York: Horizon Press, 1957).

Huftier, Arnaud, 'Poe dans le *Magasin pittoresque* (1845): L'Esprit de la *Lettre volée*', *Le Rocambole*, n.s. 11 (été 2001): 157–67.

Hughes, Winifred, *The Maniac in the Cellar: Sensation Novels of the 1860s* (Princeton, NJ: Princeton University Press, 1980).

Hurley, Kelly, *The Gothic Body: Sexuality, Materialism and Degeneration at the* fin de siècle (Cambridge: Cambridge University Press, 1996).

Hutcheon, Linda, *A Poetics of Postmodernism: History, Theory, Fiction* (New York and London: Routledge, 1988).

Hyder, C.K., 'Wilkie Collins and *The Woman in White*', *PMLA*, 54 (1939): 297–303.

Jackson, Rosemary, *Fantasy: the Literature of Subversion* (London and New York: Routledge, 1981).

Jean, Georges, *Voyages en Utopie* (Paris: Gallimard, 1994).

John, Juliet (ed.), *Cult Criminals: the Newgate Novels 1830–1847* (London: Routledge, 1998).

Kalikoff, Beth, *Murder and Moral Decay in Victorian Popular Literature* (Ann Arbor, Michigan: UMI Research Press, 1986).

Kaplan, Fred, *Dickens and Mesmerism* (Princeton, NJ: Princeton University Press, 1975).

Kayman, Martin, *From Bow Street to Baker Street: Mystery, Detection and Narrative* (London: Macmillan, 1992).

Klaus, Gustav (ed.), *The Rise of Socialist Fiction 1880–1914* (Sussex: The Harvester Press, New York: St Martin's Press, 1987).

Klaus, S. Gustav and Stephen Knight (eds), *The Art of Murder: New Essays on Detective Fiction* (Tübingen: Stauffenburg Verlag, 1998).

—— (eds), *'To Hell with Culture': Anarchism and Twentieth Century British Literature* (Cardiff: University of Wales Press, 2005).

Klein, Kathleen Gregory, *The Woman Detective: Gender and Genre* (Urbana and Chicago: University of Illinois Press, 1995 [1988]).

Knight, Stephen, *Continent of Mystery: a Thematic History of Australian Crime Fiction* (Victoria: Melbourne University Press, 1997).

——, *Crime Fiction 1800–2000: Detection, Death, Diversity* (Basingstoke and New York: Palgrave Macmillan, 2004).

——, *Form and Ideology in Crime Fiction* (London: Macmillan, 1980).

——, 'Introduction', in A.C. Doyle, *The Hound of the Baskervilles* (Napoli: Loffredo, 2002).

——, *Robin Hood: a Mythical Biography* (Ithaca and London: Cornell University Press, 2003).

—— and Heather Worthington (eds), *Murder and Mystery: Nineteenth-Century Short Crime Stories*, Cardiff Papers in English Literature, 5 (2001).

Knox, Ronald A., 'Studies in the Literature of Sherlock Holmes' (1911); online at http://www.diogenes-club.com/studies.htm (visited 10.04.06).

Kucich, John, *The Power of Lies: Transgression in Victorian Fiction* (Ithaca and London: Cornell University Press, 1994).

Lonoff, Sue, *Wilkie Collins and His Victorian Readers: a Study in the Rhetoric of Authorship* (New York: AMS Press, 1982).

Lovecraft, H.P., *Supernatural Horror in Literature*, Introduction by E.F. Bleiler (New York: Dover, 1973 [1945]).

Maik, Linda L., 'Nordau's Degeneration: the American Controversy', *Journal of the History of Ideas*, 50:4 (Oct–Dec 1989): 607–23.

Malmgren, Carl Darryl, *Anatomy of Murder: Mystery, Detective, and Crime Fiction* (Bowling Green, OH: Bowling Green State University Press, 2001).

Mandel, Ernest, *Delightful Murder: a Social History of the Crime Story* (London: Pluto, 1984).

Mansel, H.L., 'Sensation Novels', *Quarterly Review*, 113 (April 1863): 482–514.

Marriott, John and Masaie Matsumura (eds), *The Metropolitan Poor: Semifactual Accounts, 1795–1910*, 6 vols (London: Pickering and Chatto, 1999).

Maunder, Andrew (general ed.), *Varieties of Women's Sensation Fiction: 1855–1890*, 6 vols (London: Pickering & Chatto, 2004).

—— and Grace Moore (eds), *Victorian Crime, Madness, and Sensation* (Aldershot and Burlington: Ashgate, 2004).

McLaughlin, Joseph, *Writing the Urban Jungle: Reading Empire in London from Doyle to Eliot* (Charlottsville and London: University Press of Virginia, 2000).

Messac, Régis, *Le 'Detective Novel' et l'influence de la pensée scientifique* (Paris: Champion, 1929).

Mighall, Robert, *A Geography of Victorian Gothic Fiction* (Oxford: Oxford University Press, 1999).

Miller, D.A., *The Novel and the Police* (Berkeley: University of California Press, 1988).

Moretti, Franco, *Signs Taken for Wonders: Essays in the Sociology of Literary Forms* (London and New York: Verso, 1988).

Motion, Andrew, *Wainewright the Poisoner* (New York: Alfred A. Knopf, 2000).

Mukherjee, Upamanyu Pablo, *Crime and Empire: the Colony in Nineteenth-Century Fictions of Crime* (Oxford: Oxford University Press, 2003).

Murch, A.E., *The Development of the Detective Novel* (London: Peter Owen, 1968).

Nead, Lynda, *Victorian Babylon: People, Streets and Images in Nineteenth-Century London* (New Haven and London: Yale University Press, 2000).

Neuburg, Victor E., *Popular Literature: a History and Guide* (London: The Woburn Press, 1977).

Ormond, Leonée, *George Du Maurier* (London: Routledge and Kegan Paul, 1969).

Osborne, Charles, *The Life and Crimes of Agatha Christie* (London: Collins, 1982).

Otis, Laura (ed.), *Literature and Science in the Nineteenth Century: an Anthology* (Oxford: Oxford University Press, 2002).

Ousby, Ian, *Bloodhounds of Heaven: the Detective in English Fiction from Godwin to Doyle* (Cambridge, MA and London: Harvard University Press, 1976).

Owen, Alex, *The Darkened Room: Women, Power and Spiritualism in Later Victorian England* (London: Virago, 1989).

Page, Norman (ed.), *Wilkie Collins: the Critical Heritage* (London and Boston: Routledge and Kegan Paul, 1974).

Phillips, Walter C., *Dickens, Reade, and Collins Sensation Novelists: a Study in the Conditions and Theories of Novel Writing in Victorian England* (New York: Columbia University Press, 1919).

Pick, Daniel, *Faces of Degeneration: a European Disorder, c. 1848–c. 1918* (Cambridge: Cambridge University Press, 1989).

——, *Svengali's Web: the Alien Enchanter in Modern Culture* (New Haven and London: Yale University Press, 2000).

Pike, E. Royston (ed.), *Human Documents of the Victorian Golden Age (1850–1875)* (London: George Allen & Unwin, 1967).

Porter, Dennis, *The Pursuit of Crime: Art and Ideology in Detective Fiction* (New Haven and London: Yale University Press, 1981).

Pratt, Mary Louise, *Imperial Eyes: Travel Writing and Transculturation* (London and New York: Routledge, 1992).

Préposiet, Jean, *Histoire de l'anarchisme* (Paris: Tallandier, 1993).

Priestman, Martin (ed.), *The Cambridge Companion to Crime Fiction* (Cambridge: Cambridge University Press, 2003).

——, *Detective Fiction and Literature: the Figure on the Carpet* (London: Macmillan, 1990).

——, *Crime Fiction from Poe to the Present* (Plymouth: Northcote House, 1998).

Prosser, Eleanor, *Hamlet and Revenge* (Stanford, CA: Stanford University Press, 1971 [1967]).

Punter, David, *The Literature of Terror: a History of Gothic Fictions from 1765 to the Present Day*, 2 vols (London and New York: Longman, 1996).

Pykett, Lyn, *The Sensation Novel from* The Woman in White *to* The Moonstone (Plymouth: Northcote House, 1994).

——, *Engendering Fictions: the English Novel in the Early Twentieth Century* (London and New York: Edward Arnold, 1995).

——, *The Improper Feminine: the Woman's Sensation Novel and the New Woman Writing* (London and New York: Routledge, 1992).

Rader, Barbara A. and Howard G. Zettler, *The Sleuth and the Scholar: Origins, Evolution, and Current Trends in Detective Fiction* (New York, Westport, London: Greenwood Press, 1988).

Rambelli, Loris, *Storia del giallo italiano* (Milano: Garzanti, 1979).

Rance, Nicholas, *Wilkie Collins and Other Sensation Novelists* (Basingstoke: Macmillan, 1991).

Roberts, Marie, *Gothic Immortals: the Fiction of the Brotherhood of the Rosy Cross* (London and New York: Routledge, 1990).

Sala, G.A., 'On the "Sensational" in Literature and Art', *Belgravia*, 4 (February 1868): 449–58.

Sayers, Dorothy (ed.), *Great Short Stories of Detection, Mystery and Horror* (London: Gollancz, 1928).

Seltzer, Mark, '*The Princess Casamassima*: Realism and the Fantasy of Surveillance', *Nineteenth Century Fiction*, 35:4 (March 1981): 506–34.

Shookman, Ellis (ed.), *The Faces of Physiognomy: Interdisciplinary Approaches to Johann Caspar Lavater* (Columbia, SC: Camden House, 1993).

Showalter, Elaine, *A Literature of their Own: from Charlotte Brontë to Doris Lessing* (London: Virago Press, 1998 [1977]).

Slung, Michele B., *Crime on her Mind: Fifteen Stories of Female Sleuths from the Victorian Era to the Forties* (London: Michael Joseph, 1975).

Smith, Nelson and R.C. Terry, *Wilkie Collins to the Forefront: Some Reassessments* (New York: AMS Press, 1995).

Stafford, David A., 'Spies and Gentlemen: the Birth of the British Spy Novel, 1893–1914', *Victorian Studies*, 24 (Summer 1981): 489–509.

Starobinsky, Jean, *L'invention de la liberté* (Genève: Skira, 1964).

Stern, Madeleine (ed.), *The Hidden Louisa May Alcott: a Collection of Her Unknown Thrillers* (New York: Avenel Books, 1984).

'Supernatural Detectives', at http://members.aol.com/MG4273/weirdmen.htm (visited 02.11.04)

Sutherland, John, 'Wilkie Collins and the Origins of the Sensation Novel', *Dickens Studies Annual*, 20 (1991): 248–53.

Swann, Charles, 'Wainewright the Poisoner: a Source for Blandois/Rigaud?', *Notes and Queries*, 35 (233):3 (September 1988): 321–2.

Symons, Julian, *Bloody Murder: from the Detective Story to the Crime Novel: a History* (New York: Viking, 1985 [1972]).

Tani, Stefano, *The Doomed Detective: the Contribution of the Detective Novel to Postmodern American and Italian Fiction* (Carbondale and Edwardsville: Southern Illinois University Press, 1984).

Tatar, Maria, *Spellbound: Studies on Mesmerism and Literature* (Princeton, NJ: Princeton University Press, 1978).

Taylor, Jenny Bourne, *In the Secret Theatre of Home: Wilkie Collins, Sensation Narrative, and Nineteenth-Century Psychology* (London and New York: Routledge, 1988).

Thomas, Ronald R., *Detective Fiction and the Rise of Forensic Science* (Cambridge: Cambridge University Press, 1999).

Thompson, Jon, *Fiction, Crime, and Empire: Clues to Modernity and Postmodernity* (Urbana and Chicago: University of Illinois Press, 1993).

Thomson, H. Douglas, *Masters of Mystery: a Study of the Detective Story* (London: Collins, 1931).

—— (ed.), *The Mystery Book* (London: Odhams Press, 1934).

Thoms, Peter, *Detection & Its Designs: Narrative & Power in 19th Century Detective Fiction* (Athens, Ohio: Ohio University Press, 1998).

Todorov, Tzvetan, *Introduction à la littérature fantastique* (Paris: Seuil, 1970).

——, *Poétique de la prose* (Paris: Seuil, 1971).

Trodd, Anthea, *Domestic Crime in the Victorian Novel* (London: Macmillan, 1989).

Tysdhal, B.J., *William Godwin as Novelist* (London: Athlone, 1981).

Trotter, David, *The English Novel in History 1895–1920* (London: Routledge, 1993).

Unsigned Review [Margaret Oliphant], 'Sensation Novels', *Blackwood's Edinburgh Magazine*, 91:559 (May 1862): 564–84.

Unsigned Review, 'Novels', *Blackwood's Edinburgh Magazine*, 94:574 (August 1863): 168–83.

Unsigned Review [Margaret Oliphant], 'Novels', *Blackwood's Edinburgh Magazine*, 102:623 (September 1867): 257–80.

Unsigned Review, 'Past "Sensationalists" ', *The Argosy*, 5 (December 1867): 49–56.

Usborne, Richard, *Clubland Heroes: a Nostalgic Study of the Recurrent Characters in the Romantic Fiction of Dornford Yates, John Buchan and 'Sapper'* (London: Constable, 1953).

Vassilatos, Gerry, *Lost Science* (Kempton, IL: Adventures Unlimited, 1999).

Vilas-Boas, Gonçalo and Maria de Lurdes Sampaio (eds), *Crime, detecção e castigo: Estudos sobre literatura policial* (Porto: Granito Editores e Livreiros, 2002).

Voller, Jack G., *The Supernatural Sublime: the Metaphysics of Terror in Anglo-American Romanticism* (Dekalb, IL: Northern Illinois University Press, 1994).

Walker, I.M. (ed.), *Edgar Allan Poe: the Critical Heritage* (London and New York: Routledge and Kegan Paul, 1986).

Walsh, John, *Poe the Detective: the Curious Circumstances behind* The Mystery of Marie Rogêt (New Brunswick, NJ: Rutgers University Press, 1968).

Wark, Wesley K., 'The Spy Thriller', in *Mystery and Suspense Writers: the Literature of Crime, Detection and Espionage I–II*, eds Robin W. Winks and Maureen Corrigan (New York: Charles Scribner's, 1998).

Warner, Marina, *Phantasmagoria: Spirit Visions, Metaphors and Media* (Oxford: Oxford University Press, 2006).

Watt, James, *Contesting the Gothic: Fiction, Genre and Cultural Conflict 1764–1832* (Cambridge: Cambridge University Press, 1999).

Watts, Cedric, 'Telling the Time for Crime: Time, Science, Pseudo-Science and the Narrator in Conrad's *The Secret Agent*', *Merope*, 18 (May 1996): 91–111.

White, Hayden, *Metahistory: the Historical Imagination in Nineteenth-Century Europe* (Baltimore and London: Johns Hopkins University Press,1973).

Willis, Chris, 'Slums, Sleuths and Anarchists: Gender Issues in the Work of George R. Sims' (January 2000); online at http://www.chriswillis.freeserve.co.uk/sims.htm (visited 11.10.05).

Winks, Robin W. (ed.), *Detective Fiction: a Collection of Critical Essays* (Englewood Cliffs, NJ: Prentice-Hall, 1980).

Wolff, Robert Lee, *Sensational Victorian: the Life & Fiction of Mary Elizabeth Braddon* (New York and London: Garland Publishing Inc., 1979).

——, *Strange Stories and other Explorations in Victorian Fiction* (Boston: Gambit, 1971).

Woodcock, George, *Anarchism: a History of Libertarian Ideas and Movements* (Harmondsworth: Penguin, 1975 [1962]).

Worthington, Heather, *The Rise of the Detective in Early Nineteenth-Century Popular Fiction* (Basingstoke: Palgrave Macmillan, 2005).

Wright, Willard Hungtinton (ed.), *The Great Detective Stories. A Chronological Anthology* (New York: Charles Scribner's Sons, 1927).

Wrobel, Arthur (ed.), *Pseudo-Science and Society in Nineteenth-Century America* (Lexington, Kentucky: University Press of Kentucky, 1987).

Wrong, E.M. (ed.), *Crime and Detection* (Oxford: Oxford University Press, 1926).

Index

Crime Files Series
General Editor: **Clive Bloom**

Since its invention in the nineteenth century, detective fiction has never been more popular. In novels, short stories, films, radio, television and now in computer games, private detectives and psychopaths, prim poisoners and overworked cops, tommy gun gangsters and cocaine criminals are the very stuff of modern imagination, and their creators one mainstay of popular consciousness. Crime Files is a ground-breaking series offering scholars, students and discerning readers a comprehensive set of guides to the world of crime and detective fiction. Every aspect of crime writing, detective fiction, gangster movie, true-crime exposé, police procedural and post-colonial investigation is explored through clear and informative texts offering comprehensive coverage and theoretical sophistication.

Published titles include:

Maurizio Ascari
A COUNTER-HISTORY OF CRIME FICTION
Supernatural, Gothic, Sensational

Hans Bertens and Theo D'haen
CONTEMPORARY AMERICAN CRIME FICTION

Anita Biressi
CRIME, FEAR AND THE LAW IN TRUE CRIME STORIES

Ed Christian (*editor*)
THE POST-COLONIAL DETECTIVE

Paul Cobley
THE AMERICAN THRILLER
Generic Innovation and Social Change in the 1970s

Christiana Gregoriou
DEVIANCE IN CONTEMPORARY CRIME FICTION

Lee Horsley
THE NOIR THRILLER

Merja Makinen
AGATHA CHRISTIE
Investigating Femininity

Fran Mason
AMERICAN GANGSTER CINEMA
From *Little Caesar* to *Pulp Fiction*

Linden Peach
MASQUERADE, CRIME AND FICTION
Criminal Deceptions

Alistair Rolls and Deborah Walker
FRENCH AND AMERICAN NOIR
Dark Crossings

Susan Rowland
FROM AGATHA CHRISTIE TO RUTH RENDELL
British Women Writers in Detective and Crime Fiction

Adrian Schober
POSSESSED CHILD NARRATIVES IN LITERATURE AND FILM
Contrary States

Heather Worthington
THE RISE OF THE DETECTIVE IN EARLY NINETEENTH-CENTURY
POPULAR FICTION

R.A. York
AGATHA CHRISTIE
Power and Illusion

Crime Files
Series Standing Order ISBN 978–0–333–71471–3   (hardback)
978–0–333–93064–9   (paperback)
(outside North America only)

You can receive future titles in this series as they are published by placing a standing order. Please contact your bookseller or, in case of difficulty, write to us at the address below with your name and address, the title of the series and the ISBN quoted above.

Customer Services Department, Macmillan Distribution Ltd, Houndmills, Basingstoke, Hampshire RG21 6XS, England